D0599139

DISCARD

DISCARD

A
GATHERING
of
WINGS

Also by Kate Klimo

Centauriad Book I: *Daughter of the Centaurs*

A GATHERING of WINGS

CENTAURIAD BOOK II

Kate Klimo

RANDOM HOUSE NEW YORK

For the gang at the barn

Text copyright © 2013 by Kate Klimo
Jacket art copyright © 2013 by picturegarden (front cover),
Kamil Vojnar/Trevillion Images (front cover background), Nick Sokoloff (back cover)

Visit us on the Web! randomhouse.com/teens

Educators and librarians, for a variety of teaching tools, visit us at RHTeachersLibrarians.com

Library of Congress Cataloging-in-Publication Data
Klimo, Kate.
A gathering of wings / by Kate Klimo.
p. cm. — (Centauriad ; #2)
Summary: Accompanied by her closest friends, Malora leaves the safety of Mount Kheiron for the bush then the bustling city of the Ka in search of Sky, the stallion who used to lead Malora's herd of horses, and finds herself faced with making decisions about her future in new ways.
ISBN 978-0-375-86976-1 (trade) — ISBN 978-0-375-98543-0 (ebook)
[1. Voyages and travels—Fiction. 2. City and town life—Fiction. 3. Horses—Fiction. 4. Centaurs—Fiction. 5. Fantasy.] I. Title.
PZ7.K67896Gat 2013 [Fic]—dc23 2012029048

Printed in the United States of America
10 9 8 7 6 5 4 3 2 1
First Edition

Random House Children's Books supports the First Amendment and celebrates the right to read.

Contents

Sometime in the future . . .

CHAPTER I

Malora Victorious

Malora sits up, her chest heaving, her hand clamped over her mouth, muffling a scream. Her rapid breathing gradually slows. She lowers her hand and looks slowly about her. She is in her cot, in her tent, next to the paddocks, in Mount Kheiron. Outside, she can hear the horses chomping on grass and, beyond that, the steady, reassuring susurration of the river flowing past. There are no voices screaming to "feed her to the Beast." No thumping spears. No glowing eyes. She inhales, taking in the safe odors of horse and field and settling dew.

"It's only a Night Demon," she whispers to herself, as once upon a time in the Settlement her mother reassured her. She flops back on the sweat-soaked mattress, where sleep reclaims her almost immediately.

It is only the next morning, on her way to work, that Malora remembers the Night Demon, stealing across her thoughts. It has visited her so many times lately that recalling it no longer has the power to stop her cold. Her teacher,

Honus the faun, has a theory that her dreams are part of her heightened instinct for self-preservation. As the last of the People, she must draw upon every tool she has, including dreams. "Dreams contain vital information if only we can learn to decode them," Honus says. She has learned to decode words, but how is she to read this dream?

"Who goes there?" a voice calls out from the gatehouse, followed by a rattling of hooves.

"It's Malora!" she calls out, thinking that they must have put someone new on the gate. Farin Whitewithers, the usual night-duty guard, not only expects her to pass through at this time, he also has a cup of wildflower tea waiting for her.

The centaur guard stumbles through the door and swings his lantern, blinding her. "Malora Victorious?" he asks, his voice filled with a stupefied wonder.

"Yes," Malora tells him, shielding her eyes. "Mind the light."

Vision restored, she sees that the sentry's canine teeth are sharp—he is a Flatlander. Although she comes through these gates twice daily on her way to and from the blacksmith's shop, this is the first time she has seen a Flatlander at the gates. Until three months ago, Flatlanders were not permitted to guard the gates or to sit in Mount Kheiron's lawmaking body, any more than Highlanders were permitted to serve on the Peacekeeping Force. Ever since Malora won the Golden Horse for the House of Silvermane, Medon Silvermane—the Apex of Mount Kheiron—has begun to make good on his Founders' Day promise to bring about equality between his Highlander and Flatlander subjects. And ever since Malora won the Golden Horse, she has been the object of the centaurs' adoration.

Now her gaze rises to the top of the gate, where she sees, mounted for all to admire and claim for their own, the Golden Horse trophy she won on the day that started it all.

"And how is the Noble Champion?" the sentry inquires shyly.

Malora responds with a question of her own. "What is your name?"

Bowing, he replies, "Margus Piedhocks, at your service."

Malora smiles. Margus's hocks are no more pied than Farin's withers are white or the noble centaurean families of the Mane Way possess actual manes. Centaurean names are colorful without being descriptive. "Well, Margus Piedhocks," she tells him, "Max the Noble Champion couldn't be happier. He has his own paddock in which he enjoys the spoils of victory."

"I am glad to hear it, Malora Victorious," Margus says. "Give him this token of my admiration, will you?"

Piedhocks hands her a chewy green candy in the shape of a spearmint leaf. When Malora let it be known that Max favored the taste of spearmint, the confectioners of Mount Kheiron began to produce "the Max." Centaurs now give her these sweets whenever they see her. Slipping the candy into the pouch at her belt, she says, "Good day to you, Margus Piedhocks," as she passes beneath the gates into Mount Kheiron.

"And the same to you, although it still looks like the nighttime to me!" he calls after her.

Margus is right, Malora thinks. Except for the dawn light

quivering on the eastern horizon, the stars still pack the sky. Through mist fragrant with ripening oranges and new-mown hay, Malora makes her way up the series of ramping streets that lead to Brion's shop on the third ring road. The windows and archways are all darkened. Her boots make no sound on the dew-slick cobblestones, boots that wrap around her calf and fasten on the side with a leather loop held by a single silver button.

Arriving at the big stone box with wooden doors and a crude chimney coming out the top, Malora hauls open the creaking door. She loves the smell of the blacksmith shop, smoke and metal and sweat, almost as much as the smell of a stable, horse and dung and hay. She reaches over to the hook on the wall, takes down her black leather apron, and ties it on. Now that Malora knows her way around, Brion has taken to sleeping late and leaves the opening of the shop to her.

The floor of the shop is covered with a deep carpet of fine gray sand. Malora pads across to the potbellied stove, what Brion calls the red-hot beating heart of the smithy. She lays her palm against the side of the forge, which still holds the heat from yesterday's fire. On the hearth, wrapped in burlap, is her special project.

Whistling softly, she packs wood shavings into the cavity just above the firepot, hearing Brion's voice in her head: "Not too tight. Fire's a living thing, Daughter. It's got to have air to breathe." She uses the firebrand to kindle the shavings. Once the fire has caught, she lays some sticks of oak on top of that. The oak is dense and holds the heat. When the fire grows bigger, she rakes the coke over it and works the wooden paddles of the bellows. The coke begins to glow red. She sprinkles water from the slag tub onto the edges of the coke to keep the heat from spreading.

Blacksmithing is Malora's Hand. At the age of twelve, every centaur chooses a Hand. The Hand, according to Kheiron the Wise—the patron of centaurs—is what sets the centaur apart from the beasts. Malora, not being a centaur, wasn't allowed a Hand when she came to Mount Kheiron at fifteen. She won the right to learn the Hand of her choice on the same day she won the Golden Horse.

Now Brion Swiftstride is teaching her the Hand of smithing. She has grown fond of him and wants to learn all she can from him, but she enjoys these times when she is alone. This is when she feels the presence of her ancestor, who—she was convinced from the moment she first visited here—worked at this very forge. She imagines that this is exactly how he started his workday, back in the time when this city was still home to the People, before the Massacre of Kamaria, when the centaurs killed off the humans and took over the city.

Malora puts on her leather gauntlets. When they were brand-new, they were stiff, fitting awkwardly over her hands and arms. Over the months the sweat of her body has broken them down into a supple and protective second skin.

"Good morning, Daughter."

Out of the cloud of hissing steam, a bristly face emerges, and Brion's familiar horse body lumbers into view as he comes around the pot to stand over her shoulder. Brion Swiftstride is dressed for work, his dappled hindquarters swaddled in a scorched leather wrap, his burly chest covered by an apron just like hers. He is gauntleted to his elbows and wears a hat whose brim has been gnawed away to the crown by flames.

"How goes the little knife?" he asks.

Malora says, "Brittle, I think."

"Time to temper it, then."

She lifts the knife out of the tub and then buries it, blade-first, on the outer edges of the fire, where there is more ash than coal.

Brion says, "Let it sit."

While the blade heats slowly, Brion and Malora move about the shop, getting ready for the day's work. While Malora assembles the tools they will need—chisels and punches and sets and hammers—Brion chooses stock from the pile of iron rods stacked in a wooden crib in one corner, their raw material. They get the iron from the pig-faced smelter in the Hills of Melea. The Suidean hibe, half man and half boar, are miners and smelters by trade.

Today they are filling an order for the noble House of Goldmane, a series of spindles for a balcony railing. Brion lays a bar across the fire so that the center point is resting over the heart of the coals. When the bar has gone from red to yellow, Malora takes the tongs and removes it from the fire. Brion catches one end in the vise, then grabs the other end with the pliers and gives the rod several sharp yanks, so that the molten center of the rod twists like a grapevine. After they have quenched the rod and laid it out on the hearth to cool, Malora takes the knife out of the ashes and again dunks it in the tub before reheating it. They work like this all morning.

At this midday break Brion and Malora eat outside, their gloves turned inside out so the high sun will dry the sweat-damp linings. They eat slabs of coarse bread slathered with goat cheese and date preserves.

"Your blade is well tempered now," Brion tells her between bites.

Malora nods. "This afternoon, I will work on the tang."

"I have been thinking," Brion says casually, "that when you've finished your little knife . . . you will be done here."

Malora lowers her bread and stares at Brion's sooty face. "Why would you say that?" she asks. "I still have so much to learn. I must be some time away from qualifying for recognition."

"Weeks, I'd say," Brion replies. "You're a quick learner. Or perhaps it is simply a case of ironwork being in your blood."

Malora has told him her theory about her ancestor. Far from scoffing at her, Brion showed her some ancient tools that he had found buried in the sand floor of the shop, a small hammer and a primitive pair of tongs, along with three rusted, U-shaped pieces of iron: horseshoes. In the mural on the monument to the People slaughtered in the Massacre of Kamaria, the horses are sheathed in armor and their hooves are shod with iron that looks just like these relics. Not even Malora's father, Jayke, a master horseman, could have imagined such a thing as shoes for horses. But then, there had been no forge and no ironworking in the Settlement. What objects of iron they possessed had come down to them from the ancestors.

"Your thoughts are very far away today, Daughter," Brion says.

Malora clears her head with a quick shake. She knows not to bring up the subject of the Massacre. Now that the centaurs know her, it shames them to think of what their ancestors did to hers. Instead, she says, "I was just thinking that after I have achieved recognition, whether it's weeks from now or months, I will stay and work for you, in payment for your having taught me my Hand."

"Custom doesn't call for it," Brion says, popping the last piece of bread into his mouth and chewing. "It's a centaur's obligation to teach the Hand he has mastered to whoever has gained the right to learn it. I have two young Flatlanders waiting to learn from me. As for you, you are expected to set up your own shop." He wipes his mouth on the back of his hand, smearing soot across his cheek. The joints of his legs creak as he straightens to a stand.

Malora envisions having her own shop, on the beautiful tract of land the Apex has granted her by the river. There, she will forge shoes for her horses, whose hooves—now that they are standing around in the riverbank grass and no longer traveling across the bush every day—are softening. She has noticed the same tendency in the horses in the other stables in Mount Kheiron. Out in the bush, her horses' hooves were hard as rock, seldom brittle or flaky. Who would have thought that life in the bush actually gave horses healthier hooves? This causes Malora to wonder: Had the bush conditioned her in a similar way? While ironwork has made her hard of body, has life here in Mount Kheiron, the Home of Beauty and Enlightenment, made her soft of spirit? Would the old Malora have let herself be spooked by a few Night Demons? In the bush, Malora rarely had bad dreams. Waking life there was so fraught with real dangers, there was no room in her head for phantasms.

As if he has read her mind, Brion asks, "Do you miss the bush?"

Malora considers her years of wandering in the wild: protecting herself and her horses from predators, having to gather her food or kill it in order to survive. The bush had moments of stark beauty, but it was a day-to-day struggle and she withstood it alone, with only the horses for company. Here in Mount Kheiron, it isn't the glorious golden domes that sustain her. Nor is it the delightful concerts, soft and beautiful clothing, and delicious meals. She values none of these as much as the company. And it isn't just the company of her good friends, she thinks, but the sheer number of centaurs that surround her every day, the astonishing perfection of their half-horse, half-human bodies, and the music of their voices, talking, shouting, singing, declaiming, arguing, calling out to one another and to her.

"No," she says to Brion, "I don't miss it."

Malora dusts the crumbs off her hands and returns to the shop, deep in thought. It seems to her that she has both feet as firmly planted here in Mount Kheiron as they are right now in the deep sand of the smithy floor. She no longer even makes daily forays into the bush as she once did with the Flatlander Neal Featherhoof to hunt for ostrich and impala and other wild game. First it was training for the Hippodrome that kept her from it. Now it is training for her Hand. The only thing she misses, living here, is time. In the bush, there was always time enough to do everything she needed to do—groom and treat the horses, fashion tools and weapons and apparel, gather leaves and roots and wild fruits, hunt, trap, skin, and dress the game—with plenty of time left over to do nothing but lie on her back and stare at the clouds while the horses munched on grass. Here in Mount Kheiron, there never seems to be enough time to do everything she wants to do, and no time at all to lie in the grass and stare at the clouds. Civilization, she often thinks, is a greedy monster that gorges itself on time. Rousing herself from these thoughts, she goes to work on the tang of her little knife.

CHAPTER 2

Surprise!

At the end of the workday, Malora climbs another seven tiers to the summit of Mount Kheiron, where Cylas Longshanks keeps his cobbler shop at one end of the Mane Way. She moves through streets thronged with centaurs. As always, the centaurs' sense of style fills her with admiration. Males and females wrap themselves in a single piece of fabric that drapes over one shoulder, leaving the other bare, and winds around their bodies clear down to the horse tails, shielding from view their private parts. She can tell a Flatlander from a Highlander on sight. Flatlanders are wrapped in cruder fabrics and wear coarser boots. Many of them are painfully self-conscious about being seen in the Heights, where up until three months ago they seldom were even allowed to set foot.

Highlanders, being very much at home, carry themselves with poise, many of them holding beneath their noses squares of colored fabric sprinkled with scents created in Orion Silvermane's alchemical laboratory. Orion says that scents have the power to alter moods and to set the tone of society. But Malora cannot help but feel that these days some Highlanders use their scent cloths to mask the earthier smell of the Flatlanders. Trailed by their Twani attendants, the Highlanders pick their way through the crowds, lifting high their elegantly booted hooves, the females girded with belts and sashes. The Highlander females wear caps adorned with fresh flowers or beads or feathers or gems, while the Flatlander females swaddle their heads in drab scarves. But all the females in Mount Kheiron over the age of twelve, except for Malora, cover their heads in observance of the Seventh Edict regarding public decency.

Flatlanders and Highlanders alike greet Malora, the Otherian in their midst, with friendly smiles, hearty rounds of "Hail, Malora Victorious!" and the centaurs' salutation— the right hand placed over the heart, then raised palm-out to her. She is so busy answering the salutations and cramming the proffered Maxes into her pouch that she nearly collides head-on with Zephele Silvermane.

As lovely as ever in a bud-green silk wrap with magenta kidskin boots, her ebony curls escaping from a pale pink cap embroidered with green butterflies, Zephele seizes Malora by the shoulders and cries, "What are you doing up here?" She takes Malora's arm and steers her onto a side street.

"I'm on my way to see Cylas Longshanks," Malora explains. "I'm going to ask him to make a cover for the handle of my knife. I finished it today. Would you like to see it?"

Malora starts to unwind the burlap bundle, but Zephele lets out a little shriek and says, "Why in Kheiron's blessed name would I want to see it? It's bad enough I have to hear you wax poetic about it every night."

"Are you sure you don't want to see it?" Malora asks teasingly. "It's very sharp and very shiny."

"I'm sure it's a fearsomely vicious implement, my dearest darling," Zephele says wearily. "I still don't understand why Honus's knife wasn't sufficient for your needs."

"It was a *butter knife,* which I sharpened on the stones of Honus's terrace," Malora reminds her. "A poor substitute for the real thing."

Zephele has beautifully shaped, very expressive eyebrows, and right now they are arched imperiously. "Yes, well, I have no doubt you'll put this new, improved weapon to ignoble use. Skinning my poor little defenseless squirrel friends and sawing off the noble heads of innocent impalas."

"I'd probably use one of Neal's axes or swords on the noble-headed impala," Malora says, then adds tauntingly, "all that muscle and gristle, you know."

Zephele looks faint. "Kindly dispense with the grisly detail."

"Why are we standing in this alley?" Malora asks.

"Because I don't want to spoil the surprise," Zephele says, her eyes going crafty.

"What surprise?" Malora says.

Zephele flings up her hands. "If I told you, it would be a sorry surprise indeed, now wouldn't it?" She gives Malora a speculative look from beneath her long dark lashes. "Well . . . if you insist, I will tell you, but only if you promise on Kheiron's wise head not to let on to Orion that I told you, because you know how my brother loves to surprise you, and he would be exceedingly Put Out with me, not to mention Downright Cross, if he finds out I have spoiled it."

Zephele takes a deep breath, and Malora is about to advise her not to spoil the surprise, but as usual Zephele is far out ahead of her. "Well! They are transporting the bed from Honus's rooms down to your charming new cottage on the Flats with its perfect view of the paddocks and your glorious band of Ironbound Furies, not to mention the adorable Max the Champion. Very soon now, you will stop bedding down in that crude little tent like some savage, bush-bound nomad and move into your cozy new quarters, Malora Victorious."

Malora smiles. "I was a savage, bush-bound nomad until recently, and I like that little tent," she says. There is nothing crude about it. It is made of the finest silk, in the colors of the House of Silvermane. It is large enough to contain her sizable chest of clothing, a scrivening table, a cot with a down-filled mattress, and a blanket with a satin border. "And please don't call me Victorious," she adds. "Max is the real victor."

Zephele shrugs gaily. "I'm sure the fetid old dear doesn't mind sharing." She catches her lower lip in her teeth and frowns, a shadow crossing her face. "I do hope they don't damage the bed while transporting it. Did you know my dear father had that bed made from lilac wood especially for Honus? But Honus shunned such luxury and chose to sleep on a hard bench instead. Isn't that just like our dear Honus?"

Honus the faun is their tutor and was Malora's host for her first three months in Mount Kheiron. A hibe of goat and man, Honus is the only Otherian in Mount Kheiron apart from Malora. Were it not for his occasional visits down to the Flats to tutor her in reading and writing and mathematics, she would never see him these days. She misses the daily contact with him.

"Lilac wood? I didn't know that," Malora says. It explains, she thinks, the streaks of pale lavender that swirled like mist across the dreams she had when she slept in that bed. It is the most comfortable bed she has ever known, with its mattress as soft as a cloud, its silken coverlet, and its dark blue canopy with golden stars forming pictures that shift when the breeze ripples the fabric. It was in that bed, after sprinkling the canopy with Breath of the Bush, the scent Orion had made especially for her, that she dreamed repeatedly of Sky, her stallion that escaped capture by the centaurs and ran off into the bush. Sleeping in the tent these last few months, there has been no Breath of the Bush and no dreams of Sky, only the Night Demons. Perhaps now she can return to the more pleasant dreams, which she has missed nearly as much as the horse himself.

"Honus is too generous," Malora manages to say before Zephele claps her hand, fragrant with wild jasmine, firmly over Malora's mouth.

"Remember, Malora Ironbound! On the head of the Wise One, you are sworn to secrecy," Zephele hisses.

Malora removes Zephele's hand and holds it briefly in her own. "Just like Orion swore *you* to secrecy?" she asks with a grin.

Zephele tosses her head and laughs merrily. "Ah, but you see the difference is, Orrie doesn't expect *me* to keep a secret. Whereas we all hold you to the very highest standards."

Malora sighs. What Zephele says is true, but it doesn't

seem quite fair. Nor is it possible for her to be as good as the centaurs would like her to be, her little knife a case in point.

After waiting for the horse-drawn wagon carrying the bed to rumble past, Zephele releases Malora back onto the Mane Way. Zephele glides off in the opposite direction toward the House of Silvermane, saying over her shoulder, "Neal Feather-hoof has an appointment with my father, and I'm going to arrange to bump into him by chance in the lower gallery."

"Be nice!" Malora reminds her, but Zephele has already met up with another acquaintance and is deep in animated conversation, the only kind she knows. Zephele is, by her own definition, wildly infatuated with Neal, the captain of the Peacekeeping Force, but to Malora's mind has an odd way of showing it.

Malora continues on toward Cylas Longshanks's store-front. Outside the doors, the cobbler has displayed on racks the usual sumptuous offering of skins. As she enters the shop, Malora savors the scents of lemon oil and cured leather. She walks past the array of boots, displayed on wooden poles carved in the shapes of centaur hooves and legs. The pair made from bright red kid lined with zebra skin strikes Malora as perfect for Zephele. Zephele might deplore the killing of wild animals, but she is not above draping her body in all manner of their skins.

"Good afternoon, Cylas," she says. "I need a favor."

A pony-sized centaur with piebald flanks, ebony skin, and a gleaming bald pate stands behind a long stone counter buried in skins three and four deep. Cylas blinks at her from behind his spectacles and says, "No favor is too great for Malora Victorious."

Malora wonders briefly if she can ask him as an additional favor to stop calling her Victorious but then puts it out of her mind. As Honus has said, "Centaurs need to have their heroes."

Malora ducks her head and hunches her shoulders, minimizing her height for Cylas's benefit. She unwinds the knife from its burlap shroud and sets it down on the counter between them. Human and centaur stare at it for a long silent moment. If Cylas is surprised or repelled, he gives no indication.

Malora has decided in advance on the explanation she will offer. "It's not a weapon," she tells him. "It's a tool, for cutting twine or fruit or cheese."

"But of course," he replies, his face inscrutable. "It goes without saying that you would never violate the Third Edict."

Gingerly, Cylas picks up the knife by its bare handle and turns it in his hands, the blade glinting in the lantern light. "I imagine that you would like me to wrap the handle of this object in leather," he says.

"The hilt," she says. "Yes."

Cylas ponders, then says, "In a medium-weight kidskin, rough side out, I am thinking, so it won't slip from your grasp . . . when you are cutting twine or fruit or cheese," he adds carefully.

"Exactly," Malora says.

"You'd like just enough of it to cushion your grip but not so much that you lose the feel of the hilt, is it?"

"Correct."

"Color?"

"Oh! Anything you like," Malora says with a wave of her hand.

Cylas gives her a look over the top of his spectacles that says this response is unacceptable.

"Undyed," she says quickly. "And I'd like you to make a sheath, also undyed. An ankle sheath built into the lining of a boot. The outer side of the right boot."

"An *ankle sheath*?" He raises a quizzical eyebrow. Not only do centaurs not possess weapons, but they lack the vocabulary of weaponry.

When he continues to look perplexed, she glances around. There is scrap leather lying on the counter that Cylas uses to jot down measurements in chalk. She picks up the chalk and points to a clear space on the scrap. "May I?" she asks.

"By all means," Cylas says, and then watches as she sketches a sheath with the knife in it, and the boot around the sheath. "The leather of the sheath must be sturdy enough so that the blade doesn't poke through the bottom and the sides and cut my leg," Malora says, "but light enough so that it doesn't throw me off-balance. The sheath must be sewn tightly into the inside of my boot so that the knife is concealed."

The sheath will be the knife's home during the day. At night it will live on the table next to her bed and serve to fend off the Night Demons. When she asks herself why she would need the knife during the day, she can offer no answer, other than that the Demons have put her on guard.

"You wish the knife to be a secret. In case you want to catch the piece of fruit by surprise?" he says blandly.

"Exactly," she says with a smile, thinking: His sense of

humor is so like mine. Dry to the point of sour. "Make the boots natural, too, so as not to draw the eye to my feet."

"With reinforced toes?" Cylas asks.

"Yes, please," she says.

"When do you require this fascinating item?" he asks.

"As soon as possible," she says with a smile.

"Are you planning to leave us?" he asks. His dark eyes gleam with suspicion.

Malora stares at him. First Brion and now Cylas.

"No," she answers, "my plan is to stay in Mount Kheiron for as long as you will have me. But I am eager to have the use of my new tool." She rummages through the Maxes in her purse to find the nubs to advance him for the job.

Cylas stops her with a raised hand. "Your nubs are not welcome here," he tells her. "Your order will be ready in two days. I will see you then."

Knowing that arguing with Cylas will only offend the old centaur, Malora thanks him and starts for home. It is dark by the time she arrives at the city gate, where the watchman is just lighting the lantern. She is pleased to see her old friend back on duty. Farin has red flanks and a matching mustache, which he waxes and twirls at the ends, giving him a perpetually cheery look that belies his steadfast gloominess.

"Malora Ironbound!" he calls out when he sees her.

"Farin Whitewithers!" she calls back to him. "Where were you this morning?"

"Alas, this is my new shift," Farin says dolefully. "A Flatlander has replaced me, of all things. Life won't be the same without our morning chats over tea." He shakes his head.

"Everything is changing. Every time I turn around these days, there's an order for change. Up is down and down is up. Flat-landers in the Heights and Highlanders on the Flats. But if that's what the Apex mandates, then I will comply."

"As will we all!" Malora agrees as she passes through the gates out onto the road that leads to the nearest bridge. Across the Lower Neelah lie her paddocks and her camp. The crowds have dispersed on the flats, the centaurs having stopped work and returned to their homes, whose firelights shine like warm beacons. A Twani nurse, herding four kits before her, scurries toward the gate, raising her pink-palmed, short-fingered hand and hailing Malora as she passes.

"Good evening, Malora Victorious!" the Twan says, and the kits echo her. Two of the kits are female, their furry tails poking out from the bottom of their tunics. When Malora saw her first Twan, not long after she saw her first centaur, they reminded her of the picture of Puss in Boots—or "Pussemboos," as she called him—that she saw in a book in the Grandparents' box of treasures at the Settlement. Orion, familiar with the story, had laughed when Malora called the Twani Pussemboos and had hastened to correct her. A hibe of cat and human, walking upright on two legs but with flat faces coated with fur and dominated by large eyes, the Twani have served the centaurs for generations. They took refuge in Mount Kheiron when a volcanic eruption buried their city in the Hills of Melea. The Twani serve the centaurs not as slaves, as Malora assumed at first, but freely, out of eternal gratitude.

When she arrives at the larger of the two paddocks, which contains most of the herd, she walks along the fence toward camp. Shadow is the first to notice her. Her head comes up from the grass, and she calls out a shrill whinny of greeting, then trots over. Malora climbs the rails and embraces the mare's long black head, breathing into her nostrils. The mare pulls back at first, offended by the vaguely dangerous smell of smoke.

"I'm sorry I haven't bathed yet. You'll just have to take me as I am," Malora says, her voice low and calm.

Not a day passes that Malora doesn't miss Sky, the coal-black stallion that was once her father's and became the leader of her herd. Beast has taken over as the lead horse, and Sky and Shadow's daughter Lightning is the lead mare.

Beast comes along and, ears flattened to his skull, chases Shadow off so he can have Malora to himself. But before long, the horses are all gathered in a clump, jostling each other and snorting and nudging with their noses the pouch at her waist. Laughing, she opens the pouch and doles out Maxes to Beast and Lightning and Shadow, to Ember and Cloud and Raven, to Coal and Star and Charcoal and Butte. She gives them gentle smacks on the nose when their velvety, quivering lips reach out for seconds.

"You boys and girls are so greedy! I have to save some for the Noble Champion, don't I?"

They snort and shake their heads in disgust at the very idea of *Max the Noble Champion*. Max's having won the Golden Horse means less to them than the dirt that wedges into the frogs of their hooves. As far as they are concerned, Max is still—and will always be—the lowest of the low.

Malora drops down from the fence and makes her way

toward the smaller paddock closer to her camp. These two paddocks of horses are all that remain of her original herd.

Max comes galloping across the smaller paddock to greet her. He might be Noble Champion to the centaurs, but he will always be the Horse of Her Heart. In the old days, whenever the loneliness of life in the bush brought her down, Max would sense her sadness, come up to her, and place his head over her heart. This gesture of sympathy never failed to bring on a cloudburst of tears, after which she always felt much better. These days, Malora scarcely recognizes the Horse of Her Heart. His chest is expanded with pride, and his once-heavy head is high, his sparse mane streaming behind him. Now that the other horses don't chase him off his feed, he has begun to put on weight. His ribs no longer poke out, and his swayback has begun to fill in. And since the wranglers have taken to bathing him in the river once a day in lavender-scented suds, he now smells much less like the carcass of a kudu rotting in the midday sun. As if attached to him by invisible ropes, Light Rain and Bolt stream in his wake. Max's tail and croup bear the foamy marks of their slobber.

"And how goes it for our Champion this evening?" Malora asks. Max smacks his lips and shows her the hodgepodge of his remaining teeth as if to say, *You know how it is, Malora, day in and day out, eating tender green grass, munching on oats and molasses, and getting my butt polished by these two beauties.*

"It's a rough life, isn't it, Maxie, old boy?" Malora says as she gives him six lumps of spearmint, doubting that even these will be enough to sweeten his rancid breath. Max then gallantly moves aside to let each of his ladies have some. "The centaurs are right, Max. You really are noble," Malora tells him.

A bright bay with two white feet and a blaze, Bolt is an Athabanshee mare from the far-off deserts of the Sha Haro. Bolt once belonged to Anders Thunderheart, the Flatlander who heads up what was, until Malora's victory, the stable with the longest Hippodrome winning streak in Mount Kheiron's history. Dividing up the last of her stash of Maxes among the three horses, she climbs down from the fence and makes her way toward the lantern burning at the entrance to her tent.

The house the Apex is building for Malora is shrouded in darkness. She has not kept track of its progress, trusting the work to the finest builders in Mount Kheiron. Malora finds the idea of anyone building her a house embarrassing. She would be just as happy to stay in the tent, but the Apex will not hear of Malora Victorious sleeping outdoors and, as Honus has counseled her, one doesn't turn down a gift from the Apex.

Malora looks around for West, her chief wrangler. By the time she gets back from the shop, he and his crew of Twani have already watered and fed the horses. She wonders where West is. He is usually here to greet her with a full report on the horses, along with a fleece robe and a cake of soap. Not only does she miss Honus, but she also misses his bathtub, the only one in Mount Kheiron. Cold river water is a poor substitute, but she won't let West rig a shower with heated water for her, however often he has begged her to let him. If the river is good enough for her horses, it will serve her as well.

"West!" she calls out.

The sound of a familiar high-pitched giggle comes from the direction of the darkened construction site, followed by the lilting notes of Honus's pipe. Suddenly, the house leaps into lantern light as her friends come pouring out the front door, across the portico, and down the wide steps toward her.

CHAPTER 3

Night Demons

"Surprise, my friend!" Orion Silvermane calls out, grinning.

Honus takes the pipe from his lips and beams. "Welcome to your new home!"

"I hope we didn't startle you, boss," West says, with a bashful swipe of his paw over his head.

"Didn't I say you had nothing to worry about, little brother?" Theon says. "Zephele kept your secret."

Zephele catches Malora's eye and winks. She has succeeded in keeping the bigger secret—that Malora's house is ready for her to move into—and about this Malora has no need to act surprised.

With Zephele at one elbow and Orion at the other, Malora finds herself being ushered up the wide, centaur-friendly steps and under the generous portico. The house is small only by centaurean standards. By human standards, it is bigger than the home she shared with her parents in the Settlement. Where that house had been made of baked clay with skins covering the entryways, this one is built of stout timbers, with a thatched roof and wide hinged doors flanked by arched windows overlooking the paddocks. On the tiled portico, there are three chairs, for her and Honus and West, and benches stout enough to accommodate her centaur guests. Inside, there is a shelf for her books, a scrivening desk beneath one window, and a large table beneath the other. Malora sees that the table is already set for the evening meal.

In a daze, she walks through a wide archway into the separate sleeping chamber, which occupies the rear half of the house. There is the bed that the Apex had commissioned for Honus, with its cloud-soft mattress and its star-spangled canopy. It has a new coverlet made of patches of many different colors and patterns.

Recognizing the style behind the rainbow coverlet, Malora turns to Theon. "Thank you," she says.

Theon smiles. His gray eyes, so like his mother's, gleam with pride. "It's a bit flamboyant, I know, but I hope you like it all the same. I pieced it together from remnants of fabrics I have woven over the years. It was Zephele's idea. I was going to weave you something with a large rearing horse on it, but Zephie says you have a sufficiency of *real* horses rearing up in your life and to adhere to an abstract pattern. I hope it won't keep you awake at night."

"It's beautiful," Malora tells the elder brother of Zephele and Orion, and kisses him on the cheek.

Above the canopy is a vaulted ceiling into which a mosaicist has inlaid a duplicate of the design in Honus's bedchamber. Sparkling with tiny golden tiles, it has an orange sun flaming at the center. Orion flings open the doors at the foot of the bed and Malora sees by torchlight a wild tangle of rose and honeysuckle and trumpet vine, fragrant in the cooling night air.

Honus clears his throat. "The garden wants taming," he says.

"I like it," Malora says. As she looks around, she is conscious of her friends' eager eyes on her, but there is no need for her to feign delight. The builders, under Orion's direction, have thought of everything: a wardrobe, shelves for her boots, and a lantern centered on the headboard so she can read in bed, another pleasurable habit she has acquired in Mount Kheiron. On the wall next to the bed, there is even a hook for the black-and-white braided rope that was once her father's: her one essential tool for training horses. There is everything in her new house, she thinks, except a marble convenience and a bathing tub.

Lifting her long braid, she sniffs, thinking she had better bathe before she offends her dinner guests. She takes her fleece robe from the wardrobe where it hangs next to her wraps and tunics and trousers, checking to make sure that there is a cake of lavender soap in one pocket and one of lime-scented soap in the other.

But Zephele waylays her, beckoning mysteriously.

The centaur's braided tail swings before Malora as she follows Zephele out into the garden. Down at the bottom, under its own broad blue-and-white-striped canopy, a tub sits on platform.

"Carved from malachite," Zephele says with pride, "to

match your lovely Otherian eyes and your memorial necklace." Malora wears the necklace every day. With its single polished malachite stone, it once belonged to her mother, Thora.

Malora goes over and discovers that the tub is filled with hot water, fragrant with rose mingled with lavender.

"I added the juice of two lemons because Honus says it soothes aching muscles," Zephele says. "And surely your muscles must ache from hefting those hideous huge hammers all day. No fear of running out of hot water, either. There's a sun-heated cistern on your roof, and another in the shade of those trees over there for cold."

On the other side of a painted screen is a marble convenience. No more squatting in the bushes. Malora drapes her robe over the chair, set before a table with a gilt-framed looking glass. On the table is a pale blue bottle. Without uncorking it, she knows what it contains: the scent Orion concocted for her, Breath of the Bush. Also on the table is an array of brand-new silver-backed brushes. She fingers them admiringly.

"You are not to use those on the boys and girls, no matter how much you are tempted," Zephele chides her. "They have their own brushes now."

In the bush, Malora and the horses shared her hairbrush until the bristles were worn to nubs. Malora sighs happily as Zephele unbraids her hair, which falls to her waist and is the reddish color of the rocks of the Ironbound Mountains.

In the mirror, she sees Zephele wrinkling her nose. "You smell like a Pantherian buffalo hunter," her friend says.

"Have you actually ever *smelled* a Pantherian buffalo hunter?" Malora asks.

"No, and I don't care to, thank you very much," Zephele replies. "Although I must admit I would very much like to *see* one. I suppose I will eventually, when my grumbleguts father finally consents to letting me visit Kahiro." Zephele gives Malora's hair a final raking with her fingers, then backs away. "There now. I will leave you to your ablutions. I promised I would help Honus and West in the cook tent."

"Where is Sunshine?" Malora asks.

"Sleeping," Zephele says cheerfully. Zephele is notorious for refusing to let her little yellow-furred Twan do very much at all for her. Since the Twani like to sleep, Zephele believes it is good to let hers have as much sleep as she likes.

"Can you guess what we're having tonight?" Zephele asks.

"Barley Surprise?" Malora says.

Zephele grins. "That, my dear, has to be the evening's least surprising detail, but I did make sure that West prepared us a creamy pood for dessert made with hazelnuts!"

When Malora emerges from her bath sometime later, bathed, scented, and wrapped in a green silken robe woven by Theon and embroidered by Zephele with purple flowers, they are all seated at the table waiting for her, the three Silvermane siblings and Honus.

"Where is Neal?" Malora asks, glancing pointedly at the empty bench.

Orion says, "Featherhoof has two new Highlander recruits he is hosting for an overnight in his hut prior to a campout in the bush, one of them being our cousin Brandle."

"Brandle will take one look at the fence Neal made from animal vertebrae and skulls," Honus says with a chuckle, "and go running back to the Heights."

West goes around the table, offering food.

"Featherhoof says he has quite the challenge before him. He says Highlanders are sorry specimens," Zephele says, "and haven't I always said as much? My dear brothers excepted, of course! But I do think our father is taking this Founders' Day promise a little too far, don't you?"

"All I know," says Theon, helping himself from the serving dish, "is that I haven't seen our father this happy since . . ." He trails off, flicking a look at each of his siblings.

"Since before we lost Athen?" Zephele finishes for him.

Theon flinches at her boldness. "Well . . . yes," he says.

The eldest of the Silvermane children, Athen, disappeared years before Malora came to Mount Kheiron. The centaurs believed him to have been the victim of a hippo attack. Malora has never said anything to any of them, but she has walked the river and swum and bathed in it daily and there are no hippos in this stretch of the Lower Neelah.

Orion says, "I agree with Theon. Father seems quite pleased with the way things are going."

"But what about all these disputes?" Zephele says. "Today, the line of complainers wound clear down to the temple!"

"Perhaps *because* of this he is happy," Orion says. "Father feels that nothing clears the air so well as a good argument."

"I agree with your brothers," Honus says to Zephele. "Medon seems to be in his element. He has single-handedly brought about what is, so far, a bloodless revolution. I predict he will go down in centaurean history as the Great Unifier."

"The Great Grumbleguts is more like it," Zephele mutters. "I think it's very unfair. How can we have true equality when our father continues to look the other way while Flatlanders violate one Edict after another?"

"Flatlanders aren't held to the same standards as Highlanders," Malora speaks up.

"That might have been well and good in the past," Zephele says, "but it's hardly fair for Flatlanders to begin to enjoy the privileges of Highlander life without having to abide by the same Edicts that bind us."

"Well put, Zephele!" Honus says, beaming with professorial pride. "But tell us, which Edicts do you believe they are violating?"

"Some of them carry weapons," Zephele says.

"Only those on the Peacekeeping Force," Orion says. "And they are authorized to do so. And in the outlying townships where wild animals are known to prowl."

Malora, who is busily shoveling Barley Surprise into her mouth, pauses. No one has authorized her to own the knife she has just made in violation of Edict Three. Then again, she was excused from covering her head in observance of Edict Seven. While Malora has not gone out of her way to violate the Edicts, neither has she adhered to them.

"What about reading?" Zephele says. "Can your average Flatlander, apart from Neal Featherhoof, read even his own name, let alone write it? You are a gifted teacher, dear Honus, but you can't very well be expected to teach them *all* to read and write."

"We are recruiting more new teachers from among the Highlanders every day. I am in the process of teaching the teachers, which leaves the two of you to study independently," Honus says, cocking an expectant eyebrow. "Which I assume you are doing with the assiduousness I would expect from you both."

"Oh, I am assiduousness itself!" Zephele says with an innocent widening of her eyes. Zephele is fiercely intelligent, but unlike Malora, she has no great fondness for lessons. "Still, you must admit that it may take years to bring about universal literacy."

"I learned to read and write in days," Malora says.

"Well, you're different," Zephele says. "You're one of the People, and the People invented literacy and all sorts of other arcane pursuits. Plus, you're the last human, and your dear little head is probably jam-packed with all manner of wisdom, like some sort of rare, sole-surviving plant pod, crammed with precious seeds."

Malora swallows hard. She isn't sure she likes this image of herself.

"And what about Edict Six?" Zephele goes on. "I'm told the workers in our own vineyard tap the vats and help themselves to flasks of spirits, and that the tasters actually *swallow* the wine they are sworn to spit out. Neal himself says they all eat meat every chance they get. And I have also heard," she adds, her voice lowering to a scandalized whisper, "that married Flatlanders have been known . . . *to swap mates!*"

"Now *that*, Sister, is a patent falsehood," Orion says in a stern voice. "It's malicious Highlander gossip, and I'm surprised you have stooped to such depths."

"No, you're not in the least surprised, Brother," says

Zephele with a blithe wave of her hand. "Because flighty minds such as mine thrive in the shallows."

"For reasons that elude me, you only *pretend* to be shallow, Sister," Orion says.

"Besides," Zephele comes back at him, "how do you know the rumors aren't true?"

"Because Neal tells me so."

"And since when is Neal Featherhoof the fount of truth?" Zephele says. "He might be the captain of the Peacekeepers— and, Kheiron knows, the light of our father's life—but he's a Flatlander, born and bred, and his fealty is to his own kind. I wouldn't put it past him to cover for his philandering fellows. Or to help himself to the favors of some nubile Flatlander wife."

"Zephele, *really!*" Honus says. "Sometimes I wish you would put that fertile imagination of yours to more constructive uses. Still, it may be time for a careful review of the Edicts. I wouldn't be surprised if a few of them could do with a little amending or even suspension. The Fourteenth, in particular, given the troubles in the north, may be the first to go."

Malora scans the suddenly grim faces around the table. By troubles, Honus means the attacks on Dromadi trade caravans en route from the west to Kahiro. The raids are believed to be perpetrated by a band of wild centaurs, an allegation at which the Apex scoffs. When the Apex scoffs, his subjects scoff, including Malora. Besides, her idea of a wild centaur is Neal Featherhoof. The Empress of the Ka has requested an armed escort comprising representatives from all the nations, which the Apex has so far refused to join. Malora listens with only half an ear; talk about the world beyond Mount Kheiron interests her little. Mount Kheiron is her world now.

Orion says, "If the Fourteenth Edict against bearing arms goes, we might as well bid farewell to all of them."

"I am simply saying," Honus continues, "that events may require us, in the not-far-distant future, to modify our views and laws. It is worth considering that other hibes indulge in spirits and stimulants, eat red meat, and take up arms—and they live in relatively harmonious and civil societies. Perhaps, in their ways, better balanced than our own."

"If you were not a scholar and an Otherian," Orion says, "I would suspect you of entertaining treasonous ideas."

"If I am guilty of anything it is of open-mindedness, Orion," Honus says with a small smile.

"In that case, I hope my father closes *his* mind to your counsel," Orion says, his voice chilly.

"Is there pood to be had?" Zephele asks, in an obvious attempt to change the subject.

Malora is relieved when the conversation turns to the up-coming Harvest Jubilation, which will be the first ever at-tended by both Highlanders and Flatlanders.

After they have eaten the hazelnut pood, washing it down with wildflower tea, Zephele rises from the table and trots out onto the portico. She returns carrying a package wrapped in crinkly blue parchment.

"The first treasure for your very own collection," Zephele says, handing the package to Malora.

Malora unwraps it to find a small exquisite statue of a horse carved from black stone. Engraved on its back are a series of stripes that radiate from his shoulders back to his haunches in perfect symmetry, scars left by the Leatherwings.

"Do you like it?" Zephele asks breathlessly.

The onyx horse has inset eyes made from sapphire. "Sky," Malora murmurs softly, stroking the black stone.

"I commissioned the finest sculptor in Mount Kheiron to carve it," Zephele says.

"Thank you, Zephie." Malora places the object on the shelf next to the books Honus has given her: the collected poems of Alfred, Lord Tennyson, a copy of *Puss in Boots* illustrated by Fred Marcellino, the writings of Epictetus, Judith Krantz's *Scruples, The Cat in the Hat* (a book with pictures, the first book she ever read), and a novel entitled *Pride and Prejudice*, which Honus has recommended highly. Then Malora makes her way around the table and hugs each of her friends in turn. "Thank you all so very much. You are very kind to me, and I'm honored to have you as friends."

"I believe that's our cue to go and let Malora enjoy her new home in peace and quiet," Orion says, rising from the bench.

When her guests have all taken their leave and West has cleared the table and retired to his tent, Malora fetches the flask of Breath of the Bush. She climbs up on the mattress and sprinkles the canopy, perhaps too liberally, for the gift of the statue has made her miss Sky with a sudden, sharp longing.

After dousing the lantern, she surrenders almost immediately to sleep.

She is standing alone, surrounded on all sides by high sandy bluffs. Sky calls out to her in a plaintive whinny, a sound she hasn't heard him make since the day the Leatherwings attacked and carried off all the horses and the hunters in the Settlement. At the foot of the nearest bluff is a big round pen with towering walls tightly woven from weatherworn sticks. Fitting her bare toes into the cracks, she scales the wall of the pen and peers over the top. In the center of the pen, Sky is bound, all four legs pegged to the ground. He strains, his body twisting and lathered with sweat and dust.

"Oh, Sky! What have they done to you?"

He looks up and sees her, his struggles growing more desperate. Where the ropes chafe, he has begun to bleed.

Malora scrambles over the top of the pen, but something sharp in the weave gouges the palm of her right hand. She loses her grip and falls backward onto the sand. And then, suddenly, her own wrists and ankles are pegged to stakes. Like Sky, she twists and struggles against her restraints, screaming in fury.

She wakes up to find her right palm is pierced and bleeding. It takes a few moments for her to calm herself, taking deep breaths. She is safe in her new house. Not even the beautiful bed can keep her safe from the Night Demons.

Outside in the paddock, she hears the pounding of hooves as the horses run frantically back and forth, calling out to her.

West appears at the foot of the bed, his face fretful in the light of his raised lantern. "Are you all right, boss?" he asks.

"Yes! No! I'm fine!" she says, realizing that both of these statements are true. She is fine, but Sky is not. "A dream . . . ," she adds faintly.

"A visitation by the Night Demons, boss. That's all it was. It must have been that second helping of pood. I had some peculiar dreams myself, and I had only the one helping. If you're sure you're all right, I think I'll go out and soothe the boys and girls."

"Did I scream very loudly?" she asks.

He looks surprised. "You didn't make any noise at all. I just figured when the horses got so stirred up, I'd need your help to calm them. But I see you're in no condition." He turns to leave.

"No! I'm coming," Malora says, climbing out of bed.

She grabs her fleece robe and, shivering, puts it on over her sweat-damp nightshirt. She will have to make an effort in front of the herd to be calm and collected. Because the fact is, she is nothing of the kind now that she knows that Sky is no longer out in the bush roaming free. Wherever he is, Sky is in grave danger—and he needs her help.

CHAPTER 4

A Visit with the Apex

It is challenging to rekindle the fire with only one good hand, but she manages, and by the time Brion enters the shop the coals are banked and glowing red. One look at Malora's face and Brion knows something is amiss.

"What is it, Daughter?" he asks, setting down his leather satchel.

"I can't work today," she tells him. "I have to go away. I started the fire for you. You'll have to bring in a striker to take my place. One of the Twani—"

"Where are you going?" he breaks in.

"To find my horse. To find Sky," she says, lifting her wounded hand to her forehead. "I had a dream—"

"What happened to you?" he breaks in, seeing that she is hurt. He takes her hand and examines the palm, which has begun to bleed through the bandage West made for her.

It occurs to her to tell Brion a white lie, but what is the

point? "I woke up from my dream and it was bleeding," she says. "I was—"

"Come over to the forge," he says, "and I'll redress it."

His big, calloused hands are gentle as he unwinds the bloodied bandage, washes her wound in the quenching pot, then applies a salve and wraps it in a clean white cloth he produces from his leather sack.

The bandage is bulky and will get in her way, but he means well. "Thank you, Brion. Thank you . . . for everything."

"I'm not finished with you yet," he says, wagging a finger at her. "Now, go and do what you must. I will be here when you return, ready to complete your training. You will be taking your knife with you, I trust?"

She nods, thinking that had she known she were leaving Mount Kheiron so soon she would have made a much larger knife.

"Of course," she says, removing her apron with one hand and placing it on the hook, she hopes not for the last time. She realizes that she is afraid, not just for Sky, but for herself. She is afraid of leaving Mount Kheiron, where Night Demons are the only threat. Something in her dreads returning to the bush. She had come in from it unscathed, but returning to it she is fearful that her good luck has run out, that her survival skills have grown rusty, that something lies in wait for her out there. For all this, she knows she has no choice. She must find Sky.

Brion sees her out and stands in the doorway of the shop, a hand raised in farewell. She has already broken into a run when she hears his voice at her back. "Kheiron be with you, Malora Ironbound!"

Moments later, Malora is in the basement corridor of the atelier, where she pauses to catch her breath before knocking. She can tell from the light under the door that Orion is already at work in his alchemical laboratory. Like her, he is an early riser. She lifts her good hand and knocks softly.

Orion opens the door. His overwrap is a mass of stains, his dark curls are in disarray, eyes glazed with distraction. Then he registers Malora's presence and bursts into a warm smile. "Malora! Come in!"

She stands back from the open door and holds the sleeve of her tunic over her nose. Behind Orion, the alchemical laboratory is dimly lit. She sees a pot bubbling over an open flame that is attached to another pot via a long twisting tendril of copper pipe wrapped in a rag. The alchemist is distilling something that smells like the earth itself being heated in a blast furnace. In her mind's eye, she sees a place where the sand drifts in layers of many colors, where murmuring figures huddle in striped robes around fires in the shadow of billowing tents. Other scents begin to unfurl toward her like long tongues, lashing her face, her nose, her ears. There are too many of them, all demanding her attention. This is the way it always is for her here. The shelves behind the distillation apparatus are chockablock with colored vials, each containing a different scent: flowery, earthy, spicy, sweet, tangy. Although Orion assures her the vials are airtight, Malora knows differently. Some of each scent escapes into the room and mingles in a single, swarming cloud.

Seeing that Malora's distress isn't just the olfactory assault of his laboratory, Orion's smile quickly fades. "What's wrong, Malora? Is it the house? Is it the horses?"

"The house is wonderful," she says, working to focus. "Everything I could ever want. And the boys and girls are fine." Then she pauses, realizing this isn't exactly true. "Can you join me out here in the hall and close the door?"

"Of course," he says. Orion shuts the door and takes her elbow, drawing her into the far corner. "You're trembling all over," he says, then sees the bandage. "And you've hurt yourself. What's happened? Tell me."

Malora takes a deep breath to calm herself. In as steady a voice as she can muster, she begins to tell him about the dream. While she speaks, he is considerate enough to step away from her, to pace slowly back and forth while he listens. It is as if he knows that the pressure of his gaze will only further unsettle her. Although Malora is the only one who is affected by his scents in this way, she knows Orion will believe her, just as he has believed all the other visions his scents have brought forth, as does Honus, who holds that her keen sense of smell is yet another overdeveloped survival mechanism. She finishes by saying, "I don't know where Sky is, but wherever he is, he's in pain and misery, and I know I must do everything I can to find him and help him."

When Malora is finished, Orion plants his hooves and frowns. "The fact that the wound you got climbing the wall of sticks has carried over into your waking life is significant," he says.

"How so?" she asks.

"I don't know exactly," he says, "but it's as if the two worlds—the dream world and the waking world—are beginning to overlap somehow."

"Then you agree with me that I must find Sky and rescue him," she says.

"Most definitely," he says. "You must go to Kahiro."

"Why to Kahiro?" she asks, his suggestion striking her as odd.

Orion hesitates. "There is this Dromadi crone in the marketplace . . . ," he begins. "Do you remember when I told you that I once had a dream about an encounter with one of the People?"

Malora nods. She remembers everything he says. "A girl. You walked with her by a river and chatted. You told me it was a very satisfying dream."

"It was. But it wasn't exactly a dream. It was a vision, much like the ones you get, except that it was brought on by a beverage brewed by this crone."

"Gaffey?" Malora guesses.

Orion nods rapidly. "How did you know?" he asks.

"Neal gave me a sip once and I had a most vivid vision . . . of Sky," she says. And also of Lume, the silver-haired man with the burnished eyes—but of Lume she has made mention only to Zephele.

"Well," Orion goes on, "in my vision, this wasn't just any human girl. This was you, Malora, years before I ever met you. Don't ask me how, but the beverage reveals things. If anyone can helps us find out where Sky is, it is this crone and her brew."

Malora wonders why he hasn't told her about his vision

before. But that is not her concern right now. Sky is. "If that's the case, there is no need to journey all the way to Kahiro. I can simply ask Neal Featherhoof to give me some gaffey from his zebra-skin flask."

"You'll need Shrouk's interpretation. Shrouk is the Dromadi crone who knows all and sees all. Besides, I believe Neal has run out of gaffey," Orion says. "Just the other day, he mentioned to me that he was due for a trip to Kahiro to renew his supply. So you see, you must go to Kahiro."

She draws in a deep breath and lets it out. She has been in a rare state of panic brought on by the dream. Having a clear course of action brings her some measure of calm. "Very well. I will go to Kahiro. Neal will draw me a map. Or perhaps Honus has one."

Orion laughs softly. "We don't need a map. I have been to Kahiro many times. It is a matter of following the Lower Neelah to the northern coast, where it empties out into the sea."

Malora nods. "Even better," she says, and now she is the one who is pacing. "I will leave West to take care of the boys and girls. I will take Lightning and a few other horses with me and set out immediately."

"Not so fast, my friend," Orion says. "By law, we must first request leave of the Apex."

"*We?*" she says.

Orion grins. "You didn't think I'd let you go to Kahiro alone, did you? Who else would give you a proper introduction to the blind seer? I am one of Shrouk's favorites."

"Of course you are."

"Let me douse the fire and clean up and I'll accompany

you to the Hall of Mirrors. We will petition the Apex together." Orion disappears back into his laboratory. She hears him rummaging, then the hiss of water on flames, after which she smells the odor of dampened wood and ashes.

Malora says through the crack in the door, "Won't there be a great long line of centaurs snaking all the way down to the temple?" she asks. "It could take us all day to be seen."

Orion laughs. "Many things in Mount Kheiron are changing, but fortunately, as far as I can tell, nobility—not to mention family—still has its privileges. And exercise that privilege you can be sure that I will . . . on your behalf," he says as he hustles her up the stairs and out the door.

Except for the Mane Way, the streets of Mount Kheiron are still relatively uncrowded. As they maintain a brisk pace, Orion says, "We can't mention visions or blind seers to my father. He doesn't entertain metaphysical methodologies of reckoning with the world. He has a highly colorful phrase for it: *elephant dung.*"

Malora thinks for a moment, then she says, "I will tell him that Dock, on his recent return from Kahiro, heard rumors of a big black stallion being held captive somewhere. And that we are going to Kahiro to follow up on this intelligence."

Dock is Captain Dugal Highdock—retired from the ranks of the Peacekeepers—the Flatlander who taught Neal Featherhoof everything he knows about bushcraft and fighting. These days Dock escorts the barges of wine barrels that float down the Neelah from the Silvermane Vineyard to the marketplace at Kahiro. Malora knows for a fact that Dock has just gotten back from a trip, because he hailed her the other day from the deck of a returning barge. And Dugal Highdock would, Malora thinks, not object to aiding and abetting Malora in her violation of the Ninth Edict. She'll have to get a message to him.

Orion favors her with an admiring look. "Zephele is right. You are most adept at fabricating falsehoods. You are a champion liar as well as wrangler," he adds, grinning.

"White lies," she says.

"What was that?" he asks.

"The writer of a book I am reading now calls certain untruths 'white lies.' They do no harm. They spare feelings or ease an awkward social situation."

"It is, nevertheless," Orion points out, "a violation of the Ninth."

"Second clause," Malora says glumly.

Before Malora can make a mental list of the Edicts she has violated since she came to Mount Kheiron, they have arrived at the House of Silvermane. The line of petitioners is already strung out into the street. A house Twan in a blue and white tunic is standing propped against a pillar. Unperturbed by the crowd, he is licking the back of his hand and running it across the top of his fur-coated head. Malora and Orion nod to him and walk along the line of centaurs that extends up the steps, across the grand portico, and into the lower gallery. Over the whispered conversations of the centaurs, Malora hears the soothing sound of water running from the wall fountain, spewing from the mouth of leaping fish carved from pink and blue stone. The air is scented with rosewater, distilled by Orion especially for his parents' household.

"He will not be happy with my request," Malora whispers to Orion.

"Don't worry, Malora. He's been in an exceedingly good mood lately," Orion says.

Even so, Malora can tell that Orion is as nervous as she is. Beneath his white silk wrap, he exudes a body odor more horse than man. Unease, she has found, brings out the horse in a centaur.

At the head of the line, at the far end of the hallway, a Twan dozes against a towering set of doors painted white and blue with golden, claw-shaped handles.

"Good morning, Ash," Orion says gently.

The Apex's attendant and the oldest living Twan in Mount Kheiron, Ash rattles the sleep from his head and fumbles for the little round glass he wears on a black string around his neck. Lifting it to his eye and peering up at Orion, Ash's neat pink lips lift into a little bow of pleasure. "Why, if it isn't young Master Orrie!" He turns the glass toward Malora. "And the Victorious One! To what do we owe this double honor?"

"We'd like a moment with the Apex, if we may," Orion says, speaking in a low voice so as not to be overheard by the centaurs at his back.

Ash, who is slightly deaf, repeats this request in a loud, clear voice—"A moment with the Apex?"—and sets off a cascade of grumbling up and down the line.

"Just a brief moment with my parents is all I require," Orion says, darting an apologetic look at the crowd. "I'm afraid it's something of an emergency." He adds in a raised voice, "The Victorious One is in need of his help."

The grumbling breaks off abruptly, and the centaurs are just beginning to crowd around Malora to offer her Maxes along with their services when the doors swing open. Two centaurs emerge, one Highlander and one Flatlander, laughing and clasping hands. Malora only hopes that her visit with the Apex will end on a note as amicable as this.

"Go right in," Ash tells Orion and Malora.

They slip through the doors, the murmured well wishes of the crowd following them.

Malora is no longer distracted by her reflection in the mirrors covering all four walls of what once was a jubilation room where centaurs danced. Now it is the room where the Apex conducts the business of state. The Apex is standing before the low stone table that overflows with tablets and scrolls and a rack of ostrich-feather quills. His horse half is bigger than Sky and his human half bigger than her father, who was a giant among the men in the Settlement. Medon is as allover gray as a bull elephant, his gray brows standing out in an unruly thatch above his fierce gray eyes. The Apex is generally a scowler, but today he has nothing but smiles for Malora, as does his diminutive wife, the Lady Hylonome, known to one and all simply as Herself. As is their custom, both the Apex and Herself are wrapped in subdued hues.

"Daughter!" Herself cries, and holds out her arms to Malora. Her ladyship has silver-gray hair that fans out like fine feathers beneath her brown cap, and eyes of a careworn gray-blue. She envelops Malora briefly in her thin arms, then bestows a kiss on each of her eyelids and her forehead. Holding Malora at arms' length, she says, "You are looking exceptionally fit and well. Ironwork obviously agrees with you, my child."

"Thank you, Lady Hylonome, I am grateful to be learning my Hand. It makes me happier than I can say," Malora says. She turns to the Apex and adds shyly, "Just as Medon has found happiness in his role as the Great Unifier, so am I happy in the forge."

"You've hurt your hand," the Apex says, frowning down at the bandage.

"It is nothing," Malora says. *It's a manifestation of elephant dung,* she wants to add, but instead tosses out the first white lie of many. "A small accident in the forge. Brion bandaged it rather excessively."

"As well he should. See that you take care," Medon says gravely. "The forge is a dangerous place. Fire and iron combined pose formidable dangers. What can I do for you, Daughter? Son?"

Malora turns to look at Orion. Now that they have their audience, where, she wonders, do they begin?

Orion clears his throat. "Malora would like—that is, Malora and I need very urgently—to take a trip to Kahiro, and beg your leave to do so."

Medon's eyebrows poke out from his brow in perplexity. "This strikes me as a singularly ill-conceived idea, my son," he says. "Compared to Kahiro, the blacksmith's forge is as safe as a Twanian nursery."

Malora is grateful to see that if the Apex is not enthusiastic about their plan, neither is he angry.

Herself says, "We had so hoped that you would be happy in your new home and no longer feel the need to wander."

Suddenly mortified that she did not begin the visit with thanks to both of them, Malora says, "The house is all I could ever want. It's so very beautiful. I will be very happy there, I know, and I am ever so grateful to you both. But I have recently learned something that threatens to undermine my happiness, and I have no choice but to act upon it. In order to do so, I must make a trip to Kahiro. You see, sir, one of the Peacekeepers—"

"Dock," Orion puts in.

"Yes, Dugal Highdock has returned from Kahiro recently with word that my horse, Sky—"

"The splendid blue-eyed stallion that was the leader of your herd?" Medon interjects, his gray eyes suddenly keen.

"The very same," Malora says, relieved at his obvious interest. "The word in Kahiro is that Sky is being held captive."

"Where and by whom?" Medon's eyebrows lower ominously.

"That's just it, sir," Orion says. "We're not sure exactly where or by whom, which is why we need to go to Kahiro because, as everyone knows, everything you need you can find in the marketplace of Kahiro . . . including *information*!"

Malora squeezes Orion's hand in gratitude.

The Apex's eyes narrow. "Let me see if I understand this. The two of you wish leave to go to Kahiro?"

Malora and Orion, sweaty hands interlaced, nod earnestly.

The Apex throws back his head and releases a roar of wordless command so powerful, Malora imagines her heavy braid being blown back. "Ash!" the Apex lets out with his next roar.

Ash pushes open the door and stands on the threshold, blinking in the aftermath of the Apex's summons. "You roared, Your Fierceness?"

"Yes, I roared. I can still roar now and then, can't I? Find and fetch me Neal Featherhoof. He's lurking about some-where, visiting with Honus, I believe. Bring me Honus, too, while you're at it. We are going to need both of them."

"Yes, Your Fierceness," Ash says as he bows his way out of the room and shuts the door.

"I will permit you to go to Kahiro on two conditions," Medon says, holding up two meaty fingers. "One: Neal Featherhoof, and a detail of the Peacekeepers, will go with you to and from the Kingdom of the Ka. And two: Honus must find a way for you, Daughter, to go amongst the hibes of that city *undetected*."

Malora blurts out, "But I don't need—"

"I WILL SAY WHAT YOU NEED!" the Apex thunders, and Malora quickly bobs her head in agreement.

Herself places a hand on her husband's biceps. Medon, heaving a deep breath, nods slowly and continues in a more modulated tone: "The last of the People on this earth must be preserved at all costs."

The doors swing open again, admitting a centaur with a golden hide and Honus the faun. Honus remains standing by the door, but the centaur ambles into the room on long ginger-colored legs. With hooves that are feathered with tufts of pale gold, Neal Featherhoof is possibly the only centaur Malora knows whose name fits him. He must be off-duty to-day, she guesses, because he is not wearing the red and white wrap of the Peacekeepers with the gold band around his neck that reminds her unpleasantly of the collars Neal has buckled onto his hunting dogs. Malora much prefers Neal out of uni-form: wrapped in ragged impala skin that covers only his hindmost quarters and, on his human half, an equally ragged buckskin vest. His scarred arms and his chest are roped with muscle. From the rawhide thong around his neck dangles the claw of a lion he slew with nothing more than the long-handled dagger called the Bushman's Friend.

"Did you need me, sir?" Featherhoof asks the Apex and then, as if just noticing the two other visitors, says casually, "Oh, hello, Orrie. Hello, pet. What brings you here?"

Medon says, "You are to outfit and provide an immediate escort for an expedition to Kahiro. Malora and Orion wish to go in search of the stallion Sky, whose whereabouts, they seem to feel, will be revealed to them in the marketplace at Kahiro."

Neal winces and says to Malora, "Pet, I must say, we all know you are as brave as our Apex here is wise, and I know that this horse holds a special place in your heart, but you've had better ideas. Kahiro is really no place for the likes of you."

Malora feels her face heating up. The Dream Wound throbs. "Why do you all keep saying that?" she says. "I am more than capable of taking care of myself."

"In the bush, I'll grant you," Neal says. "But in the Kingdom of the Ka there are dangers you have never dreamed of."

Something about the way Neal says this—the unusual note of gravity perhaps—makes Malora swallow her retort. The Hall of Mirrors falls into an uncomfortable silence that is finally broken by Honus.

"I think I might have a solution," he says, "that will permit Malora to enter Kahiro and yet keep her safe."

CHAPTER 5

Malora's Horns

Malora and the four centaurs listen as Honus explains his solution. The others are struck by its cleverness, while Malora
finds it bizarre and utterly incomprehensible.

"All will become clear," Honus says to her when he sees
the baffled expression on her face.

Malora nods uncertainly. So long as she can go in search
of Sky, she will put up with any amount of foolishness.

Orion and Neal depart immediately to make arrange-
ments. Honus and Malora have their own errand to run.

"My dear, I owe you an apology," Honus says as they set
out for Longshanks's shop, Malora striding, Honus tripping
along on his cloven hooves.

"For making me wear some foolish disguise?" Malora
says. "I will trust you when you all say it is for my own good.
Kahiro is a dangerous place, as Neal says. It's best that I blend
in and not call attention to myself."

"Clearly I have done an incomplete job of explaining to you how things are in the greater world outside Mount Kheiron," Honus says as they walk. "I never imagined you would ever be leaving Mount Kheiron and, even if you did, that you would be doing so this soon. I thought there would be ample time to explain, to educate and prepare you."

"I understand that the other hibes hate and fear the People as much as the centaurs once did," Malora says.

"It's not as simple as that," Honus says. "The Massacre of Kamaria represented the People's last-known stand. But before that, there were hundreds, even thousands of years of war waged between the hibes and the People."

Malora knew this, too, but it always surprises her to hear of it. "Why did the hibes hate the People so? What did we ever do to them to deserve such hatred?" she asks.

"You created them," Honus says.

Malora stops walking and turns to stare at him. "I don't understand," she says softly. "I didn't do any such thing."

"*You* didn't, specifically, but thousands of years ago, the Scienticians did, and the Scienticians were People," Honus says, "at the very height of their scientific powers."

"I still don't understand," Malora says. "How did they do this?"

Honus heaves his shoulders. "With science . . . and perhaps some amount of magic. No one knows. For the longest time, the hibes believed they were creatures of nature, like the beasts of the bush, the birds of the air, and the fish in the streams and the sea. But when the information leaked into the world that we were unnatural species, *scientific* creations—

bizarre synthetic combinations of human and animal—they turned upon the People, their creators, and set out to destroy them. They did an excellent job of it, too, I might add. The People were herded together into camps, where many of them died of starvation and disease. At least your tribe, the Kamarians, died free. Just as you and your parents lived free in the Settlement."

Malora feels torn asunder. "Why did my parents never tell me . . . ?"

"Parents want to protect their children, much as we here in Mount Kheiron want to protect you," Honus says.

Part of Malora wants to forge ahead and prepare for her journey to find Sky, while another part of her wants time to stop so she can hunker down with Honus and learn more.

"After the People had virtually perished from the earth, the hibes began to believe, for reasons I will save for another time, that what they had done—systematically destroying the People—was a fundamentally bad thing. They began to repent and to revere the memory of the People, their artifacts, their relics, their likeness, and the very brilliance that had enabled the People to create the hibes in the first place. The People, in death, were worshipped as martyrs, as gods. The centaurs alone—perhaps because they live in such isolation—never subscribed to this religion. They had their own rather more secular god in Kheiron. But the hibes of many of the other nations, those who throng the streets of Kahiro, almost all worship in the Church of the Latter Day Scienticians. If they were ever to lay eyes on a genuine, living, breathing human being, who is to say what they would do? Either kill you with kindness or attempt to preserve you as a living relic in their temple. In either case, it would be a most unhappy fate for you. And that, my dear, is why we in Mount Kheiron know we must guard the secret of your existence and, when we bring you out into the world beyond Mount Kheiron, give you a most convincing disguise."

Malora, who has previously only been humoring Honus and the centaurs by going along with this plan, is, by the time they reach Cylas's shop, heartily in favor of it. Something new to fear, a bitter voice inside her head says.

"You will be happy to know that your order is nearly ready," Cylas says when he sees her coming through the door.

"Thank you, Cylas," Malora says. "But we are here on other business."

Honus explains what they need. Cylas listens with his usual attentiveness. When Honus finishes, the cobbler says, "You wish me to appropriate the horns of a goat, approximately the same size and shape and color as your own quite distinguished pair?"

Honus nods. "Yes, and find a way of affixing them to a band—I am thinking one made of tortoiseshell—that fits over the crown of Malora's head and can be well concealed beneath her hair," he says.

"This would be a disguise," Longshanks says softly, "for Malora to wear on the streets of Kahiro."

Honus nods. "Just so. To the milling crowds it will appear as if she were a relative of mine. A faun maiden. My daughter."

Always the daughter, Malora thinks. Thora, her mother, would think her in very good hands with Honus.

"An excellent notion," says Cylas. "I go to Kahiro once a year, to study the fashions and derive aesthetic inspiration, and every time, I feel positively menaced. Hold on to your nubs, too, for I don't know who's cleverer or more bent on picking your pocket: the tradesfolk or the thieves! However," he says, clearing his throat, "there is the not insignificant matter of her *uncloven* feet, not to mention her ankles."

Malora glances down at Honus's trouser-clad legs, which are differently jointed at the ankle and in this respect more horselike than human.

"I have thought of that," says Honus, "which brings me to my second request. And that is a saruchi."

"A saruchi?" Malora asks. "What is that?"

"Ah yes! The wildly popular sheKa fashion," Longshanks says. "A wrap for the lower body of the female two-legger. It wraps around the waist and drapes to the ground."

"But how am I to get around in such a garment, let alone ride a horse?" Malora says.

"You will learn, just as your lady forebears did so long ago," Honus says. "You might even find it has its advantages."

"But aren't strangers bound to see my feet *beneath* this saruchi and notice that I have no cloven hooves?" Malora says doubtfully.

"The saruchi will cover your feet. Besides," Honus adds, "staring at the feet of sheKa is considered disrespectful, so most have trained themselves not to stare at the feet of any female bipeds. Besides, they will see the horns on your head and most of them will assume the rest. I will have to coach you how to walk, of course," he adds, "but one thing at a time."

Honus turns to Longshanks. "We are leaving at daybreak tomorrow on a mission of utmost importance. Can you help us, my old friend, by expediting this order?"

"I will set aside all other jobs. I should have the saruchi, the headdress, and the holder for the knife ready by this evening," the cobbler says.

Honus turns slowly to Malora with an upraised eyebrow. *"The knife?"*

"A tool," Malora says, blushing.

"For cutting cheese and twine and bread," Longshanks says smoothly.

"I see," says Honus, unsuccessfully concealing a smile.

"I made it in the shop as a special project," Malora tells him. "It's much sharper than the butter knife I borrowed from you."

"That is excellent news, indeed," Honus says. "This way, when we are accosted by brigands on the road to Kahiro, you won't have to resort to *buttering* them to death."

It is his favorite joke. Malora responds with a laugh and wonders whether laughing at a joke she doesn't find funny constitutes a white lie.

At dawn the next morning Malora stands outside the big paddock. She is dressed in buckskin trousers and the new boots with the ankle-sheath, a white cotton tunic, and a wide-brimmed impala-skin hat, with the black-and-white braided rope slung over her shoulder. She has already made her rounds, said her good-byes to the boys and girls, and assembled those horses she will take with her. She has decided to bring only mares, because they are more intelligent and have greater stamina, and she wants no equine flirtation going on. Besides, when she finds Sky, the mares will be her gift to him.

Lightning will be her principal mount. Malora has tacked her up with a bit and a bridle and a saddle that Longshanks made from cow leather and bone, with cow-leather stirrups and saddlebags. In one bag, she has packed an extra pair of suede trousers, three tunics, and the long pale-blue saruchi Cylas made for her. The other bag contains *Pride and Prejudice,* a silver-backed hairbrush, and the goat-horn tiara. Cylas adjusted it several times, but the tortoiseshell band hurts her head, so she does not intend to wear it until they reach the outskirts of Kahiro. In addition to Lightning, she is bringing Light Rain and Charcoal. Light Rain will be her second mount—leaving Bolt to enjoy Max all to herself—and Charcoal will serve as a packhorse because she and Raven, the horse that Honus will ride, are inseparable. Malora has tacked up Raven with Honus's sidesaddle.

Malora is just going over some horse-keeping details with West when Neal and Dugal Highdock arrive, followed by Orion. Neal and Dock carry bows and sheaths of arrows on their backs. Neal also carries a sword in a scabbard on his belt, whereas Dock carries a coiled bullwhip made of rhino hide. Orion is unarmed.

"Thank you for coming," Malora says to Dock.

"My pleasure to serve," he says gruffly.

A centaur of few words and fewer smiles, Dugal "Dock" Highdock is small but tough and stringy. He has scarred brown flanks, and the hair on his head stands out like tufts of white cotton. Dock walks with a hitch in his right hind leg where a crocodile savaged him.

Honus is the next to arrive, riding in the back of a wagon piled high with supplies. Pulling the wagon is a team of two stout Beltanian draft horses driven by Lemon, who has replaced West as Orion's Twan. Lemon's mate (and Zephele's Twan), Sunshine, sits next to him in the high seat.

"How will Zephele manage without you?" Malora asks Sunshine. She says this to be polite, since Zephele rarely calls upon her Twan to perform services.

"Ah, but Zephele is coming, too!" Zephele says, stepping out from behind the wagon. She is wheeling a cart containing a painted wooden chest and a tapestry bag that is bulging at the seams.

Neal cuts short his discussion with Dock and says, "Zephele is not going *anywhere* but back to the House of Silvermane, where she belongs!"

"I respectfully beg to differ, Captain Featherhoof," Zephele says, her dimpled chin held high. "Last night, Herself and the Apex approved my request to join the expedition. Feel free to march right up the mountain and ask them yourself if you don't believe me. I persuaded them that it was high time I visited Kahiro, and they both agreed, as well they should, since I have only been begging them for the privilege since the day I turned ten. How exciting it will be, not just to visit Kahiro but to do so with one of the People in disguise! I wonder if I should wear a disguise as well? Unfortunately, as we learned at the last jubilation, it is difficult, nigh onto impossible, to disguise a centaur as anything but a centaur."

Sunshine has climbed down from the seat and tugs unsuccessfully at the handle of Zephele's trunk.

"Don't strain yourself, my dear," Zephele tells the Twan. "It took three of our stoutest Twani to load it in there. I'm sure it will take at least three to unload it. Unless one of these muscular young bucks will volunteer for the job?"

Neal ambles over and stares down at the trunk. Then he looks up into the wagon, which is already loaded to the point of toppling. He strokes his chin thoughtfully as if making a serious assessment.

"Show me what's in this chest," he says.

Drawing herself up primly, Zephele replies, "Kheiron shuns your impertinence! My garments are none of your concern."

"Oh, but didn't your father explain to you how it is? *Everything* about this expedition is my concern," Neal says.

Zephele holds out for a fleeting moment, then relents. "Oh, very well!" she says, yanking open the trunk. Shimmering garments spill out as if they had been waiting for their chance to escape.

"Tell me, Zeph, are there any *sensible* garments—suitable for the rigors of the bush—in among this frippery?" Neal asks, poking the point of his sword into the jumble, causing some garments to slither onto the ground like colorful, silken snakes.

"The sensible garments are in the satchel," Zephele says huffily.

"I'm encouraged." Neal stuffs the clothing unceremoniously back into the trunk, slams the lid, and thumps it. "Leave the trunk here, Zeph. We'll make room on the wagon for the satchel."

"But—" Zephele starts to protest.

"Zephele Silvermane," Neal says to her, softly but distinctly enunciating each syllable of her name, "let us agree on this at the outset. This is an expedition into the bush. I am the captain of this expedition. I will say what you can and cannot do. It is not a matter of fancy. It is a matter of safety—often as not a matter of life and death—which is why you will do *exactly* as I say and endeavor not to protest, contradict, or wheedle me into granting you your every whim, however much your adoring father and mother and brothers and cousins and friends have all accustomed you to getting it since the day you were born. *My way* is the law, is that understood?"

"Very clearly," Zephele says, looking thoroughly abashed, her eyes cast downward.

"Good! It's settled then. Let's find room on the wagon for this satchel," he says to Sunshine.

Then Zephele puts in timidly, "If I might first request a single boon, Captain?"

Neal folds his arms across his chest. "What?" he asks flatly.

"I should like to transfer just *one* of the frivolous wraps into the bag I'm taking." She hastens to head off his objection. "I will need something to wear when we get to Kahiro, where the sheKa, I am told, dress in the very latest fashions. Surely you wouldn't want the daughter of the Apex of Kheiron to stagger into Kahiro looking like a Suidean slattern, now would you?" she asks, eyeing him from beneath her velvety lashes.

"As if such a thing were even remotely possible," Neal says, throwing up his arms. "Choose one piece of finery and we'll be on our way. And make it quick. We have a good twenty days of travel ahead of us."

Zephele catches Malora's eye and winks.

When Malora first approached Mount Kheiron from the south, it went from not being there one moment to filling her sights the next. But the terrain to the north, except for the mountains to the west, is as flat as a piece of pounded iron, and Mount Kheiron remains at their backs almost the whole of their first day, as if reminding them that if the bush proves too daunting they can still about-face and go running back to the Land of Beauty and Enlightenment.

Neal and Orion lead the way, followed by Zephele, Malora, and Honus walking three abreast. Behind them roll the Twani in the wagon, hitched to the back of which are Light Rain and Charcoal, with the bullwhip-wielding Dock bringing up the rear.

They tread the well-worn path that traders have traveled for generations making the journey from Mount Kheiron to Kahiro. The Lower Neelah flows sluggish and brown on their left, and the Hills of Melea rise like a wall to their right, changing colors with the position of the sun. Zephele spends so much time swiveling her head to look behind her that she might as well be walking backward, Malora thinks, and finally tells her so.

"But Mount Kheiron is so small, Malora! Look at it compared to this great, wild vastness!" Zephele says, her voice filled with something Malora has never heard in it before.

Fear? Or perhaps simply respect for something she has not conquered, and never will be able to, with her beauty, her charm, or her status as the daughter of the Apex.

"It *is* small," Malora agrees thoughtfully. For herself, she is content to be on the back of a horse and is surprisingly happy to be in the bush again. Why was she so afraid of returning? Perhaps just as absence from the bush made her fearful of it, returning to it has restored her confidence. And then there is the anticipation of finding Sky, which thrills her.

"I've spent my whole life in that small place," Zephele muses.

"Well then, it's a good thing you're finally getting away from it," Malora says. The fact is that since Malora's arrival, Mount Kheiron has become her entire world, too. The thought that Mount Kheiron will be waiting for her when she returns fills her with a sense of comfort and security. That she will be bringing Sky with her makes it all the more exciting. Both worlds—the wild world of the bush and the civilized one of the centaurs—she is now able to move about in and inhabit.

"That you survived out here—in fact, positively thrived!— for as long as you did only increases my deepest respect and admiration for you," Zephele says. After a brief silence, she adds, "One only has to look down to see that death is everywhere."

Malora looks down. Zephele is speaking of the bones and skulls littering the trail.

Honus is so stimulated, he slides from his saddle constantly to gather specimens for his collection: kudu horns, rabbit and impala skulls, porcupine quills, sparkling rocks, and feathers of all kinds. Honus's slipping from the saddle is Malora's cue to shout ahead to Neal to call a halt. Honus hands Malora Raven's reins and then retrieves the specimen that has caught his eye.

After the fifth halt, Neal circles back and says to Malora in a low voice, "With all due respect to the Learned Master, and I personally don't care if we stop a hundred times, but this trip is, I understand, a matter of some urgency to *you*. I'm sure if you were to remind Honus of this fact, he would curb his naturalist's ardor."

"Don't worry," Malora says. "Tomorrow he'll be so saddle-sore he won't be able to dismount without a great deal of pain."

Neal nods and grins, then rejoins Orion, who—like the Peacekeepers—wears a wide-brimmed straw hat, while Zephele has turned in her centaurean maiden's cap for a bright pink head scarf. The Silvermanes have gone Flatlander in the bush, Malora thinks wryly.

Zephele's enthusiasm for the wonders of the bush is as boundless as Honus's, although she restricts herself to pointing and asking questions. "What is that sweet little flower over there?" she asks.

Malora squints at a little blue flower not even her mother gave a name to. "I know the names of the *useful* plants," she tells Zephele. "But that one has no use so it has no name."

Honus speaks up: "It is *Triteleia grandiflora.*"

Zephele repeats the flower's name and asks Honus to spell it so she can copy it down on the small, leather-bound tablet she keeps in the pouch on her belt. No sooner has she written down the name than she points to the herd of striped antelope leaping clumsily about in the cloud grass just to the west of them. "And what are those?"

"Wildebeest," Malora says.

"How comical they are," Zephele says, laughing. "Why do they run in such an antically irregular fashion?"

Neal, having overheard, calls back, "For your ladyship's amusement!"

Zephele rolls her eyes.

Malora says to Zephele, "No reason I can think of. That's just the way wildebeest run. Perhaps they run this way to elude predators with their unpredictability."

"Wildebeest," says Zephele, rolling the word on her tongue. "The name suits them, doesn't it?" Her declared goal is to memorize the names of every plant and creature she sees on the expedition.

Shortly following their midday halt to eat nuts and fruit, hard bread, and cheese, Malora spies a lone dark brown antelope lurking behind a bush. Tapping Zephele on the shoulder, she points. "See that brown animal over there? That's the sable antelope. It was skinned to make that luxurious winter cape of yours."

"No!" Zephele stares at the cowering creature, aghast. "The poor dear thing! But it's so shy and sweet!"

"And so warm and soft!" Neal calls back loudly enough to spook the sable and send it bounding off, horns flashing in the sunlight.

Zephele shudders. "That decides it. As soon as I return home, I will donate all my furs to the Flatlanders Fund and have Theon weave me a thick woolen cape. I don't care how frumpy I look. From now on, I will foreswear the wearing of animal skins."

"I'll believe that when I see it," Orion calls back. And he and Neal laugh.

"Orion Silvermane, how dare you share laughter at my expense with the Flatlander," Zephele says imperiously, setting off still more laughter.

Later, when a snake the size of a large tree branch slithers across their path, Zephele screams. Everyone stops. Malora drapes her reins over Lightning's saddle horn and dismounts. Clamping the rock python's massive jaws shut with one hand, she hoists the upper half out of the grass to give everyone a good look at it. She strains beneath its weight. It is as big around as an elephant's leg and as long as three horse-lengths. She is showing off, she knows it, but she can't help herself. They have shown her their world. Now she wants to show them hers.

"Utterly magnificent!" Honus says. "And a marvel of natural engineering. I imagine knights of yore modeled their segmented armor on the scales of such creatures as these."

"I seem to remember that you have a pair of cunning boots made from the skin of one of these marvels," Orion says to Zephele.

"In that case, I will bid farewell to my snakeskin boots, as well as my sable cape," his sister says.

"And your zebra- and your leopard- and your kid- and your giraffe-skin boots as well?" Neal adds, grinning.

"You seem to be paying rather close attention to my footwear, Flatlander," Zephele says tartly. Then to Malora: "Oh, take care, Malora. Does it bite?"

"Not exactly," Malora says. Her strength giving out, she eases the snake back down, releasing it and standing back to give it a wide berth as it slithers off into the grass. "It strikes with the points of its teeth to knock its prey senseless, then it squeezes the life out of it and gobbles it down whole. I've lost more than a few colts to these monsters."

"Snake, dear, do you hear me?" Zephele says, looking off into the grass. "If I promise never to make a pair of boots out of you, do you promise not to hurt me?"

CHAPTER 6

Too Beautiful to Kill

In the lowering rays of the sun, Neal leads them past a massive termite mound where a fully grown female leopard lounges, staring at them with her great, unblinking golden eyes.

Zephele shrinks away, but Malora reassures her. "Don't worry. She's already eaten. See?" And she points to the tree from which hangs the carcass of a half-eaten eland. The she-leopard has obviously just sated herself and then dragged the remains of her meal up into the tree, out of reach of hyenas, wild dogs, and other poachers. Zephele shudders. Neal calls back to them in a way calculated to make Zephele shriek yet again. "Now *that's* a sight to make a Flatlander's mouth water for dinner. I think it's time to look for a place to camp."

"What an excellent idea, Captain Featherhoof!" Zephele calls back to him serenely.

They continue at a slower pace, giving Neal a chance to size up the terrain as they go.

"What's taking him so long?" Zephele says, her stride flagging.

"We need a place close enough to the river so we will be able to have cooking and bathing water," Malora explains, "but not so near that we are overrun by the wild animal traffic going to and from it."

Zephele replies wearily, "Oh. Well, in that case, let him take his time and choose with the greatest possible care."

Neal settles for a hard, barren swath of earth studded with sparkling pink rocks.

"Here?" Zephele asks. "Isn't it a bit bleak?"

"It's hardly that. Rose quartz!" Honus cries. No sooner has Honus slipped off Raven's back and turned her over to Malora than he hobbles off to fill his arms with glittering mineral specimens.

With Lemon's help, Malora rigs a roped enclosure for the horses, strung with bells that will jingle should a predator attempt to broach the perimeter. Then she fetches a bow and quiver from the wagon and goes off with Neal to hunt dinner, leaving Orion and Zephele to collect firewood, Dock to guard the camp, and Lemon and Sunshine to erect the tents. There is one tent for the Twani, another for Zephele and Malora, and a third for Orion and Honus. The Peacekeepers will sleep outside and take turns standing watch. When Malora and Neal are out of earshot of the others, Malora says, "I think Zephele did quite well on her first day, don't you?"

Neal grunts. "We'll see how she fares tonight. I don't think she's quite realized that the bush does not come equipped with a marble convenience."

"Aren't you being a little hard on her?"

Neal's lips twist into a smile. "I've been teasing Zephie since she was three years old. She's used to it."

"But she's grown up now. Isn't it time you stopped?" Malora asks.

"When she acts like a lady, I'll treat her like one," Neal says shortly. He takes out the familiar zebra-skinned flask and holds it to his lips, drinking sparingly.

"Is that gaffey?" Malora asks.

He nods and wipes his mouth.

"Orion told me you had none left."

"This is the dregs," he says. "I've been nursing it for weeks. Care for a sip? It's quite potent."

Knowing that visions derived from drinking this beverage, according to Orion, may hold the key to Sky's whereabouts, she reaches for the flask. Perhaps this will save them a trip to Kahiro. Zephele will be disappointed, but Sky will be located that much sooner. Closing her eyes, she puts out the question silently—where are you, Sky?—then tilts her head back and lets some of the bitter liquid trickle down her throat. She swallows slowly, her eyes still shut.

The air smells freshly scrubbed. Suddenly, she is wrapped in his arms, his mouth pressed to hers, his sweet breath coursing through her body. She gasps and pushes him away, staring up into eyes that are huge and burnished and as silver as his hair. Lume whispers, "Good. You're alive."

Malora opens her eyes and says, "Of course I'm alive."

"I did not expect otherwise," Neal says, eying her strangely as he snatches the flask from her grip and pounds in the cork with the heel of his hand. "Don't tell me. You saw elephants with pink wings dancing on the tops of daisies? Or is it putti frolicking in the clouds?" he says.

"No," Malora says, laying a hand to the side of her face, which feels hot. "But I did see a man."

"Did you now? Would this be a fellow human being?" Neal says.

Malora nods.

"Well now. That's very nearly as fanciful as the elephants and the cherubs. But I suppose you're entitled to your dreams. I hope he's everything you want in a mate."

"He is," she says faintly. She wonders, not for the first time, where he is, who he is, and when she will meet him.

"Back to reality with you, my pet," Neal says, pointing to a herd of impala in the high grass. Neal fits an arrow to his bow, raises it, and pulls back the string, sighting his target. Malora holds her breath until Neal releases the arrow. It whistles through the air, and seconds later a small impala falls, the rest of the herd leaping off in all directions.

They retrieve the dead animal, which Neal hoists with a rope, its head hanging down, from the branch of a nearby tree. Then Malora takes out her knife and skins it just enough to carve off the meat from the tenderloin. She is pleased with the way her knife slices through the still-warm flesh. Then she cuts down the carcass and leaves it for the scavengers. By the time her work is finished, the bandage on her hand is soaked in impala blood. She strips it off, and Neal helps her wash it with the water in his canteen.

"Nasty gouge," he comments.

Malora holds up her hand. "This? I got it in a dream," she says.

He raises an eyebrow. "If you say so, pet."

He washes the blood off her knife, too, then hefts it. "You handle the knife well. Do you know how to use it?"

She stares at him blandly. "I believe I just did," she says.

"I mean to *defend* yourself," he says.

"Of course I do," Malora says, taking back the knife and returning it to her boot.

"It's a fine weapon," he says.

"If you'll stop teasing Zephele, I'll make one for you when we get back to Mount Kheiron," she says.

"In the marketplace at Kahiro there are endless displays of Bushman's Friends for sale," Neal says.

"The only thing I hope to find in the marketplace is the way to my horse," Malora says grimly.

Neal says, "Why a levelheaded young woman like you would think some old crone in possession of useful informa- tion . . . She's a gaffey brewer. Gaffey is a stimulant, not a magic potion. And the visions it gives rise to are figments of an overactive imagination and nothing else. I hate to be the one to disappoint you, pet."

Malora stares at him coolly. "If Shrouk and her gaffey don't yield up the information we need, maybe you can help me find Sky."

"I will do what I can," Neal says, and Malora is glad to see that he has wiped the mocking grin from his face.

While Lemon brews nettle soup in a pot, Malora and Neal spit the impala tenderloin and roast it over the fire.

After everyone has finished eating, the carnivores on one side of the fire, the herbivores on the other, they all sip cups of red bush tea while darkness lowers and the stars begin to poke through like slivers of diamond through dark velvet. They gather their wraps around themselves and stare at the fire, their thoughts lost in the flames.

A loud, cackling cry rouses everyone. Wide-eyed, Zephele scoots closer to Malora. "What was that?" she asks.

"Hyena," Neal says, picking his teeth with a twig.

Green lights flash in the darkness.

"And what are those?" Zephele asks.

"Bush bunnies," Malora says. "Their eyes glow."

"They look rather sweet," Zephele says.

"They taste like berries and wild sage," Neal says.

"Haven't you already sufficiently gorged yourself?" Zephele says.

Darkness deepens and the air grows chilly, drawing them closer to the fire. A powerful musk fills the air and causes the horses to stop munching their feed and fall still.

Malora lifts her nose and sniffs. "I wonder," she says slowly, rising to her feet. She lights a stout stick and takes a few steps with the torch away from the fire and into the darkness. "I thought so! Look!" she whispers, as she holds up the torch and illuminates a family of rhinos: a bull, two cows, and a calf, all grazing placidly while peering at the travelers with their tiny curious eyes.

"Oh my! They're like living rocks!" Zephele says. "Are we in any danger of being gored by those fearsome horns?"

Malora returns to the fire, tossing the torch into the flames. "Not really. They're just as curious about us," she says, "as we are about them."

"Those would be black rhinos, if I'm not mistaken," Honus says. "As opposed to white."

"Really?" Malora says. "They all look gray to me."

"*Diceros bicornis* is the scientific name. I believe the name *white rhino* came about as a result of a misunderstanding of the word *wide,* for the white rhino has a wider head than the black. Ancient safari hunters designated the black rhino to be one of the Big Five, which were held to be the most difficult animals to hunt: lion, elephant, Cape buffalo, black rhino, and—I believe—that spotted creature we saw earlier today, the leopard."

"The Big Five," Zephele says musingly. "To think that we've been in the bush only one day and already we've sighted two of the Big Five. I wonder if we'll see the other three before we get to Kahiro? We must all pay very close attention."

"I could do without coming across a Cape buffalo," says Neal. "The Cape buffalo is, as far as I know, the only animal driven to seek revenge. When they're wounded, I've seen them lay waste to entire camps."

"Then there's the Ugly Five," Honus goes on. "Can you guess what they might be?"

"Hmmm," says Malora. "Well, the bush pig is *very* ugly."

"But equally as succulent," Neal puts in.

"Very good! The bush pig is one of the Ugly Five," Honus says. "The other four are the wildebeest, the marabou stork, the hyena, and last but by no means least, the hippopotamus."

A short awkward pause follows the mention of hippos, the beast that savaged Athen Silvermane. Zephele breaks the silence: "I think it's cruel to say that some animals are ugly. Surely each creature is, in its own way, beautiful. I'm quite positive that the mother bush pig finds her little bush piglets the most adorable things in the world."

Neal spits into the fire. "How about the Ridiculous Five?" he says. "Let's see . . . that would be the Sniveling Coward, the Boasting Windbag, the Relentless Expert, the Conniving User, and last but not least, Zephele Silvermane, the Hopelessly Sentimental."

Zephele narrows her eyes at him. "At least I am not one of the Cruel Five, a Rude and Heartless Brute," she retorts.

Neal appears to take this as flattery. Zephele's eyes blaze.

Honus says, "I think I'll retire before any centaur blood is spilled."

"Me too," Malora says, rising to her feet and stretching her saddle-sore muscles.

Zephele follows Malora to their tent. "What if I have to get up to relieve myself in the middle of the night?" she whispers.

"Wake me up and I'll escort you to the great dirt convenience," Malora says, yawning.

Just outside the tent, Sunshine has left a flask of water for drinking and a bowl of heated water for washing. Centaur and human share a small bar of soap and huddle over the bowl, washing themselves by lantern light only as far as modesty and the water will take them. Then Malora flings the dirty water into the darkness and leaves the bowl for Sunshine to refill in the morning. They enter the tent.

"Great Hands but this rusticity is extreme, is it not?" Zephele declares, surveying the inside of the tent. "And small. Somehow, it seemed bigger when it was light out."

"You'll get used to it," Malora says, setting the lantern on the camp table between their cots and stretching out on her own, folding her hands behind her head. "You'll be so exhausted at night, I promise you won't even notice the size of your quarters."

"Are you going to sleep in what you wore today?" Zephele says.

"Why not?" Malora says. "Besides, I didn't think to bring any nightclothes. I never wore them before I came to Mount Kheiron."

Zephele nods thoughtfully. "It seems foolish now that I think of it, to change one's clothes for sleep out here. I mean, what if a herd of wild elephants rampages through the camp in the middle of the night? I wouldn't want the others to see me in my night wrap." In the lantern light, she sets up a looking glass on the camp table and bends over it to examine her reflection.

"Why didn't you tell me I was turning as pink as a boiled beet!" she cries. She puts the back of her hand to her cheek. "My skin is so hot. I never realized the sun had such power."

She pulls off the head scarf. Malora is surprised to see Zephele's head bare for the first time, as she tugs a brush through her short but unruly curls. "Such snarls! You're lucky. You can keep your hair in a braid. One of the problems with wearing a cap or a scarf all the time is that you wind up with the most stubborn tangles in the back of your head at the end of each day."

"I think your hair is beautiful," Malora says. "See how it shines!"

"Ha!" Zephele says. "My meager little crop . . . I wonder

if I should let it grow long like yours. Who would be the wiser?" she muses.

"Wouldn't it be hard to fit long hair beneath a cap?" Malora asks.

"Maybe I'll stop wearing a cap altogether!" Zephele says. Then she laughs, "Listen to me: one day in the bush and I've turned into an upstart. Herself would say that I am behaving like a small child with a high fever. I feel rather like that. All this *excitement*! I do hope I'll be able to sleep."

Zephele is just about to lie down on her cot when she says, "I nearly forgot." She removes a green flask of scent from her bag and dabs some behind each ear. "Wild jasmine for courage." Then she lies down and covers herself with the blanket. Malora leans over and douses the lantern.

"I think you're very brave, even without the aid of the scent," Malora whispers in the jasmine-scented darkness.

"Do you really?" Zephele asks, her voice weary but eager.

"Yes. My first night in the bush, I slept in a ditch I had dug beneath a mashatu tree. I hid beneath a blanket, and I was terrified."

"Were you really?" Zephele asks. "You were just a child, though. And alone."

Just then, something touches the roof of their tent. "What was that?" Zephele asks in a tense voice.

"An insect of some sort. It's nothing to worry about. I understand how you're feeling. Nervous and jumpy, like I was. Every time something landed on my blanket I'd start. Sometimes I even screamed. Then Sky would spook. I thought the night would never end."

"Did you really scream?" Zephele asks in delight. "Or are you just saying that to make me feel better?"

"Oh, I screamed quite loudly," Malora says. "The first night in the bush is always the hardest."

"It doesn't seem so bad to me. . . ."

From a distance comes a high wheezing *blat,* followed by a succession of *blats.*

"What was that?" Zephele asks, sounding slightly less brave now.

"Elephants," Malora says, "very far away. From back where we came. We passed a dead one a ways back. The elephants are probably coming to mourn it."

"What dead elephant?" Zephele says. "I saw no dead elephant."

"I didn't either, but I smelled it," Malora says.

"I wonder why I didn't smell it?" Zephele says.

"Wild jasmine."

A little later, they hear a growling snigger. "What's that?" Zephele asks.

"Baboons."

The jabbering escalates into a spirited discussion.

"They sound like Flatlander louts, don't they?" Zephele says. "Thugs and hecklers."

"They're just staking out their territory," Malora says.

"Like the guard at the city gates of Mount Kheiron," Zephele says.

"I suppose you could say that," Malora agrees. "Although you can make too much of the similarities of animals and sentient beings."

"I don't know . . . animals speak to each other, just as we speak to one another, don't they?" Zephele says.

"They *communicate,*" Malora says. "They don't speak. There is a difference."

After a brief silence, Zephele says, "When Sky comes to you . . . in your dreams . . . does he *speak* to you?"

"Yes, he does, I suppose," Malora says.

"In words?"

"Yes, but that may be just me, putting his thoughts into words. When we were together, we understood each other without words. We were that close." She smiles to herself. "I now see . . . like a centaur separated into two."

"Did you bring some Breath of the Bush with you so you could conjure him?" Zephele asks.

"No," says Malora. "I don't like to use scents in the bush. It interferes with my ability to smell danger."

"And dead elephants . . . Orrie doesn't use them anymore, either, modeling himself on you," Zephele says. "It's too bad, because I was thinking that perhaps the next time Sky visits you in a dream he might do you the courtesy of telling you exactly where you might find him. And save us all this time and trouble, if you see what I mean . . . not that I don't welcome this opportunity for adventure. And not that Sky isn't worth any amount of effort on our parts."

"I couldn't stand to see him again, hobbled and pegged," Malora says. "And when he saw me, he thrashed about so wildly I was afraid he would hurt himself. I am trying to remain very calm, hoping that wherever he is, he will remain equally as calm, knowing that I am on my way to free him."

Zephele doesn't respond.

A few moments later, Malora hears a familiar bone-jarring roar. She is just about to tell Zephele what the sound is when she realizes that Zephele has dropped off to sleep. It is just as well that Malora doesn't have to tell Zephele that the roar belongs to a lion. Even though she would delight in adding to her list of the Big Five, Zephele has had enough excitement for one day.

Malora wakes up the next morning to the sound of the ring-necked turtledove calling her name, "Ma-lo-ra! Ma-lo-ra!" In the next cot, Zephele is still fast asleep. The tent smells more of horse than of wild jasmine, as if Zephele's horse half took over at night.

Sunshine pokes her head into the tent and sets down two cups of steaming mint tea and the tub of heated bathwater. "Good morning, ladies!" she says in a loud clear voice.

"Shhh!" Malora says, pointing to Zephele's huddled form.

"With respect," says Sunshine, "the Captain says to make sure you are both up and moving."

"The Captain," says Neal, poking his head into the tent, "wants us under way while the sun is still low in the sky. It's going to be a hot day. Let's get going, shall we?" He claps his hands loudly. "The rest of us have been up for quite some time."

Zephele emerges, groaning, from her swaddling of blankets, blinking blearily.

"Is that the nest of a marabou stork or Zephele Silvermane's curly head that I see?"

Zephele struggles to sit up, scrubbing her face with her

hands. "I am thoroughly awake now, thank you, drummed up from a sound sleep by your insolent patter."

After a breakfast of cold impala meat and cold nettle soup, the travelers pack up camp and set forth once again.

Except for Neal and Dock, everyone is sore. Requests to stop and rest are frequent. Neal is surprisingly sympathetic. It is Malora who notices, halfway through their second day, that they are being followed.

"It's nothing more than a swiftly moving cloud," Orion says, after squinting up at the sky for a long moment.

The sun is bright and the air shimmers with heat. Honus has tied a strip of cloth around his head to keep the sweat from dripping into his eyes. "Surely not," he says to Orion. "The sky is cloudless."

"Honus is right," says Neal. "It looks like some sort of a bird."

They all stop and look up. Holding the top of her hat, Malora tilts her head back and, squinting against the sun's glare, sees a creature with enormous white wings wheeling directly overhead, much higher in the sky than most birds venture. And although, as Honus has already pointed out, the sky is cloud-free, Malora feels a cool gust of wind that carries the fresh smell of an oncoming thunderstorm.

"That is the most beautiful thing I've ever seen," Zephele says. She has appropriated her brother's straw hat, which she has tied on to her head with the pink scarf. Her nose and her one exposed shoulder are raw with sunburn.

"A raptor of some sort, from the looks of it," Orion says. "Lord of his own domain and preparing to swoop down on his prey."

"Yes," says Honus, "but what order of raptor? Look at the size of him! And not just his wingspan but his body as well."

"Whatever it is, it's certainly taking its time," Neal says. "It's obviously very choosy about what it eats."

Honus fumbles for his mother-of-pearl opera glasses and focuses them upward. "Perhaps it's an oceangoing raptor blown inland off its course. Its wingspan is monumental," he murmurs. "And I'd give my left horn to have one of those feathers."

"Why didn't you say so?" Neal says. He pulls his crossbow out of its sling, loads it, cocks it, and draws a bead on his target.

"It's quite far away. I doubt even *you* could hit it from here," Orion says, a note of caution in his voice. "What's more, I suggest that you don't even try. The arrow may miss its mark, fall back to earth, and wound one of us instead."

"That would never happen. This is my most powerful bow," Neal says, his eye still on the target. "If my arrow hits home, I should be able to get Honus and Zephele a whole brace of splendid white feathers."

"Don't do so on my account," Zephele says warily. "Really, Neal, it's much too beautiful to kill. Please don't."

Neal, not taking his eye off his target, says, "Oh, but it's far too tempting to pass up. It looks like it's got a lot of meat on its bones, too."

Malora brings Lightning swiftly up alongside Neal and forces the crossbow down with the full force of her arm. "Do *not* kill it!" she tells him through gritted teeth.

Neal glares at her. "Don't ever do that again, pet."

"If you try to kill it again, I promise you I will."

Neal smiles sadly. "Don't tell me you've gone all sentimental on me, pet. We could have lived off that meat for days. Can't I at least take a shot at it?"

"No," Malora says.

"Why?" Neal asks.

"Because if you did, you would be a murderer," Malora says. "And I can't be friends with a murderer."

CHAPTER 7

Zephele Takes Up Arms

On their fifth day in the bush, Zephele is collecting wild-flowers to sketch for an embroidery design.

With *Pride and Prejudice* propped open on her saddle horn, Malora is reading as she rides.

"I am impressed that you can do that," Honus says. "It is all I can do to stay on the beast's back."

Malora smiles. "If there is trouble, I will toss the book aside and grab the reins with both hands."

"For the sake of the ancient binding, let us hope trouble remains at bay. Meanwhile, are you enjoying the book?" Honus asks.

"It is very strange," Malora says. "If this writer, Jane Austen, did not state at the beginning of her book that she writes about humans, I would have thought that her subject was centaurs. Highlanders, mostly."

Honus, whose face beneath the bandana has darkened to

the color of a hazelnut, closes his eyes and recites from memory, "It is a truth universally acknowledged, that a single man in possession of a good fortune must be in want of a wife."

"Man and wife being the People and fortune meaning nubs," Malora says.

"In essence, yes," says Honus.

"Mrs. Bennet, while much more irritating and meddlesome, is every bit as concerned with her daughters' making a good match as Herself is about Zephele and Orion marrying well. She has told me that she expects Theon to remain a bachelor."

"A mother senses these things," Honus says. "Tell me, does it sadden you to read about a society in which all the humans are engaged in the act of pairing off?"

"Not really," Malora says. "But maybe that's because I feel there is someone for me." She is thinking, of course, of Lume.

Honus wags his head. "Entertaining such hopes can only lead to disappointment in the end."

Malora feels a flash of anger. "Why are you all so sure I'm the last human? If I exist, then others could."

"Your Settlement was most likely the last of its kind. And you are the last of the Settlement." There is a look of pity in his eyes. "It isn't healthy for you to entertain hopes to the contrary."

Malora, stung, deflects the conversation back to Honus. "And what about you?" she asks. "Is there no faun mate for you?"

"When Medon first bought me, I was the only faun anyone had ever seen. Since then, my hibe has begun to stream down from the frozen wastes of the north, and now we fauns are far less exotic. Still, for me, going without a mate is a choice. Some of us," Honus says, "are destined to be alone."

But Malora scarcely hears him. She has lifted her head into the breeze, nostrils twitching. "I smell lion," she announces in a loud voice.

Neal gives the air a sniff. "Good nose, pet."

The pace of the group immediately picks up, as if lions had begun to stalk them, although Malora continually reassures both Honus and Zephele that this is probably not the case. "If lions were following us, Dock would tell us." And, in fact, the afternoon proceeds without incident.

That evening after dinner, Neal drills them all on what to do in the event they cross paths with a lion.

"I don't see that we have anything to worry about!" Zephele says blithely. "We have Malora the lion-killer in our midst."

"That lion was *old*," Orion reminds his sister, not for the first time. "And Malora didn't kill it. She simply scared it off."

"That's true," Malora says.

"We might not be as lucky next time," Neal says. "The next lion might be young and fit and hungry, which is why I am taking the trouble to instruct you all accordingly."

Zephele, who is embroidering by the firelight, speaks without looking up from the figure of an impala whose head and forelegs she has completed. "Tell us, wise Captain, what must we do to preserve ourselves."

"The first rule is," says Neal, "if you see a lion, do *not* run."

"Which is harder to do than it sounds," Malora says.

"Your first impulse will be to scream and run. But you have to resist running with everything you have."

"Your running is the lion's signal to attack," Neal says.

"Run like an impala," Malora adds, "get eaten like an impala."

Zephele's needle hand has frozen. "So what must we do if not run?" she asks.

"Turn around," Neal says, "and very calmly walk—do not run—in the opposite direction. Then follow Dock and do whatever he tells you. I'll stay behind and deal with the lion."

Later, Zephele whispers to Malora as they make their way to the tent. "Do you think Neal is competent to defend us?"

Malora shrugs. "He and Dock are both good hunters. They've got quick reflexes. Neal won that lion's claw in a fair fight. And if they should fail, I'll do my best to protect you."

"I am so glad that I am sharing my tent with you. Not only does Honus snore, but he would be very little help defending me from a lion. He'd probably smack it on the head with a book. And Orion would want to sprinkle it with scent."

"A lion-taming scent," Malora says thoughtfully. "I'll have to suggest that to him."

The next morning, they wade through grass so high, it brushes the withers of horse and centaur alike. It is eerily quiet, except for the steady *swish-swish-swish* of the grasses parting and the occasional horse nervously flushing its nostrils. When a flock of guinea hens explodes in their path, the horses all spook. The Beltanians rear and take off with the wagon, Lightning throws a buck, and Raven goes into a frantic little tailspin that flings Honus off into the grass.

Malora leaps from Lightning's back and runs to Honus.

"Are you all right?" she asks.

After a dazed moment, Honus laughs. He appears more embarrassed than hurt as he staggers to his feet and dusts off his trousers. "You know? I think I might have dozed off," he confesses.

"That probably saved you from a broken bone," Malora says. "You were asleep when you fell. A relaxed fall hurts less because the body isn't braced for impact." She pauses for a moment and realizes she has just uttered the words of Jayke, her father, the master horseman. She has a sudden longing for him so sharp that for a few moments she cannot move.

Raven has stopped a short distance away, munching grass. Malora inhales, then lets it out. She goes over to gather up the trailing reins and stroke Raven's neck. "Silly filly. Those were just birds. Nothing to work yourself into a state over." Gently, she leads Raven back to Honus. She tightens Raven's girth and then says to Honus, "Up you go, Honus. Try and stay awake this time."

After she has placed the reins back in Honus's hands and murmured a few more calming words to Raven, she says to Neal, "From now on, I think we should let the horses graze when they like. It will have a calming effect on them."

"You're the horse expert, pet," Neal says.

"Horses eat grass to calm themselves," Orion says ominously, "but what are we to do?"

"Pay attention," Neal says. "We're entering lion country. The horses smell it."

The air is suddenly rank with the musk of big cats. Any one of the clumps of bushes they file past might conceal the den of a lion. And in grass this tall, they may not be able to see a lion until it is upon them. Every muscle in Malora's body is tensed. If a lion showed itself now, she would be forced to defend herself with the knife. But in the end, there is no need. By midday, the air has cleared. A brisk breeze has washed all trace of lions away. They all breathe a little easier when they break out of the high grass into open savanna. No one is interested in stopping for the midday meal, so they eat while they move.

As if celebrating, wildebeest buck and caper, tagging along in their wake. Giraffes, with their fluid lope, crisscross their path. Herds of zebra, impala, and baboon convince Malora that, even if the lions were to return, there is more than enough meat on the hoof for a hungry lion to choose from without having to resort to a repast of centaur, horse, or human.

Honus speaks up. "The sheer number and variety of these beasts continue to astound me. To think that there was once a time when human interference brought their numbers so low, many were even threatened with extinction."

"How did that happen?" Malora asks.

"Hunting and poaching and disease. Some of it was simply a matter of displacement. Once upon a time, the People occupied large Settlements. Impossibly large cities. The bigger the cities grew, the more they encroached on the animal habitats. As their grazing lands were turned to farm and homelands, the animal population began to dwindle. There is a theory that the reason the Scienticians created hibes in the first place was to encourage empathy in human beings for the dwindling beasts of the earth. What better way to bind humans to animals than to link them, genetically, to the species they were destroying. Ironically, today the humans are extinct—but for you, my dear—and the animals have rebounded."

They soon come upon a series of dried mud beds overwritten by a scribbling of animal tracks, which Malora reads like the print on the page of a book.

"Hippo wallows," Malora says. "See here? That is the track of the bird that lives on the hippo's back and eats the insects that infest its body."

"Ugh!" Zephele says, covering her mouth with her hand.

"Hippos aren't so bad. They kill only if they feel their calves are being threatened," Malora reminds her friend, although she knows where Zephele's fear comes from. Had Malora lost a brother to a hippo, she might fear them equally.

Just above the wallows they come upon a small grove of trees surrounded by a flat grassy landing. Neal declares this to be a perfect campground. The Twani erect the tents, while Honus sorts through the day's treasures and Zephele arranges the wildflowers she has picked into a wreath for sketching. Orion and Dock travel to and from the river, returning with buckets of water for the horses and for washing and cooking. Malora runs the rope strung with bells around the trunks of the outermost trees to form a makeshift paddock in the shelter of the grove. Once the tents are set up, Sunshine gathers stones for a fire pit and Lemon goes off in search of firewood. Malora is beneath the trees, currying the horses with her new hairbrush, when Lemon comes racing back to the camp.

"Come!" he says breathlessly. "You must all come see."

Neal tells Sunshine to stay behind to watch the camp while the rest follow Lemon. The Twan leads them to a stand of bushes and points to a large wallow on the other side. Peering through the bushes, they all watch the scene: two young male lions, with shaggy golden manes, are draped across the back of a large hippo bull. The hippo, still alive, stands in the mud while both lions dig their claws into his hide and, with their teeth, tear big pieces of flesh from his lower back.

His voice low and grim, Neal says, "Well, Zephele, there's your deadly centaur-eating hippo for you. It just goes to show you that in nature everyone has an enemy."

Zephele, gnawing at the base of her thumbnail, seems transfixed by the gruesome sight.

Honus says in a soft voice, "A brave man is always frightened three times by a lion: when he first sees his track, when he first hears him roar, and when he first confronts him."

"Who said that?" Orion asks.

"It's an old proverb cited by the ancient known as Hemingway."

"Why doesn't the hippo run away from those brutes?" Zephele asks.

Malora feels a keen sense of pity for the hippo. His great mouth opens in a wide, gummy yawn of silent agony, and yet he simply stands there, patiently allowing the lions to help themselves to his flesh. "He knows this is the end for him. He's outnumbered," she says.

Orion staggers off a short distance and, gagging, empties the contents of his stomach.

The others continue to look on. Finally, Malora can stand

it no longer. "Enough!" she explodes in a harsh whisper, and begins to herd them back to camp. To Lemon, she says, "Did you actually think we'd find this amusing?"

Lemon sulks.

"Don't be too hard on him," Neal says. "Perhaps it is just as well that we all see what there is to fear from lions."

Zephele comes striding up alongside Malora. "I want you to teach me," she says in a fierce undertone.

"Teach you what?" Malora asks.

"Teach me how to kill," she says.

Malora turns and stares at her friend. "What are you talking about?"

Zephele's eyes are wide and pleading. "I'm not talking about murder, you needn't worry about that. I'm talking about self-defense. Malora, I don't *ever* want to be like that hippo. I don't ever want to stand by and let myself be savaged by some wild beast. I won't hunt them. But neither will I let them hunt me. I want to be able to defend myself without having to depend upon you or Neal or Dock or anyone else. I want you to teach me how to kill so I can protect myself."

Malora searches Zephele's face and sees that her friend has never been more serious. "What about the Edicts?" Malora says.

"I'll follow the Edicts in Mount Kheiron, but out here in the bush I can't afford to. Will you help me? I'd ask Neal, but he's too fearful of my father."

"Very well," Malora says at last. "But please don't ever tell the Apex. Neal isn't the only one who fears him. I know he'd never forgive me. He might even turn me out." As she says this, she realizes that in spite of the fact that she knows how to make her way in the bush, she fears being turned out as much as any centaur—that's how powerful the claim civilization has made on her.

That day, and every day after that, Malora gives Zephele lessons in archery. After they have made camp, Malora leaves Dock and Neal to hunt while she stays behind and sets up a shooting range for Zephele. All the while Malora is doing this, she finds herself thinking of her mother, who taught her how to use a bow. As she instructs Zephele, she hears her mother's voice in her ear: "Feet shoulder-width apart, weight equally distributed on your feet. When you pull the string back, you want to use your bones, not your muscle. . . ."

The first time she does this, Malora takes a stub of charcoal and makes a target on the wide smooth trunk of a baobab tree. Zephele misses the target the first few times but keeps trying with a determination Malora finds impressive. When the arrow flies wide of the target, Malora tells Zephele, "Remember always to look at what you are aiming at, never at the arrow. Burn a hole with your eye into the target and the arrow will seek it."

Just as this advice made a difference for Malora, so does it now serve Zephele. As the days pass and the practice sessions pile up, the centaur maiden starts hitting the target more often than missing it. On the eve before their arrival in Kahiro, Neal returns early from hunting and watches as Zephele hits the direct center of the target at twenty-five paces. Malora notices a new expression in Neal's eyes when he looks at Zephele.

"What you lack in the strength of your arm you more than make up for in the acuity of your aim," he says to

Zephele. "All that time spent in the stitchery has sharpened your eye and steadied your hand."

Zephele lowers her bow. "Thank you, Master Feather-hoof," she says primly. "And I intend to strengthen my arm."

Neal merely nods as if he didn't doubt her.

That night, they camp in fine white sand near a stand of towering date palms. Monkeys chatter in the treetops, and Malora hears the cries of birds she doesn't recognize. The next morning, when she emerges from her tent, she spots big, bright-red-and-green-plumed birds flapping in the treetops.

"Parrots," Honus says, eyeing them through his opera glasses. "They look comical, but don't be fooled. They can snap your finger with those hooked bills."

For the first time, Malora is wearing the disguise, the horns and the saruchi, but Honus seems more interested in the parrots than in her transformation.

The centaur bucks are equally sanguine as they stand around the morning cook fire.

Zephele, returning from the river where she has washed her hair, claps a hand to her chest. "Remarkable! No one looking at you will ever be able to tell you're human!" she says.

"Unless you give her away, dear sister," Orion says.

Zephele covers her mouth with her hands. "Oh dear! This will require practice."

"And subtlety," Neal says. "A bold new concept."

Zephele attempts a subtle nod.

They are soon under way and by midmorning are wading through drifts of fine white sand. The sun's rays bounce off the dunes and nearly blind Malora and the centaurs. They all covet the spectacles with tinted lenses Honus donned this morning.

As they crest a sandy rise, Malora blinks to bring the image before her into focus. Below lies the Caldera of Neelah, a vast deep tidal lake, Honus has explained to them, where the River Neelah pools just before the delta. Rising up from the middle of the lake are three small stone peaks. Malora sees the heads of bathers bobbing in the water. Other two-legged figures are diving off the peaks.

"What are they?" Malora asks.

"Ancient pyramidal structures that once contained tombs, now almost completely submerged by the tides," Honus explains.

"No, I mean, what are those beings diving into the water? They look like People." From this vantage point, they look like tall, slender, scantily clad men. Could it be that Honus is wrong? Could these be fellow humans?

"From a distance, perhaps they appear human," Honus tells her. "But you won't think that when you see them at close range. They are the Ka—the males of the hibe. The sheKa rarely venture out during daylight. The Ka are a semi-amphibious hibe that can remain underwater for long periods of time. They have a nictitating membrane that comes down over their eyes, enabling them to keep their eyes open underwater, a trait they share with the crocodile with which they coexist peacefully on the delta of the River Neelah."

"Really?" says Malora. She is excited now. New hibes might not be as wonderful as other humans. But the prospect is fascinating.

The road leads them down a loose, sandy embankment. The sand is white and the sky is azure. Malora feels her pulse quickening as it once did as she approached Mount Kheiron for the first time. Here the air is filled with an indescribable smell. Malora looks around. Her companions are all inhaling deeply.

"What is in the air?" Malora asks. The only way she can describe it is that the air smells of clean horses sweating on a hot, dry day. It is one of her favorite aromas on earth.

"I think it must be the sea!" Zephele says, her little nose twitching.

"Right you are!" Honus says.

"Of course!" says Malora. "I smell it, but I don't see it. Where is it? Race you to the sea!" Malora urges Lightning off the road and down the sandy slope with Zephele not far behind. They will follow their noses to the sea.

"Stay on the path!" Neal's voice booms at their backs.

Malora stops and swivels in the saddle.

"Why?" she asks mutinously.

"Sinkholes," Neal says in a voice of controlled calm. "The natives know where they are, but you don't. Nor do I. You might step into one, and you—and your horse—would disappear in a matter of seconds and we would never see you again."

Zephele turns pale.

Malora quickly guides Lightning back onto the path.

"Now that you have finished scaring our tails to stubs, can you kindly show us the safest route to the sea, Neal?" Zephele asks.

"All in good time," Neal says. "First, we must stop and

stable the horses. Then we must enter the city and claim our rooms at the inn."

"You'll see the sea soon enough," Honus says. "More than enough of it, I daresay."

Zephele catches Malora's hand and squeezes. "Can you wait? I can't wait! Oh, and after we have seen the sea," she says, "I should like to set eyes on the sheKa."

"If they look anything like the males, they are very beautiful," Malora says. "Just look at them all. How graceful and long of leg they are."

As they approach the shores of the Caldera, where a flock of flamingos wade in the shallows, they ride past a row of the Ka. They lie belly-down on colorful striped mats, their backs dark and oily, the soles of their long feet as pale as fish drying in the sun. One of them turns over and all the others flip over, as if following the leader.

A hiccup of surprise escapes Zephele. "They are frog people! Why did no one tell me that the Ka were so utterly *homely?*"

Honus flicks the reins and brings his horse up beside Zephele, saying in an urgent undertone, "My dear, understand that you will be seeing all manner of exotic-looking hibe while in Kahiro. Many thoughts, impressions, and opinions may rise in your mind. But it is of paramount importance that you not give voice to every observation that enters your head. The Ka are most sensitive about the amphibiousness of their facial features."

"They ought to be," Zephele says flatly. "They look like great big croaking frogs."

Malora regards Zephele thoughtfully and wonders how

this can be the same maiden who said about the bush pig: "I think it's cruel to say that some animals are ugly." How is it any less cruel to say that some hibes are homely?

"They may look like frogs to you," Neal says to Zephele, "but you must no more tell them that than you would point out to a centaur, for instance, that she has a horse's ass."

Malora's laughter is cut short by a wounded glare from Zephele. Returning her gaze to the row of heKa, Malora says, "*I* think they're beautiful! I can see how they might make superior warriors."

Considering this, Zephele says, "They say that the sheKa have the bodies of goddesses."

"Who told you that?" Orion asks sharply.

"A maiden at the stitchery, whose brother came here and visited a House of Romance," Zephele says.

"What is a House of Romance?" Malora asks.

No one responds as she looks around for an answer, nor do they meet her gaze.

"Can someone please answer my question?" she repeats.

"You'll learn . . . soon enough," Honus says grimly.

"Yes, but for once," Neal says, grinning, "not even Honus is willing to lecture."

"I can explain," Zephele says cheerfully. "A House of Romance is a delightful place where poetry is recited, plays are performed, and soft music and perfume fill the air."

"Well," Honus says, clearing his throat awkwardly, "that's certainly *some* part of it."

Zephele breezes on. "Another of my stitchery friends told me that she heard that in some of the houses the sheKa have actually had their faces altered to make them look more like the People. Because of their bodily similarity to the People, they say that males of all hibes desire the sheKa more than the females of their own ilk. I should like very much to see the sheKa. Will I be allowed to stay up late and see them? They come out at night like the stars."

Honus and Orion exchange a helpless look.

Malora suggests, "Why don't we visit a House of Romance and see for ourselves?"

"Oh, brilliant!" Zephele declares.

"Never!" says Orion.

"Why not?" Malora and Zephele both say.

"Because," Honus says carefully, "it would be neither seemly nor safe."

Neal shakes his head, wiping tears of mirth from his eyes. "I can see this is going to be a very *interesting* trip."

CHAPTER 8

The Kingdom of the Ka

The block stone city walls of Kahiro rise up many times higher than the wall that surrounds Mount Kheiron. It is by far the largest and most imposing structure Malora has ever set eyes on. She cranes her neck, one hand holding the horns in place. High up, along the crenelated parapet, Ka guards with long spears march, looking no bigger from where she is standing than an army of ants holding sticks.

"How do they get up there?" Malora wonders aloud.

"Impressive, isn't it? They are hoisted," Honus says, "on wooden platforms. From the wall facing the sea, they are known to dive into the ocean when the tide is high. These many-colored rocks you see that comprise the wall come from the north, where the Great Ice crushed many of the large buildings and carried the detritus southward. I daresay there are blocks here from all the capitals of what was once known as the European continent."

Hunkered down in the shadow of the wall is a squat sand-stone structure where they will stable their horses.

"The hostlers are Dromadi," Honus says quickly under his breath to Malora and Zephele as they approach the sta-bles.

Malora is unprepared for the sight of her first Dromad. Later, after she has seen the camels in the marketplace, she will understand that, just as the centaurs are half human and half horse, the Dromadi are half human and half camel. Where a centaur's back is smooth and sleek, the Dromadi have high, ragged-looking humps. Most have one, but some have two.

As one of them lopes toward them on impossibly long and knobby legs, longer in the front than in the back, Zephele whispers to Malora, "See how his hump wobbles when he moves? How very *awkward*!"

"The humps store fat and water," Honus explains. "Like their camel cousins, they can survive for long periods of time without food or water."

Malora gazes up at the hostler as he arrives, looming a good five hands taller than any of them. Beneath her, she feels Lightning's back muscles bunch, registering the presence of this strange new creature and making a valiant effort not to spook. She hugs the mare with her legs and sends her a silent message: You'd better get used to them. I'll be entrusting you to the hands of these strangers.

To keep from staring at the undulous hump, Malora con-centrates on the hostler's face, which is surprisingly hand-some: golden-skinned, with golden hair shaved close to the scalp. His large eyes are a soft brown, framed by long golden eyelashes spangled with sand. Unlike the centaurs, the Dromad wears no clothing. His arms and torso are muscular and baked by the sun to the same golden color as his camel parts. All of him is covered in a thin, sparkling coating of sand, like an enormous date dipped in sugar. She wants to tell him: *Even though a Scientician made you, I find you beautiful.*

"Isn't he perfectly *hideous*?" Zephele whispers in Malora's ear, and again Malora wonders with a flash of irritation she doesn't usually feel toward her friend, why this unkindness?

Honus raises his arm and speaks in a strange tongue that sounds as if he were trying to bring up a piece of gristle caught in his throat. The Dromad answers in kind.

"We are lucky to be traveling with Honus," Zephele says in a normal voice. "He is a prodigy of languages."

Malora, waiting for a gap in the talk, leans in to Honus and says, "Ask him if he has heard of a big black blue-eyed stallion anywhere hereabouts."

"First we must settle on a price for boarding," Honus whispers back. "Leave your horse here and explore the facility. I think you'll find it meets your stringent standards."

Malora slips off Lightning and whispers words of encouragement before leaving the reins with the hostler. Absently, the hostler runs big, leathery hands over Lightning's flanks and calms her instantly. Satisfied, Malora joins Zephele and Orion as they walk toward the stables.

"Everything is bargained for here, they say," Zephele explains. "I cannot wait to try my hand at it. I suspect I will excel at it. I come prepared, for I have brought great quantities of nubs with me, and I intend to purchase mounds of goods and, of course, gifts for everyone back in Mount Kheiron."

The stalls are whitewashed, clean, and airy, nearly every stall filled. There are four identical gray dappled steeds with curly manes like silver shavings, a row of bashful Athabanshees, as white as ivory, three draft horses, and two full-grown horses no bigger than Neal's hunting hounds.

"How tiny and cunning they are!" Zephele says, reaching in to pet their velvety little noses.

"They pull small carts for vendors and, small as they are, are cheaper to feed," Orion explains. "This is the most reputable stable. The Apex boards his Beltanians here when he visits, and has never complained."

Honus and Neal and the Dromad must have arrived at a satisfactory price, because two more Dromadi are leading the Beltanians into a stall, where they have begun to wash them down with buckets of soapy water and large foamy pads. Next to the Dromadi, the draft horses look like stocky ponies.

"Those are sponges," Orion tells them. "They come from the sea."

"Really?" says Zephele, giving the pads a closer look.

"They were once living things," Orion adds. "They are much more absorbent than cotton cloth, and very useful."

"Remarkable!" says Zephele. "Where might I purchase some for my convenience?"

"From the marketplace," says Orion.

"Of course!"

Sunshine and Lemon unload the luggage from the wagon and place it in a handcart. Malora removes the saddlebags from Lightning and slings them over one shoulder.

"Enjoy your rest here," she whispers into the mare's twitching ear, feeding her a Max. "I will see you very soon . . . I hope with news of Sky or perhaps even with our big boy himself."

After doling out more Maxes to Raven and Charcoal and Light Rain, she joins the others on the last stretch of road that winds through the dunes between the stable and the city gates. Honus is in deep conversation with Orion and Neal. They fall silent when Malora catches up to them. Malora looks from one to the other. "Did you discover anything useful?"

Honus looks to Neal for approval before saying to Malora, "The hostler says there are rustlers who steal horses and that a horse of Sky's description would potentially be very valuable."

"Are my horses in danger here?" Malora asks, casting a wary look over her shoulder.

"Don't worry," Orion says. "They post guards."

Neal adds, "He says most of the raids occur in the outlands, in the big ranches along the northeastern seaboard and on the Dromadi caravan route from the west."

"And who are these raiders?" Malora asks.

She looks around at Orion, Honus, and Neal but their eyes are busy elsewhere.

"Can someone please answer her question," Zephele demands.

"It has been confirmed," Neal says reluctantly. "The raiders are wild centaurs."

"No!" says Zephele, clapping a hand to her mouth.

"Really?" Malora asks.

Neal nods. "Apparently rumor has evolved into hard fact since my last trip."

Honus nods. "It appears that someone survived the most recent raid and offered a vivid account. The raiders of the caravans are, indeed, centaurs, of an altogether different nature than those of Mount Kheiron."

Zephele says in a dazed voice, "So it's all true!"

"A savage lot they are, the Dromad tells us," Honus says. "They are said to go about naked, their bodies elaborately painted, their flesh pierced with bones, stones, rings, shells. They'll lay claim to any cargo they find, but it's horses that interest them the most."

"Interesting," Malora says, "that they have something in common with the centaurs of Mount Kheiron."

Rather than finding comfort in Malora's words, her companions seem exceedingly uneasy. Malora continues, "Who knows? Perhaps you have even more in common than horses." She gazes at them provocatively but sees this comment has only made them even more uncomfortable.

"You don't understand, Malora," says Zephele. "When word gets back to Mount Kheiron, the Apex will have to volunteer Peacekeepers for the escort. Especially if the wild centaurs are targeting horses. We all know how soft Father is on horses. Before we know it he'll have us all up in arms. And once the Fourteenth Edict falls, anything could happen! Our wonderful, peaceful way of life is in dire peril!"

"Calm yourself, Zeph," says Orion.

"I agree with Orrie," says Neal. "There's no need to anticipate. If I know the Apex, he will uphold his policy of noninvolvement. So long as the wild centaurs leave the civilized ones in peace . . ." He stops and strokes his chin, adding with a bemused smile, "Odd, I've always thought of *myself* as being the wild centaur. . . ."

"*And* with good reason," Zephele says.

"So do we think it likely," Malora says carefully, "that the wild centaurs have captured Sky?"

"It's only a theory," Honus says. "We don't know for certain."

Malora warms to the theory. "In my dream, Sky was in a place of sandy bluffs. Didn't you once tell me that a tribe of warlike centaurs broke with the centaurs of Mount Kheiron and settled in the Downs? Downs is another word for dunes, is it not?"

"True enough, but surely they haven't been able to stay hidden all this time," says Orion.

"I don't know," says Neal, flicking the tip of his beard. "The Downs would offer the perfect stronghold."

"We will go into the Downs," Malora says. "I'll go get Lightning."

"Not so fast, pet," Neal says, stopping her with a hand. "Those sinkholes I warned you about? The Downs are riddled with them. No one who has ever gone in there has come out alive."

"Except, apparently, an entire tribe of wild centaurs," Malora says.

"That doesn't mean you will," Neal says, "with all due respect to your skills."

"I have an excellent idea," says Orion. "Instead of dashing off into a maze of sinkholes—into which Lightning would surely sink, even if you managed to scramble free—and taking on the entire wild centaur tribe, let's adhere to our original plan. Let's first visit Shrouk and see what she has to tell us."

"I agree with Orrie," says Neal. "Let's avoid the Downs if at all possible. They say horses and centaurs are particularly prone to fall into the sinkholes."

"Not *wild* centaurs," Malora points out again.

"All right, I'll admit it! There are wilder centaurs than me. And they know the safe routes through the Downs," Neal says.

"The Flatlander makes sense," Zephele says. "Let us please eschew the Downs. I, for one, detest getting sand in my hair."

Neal bows to Zephele. "For this reason alone, my lady, we will stay well clear."

Everything in Malora cries out to head immediately for the Downs. But the idea of drowning in sand fills her with dread. Sand in her mouth. Sand in her eyes and ears. Desperately clawing away at it as she slides farther down into the airless, endless darkness. "All right. Shrouk it is," she says.

As one, the others heave a sigh of relief.

They proceed to the gate, which is raised. Its heavy iron bars, closely set, hang overhead, ending in a row of spikes. This gate is as unlike the welcoming entrance to Mount Kheiron, Malora thinks, as a Twan is from a lion.

"They lower the gate at night," Honus says, "to keep out wild animals."

Neal removes a sheaf of parchment from his pouch and hands one sheet to each of them. Malora examines hers. It looks like a miniature flag, with the Eye of Kheiron stamped in bold red and black ink on a field of blue.

"Keep track of your pass at all times," Neal says to the group. "Put it somewhere safe, where no pickpockets can pluck it from you. These passes, which are called Eyes, offer proof of both your Kheironite citizenship and your authorization by the Apex to travel abroad. It will permit you to pass through these gates, and you will be asked to show it again when you claim your room at the inn. If you lose your Eye, the guards will not allow you to leave."

Zephele hugs her elbows and looks up at the stone parapet. "Imagine! Spending the rest of one's days walled up in here!"

"What do you bet she takes one look at the marketplace and *begs* never to leave?" Neal says to Orion in an undertone.

"I heard that, impertinent lout!" Zephele calls out.

There are six armed guards standing along the gateway. The nearest one swivels his head when he hears Zephele, giving her a hard stare.

"Oh, I didn't mean you," she says. "I was speaking to *that* lout." She points limply to Neal.

The head swivels away, indifferent. The Ka are haughtier than Highlanders, Malora thinks. Even Zephele, the haughtiest of the haughty, is intimidated. But Malora isn't intimidated so much as she is fascinated. These Ka are clad in shiny loincloths and hoods striped bright green and blue. They have long, taut leg muscles and smooth, hairless skin that holds the faintest tinge of green.

Honus walks up to one of them and speaks in a voice that sounds as if he were gargling water. The Ka gargles back at him briskly. They speak at length, after which the Ka nods and holds out his hand toward the rest of them, wiggling long spatulate fingers that are webbed at their base.

"He is requesting to see our Eyes," Honus says.

One by one, they file past the guard and place their Eyes in the palm of his hand. The guard examines each of their papers before handing them back. When he is finished, he waves them through the gates. Malora marvels at the long, slender arm moving as gracefully as the tendril of an underwater plant.

No one notices or even checks their many weapons as they pass beneath the gates into the city. Malora adjusts her eyes to the dimness, for the city wall to the west blocks out the lowering rays of the sun and mitigates the desert glare. In here, the white sand has been trampled to gray beneath the feet of a crowd so vast Malora catches her breath. It is like wading into a powerful river of hibes, as frightening as it is exhilarating. The current sweeps down into a deep bowl filled with low, simple block buildings all tightly packed in on top of one another. The northern wall opens in the center in a soaring arch that faces out to the sea. At least that's what Malora thinks it is, because all she sees is billowing mist through which she can make out the bobbing masts of the sailing ships docked beneath the arch.

"Shall we dive in?" Neal says with a crooked grin. "Look lively and stay close to me."

Malora counts five roads running down into the bowl. The middle one, the widest, leads directly to the arch and, for all its width, the buildings on either side join overhead and give the impression of a tunnel rather than a thoroughfare. The tunnel is so packed, it looks as if the heads of the walking pedestrians are bobbing in place. Neal ducks into the road west of the main one, which is narrow but every bit as crowded. The buildings on either side have arched windows and doors covered with curtains of colorful glass beads. It is as if the buildings here have been dipped in vats of colorful dye: indigo, magenta, turquoise, yellow. Malora notices that the wooden shutters, porches, and doors stand out in the mist, painted bright blue.

"Why blue?" Malora asks Honus, pointing to a shutter in passing.

"The color is said to fend off evil spirits," he says, "but I believe that it discourages the biting bugs that swarm at low tide."

"Keep a brisk pace and don't speak to anyone outside the group," Neal calls out to them.

Honus turns to Malora and says, "Your stride is perfect."

She nods, pleased to hear this. It ought to be good. She practiced it enough on the last days of their trek, dismounting every so often and walking on the balls of her feet with her body tilted forward, leading with her chin, bottom sticking out behind her, imitating Honus's cloven-hooved trot.

The variety and number of hibes make Malora's head spin. Honus holds Malora's elbow in a fatherly fashion and steers her along while Zephele clings to her other arm. By force of habit, they fall into the same formation they followed in the bush: Neal and Orion leading the way, followed by Honus and Zephele and Malora, then the Twani wheeling the handcart, with Dock bringing up the rear, glaring, gripping his bullwhip in threatening fashion.

"I like the open road," Dock says through gritted teeth, "but I dread the destination. I hate this place."

How could anybody hate this? Malora wonders. There is

so much to look at. Ka are by far the most plentiful hibe, followed by Dromadi, and then sprinkled throughout are all manner of others. She sees squat, husky bipeds that seem human at first glance but on closer inspection have snouts flanked by short tusks and ears tufted with coarse fur.

"Suideans," Honus says in passing.

Malora nods. "The pig-faced smelters from the Hills of Melea," as Brion described them.

She sees bipeds with hooves like Honus's but with heavy horns that curl around their ears.

"Capricornias," Honus says. "We fauns are lucky to have our much smaller horns. I'm told the Capricornias suffer chronic neck aches, owing to the weight on their skulls of those great hulking sheep horns."

Malora thinks her eyes are playing tricks on her when she first sees a large striped cat padding along with a human face, followed moments later by a group of cats walking on two legs. The latter are more muscle-bound versions of the Twani but with a far fiercer demeanor. Both the males and females wear beaded leather strings with small triangles covering their private parts, the females letting their three tiers of breasts swing free. Their hair is long, dark golden streaked with brown, with all manner of beads and bones and bells worked into its weave. Their beaded belts and shoulder slings bristle with daggers and knives and spears. To Malora, they seem far more human than the Ka, but it is a profoundly *wild* humanity. She wonders what draws her more to them, their wildness or their humanity.

"The catlike quads are Aleurs," Honus explains. "Very rare, I'm told, because the biped cats wiped them out centuries ago. The bipeds are Pantherians. They hail from the far south-east, where the jungles run down to the sea and there are more wild animals than anywhere else in the known world. The Pantherians are masters of their domain and superb hunters. They still spurn the Aleurs, but they let the few survivors live."

Ahead of them, Neal takes a sharp turn. They follow him around the corner, where a small crowd of ragged creatures sets upon them, chattering and jabbering.

"Tads," Honus says.

"What?" Malora shouts over the din.

"Juvenile Ka!" Honus replies. "These are beggars. Unlike their wealthier counterparts, their parents abandon them early. Steel yourselves, ladies. They're very persistent."

The tads are male and female, their faces grubby and their loincloths soiled.

"Meester, meester!" they say to Honus. "I show you da sea! Twenny nubs, I show you all!"

"Goat laydee! Goat laydee!" With a start, Malora realizes they are addressing her. They hang from the hem of her tunic and tug at her hair. Fearing that her horns will slip, Malora clamps one hand over the tortoiseshell band and shoos them away with the other.

They cheerfully persist. "You want camel saddle? I give you da best price!"

"I'm sorry. I don't own a camel," Malora explains.

"No matter how they may tug at the strings of your heart, just shake your head vigorously and say no," Honus says, demonstrating his technique to tads on all sides. "Do not engage in dialogue."

They are everywhere, bantering, cajoling, arguing, cheerfully undiscouraged by the traveling party's repeated head shaking. Even when Dock rushes at them with his whip, they slap each other and point to the scowling Dock as if the old centaur were putting on a performance for their amusement.

One of them jumps in front of Malora, hands clasped beneath his chin. "Mees! Mees! I show you relics of the Scienteeeshan! Only two nubs, pleeeeeease, Mees!"

"No thank you," Malora says, laughing at the earnest expression on his face. She finds their antics funny and touching, but Zephele is clearly distressed.

"Make them go away!" she begs. They cling to Zephele's horse half, stretching her khaki wrap and peeling her boots down to the hoof.

Malora brushes them off Zephele like burrs, including the one who is swinging from her tail as if it were a bell pull.

"Go away!" Malora says. "Don't bother her. Where she comes from, she is a noble lady." Malora lifts her black-and-white rope and gets them to back off, as she would a small band of unruly horses. Eventually they fade into the shadows and lie crouching in wait for the next new arrivals.

In spite of the crowds and the noise, the briny air is shot through with moisture, giving everything a pale, dreamy look, dulling the edge of Malora's alertness. Zephele, on the other hand, looks frantic. Orion takes his sister's arm firmly in his.

"Poor Zeph. Drowning in a sea of Otherians. You'll get used to it," he tells her.

"Of course I will!" Zephele says, with ragged determination. "It's just that I feel sorry for the poor little things. They obviously have nothing."

Neal calls back, "As beggars go, they live like little kings and queens. There's enough garbage in Kahiro to feed a whole city of tads. Stay with me now. We're almost there."

"Are we walking in circles?" Malora asks.

"It is entirely possible," Honus says.

Meanwhile, a fresh wave of beggars and street hustlers has risen up around them.

"It's because of you two," Honus explains. "You and Zephele are new to Kahiro. It happens to everyone their first time. It's as if the city senses new blood. It's all in your faces. Your faces are open. Soon you will learn to close your faces, to walk with your eyes hard, and the beggars won't bother you."

A beggar dances before Malora and Honus, a scruffy Capricornia with a patch over his eye and one raffishly cock-eyed horn. "You two there, with the horned heads, welcome to the Mother of the World, cousins! I will be your guide! Follow me!" he says, his voice as nasal as a nanny goat's.

Honus responds with a flip of his hand. "We require no guide, my ovine friend. Be off." Then Honus turns to Malora. "Mother of the World is apt," he says, "for Kahiro is the most ancient city on earth. Countless civilizations have risen and fallen on this very spot and left their mark like the alluvial sands deposited by the river. The Ka are merely its most recent inhabitants. The Ka won it. Whether on land or in the water, in battle or on the playing field, rich or poor, the Ka are supremely sportive."

"And what of the sheKa?" Zephele asks.

"One rarely sees them on the street during the daylight. The poor are in their hovels, the rich in their villas. The wealthy sheKa are the world's finest hostesses. The Ka are intensely jealous and many a duel is fought between jealous heKa over the favors of a sheKa," Honus says.

"I sell you statue of zaffinks for cheap. Two for one nub," the same Capricornia beseeches them.

"What are *zaffinks*?" Malora asks.

"Ha!" says Honus. "He means *the Sphinx*. It is a giant ancient statue that lies somewhere outside the city walls far beneath the earth. The stone likeness of a lion-human hibe— carved many thousands of years before the living hibes ever walked the earth—is now lost to the sands of time. This horn-headed fellow is bluffing. He will take you to a mound of sand in the middle of nowhere and tell you this is where the Sphinx lies, buried beneath it. Then he will dig and dig and dig and eventually, he will unearth a few worn rocks and attempt to sell them to you as true relics of the sphinx. Oh, they'd sell the very sand if they thought they could find a buyer for it."

They scurry to catch up with Neal as he disappears around another corner. They have passed into a residential neighborhood where the crowd is sparser, more composed and quiet, consisting mostly of Ka, their long narrow feet encased in leather sandals whose papyrus straps crisscross their muscled calves and tie off at the knee. They wear embroidered cloth headdresses that cast deep shadows over their green-tinted faces and make them seem noble and mysterious. Unsmiling, they stride with purpose, carrying long sticks that have knobs carved and painted like brightly colored serpents.

"Those sticks are multipurpose," Honus explains. "The Ka use them for dancing, dueling, fishing, poling barges, digging clams, and conjuring their gods. They have also been known to save lives with them. If one of them chances to step into a sinkhole, his mate offers him the end of the stick to pull him to safety."

"Perhaps I should get a stick of my own," Malora says. She has not given up on the idea of having to enter the Downs. If that is what it takes to find Sky, she will do it.

"In the marketplace of Kahiro—"

"I know," says Malora, rolling her eyes, "I can get anything I want." But all I really want, she adds silently, is to find my horse.

The street comes to a dead end at the wall, in what Malora calculates is the northwest part of the city. A structure rises, built into the wall and extending halfway up.

"We have arrived!" Honus announces. "The Backbone of Heaven!"

CHAPTER 9

The Backbone of Heaven

"What an odd name for a place," Malora says to herself as she stares up at the inn, the beads at its many windows rattling in the breeze. Then she looks down. Surrounding the inn and bubbling up from beneath the wall at its back is a trench filled with water.

"Over the years, the inn has acquired a moat courtesy of the ever-encroaching seawater," Honus explains.

There is a stone footbridge over the trench leading to the wide arched entrance. On a terrace in front of the inn are large round tables at which are seated a variety of hibes drinking strangely colored beverages and dropping strange-looking food with their hands into their upturned mouths.

"Seafood," Honus says. "It takes some getting used to."

"Give me your Eyes and wait here," Neal says to them. "I'll make sure our reservations still hold. We're a day early." Neal collects their documentation and strides across the bridge and into the inn.

"Where will we stay if they can't put us up?" Zephele asks fretfully. There are smudges of fatigue beneath her eyes.

"Don't worry," Orion says. "Kahiro is full of inns and hostels. Still, I hope they can take us. I am fond of this place."

"These are not particularly luxurious accommodations, mind you," Honus puts in. "But it is quiet and clean, and at night you can hear the sea as well as see a small sampling of it right here." He gestures to the pool. "From the depth, I am judging that the tide is high."

Malora bends down and dips her finger in the water. It is a milky pale green color and shockingly cold. She raises her finger to her mouth and sucks it. It is as salty as tears.

"Try it," she says to Zephele.

Zephele bends and cups some in her hands, sampling it on the tip of her tongue. "It is most flavorful," she says.

"I don't suggest you drink it," Orion says.

"Or swim in it," Honus says.

"Why not?" Malora asks.

"It is full of all manner of creatures," Honus says.

Orion intones, "Fish and poisonous seagoing snakes. Whales and sharks and octopi and eels and all nature of cold-eyed creatures. Not to mention the coldest-eyed of all, the aquatic hibes."

Zephele hugs her elbows and shivers, but Malora is intrigued. "I have swum with hippos and crocodiles. I would like to swim in the sea."

"Always the fearless one," Zephele says, "wherever she may find herself."

"I have fear," Malora says defensively. "Only a fool has no fear. For instance, I fear for Sky."

"Fear for the safety of others is simply another form of empathy. Valor, even," Zephele says.

Malora feels nettled. She knows she is not as good, or as noble, as her friends think she is, but it is hopeless to point this out to them. They refuse to believe that a human being could be flawed. In their own way, they are as bad as the worshippers in the Church of the Latter Day Scienticians.

"Easy, my friend. We know you're afraid for Sky," Orion says gently, "and we will do everything we can to help you find him."

Neal appears on the other side of the bridge and beckons. They cross over and go through the arch into a palm-shaded courtyard in the center of which a round stone fountain splashes. Across the courtyard is a high desk, and behind it the Ka innkeeper nods at them cordially.

"Welcome to the Backbone of Heaven! I am Akbar, at your service," the innkeeper says in a voice that flutters through his fleshy lips. "I have three rooms available on the ground floor for the quads. And a suite on the top floor for the two bipeds." He doles out iron keys to each of them. "Thank you for choosing the Backbone. There will be an evening buffet served in the courtyard at the sound of the bells." Then he crooks a long webbed finger at Neal and adds, "A word with you, my fine young quadruped?"

As Ka and centaur confer, Malora wanders over to an arched indentation in the wall where a statue of a man and a woman, draped in lapis-blue hooded cloaks, stand side by side, palms upturned, sweet smiles on their lips, eyeglasses perched on the ends of their noses.

"Who are they?" Malora asks Honus, who has joined her.

"Doctor Adam and Doctor Eve," Honus says. "The last People."

"No, they're not," Malora says automatically, then catches herself immediately. "I see. They look so . . ."

"Insipid?" Honus suggests.

"Dim-witted," Malora says with an apologetic shrug.

"Yes, you wouldn't know it to look at them, but they were brilliant Scienticians, the patron saints of the Latter Day Church of the Scienticians."

Malora makes a face. She prefers Kheiron to these two. At least Kheiron looks wise and kind in the art and statuary dedicated to him, a god who demands not faith but the diligent adherence to Edicts.

Neal has returned from his brief conference with the innkeeper. "Akbar strongly recommends," he says, "that we keep our two females under close watch. The streets of the city are crawling with scouts. I had forgotten that it's recruiting season."

Dock growls and clutches his whip handle. "Let 'em *try*."

"Try what?" Malora asks. "Who are these scouts?"

"*Talent* scouts," Neal replies. "Agents who roam the streets in search of fresh talent for the Houses of Romance."

"How exciting!" Zephele says, her eyes flashing. "Might they choose Malora and me? Surely, our beauty and cleverness qualify us."

Malora squeezes Zephele's hand, happy to see that her friend's spirits are rekindling.

"This is not a competition you would wish to enter, much less win," Neal says.

Zephele draws herself up tall. "And why not?"

Malora adds, "From the way Zephele has described these places, they sound like fun."

"Most entertaining," Zephele adds.

"I'm truly sorry if anyone has said anything to give you that impression," says Neal. "Nothing could be further from the truth. While many hibes run away from home to join them, they live to regret their decision. In the Houses of Romance, the females—and the males—are poorly treated. Their individual wishes and their very identities are subsumed by the house, and they become mere commodities, objects to be sold and sold again to the highest bidder until their value and usefulness, their youth and their beauty, are exhausted and depleted."

Malora feels as if she has just lifted a beautiful rock only to discover a scorpion with an arched tail. When she finds her voice, she says, "Thank you for finally telling us the truth, Neal. In that case, we are not interested in visiting these places."

"*Definitely* not interested," Zephele agrees, chin upturned. "Moreover, we shall not hesitate to express our feelings to any scout who has the temerity to approach us."

Neal shakes his head wearily. "You still don't understand. Your *interest* is the furthest thing from their minds. They say that one moment you are standing in the bazaar fingering some exotic piece of goods and the next, you are lying bound and gagged and drugged in a room that, for all its finery, is little more than a prison."

"We'll be vigilant," Malora says, squeezing Zephele's hand harder now, less afraid for herself than for the centaur maiden.

"As will the rest of us, pet. Rest assured," Neal says. "I wouldn't want to be the one who had to tell the Apex his daughters had been pulled into a House of Romance. If anything would make him toss the Fourteenth into the Neelah that would be it."

"We can't let that happen!" says Zephele.

"Pay no heed to Featherhoof," Orion says. "Father would be more than willing to pay whatever ransom was demanded."

"Ransom?" Malora asks.

"It is customary," Orion explains, "for the wealthier families to pay for the release of their sons and daughters. It's a valuable source of income for the Houses."

"Families pay handsomely," Neal says, then adds with a wicked grin aimed at Zephele, "unless their sons and daughters are more trouble than they are worth."

Neal is the only one who finds this funny.

"What kind of a place *is* Kahiro?" Malora bursts out.

"Not Mount Kheiron, that's for sure," growls Dock.

"Actually," Honus says, "the Houses lie outside the walls and are therefore not subject to Kahiran law—or any other."

"Makes you appreciate the Edicts a bit more, doesn't it?" Orion says. "I suggest we retire to our rooms and refresh ourselves before the evening meal."

As exhausted as she is, Malora must ask, "What about Shrouk?"

"It's nearly dark," Orion says. "The streets will soon be unsafe and the marketplace is closed. There will be time enough to see Shrouk tomorrow."

Tomorrow, Malora thinks, I will learn about Sky.

* * *

Serving them their evening meal is a pink-skinned, broad-bottomed hibe. Her tiny head, with its protuberant eyes, is set on the slender stalk of her neck. An ostrich woman, Malora thinks. I wonder how fast she can run.

"What I wouldn't give to have eyelashes like hers," Zephele whispers to Malora.

"Me too," Malora says. This is a white lie. She is indifferent to the length of eyelashes but encouraged to hear Zephele say anything positive about another hibe.

The server sets down cups of sea broth, then slips Honus a small sheet of paper and bustles away. Neal leans in to read what is written on the sheet, shaking his head in disgust.

"What is it?" Malora asks.

"A small setback," Honus says. "We made an inquiry at the desk earlier, and this is our response. It seems that Shrouk has radically reduced her custom."

"What does that mean?" Malora asks, setting her cup down so hard that broth sloshes onto the table.

"It means we will not be able to see her until the day *after* tomorrow," Neal says. "She now limits her practice to once a week."

Malora sits back. She feels their eyes on her, sympathetic but helpless.

"Is there no other recourse?" Orion asks Honus.

Honus says, "I'm afraid not. She is ancient. We are lucky she is still alive and practicing."

"The day after tomorrow will have to do," Malora says, even though inwardly she is screaming. The day after tomorrow, Sky could be dead! I should not have listened to them. I should have insisted on going into the Downs.

Malora folds her hands to keep them from shaking. She wants to pound them on the table. To have come this far, to have traveled all these many days, only to have to wait one more day, is nearly intolerable.

Zephele rises from the bench and wraps her arms around Malora's shoulders. "Please don't fret," she says softly. "We will find Sky and all will be well. And in the meantime, we will go shopping in the marketplace of Kahiro."

Malora sighs. How can she explain to her friend that the idea of shopping instead of visiting Shrouk makes her want to pick up the table and heave it into the fountain? But she says nothing. She doesn't trust herself to speak. She passes the rest of the meal in silence. The seafood, which she might under other circumstances have enjoyed sampling, is gritty and tasteless. Although Honus makes an effort to explain what each dish is, Malora doesn't really listen, and most of it she leaves on her plate.

Dock, whose own plate goes largely untouched, growls, "I don't blame you. Slimy grub's not fit for scavengers."

The others carry on, a forced fellowship in which Malora takes no part. She misses the horses. Not just the horses they left in the Dromadi stable but the ones in Mount Kheiron. She misses the warmth of Max's long, faintly rank head. And she misses Mount Kheiron itself.

When she expresses these thoughts to Honus, he says, "Ha! Mount Kheiron and its centaurean homogeneity. Yes, indeed. I do believe you are suffering from Kahiro Syndrome."

"What's that?" she asks.

"A temporary condition that comes about as a result of being exposed to a surfeit of strange food, strange language, and strange hibes. You want to curl up in a ball and breathe only the air from your own lungs and shut out all this jarring strangeness. Is that how you feel, my dear?"

"A little," she says, just to humor him. It is Zephele who suffers from the syndrome. Malora's suffering has a different cause. It is Sky's suffering she feels in her very bones.

Honus pats her hand. "You'll see. Your mind will widen again to encompass all this. Everything will seem much more acceptable in the morning. You'll get a good night's sleep and face tomorrow refreshed and once again open to new things."

Later, in her room, Malora removes the horns and rubs her scalp, then her calves, sore from walking on the balls of her feet. She looks around. Tucked up under the eaves, the room is small and modest by centaurean standards. There is a rectangular box of netting encasing a narrow bed and a wooden stand with a white bowl filled with water for washing. Once the home of a sea creature, Honus has told her, the bowl is called a seashell. She will find more seashells, of all shapes and sizes, on the shores of the sea tomorrow, where Neal has promised to take them *after* Zephele has sated herself shopping. She takes the sea sponge and drops it into the bowl. Then she strips and washes everything but her hair. Dirty hair is wild hair, and the more wild her hair, the more successfully it will conceal the tortoiseshell band.

Drying herself and slipping on only a tunic, she goes over to the window, parts the blue-glass beads, and looks down. The street below is in near-darkness and, except for the cats flowing in and out of the shadows, deserted. A few streets over to the east, she can see the aura of blazing torches and hear the endless shuffling of feet, the constant murmuring of many strange tongues punctuated by an occasional wild hoot of laughter. Somewhere, farther off, she hears music, as strange-sounding as the babble.

Honus has told her that the city, its streets and clubs and eateries, stays awake until sunrise. She should be out there prowling, asking everyone she sees about Sky, holding up the charcoal portrait Zephele drew of him—with the eyes rendered in the same vivid blue paint Zephele uses to accent her own eyes. But the thought of the scouts keeps her indoors. It isn't fear so much as if something were to happen to her, there would be no one to save Sky.

She stands up, letting the beads fall back over the window. Dousing her lantern, she climbs into the narrow bed. The net and the walls of the small room press in upon her. She closes her eyes and imagines she is in the tent, a closeness that is comforting rather than oppressive. But she isn't sleepy even though she needs to sleep. A day in the marketplace, her friends have told her, will be far more exhausting than any of their days in the bush. In the darkness, her hand wound throbs. She sits up and tears away the coverlet. She will never be able to sleep here! Then she remembers the ladder in the hallway that Honus told her led to the roof. She rips aside the netting, claps the horns back on her head, and slips on her boots. Rolling up the mattress and bedding, she carries them into the hall.

One-handed, she climbs the ladder and eases the hatch open with her horns. As she emerges onto the roof, she inhales the pungent sea air, an instant balm to her frazzled nerves. She looks around. White wisps ride the breeze like trailing scarves. The roof is an enormous square, the tiles still warm from the day's sun, surrounded by low walls with, here and there, a potted palm. She sees a figure in the mist and is glad of the knife in her boot, then realizes it is Honus. He is leaning against the wall, smoking a pipe. Choosing a spot between two palms, she lays out her bedroll on the tiles, then joins Honus.

He speaks without turning his gaze to her. "I knew you'd choose the roof over the room. The air is close down there."

Malora rests her elbows on the wall and looks out. Holes in the mist reveal the water below, black as oil. "So that's the sea," she says, feeling oddly disappointed.

"Wait until the mist blows off," Honus says. The next moment, as if on cue, a brisk wind scatters the mist to reveal an enormous, craggy mountain rising up out of the sea, etched in torchlight.

"Behold," says Honus, "the *true* Backbone of Heaven!"

"Why do they call it that?"

"Because it fell from the heavens and landed on the earth. The Scienticians predicted the occurrence hundreds of years before it happened. The Prophecy unhinged the People, even more than the proliferation of the hibes. They thought it boded the world's end. Knowing that the world might be ending made them half mad at worst, heedless of their welfare at best. The Scienticians built massive subterranean shelters all over the earth. They were intended originally for the People, but by the time they were finally put to use, there were more hibes than People and the hibes took most of them.

"There is a story in an ancient book called the Bible about a flood that once covered the earth and a man named Noah who was told by his god to build a great boat called an ark to hold two each of every animal on the earth. Aptly enough, the Scienticians called these shelters arks. Ironically, there was no room on the arks for the animals, which were left to fend for themselves. Many of them, the ones on this continent, went unscathed. On other continents they were rendered extinct and live on only through the surviving hibes. In the north, the impact of the rock colliding with the earth caused a deep freeze called the Great Ice. A vast sheet of ice covered the northern half of the world—and still does, or so the sailors say. Elsewhere, volcanoes erupted, the earth heaved, tidal waves swallowed whole coastlines, and great cities were buried. It is even said that on other continents, the land dissolved into great lakes of molten fire. Kahiro, which had once been an inland city, instantly became a seaside one with this great rock lying in the middle of its harbor."

"That rock out there caused all that destruction?" Malora asks.

"That rock is probably only a chip off the one that crashed to earth. Still, it was impressive enough to inspire the hibes of Kahiro, and all of the surrounding territories, to found the Church of the Latter Day Scienticians."

"Why?" Malora asks. "Because the Scienticians predicted the disaster and built the arks?"

"Not that so much as that the Scienticians were People and the hibes believed that their centuries-long persecution of the People had angered their god and caused him to bring down the very spine of heaven. Hence . . . the Backbone you see here before you."

Malora was not raised to worship. Except for a reverence for the Grandparents, the Settlement had been godless. The concept of gods—Kheiron, the god of the centaurs, and these bespectacled Doctors—is alien to her. "Do you think it's true," she asks Honus, "that their god punished the hibes?"

Honus taps out his pipe on the edge of the wall. Sparks fly toward the sea. "I believe that a great rock hurtling randomly through space collided with the earth, upsetting the balance of a planet that was already in calamitous imbalance. Hibes, just as the People did before them, need to find reasons for occurrences. The bigger the occurrence, the more powerful and compelling the reason."

The mist rises, revealing a sky full of stars. Looking up, Honus points. "Centaurus," he says.

He has pointed out the star picture to her on previous occasions, but this is the first time she can actually see, in the collection of stars, the outline of the body of a centaur. "I see it!" she says softly.

"Just as the ancient astronomer Ptolemy saw it thirty centuries ago," Honus says.

"I don't understand," Malora says. "That was long before the hibes. Were there once *natural* centaurs on earth?"

"It's hard to say," Honus says. "But I'm much more inclined to believe that the centaur sprang from the imagination of mankind, along with fauns and the Ka and so many of the other hibes you saw today. The Scienticians simply made flesh and blood what had once existed only in the deepest, darkest recesses of the human consciousness. You might say that we, the hibes, are a dream made real." Honus shivers and then stifles a yawn with his hand. "And speaking of dreams, it's time you got some sleep. Apologies, my daughter, if what I have just told you makes for a poor bedtime story." He turns to her and takes her arm. "Walk me to the door and then shut it and lock it behind me. That way no one will bother you tonight."

Before he descends the ladder, he plants a kiss on Malora's forehead. "Sleep well, my child."

Malora smiles at him. "I enjoyed my bedtime story," she says. For that is all it is to her: something that happened long ago and far away. Her own story, rolling out before her like one of the scrolls in Honus's library, is what interests her.

CHAPTER 10

The Marketplace

On the way to the marketplace the next morning, they pass no less than a dozen altars to the Doctors. They cross a square dominated by a marble temple, with a blue-robed statue of Adam standing on one side of its entryway and one of Eve on the other, both wearing the same dim-witted smiles. A steady stream of hibes, all wearing white jackets, pours through the doorway.

"The garb is called lab coats," Honus explains. "They are worn out of respect for the humble, everyday attire of the Scienticians."

Malora looks up at a big round stained-glass window above the door of the temple, the colors vibrant in the morning sun, depicting a river of hibes fleeing before a giant flaming ball.

"If you'd care to observe the service . . . ?" Honus says, indicating the doorway.

"No!" Malora says emphatically. Last night, she dreamed

that the Doctors Adam and Eve had stepped off their pedestals to scold her for marring her human head with horns. She had torn off the horns, leaving bloody stumps. Her head still aches this morning.

"The marketplace is a city unto itself," Honus explains as they approach the gateway. "It has its own laws, its own security force—dedicated to keeping beggars out—and many of the vendors never leave its jurisdiction, living out their lives in tents set up behind their booths."

They pass through a set of iron gates whose Ka attendant takes his time examining their Eyes before permitting them to enter. Overhead, the sun hangs like an orange suspended in the haze of dust kicked up by the browsers who have arrived well ahead of them, wandering the aisles of booths and stands that run from west to east. Malora is astounded at the sheer size of it. The marketplace of Mount Kheiron occupies a town square. This seems as big as all of Mount Kheiron and the Flatlands combined.

"It is all too easy to get lost in here," Honus says.

He is on one side of Malora and Orion on the other. Behind them, Sunshine and Lemon push the empty cart, which Zephele has sworn, by the end of the day, to fill to the brim with her purchases. Ahead of them, Dock and Neal have a firm lock on Zephele's arms. She manages to drag them from one side of the aisle to the other as she examines the wares on display. Still dressed for the road in a plain khaki wrap and boots and a matching cloth wrapping her head, Zephele looks radiant this morning. The marketplace of Kahiro is truly her element. Any revulsion Zephele might have had yesterday about the other hibes seems to have been obliterated by her enthusiasm for their wares.

"Oh, look!" she says. "An entire *aisle* of essential oils!"

Malora hangs back, knowing that experiencing the gamut of glass vials will wreak havoc on her heightened senses. Dock takes Orion's place as Orion joins Zephele, apologizing to Malora. "I'm sorry but this is the only aisle that interests me," he says.

"Of course," Malora says. "I'll wait here."

While Malora waits—watching from a safe distance as Zephele lifts and uncorks the many colored vials, running them beneath her nose and then beneath Orion's—Dock wards off the carters, swatting at them as if they were flies.

"Poor fools can't afford booths so they cart their wares," Dock explains. One of them, a Dromad, thrusts his wares in Malora's face and babbles.

"Anglish!" Honus tells them in a surprisingly churlish voice.

Malora sees what the Dromad offers and isn't interested: salt crystals, palm dates, items woven from palm leaves. Another Dromad joins him pushing a cart with a rack of fine-looking woven halters that interests her more.

"For camel and horse!" a third Dromadi carter promises, from behind a cart carrying a single saddle tooled with silver and turquoise.

"No need to be hasty. There is an entire aisle devoted to saddlery," Honus tells her over the noise of the hawking Dromad.

Malora considers buying a beautiful saddle for Sky, but

Sky isn't there to be fitted for it. Nor does she want to run ahead of herself. If she finds Sky, she won't need a fancy saddle to enjoy being on his back again. If only she *can* find him. One more day, she thinks.

Zephele is bargaining with the Dromad at one of the scent counters. The Dromad looks affronted. Orion, smiling sweetly, intervenes, holding out a handful of nubs. The Dromad sweeps them from Orion's palm and into a pocket that appears to be sewn right into the hide of his hump. Then he begins to wrap the vials, more than a dozen of them, in paper. Orion instructs the Dromad to wrap them extra thickly, and Malora is touched by his consideration for her sensitive nose.

"There are alchemical ingredients here that Orion can't obtain locally, like clove and myrrh and sandalwood and eucalyptus," Honus explains.

Zephele returns and hugs Malora for joy as Orion lays their parcels in the cart. "I have *stockpiled* wild jasmine!" she tells Malora gleefully.

They pass into an aisle that appears to be composed of livestock: pens of sheep and goats and cattle; rows of camels, hunched in a long disgruntled line, their long, gangling front legs tied together. There are horses, too, yoked together like beads in a long string, their hides rimed in dust. Malora moves up and down the rows, searching for Sky. The Dromadi vendor, chewing a black viscous cud, observes Malora from beneath his dusty lashes and says something to her in his harsh, guttural tongue.

Honus says, "He wants to know if you wish to purchase a horse."

Malora laughs. The idea is absurd to her. "No thanks,"

Malora says. "Tell him I get my horses for free." Then she removes the portrait of Sky from her pouch, smooths it out, and shows it to the Dromad while Honus explains. "Tell him how big Sky is," Malora says, gesturing with her hands.

Staring briefly at the picture, the Dromad spits into a nearby copper pot, wipes his lips on his arm, and says something to Honus. Honus smiles.

"What?" Malora says.

"He says if it's *big* you want, he can sell you a camel with a fine saddle with bells on it."

The Dromad nods, as if confirming Honus's translation.

"No thank you," she tells the Dromad. "I don't ride camels."

Honus steers her away from the booth. "He says it is your loss. But believe me, you would *not* be happy with the gait. Very bumpy, even with a saddle. And they have notoriously foul dispositions."

Zephele nabs them and hustles them past the livestock into the next aisle, where the vendors wear colorful vests sewn with mirrors through which the hair on their shoulders and torso pokes. They have triangular faces with broad flat noses, the points almost meeting above the crowns of their heads. In the center of their broad foreheads, precious gems glint. Before them, piles of gems rise up like small glittering mountains—rubies and sapphires, aquamarines and tourmalines—mound after mound, flashing in the sunlight.

Breathlessly, Zephele works her way up and down the aisle, sifting her fingers through the gems, beneath the disapproving eyes of the vendors. But Malora is more interested in the vendors than their wares.

"How are the gems on their heads held in place?" Malora whispers to Honus.

"Embedded in their skulls at birth. They are Bovians from the east," Honus whispers back.

"Cow-heads," Neal mutters over his shoulder. "They carry on like princes royal but they are really just miners with airs."

Except for their horns, they look like men. Malora peers over the counter and sees the hairy legs and blockish split hooves of cattle.

Zephele swoops down upon Malora and waves a sapphire as big as a wren's egg in her face. "What do you think? Should I buy it?" she asks.

"What for?" Malora asks.

"For its beauty, of course, why else? *I know!* I will buy it for you for your collection!" Zephele says.

"Please don't," Malora says.

But Zephele is already bargaining with the bovina behind the counter.

"Don't bother arguing with her," Orion says. "She's enjoying herself immensely. Shopping is like a sport for her, and she has entered with great gusto the greatest arena on earth."

The travelers now pass vegetables and fruits piled high, melons and pineapples and pomegranates and apples of all kinds, berries glistening like gems, bunches of green bananas and other fruits Malora has never seen. Feeling the first pangs of hunger, Malora wonders when they will eat. Her palm—beneath a bandage that was fresh this morning but is already brown with dust—aches, as do the balls of her feet.

Zephele leads them over into the next aisle. Malora gets a

quick impression of knitted goods and great spools of thread presided over by thick-legged hibes with baggy gray skin and sorrowful human faces with ragged, oversized ears.

"Loxidants," Honus says. "A homo-elephantine hibe. Mostly textile merchants."

By the time they extricate Zephele she has purchased six bolts of fabric. To get her to leave the aisle, they have to promise to return later. It is not yet midday and already the cart is nearly full.

"We arc approaching the only truly worthwhile aisle of the marketplace," Neal says.

"It's called the Arsenal," Honus says with an ominous flash of his eyes.

For the first time, Malora's desire to shop bursts into flame. The booths are run by Pantherians, who nod at Malora when she eyes the goods as if they recognize a kinship. With muscular arms crossed over their bare chests, males and females stand proudly before racks of intricately carved spears, swords, daggers, bows, and arrows. Orion points to one of the spears, painted with a red and black design and wrapped in muslin strips from which hang beads and what look like the teeth of small mammals. "What do you think of that, Malora?"

Malora picks up the spear and hefts it, rattling the teeth and shells. "The point is sharp enough, but with these noisy decorations hanging off it your prey would hear you before they saw you." She replaces the spear.

"The faun maiden is right," the nearby Pantherian says in a deep voice as refined as Honus's. "It is ornamental in nature. Would you care to examine some *real* weapons?" she asks

Malora. "We keep the pretties out front and the deadlies in back."

Malora follows the Pantherian behind a curtain made of tiny painted bones into a long gallery. On either side of the gallery hang more weapons, plain and lethal-looking: deadly, indeed. At the far end stands a skin target pierced many times over. The rest of the party has joined Malora.

Choosing a wooden spear, Malora hefts it, then shifts it to her right hand, feeling only a mild twinge in her palm. "Now *this* is what a real spear looks like."

Orion nods. "I will take your word for it."

"May I?" Malora asks the Pantherian, indicating the target.

The Pantherian nods.

There is a line of stones in the sand. Malora stands behind the line, and everyone else gathers behind her to watch.

Malora flexes her right hand. She will have to get used to using the hand in spite of the wound. Balancing with her left hand, Malora draws the spear behind her right shoulder and executes a few test passes with it. It is light, but the balance of the spear carries it forward without weighing it down. Malora inhales, drawing her arm back and then bringing it forward with a quick rush of breath, releasing the spear. It whistles through the air and sticks in the target, handle wobbling, at the exact center.

"Nice arm," purrs the Pantherian. "In spite of the wound."

"Nice spear," Malora replies. "It throws itself."

"Hardly." The Pantherian goes to retrieve the spear from the target.

"Would you like to buy it?" Neal asks.

"Of course she would like to buy it," Zephele says. "Did you see the way she threw it?"

Malora gives Zephele a look. A month ago, Zephele would never have expressed admiration for the handling of a weapon. A month ago, Zephele would never have set foot in the Arsenal. "No thank you," she tells the Pantherian, "but I would like to buy one of those sticks like the Ka carry."

"A Kavian serpent staff?" the Pantherian says with a scornful snort. "Over that way. Come back when you want something *real.*"

Two aisles over, Malora chooses from among hundreds of brightly painted wooden sticks, one that is the right size and heft for her. Painted like a red cobra, the smooth hooded head fits nicely in her left hand and supports her weight.

Neal says, "You have me baffled, pet. You had your choice of any number of magnificent weapons and yet you choose a decorative stick? The affectation seems most unlike you."

Malora leans in to him and whispers, "My feet are sore from trotting like a faun. The stick supports my weight. Do you consider *that* an affectation?"

"No, I consider that sensible," Neal says.

Malora has another use in mind for the stick, one that she keeps to herself: it will help her detect sinkholes if she has to go into the Downs to search for Sky. "I'm hungry," she announces.

Neal sends the Twani back to the inn with their brimming cart while the rest of them make for the food aisle. Not even at the Founders' Day feast has Malora seen such quantity and variety of foods. Neal suggests that they take a quick tour of the booths before ordering. They tour the platters on offer beneath white canvas awnings. There are refreshing-looking glass pitchers of beverages from which Neal steers them away.

"Spirits," he explains.

There are big colorful bowls of cut-up mixed fruits and others of vegetables. There are pots simmering over fires filled with stews, smelling delicious and savory. Zephele asks Honus which ones have meat in them. Then there are platters of roast antelope with their horns still attached, roast peacock with their feathers restored, whole cooked horned sheep, and tubs of great cheesy lumps.

"Dormice," Honus says. "It is camels' hump fat, floating in saffron sauce." The description makes Zephele gag into her hand.

Suideans ladle buffalo stew from big cauldrons; Pantherians offer bush meat on a stick and served in a bowl made of hard, shiny-crusted bread. Malora is tempted to order this.

"I wouldn't if I were you," Honus says.

"Why not?" Malora says.

"Anything that's called bush meat is very likely monkey meat."

Malora recoils. One of the first things her father ever taught her was that monkeys were not for eating.

"Why are they permitted to sell tainted meat?" Malora asks.

"It's the marketplace in Kahiro," Honus says with a shrug. "Buyer beware."

"That doesn't sound like a very nice philosophy to me," Zephele says with a deep frown.

"It's not," says Orion. "Not everything in Kahiro is nice, Sister, as you may have gathered by now."

"Would either of you ladies care for the jellyfish parfait this nice merman is selling?" Neal asks.

A handsome, barrel-chested hibe with the head and torso of a man and the tail of an enormous fish sits with his lower half immersed in a great wooden vat of water. He offers deep glass bowls filled with something gelatinous and grayish green.

"What happens if the merman gets out of the barrel?" Malora asks.

"On dry land, he dies," Neal says.

"Then how did he get here?" Malora says.

"He probably paid some strapping quad or biped to wheel him up from the sea. Live sea snakes are always tasty," Neal says, indicating the bowl held up by the next merman.

"Then eat one of them," Zephele says, slyly challenging.

Neal tosses a nub to the merman and dips a hand into the bowl. He selects a small snake that whips wildly about as he dips it into a bowl of bright red sauce and then drops the sea snake, wriggling, down his throat. He chews, then swallows hard and grins. "The sauce is really very good."

"What does it taste like? The sea snake, I mean," Zephele asks.

"Like chicken," he says.

"A meaningless analogy, Flatlander. You know I've never eaten chicken," Zephele says, giving Neal a rather unladylike elbow jab to the ribs.

"It tastes a bit salty and a bit bitter at the same time," Neal says.

"In the bush," Malora says, "if something tasted sweet, I

knew it would give me vitality. If it tasted salty, I knew it would nourish me. If it was sour, it wasn't ripe. And if it was bitter, it would probably kill me."

"From now on," Neal jokes, "we'll let you be our official taster. If it doesn't kill you, it's bound to be safe for the rest of us to eat. Do, by all means, tell us what looks good to you, Malora."

After they have eaten, Honus says, "In my experience, nothing revives one from a postprandial swoon quite so well as a breath of fresh sea air."

"Finally!" says Zephele.

"Take us there!" says Malora.

Neal leads them to a worn wooden door in the wall where a Ka stands sentry. When they flash their Eyes, the Ka throws the bolt and lets them pass through.

On the other side of the wall, a blue and green flag hangs limply from a high pole.

"Are we leaving the marketplace, or are we leaving Kahiro?" Malora asks.

"Both," says Orion. "The shore is considered international territory."

But Malora sees no shore. There is only a high, steep ridge of sand running parallel to the wall as far as she can see. "Where is the sea?" she asks.

"On the other side of these sand dunes," Honus says.

They follow a well-worn path that runs between the dunes and the city wall. The noise of the marketplace has suddenly disappeared. But where is the sound of the sea? The constant murmuring that accompanied Malora's sleep is not audible here. Instead, there is eerie silence and the air is dead.

"What happened to the sea?" Malora asks.

"It's there," Orion tells her. "It's just over the crest of the dunes."

Flocks of gray-and-white birds swirl and dive at them, pulling up at the last moment and careening away with sneering caws.

"Winged scavengers," Dock says bitterly.

The path gradually steepens and begins to rise up the side of the dunes. Malora thinks she was hot in the marketplace. Here she swelters. Sweat drips down her back and her legs. Zephele is pale and looks faint. Orion takes his sister's arm and supports her the last few steps to the top. Their hooves sink into the loose sand and they scramble. Malora takes Zephele's other arm, and together she and Orion keep her upright. Neal stands at the crest of the dune, his golden hair ruffled by the wind. Honus stands beside him. Behind them, Dock huffs and curses with every step.

Finally, they achieve the summit of the dune.

"Behold, my friends," says Honus, sweeping an arm before them, "the wine-dark sea!"

A Close Call

Moments before, the sun beating down on the dunes was hot and still, the air as dry-baked as a furnace. Now the wind whipping off the water flings cold moisture into Malora's face. She licks her lips and tastes salt.

She stretches out her arms as if to embrace the whole of the watery expanse spreading out to the horizon. She imagines herself riding on horseback along the shore with the wind whipping her hair.

Whereas moments ago the sea was dark, now it is blue. It is a blue different from any that Malora has ever known. River water is muddy, or it is green, but it is almost never blue, and if it is, it isn't quite *this* blue. This is a blue that is alive and moving, running at a rapid clip. Rows of waves speed toward the shore for as far as she can see in both directions, foamy and swirling, like the wind-tossed manes of galloping horses.

"Well, ladies," Orion says, his eyes moving from one to the other, "what do you think?"

Zephele huddles, clasping her elbows and shivering. "It frightens me," she says in a small voice.

"Ha! You would do well to fear it," Honus says, "for its tides are fearfully powerful."

Neal shakes his head slowly. "I don't mind looking at it. I don't mind eating the fish that swim in it. And there is nothing like a sea breeze to clear your head after a night of carousing. But you would not catch me in it or on it or under it or crossing it anytime soon."

Malora says, "I *will* swim in it before I leave this place."

This declaration is met by a brief silence.

"I think not," says Orion with a nervous laugh.

"Why would you even *want* to?" Neal says.

Malora says, "Let's get closer," as she leads the way down the steep path toward the sea.

"I'll be staying right here," says Dock, arms folded across his chest, hooves planted in the sand.

"Suit yourself, old man!" Neal calls. "We'll meet you back at the inn."

Malora picks her way down the path. The dunes are more solid on this side, with boulders and grass poking up like sharp little swords. Further down the shoreline, Honus stops and points. She doesn't see at first, and then suddenly she does: there are stone structures tucked in among the rocks. "The homes of the sealies and merfolk," he says.

Malora watches as the sea boils into the doors and windows and then pulls away with a rattle and clatter of stones.

"Twice a day, their houses are completely submerged by the tides," Honus says. "That's when they return home. The rest of the time they spend in the sea."

"Oh, look in the water!" says Zephele, clapping delightedly. "How adorable! They're so tiny. Are they children?"

"Sealie pups and merkits," Honus says, nodding. Little figures wriggle about in the shallows. There are crude baskets cradled in their arms. They are gathering up sopping hanks of yellow and pink and blue and green and filling their baskets.

"What are they doing?" Malora asks.

"Harvesting seaweed to sell in the marketplace," Honus explains. "It is very healthful. Some of it is edible. Other kinds fertilize crops. The sea is the cradle of all life. It nurtures just as it destroys."

A few of the children pause to stare back at the strangers. The pups have human faces and arms and shoulders but their skin is black with a bluish sheen and they have stout torsos that split into legs ending in short fins that look like a fat dog's paws. The kits' tails are covered in scales, some golden, others tending more toward green and blue. As they draw nearer, Malora sees that both pups and kits have long, muscular necks with gills running behind their tiny budlike ears.

"I've always been vaguely revolted by those gills," Orion says thoughtfully.

"I know what you mean. They call to mind bloodless incisions," Honus says. "I think it's their cold-bloodedness that puts us off. Most of the rest of us are warm-blooded. Even the Ka are equally as comfortable on land as in water. But these hibes are, in the truest sense of the word, *Other*."

The shore is steep where the waves sweep in. While the centaurs stay where the footing is more level, Malora and Honus walk closer to the water.

"This is where the treasures fetch up," Honus explains.

Malora finds a fragile spiral object and holds it in the palm of her hand. It looks like a flower made of delicate bone. "Is this a seashell, too?" she asks.

"Yes. It is no longer occupied, so now it is yours, if you like."

Malora slips it into her pouch.

They make their way slowly, Honus bending to pick up a seashell or a brightly colored stone to place in his own pouch. Malora walks with her eyes on the ground, as greedy for sea treasures as Zephele was for items in the marketplace.

The next time she looks up, she is surprised to see that the dunes have disappeared and that they and the centaurs are now walking on a flat, even stretch of sand.

"Around the next bend," Honus says, "is the port."

They come to a high stone wall with steps running up the side. Malora and Honus climb up them, and from the top of the wall Malora stares down into water that looks black and fathomless and sucks against the mossy sides of the wall. Then she gazes up to where the arch of Kahiro soars high overhead. Under the arch, boats and ships bob at their moorings.

"The boats enter and leave beneath this archway," Honus explains.

"I've never seen a structure so high," she says.

Honus replies, "The wall is even higher on the sea side of Kahiro. That is so that ships with very tall masts can sail beneath the great port arch. It's high tide now. If we wait here long enough, maybe we'll see it."

"What will we see?" Zephele asks, as the centaurs join them on the pier.

"Wait!" Honus rests one hand on Malora's arm and points

upward. She sees a tiny figure on the top of the arch. The idea of standing up there makes Malora's head reel. As she watches, the tiny figure launches itself into the air and dives gracefully down, down, down, landing with a neat splash in the pool beneath them.

When the Ka's head bobs up, Zephele bursts into applause. "Oh, excellent!"

"This is the Kahiro Pool. As you can imagine, the water is very deep here," Honus says. "Shall we walk a ways out onto the pier?"

The pier is covered with dark green seaweed and juts out into the water. Threaded through iron rods sunk into the pier is a long mossy rope.

"Grab on to the rope," Neal instructs them. "The footing is dicey. Farther out, it's treacherous."

The rope feels cold and slimy in Malora's hand. The sea sloshes over the pier. White-lipped and determined, the centaurs hang on to the rope and pick their way along. On the other side of the pool, another pier runs parallel to this one. Ka tads leap from it into the water and haul themselves out on long ropes.

"These piers are known as the Arms of Kahiro," Honus says.

The Backbone of Heaven, rising up from the center of the harbor, looks smaller by day but is alive with nesting seabirds. Malora begins to feel slightly queasy. The water, which had looked so blue and inviting from the dunes, is black and afloat with objects rising and falling with sickening regularity, including long, sinister tendrils of seaweed.

"Still want to go swimming, pet?" Neal asks.

When Malora doesn't respond, Orion says, "It's not what you see that bothers you so much as what you don't see." His pale eyes have darkened, absorbing the water's darkness.

"What's that?" Zephele asks suddenly.

They all break off gazing into the water to see Zephele pointing to another rock slightly to the east of the Backbone of Heaven. It rides lower in the water and has some sort of structure occupying most of it.

"That ziggurat on the small island?" Honus says. "That, my dears, is the Beehive, the most famous of all the Houses of Romance. A boat leaves from the end of this pier on a regular basis to deliver customers to and from the Beehive."

"Well," says Zephele, turning huffily away, "the less said about *that* the better. I believe I've had enough of the sea *and* Beehives. I'm tired. Are you tired, Malora?"

"Yes," says Malora. "Let's go back to the inn."

"An excellent idea," Neal says.

They all turn around slowly on the pier and work their way back to the shore, passing beneath the arch and proceeding along the promenade. Dockworkers, Ka and burly Bovians, are loading and unloading goods from the ships. Overhead, nets of cargo sway.

Mount Kheiron has a small river port where flatboats and barges load and unload, but that is a modest enterprise compared to the Port of Kahiro, with its forest of clinking masts. The ships, hulls creaking as they rise and fall on the swells, smell of the sea and of their cargos: spices and oils and hides, olive oil and wine and oranges. As Malora's nose takes it all in, she gets hints of the lands from which these ships have sailed, crowded waterfronts with white-capped mountains rising from the mist, tiger-eyed hibes padding along the decks, monkey-tailed hibes scaling the rigging. The decks and rigging here are all empty of crew.

"Where is everyone?" Malora asks.

"Probably at the Beehive," Neal says with a bark of laughter. "Who knows how long they have been at sea? Oh, you wouldn't catch me on board one of these things. The sea's no place for a centaur."

They leave the port and enter onto the wide main street, moving against the tide of the crowd, which is headed toward the port.

"Where are they all going?" Malora asks.

"Believe it or not, to watch the sun set into the sea," Honus says. "It is a daily ritual here. They bring beverages and simple foods and stand on the piers. They watch the sealies swim out with their torches to light up the Backbone of Heaven. And when the sun finally drops into the sea, they cheer and applaud as if it were a dramatic performance put on for their amusement."

"Painters depict the sunset at Kahiro and sell them in the artists' aisle at the marketplace. These sunsets on parchment are a very popular souvenir of Kahiro," Orion adds.

"Can we watch the sun set into the sea some night?" Zephele asks.

"I will think about it," Neal says.

"What is this?" Malora asks.

They are passing a building twice the size of their inn, made of rose-colored blocks of stones and topped by a polished gold dome that is easily ten times larger than the dome on the temple of Kheiron.

"The Empress's palace," Neal says.

A sudden blare of trumpets pierces the air and sends the crowd scurrying. Pedestrians grab hold of one another and haul each other into the shelter of doorways and porticos. Malora pulls Zephele to one side of the street while Orion, Honus, and Neal wind up being shoved by the crowd to the other. Neal is struggling to make his way across to join Malora and Zephele when two lines of Ka come down the street. Clad in green and blue loincloths and matching headdresses, they bang their serpent sticks on the pavement, linking their arms and forming a double barricade to keep the crowds on both sides from surging back into the streets.

"What's happening?" Malora asks.

Zephele hugs herself happily. "Who *knows*? But isn't it *exciting!*" She wiggles her fingers teasingly at Neal across the road. He scowls and gestures to both of them to stay where they are.

Malora turns to watch a procession of Ka in golden loincloths holding two long, ribbon-wrapped poles bearing a big gilded box festooned with fresh flowers, its sides covered with brightly beaded curtains. Through the swaying beads, Malora catches sight of a single sheKa within, perched on a golden throne. She wears a golden headdress and a purple veil over her lower face. Hands folded demurely on her lap, her huge, moist amphibious eyes stare haughtily ahead.

"It's the litter of the Empress of the Ka. It is just as it has been described to me, but I never dreamed we'd actually see it. Oh, we are so lucky!" Zephele says breathlessly. "Did you see her?"

Malora nods.

"I did, too, and she's absolutely divine, is she not?" Zephele cries.

Malora smiles at her friend. Zephele's former intolerance seems to have vanished. The horns blare again and the crowd's roar of approval follows the litter as it files past Zephele and Malora. Behind the Empress's litter are more Ka, these wearing red loincloths, some holding horns to their fleshy lips, others beating drums strapped to their slender hips.

Malora reaches out for Zephele's hand and, groping around, turns to find a bovina standing where Zephele had been moments before. She is waving a small blue and green pennant and cheering with the others. Her heart hammering, Malora's eyes skitter over the crowd. Zephele is nowhere to be seen. Malora turns to signal to her companions across the street, but the parade blocks her view of them. She pushes her way back through the crowd, searching for her friend. Finally, she picks up the faintest trace of Zephele's wild jasmine scent. Malora tracks it along the pavement, shoving aside anyone in her way. Then, over the din of the crowd and the music, she hears Zephele's voice.

Crossing the mouth of a narrow alleyway, Malora sees Zephele at the far end. She is speaking with a stout, dapper-looking Capricornia wearing a white robe and white knee breeches. His hooves are gilded, along with the horns that curl around his ears, and his white beard comes to an oiled point beneath his chin. He is holding an object in his hand that looks like an apple but cannot be one, for even from a distance Malora can tell that Zephele, fists to her mouth, trembles with the desire to touch it. Zephele looks up briefly and sees Malora, waving her over excitedly.

"Come and see, Malora! Come see the treasure!"

The Capricornia turns and eyes Malora with a look she instantly dislikes. It seems to see clear through the saruchi to her human legs. Impossible, she tells herself, as she takes extra care to mince faunlike toward him, hand leaning on the head of her cobra stick.

"What is it?" Malora asks. Her bandaged hand reaches out to swipe from his palm the object Zephele covets. He huffs indignantly and she smells spirits on his breath.

"It's a pomegranate," Malora says dismissively. Why all this fuss, she wonders, over a piece of fruit?

"Oh, but peel back the skin and you will see that it is no ordinary pomegranate," Zephele urges her.

Lifting a triangle of skin, Malora now sees that the object she is holding is an artificial pomegranate, covered in red leather skin, bursting with what must be hundreds of small, perfect rubies, each shaped like a shimmering seed. "It's very beautiful," Malora concedes. "Let me buy it for you, Zephie."

"It is not for sale, this kind gentle Capricornia tells me," Zephele says.

"Oh?" says Malora, shifting her gaze to him. "Why not? Isn't everything in this city for sale?"

The Capricornia's eyes stare back at her, as pale and cold as gold nubs. "It is free," he says. "And there are more where it comes from, in a magnificent palace in the middle of the sea. There you will find bunches of grapes made from amethyst and emerald. Oranges with succulent topaz wedges. It's all waiting for you, only a short boat ride away."

Malora raises an eyebrow. "Leaving from the end of the easternmost Arm of Kahiro?"

"Exactly!" the Capricornia says. "And if we hurry along, we won't miss the next launch."

Malora tosses the pomegranate back to him and he fumbles to catch it. "No thank you. Our friends are expecting us. They are just around the corner. As a matter of fact, I think I hear them calling us now."

Zephele's face falls, but her eyes never leave the pomegranate. "Another time, perhaps, kind sir?" she says.

Malora grabs her arm and pulls her away from the Capricornia. "Not anytime soon," she whispers to Zephele between clenched teeth.

"By all means," says the Capricornia, returning the pomegranate to a green satin sack and tugging the drawstring tight. "I shall look forward to it."

"As shall I!" calls Zephele over her shoulder as Malora all but drags her out of the alley.

"Will you please stop speaking to that *predator!*" Malora whispers harshly.

"What do you *mean?*" Zephele asks, wide-eyed.

Malora stops long enough to throw up her hands. "Were you so smitten by his wares that you forgot absolutely *everything* that *everyone* has been telling us about the scouts?"

Malora can see the thoughts flashing behind Zephele's wide eyes, culminating in a dropped jaw. "You mean . . . !"

Malora nods. "That, my dear girl, was a talent scout."

"Surely not. They bind and gag and drug their victims," Zephele says.

"Obviously this one knew he didn't need to resort to such measures. All he did was show you a ruby pomegranate and you were so dazzled, you were ready to follow him anywhere."

"Straight to the Beehive," Zephele says in a dull voice.

"Exactly," Malora replies, continuing to herd Zephele along.

Zephele throws an arm over Malora's shoulder and kisses her cheek. "Thank you, dear friend, for saving my honor. I don't know how I shall ever repay you."

"You can repay me," says Malora, "by swearing never to speak to another stranger as long as you are here. And by remaining at my side."

Zephele nods. "On the Wise Head of Kheiron, I swear. I know I'm in no position to extract any promises from you, but will you please promise not to tell the others—Neal especially—about this little encounter? I'd never hear the end of it."

"I promise," Malora says.

CHAPTER 12

Food for Sharks

Malora wakes early the next morning as the sun is rising and feels a surge of happiness. *Today I see Shrouk!* Rising from her rooftop bed, she dons horns, saruchi, and boots and trots over to the seaward wall.

Just as she hoped, the water is as smooth and green and inviting as a meadow this morning. Even the Backbone of Heaven, with its blanket of roosting birds, seems more domesticated today. My last chance to swim in the sea, she thinks. Tomorrow, we will be on our way to Sky.

Before she leaves, she puts on a cape, leaving the hood down so her horns are visible. Slipping a note beneath Honus's door to say that she has gone searching for seashells, she creeps down the stairs and out into the city. The streets are empty and still. It is as if the city has stopped to take a breath. Even the beggars are asleep, huddled in doorways. Ka in dusty white loincloths working long brooms are the only ones out.

When she reaches the port, she heads west. Honus has told her there is a long, flat strand where he has found his best treasures.

Malora walks along the curved shore until the Arms of Kahiro, the Backbone of Heaven, and the Beehive are all lost to sight. The water looks as inviting as it did from up on the roof. Malora looks up and down the shore. Seeing no one, she strips off her clothing and removes her horns, leaving her things in a neat pile above the wave line. Then she slips into the water. It is surprisingly tepid and smells faintly of fish. Taking a deep breath, she immerses her head and begins to swim. The salty water is dense. It stings the Dream Wound in a way that feels healing. She swims underwater, eyes open to the lime-green depths, afloat with scraps of seaweed and flitting little fish as vivid as wildflowers. She swims along the shoreline until she rounds the point. There she sees the pier and the Backbone of Heaven blotting out the Beehive. Before anyone can see her, bareheaded in all her humanity, she turns around and swims back the way she came.

Climbing out of the water, Malora lies down on top of her cloak and lets the morning sun bake the beads of moisture off her skin. Eyes closed, wiggling her toes in the warm sand, she wonders idly what Brion is working on today. Wagon spokes? Fence finials? Pitchfork tines? A cloud moves over the face of the sun and blocks out the warmth. She opens one eye to see just how big the cloud is, and how long she will have to wait for the sun's warmth to return.

Standing over her is the Capricornia scout, his face in shadow. Suddenly Malora feels like the world's biggest fool.

"Good morning, beauty," he says.

Malora yanks the cape over herself and offers no greeting in return.

"This is not a safe place for a young maiden to be alone," he says. He extends his hand. "Allow me to escort you to safety."

Malora sits up. She isn't sure what she is going to do. Under cover of the cloak, she works her way into her saruchi and tunic and boots. She considers drawing the knife from her boot but thinks better of it. Bide your time, she coaches herself. She stands and places the horns back on her head, arranging the wet hair over the band.

The Capricornia chuckles. "How long did you think you could go on keeping your identity secret from the world?" he asks, offering her his arm.

Malora doesn't reply. There is no good answer. She stares at the arm. It looks strong. Inside the sleeve of his robe, a dagger glints. Her own knife is sharp, but it is in her boot, and she has never faced off against a hibe.

"You needn't look so worried," he tells her. "Where I am taking you, you will be safe and highly prized. The Queen of the Hive."

"The *Bee*hive?" she asks, widening her eyes innocently. "I have heard wonderful things about the Beehive. I'd like to see it. Will you take me there?" She puts an eager smile on her lips.

"It will be my pleasure," he says.

She takes his arm, and like old friends they stroll toward the pier. It has come to her that her best defense is to imitate Zephele at her very silliest.

"I was watching you while you were in the water," the Capricornia says. "You are a strong swimmer, but the sea is dangerous at this time. The morning is when the sharks come in close to the shore to feed."

Malora pulls back and claps a hand over her heart. "Sharks! I have never seen a shark before. Are they just too, too fierce?"

"Indeed, they are. The skates, too," the Capricornia goes on. "I saw them, leaping all about you as you swam, like a demonic escort. They carry a paralytic poison in their tails. One touch is death."

Malora feigns a shiver. "How dreadful!" she says, suspicious that he is just trying to frighten her.

"Well, well, well," he says with a gentle laugh, "you almost learned the hard way, didn't you?"

"This surely must be my lucky day," Malora says.

"We are both lucky," says the Capricornia. "You, for avoiding the sharks and the barbs of the skates, and me for finding *you* before they did. You must take better care of yourself. I will make it my business from now on to see that you do."

"You are too kind, sir," she says, fluttering her eyelashes, sounding more like Zephele than the dear girl herself. "And I thank you for looking after my welfare so gallantly."

"You are most welcome," he says, patting her hand.

They are nearing the port. A crew of Suideans on the docks unloads sacks into a large pushcart. She could scream for help and they would come running, but the Capricornia would only reveal her identity to them, and then her secret would be made even more public. She envisions word spreading throughout the city until all of Kahiro comes rushing in upon her. She feels beads of perspiration gathering on her upper lip and wipes them covertly away before the Capricornia can see them.

Malora asks, "By any chance, do you still have that rare and precious bauble you showed my friend yesterday?"

"Why yes, I do, as a matter of fact," he says.

"Oh, I would love to see it again," Malora says. "I only feigned disinterest yesterday because I was jealous you hadn't chosen me to share it with first."

"Oh, you have nothing to be jealous about, my dear," the Capricornia says. "Had I known the truth about you, I would have snatched it from the quadruped wench's greedy clutches and bestowed it upon you and you alone."

As she watches him reach into the folds of his robe, Malora bites back a smile to think how Zephele would take to the name *quadruped wench*. The Capricornia produces the green satin sack and removes the ruby pomegranate. He places both in her cupped hands, then wraps his own around hers.

"The first of many gifts that I will bestow upon you," he says, squeezing her hands.

"I am speechless with gratitude, kind sir," Malora says. "I've never been in a boat on the sea before, you understand, and I think it would comfort me to cradle such a treasure in my hands."

"It is you who are the treasure, my precious one," he says.

She turns her head away in disgust. "Oh, sir! How you make a girl blush!"

As they resume their walk toward the pier, Malora wonders how Zephele can stand acting this way. Is it, as it is now for Malora, a means of self-defense? A way of cloaking one's real intelligence?

The Capricornia says, "While we wait for the boat, I have a treat in store for you."

"*Another* treat? You spoil me!" Malora says. Her left hand is trapped in his, her right cradles the pomegranate. The Dream Wound throbs.

"Wait here," he says.

She watches as he goes over to a sealie in the shallows near the pier. I could easily run away now, she thinks. But it wouldn't matter; her secret will never be safe with the likes of him. No, somehow she has to solve the problem permanently.

He returns carrying a net bag filled with butchered fish parts. "For the sharks," he says, grinning. One of his teeth glints golden.

"Is it really?" she says, her hand going to her mouth.

"Come with me and see."

The net bag hanging from his arm by a string, he grabs hold of the rope railing and leads her by the hand out onto the pier. The farther from shore they go, the more slippery the rocks. She tries to extricate her hand and reach for the rope, but he won't let her. He would rather she depend upon him than the rope. Her resentment of him simmers.

At the end of the eastern Arm of Kahiro, the width of the wall widens. There is a dry space in the middle where the waves can't reach. Malora carefully sets down the pomegranate in its green bag within the dry space. She eyes the fish parts.

"Am I permitted to feed the sharks now?" she asks, batting her eyelashes.

"First I must signal for the boat," he says. He waves his arm in a wide arc.

"The Beehive is so very far away," Malora frets. "Are you sure they will see you?"

"They will see my signal. And when they set eyes upon you, how they will rejoice! I will be the most celebrated scout in the world. They will write songs about me . . . *and* you."

Malora smiles as if his notion were deeply gratifying. "Shall we feed the sharks?" she says with a mock sweetness that matches his own. "However do we accomplish such a task?"

"It's simple. Toss some of the fish chunks into the water. The sharks will come calling and put on quite a little display for us, as you will see," he says.

"Really?" she says, her eyes going round. "But won't it be frightfully dangerous?"

"In the water, it will be treacherous," he says. "But you will be safe up here on the pier with me to protect you."

Malora begins to pull out bits of the foul-smelling fish and throw them into the sea. The Capricornia praises her actions as if she were a prodigy.

"But where are the sharks?" she asks, staring down into the water, thinking, If the boat arrives before the sharks, what will I do then?

"Wait," he says. "Be patient, beautiful girl."

The next moment, the sea begins to boil and foam as the water erupts with the shiny, dark gray fins of sharks. Malora has never seen sharks, only heard them described by Honus. They are an ancient species, more ancient than the People. She observes their gray-green bodies angling through the water, their heavy tails and fins, their jagged rows of teeth, their small black beady eyes. There are no predators on land with eyes as dead as these, she thinks.

"See?" he says with an elated smile. "There are at least six of them. What if it were you down there in the water, instead of the fish? You are at least as tender and tasty as fish guts. Aren't you glad I came along in time to warn you of the dangers of the deep?"

"How will I ever thank you!" she says, giving him a tremulously grateful look. "But I'm afraid there's not enough fish to feed them all. Will the sharks be very angry with us?"

"They'll start in on each other when they have run out of fish," he says in a distracted tone. He is looking out to sea now, not down at the sharks. "Where is that launch?" he mutters to himself. He steps to the end of the pier and raises both arms over his head. The moment has arrived. Malora hears a roaring in her ears louder than the sound of the feeding sharks' snapping jaws.

She tosses the rest of the fish, net bag and all, into the roiling sea. She feels a curious calmness as she rises up onto her toes and walks toward the Capricornia's broad back. Stiff-armed, palms flat, she shoves him off the end of the pier and into the water. He lets out one brief cry before the sharks cut him off. The sea bubbles red, like a pot of beets on the boil.

"It nurtures as it destroys," she whispers. Nausea coils in her gut. Looking beyond the bloodied water, she remembers how she stopped Neal from murdering the big white raptor. But that had been a bird. The Capricornia was a sentient being, half human, with thoughts, plans, aspirations, a home, perhaps even a family. Does this make me a murderer now?

Then she bristles as she thinks, He was a predator, like a leopard or a lion or a shark. I had to kill him to save myself.

She swallows her nausea, bends down, and picks up the bag holding the ruby pomegranate. Then she edges back along the pier toward the port where no one—not the Ka tads diving off the pier nor the Suidean cargo mates—is aware of what she has just done.

At the morning meal, Malora presents Zephele with the pomegranate.

Zephele's eyes pop. "How did you . . . ?" she starts to ask, then stops herself. "Never mind. I don't want to know. Oh, wonderful you, to have thought of winning me such a prize— the one thing I wanted more than anything in all the marketplace of Kahiro!"

"That's quite a statement," her brother says.

When Neal sees the pomegranate, he holds out his hand for it. Reluctantly, Zephele places it in his palm. He turns it curiously in his hands. "You know, there are baubles such as this—fruits made of gems—in bowls in the salons of the Beehive," he says. He lifts his eyes to Malora speculatively. "That's the only place I have ever seen them."

Before Malora can manufacture a white lie, Zephele explodes: "Neal Featherhoof! Do you mean to say that you have actually *been* to the Beehive?"

"Only once," Neal says smoothly, "to satisfy my curiosity."

"*Liar!*" Zephele says, snatching the pomegranate.

CHAPTER 13

Shrouk Speaks

"Is that gaffey I smell?" Malora asks as her nose picks up a pungent aroma emanating from the saffron-colored tent just ahead.

"It is indeed," Orion says. He turns to the others. "The rest of you wait outside until Malora has finished her consultation."

Neal holds up two zebra-skinned flasks. "So long as I get my refill."

"Of course," Orion says. "But business first."

"Are you sure you don't want me to stay with you, Malora dear?" Zephele says in a low voice.

"I'll be all right," Malora says. It has been decided that only Orion will accompany her into the tent.

"You look fetching," Zephele assures her, as if this were a jubilation or a banquet.

Malora is wearing the apricot silk saruchi Zephele purchased for her in the marketplace yesterday, along with a turquoise tunic made of nubby cotton. After so many days of waiting to see Shrouk, Malora now finds herself light-headed and anxious.

Orion raises the flap and, with a lift of his chin, bids Malora to enter first. Ducking low so as not to snag her horns on the flaps, she steps into the warm darkness where the aroma of gaffey is so strong her glands prickle. In the center of the tent, a wrinkled miniature Dromad crouches on cushions, her camel-self hidden beneath a saffron-colored robe. Before her is a low table arranged with a copper ewer and a row of tiny gilded cups and saucers. Her blind, filmy eyes shining like mother-of-pearl in the gloaming, the Dromad beckons Malora forward with a long brown finger.

"Hello, Shrouk," Orion whispers.

Shrouk's face turns sharply toward Orion and she breaks into a wide, gummy smile. "Silvermane!" she says in a hoarse whisper, holding out a warty hand for Orion to kiss. "Gentle centaur, come in and imbibe of a freshly brewed pot of Shrouk's very finest. Sit, sit." She points to the pink and orange silken cushions scattered on the floor around the long, low table. Malora sinks into one of them, cross-legged, while Orion folds his legs beneath himself on the bare ground beside her. The under-scent of Orion's anxious sweat—human and horse—grounds Malora.

Shrouk tips the copper ewer and pours a thin stream of dark brown liquid into a cup, the liquid spilling over the tips of her fingers, which are stained as dark as the brew. She fills both cups, stirring a lump of sugar into each with a small filigree spoon and adding parings from the rind of a fat ripe lemon. She serves it up to them, a cup in each hand, her rheumy eyes sparkling with gentle mischief.

"Gaffey," she cackles. The eyelashes that brush her dark cheeks are white.

"This is Malora," Orion says. "The faun maiden has need of your all-seeing eye." He takes his cup and nods to Malora to take the other.

"Is that a fact?" the Dromad croaks, then cackles.

Malora bobs her head. "It's a fact," she says softly.

The Dromad hocks a wad of phlegm into a nearby copper spittoon and wipes her lips on the sleeve of her robe. "True, you may have need of my sight, but you are no faun. Shrouk knows when she is in the presence of . . . the *People*."

Malora sets down her cup with a clatter. She whispers to Orion, "I thought you said she was blind!"

"Shrouk sees with the Inner Eye," the ancient Dromad says, tapping her forehead. "Now, why have you come?"

"I have lost a stallion," Malora begins. "His name is Sky, but he is so much more than a horse. He is my family, my heart, my soul's companion—and I must find him because I know he is in danger. Orion thought you might be able to tell me where he is."

Shrouk smiles as her head wobbles. "Drink up, my beautiful children. Drink up!"

Malora feels Orion's anxious eyes on her. He has not touched his gaffey. She picks up the cup and saucer and holds them beneath her chin, inhaling deeply. She sips. The beverage is bitter, sweet, nutty, earthy, tart. It seems to tug and stroke her tongue every which way, from sweet to salty to sour to bitter and back to sweet again. As if illuminated by a flash of lightning, she sees Sky rearing, straining against ten ropes held by ten naked male centaurs with wild hair, inked skin, and pierced flesh. As quickly as it appeared, the vision vanishes.

"The wild centaurs have him," Malora says, setting her cup and saucer on the table. She is put out, because she wasted three days finding out what she had already suspected before she ever passed beneath the city gates.

"I was afraid you'd see that," Orion says, dropping his chin onto his chest.

"What she doesn't see," says Shrouk, "is that the wild centaurs worship the horse as a living god. Shrouk urges the human not to seek his liberation. It is for the best."

Malora's anger grows. "Why is that?" she asks.

"Shrouk foretells *death*."

Orion's head jerks up. "Whose death?"

"If she sets out to rescue the horse, Malora will *perish*. Shrouk sees the whole centaurean nation mourning her. Shrouk sees a faun, with tears streaming down, soaking his pointed beard. He is trailing the procession, piping a dirge."

"Shrouk!" Orion says, his voice cracking with outrage. "How *dare* you?"

"Shrouk has no choice," she says with a lift of her frail shoulders. "It is what she sees. Shrouk is very tired. . . ." She trails off, settling into the folds of her robe, and is soon snoring lustily.

Malora rises and blunders her way out of the tent. Outside, she blinks against the lemony midmorning sun.

Zephele points to Malora's hand. "Your Dream Wound!" she says in a stricken voice.

Malora looks at the bandage. It is saturated with blood. She peels it off and wipes the palm of her hand with it. "It's nothing," she says.

Orion follows her out of the tent. "It is *not* nothing," he says. He draws the others off to the side and speaks to them in hushed tones.

Meanwhile, Malora wonders what to do. She can go after her horse and tempt death. Or return to Mount Kheiron, where it is safe.

Neal backs away from the huddle. "And you all actually believe that steaming heap of elephant dung!"

"Thank you, Neal," says Malora, relief flooding her. Neal is right. Shrouk is just another market vendor. Sometimes her goods are worth something, and sometimes they are shoddy. The words *buyer beware* ring in her ears.

But Zephele believes Shrouk. Tears roll down her cheeks as she says, "But, Neal, everything Orion has ever learned from Shrouk has come to pass. Oh, what if it's *true*?" She stares at Malora in misery. "The thought of losing my dear, sweet friend is more than I can bear."

"And what is your thinking about this, Silvermane?" Neal asks Orion.

"I don't know *what* to think," Orion says as he gazes back at the tent. "All I know is that I am very much to blame. If I hadn't suggested coming here, if I had let Malora simply comb the bush in search of her horse, we would not now be faced with this distressing dilemma. I'd like to disbelieve Shrouk. Perhaps the ravages of age have clouded her inner sight, but I am afraid that we do this at our own—at Malora's—peril."

"I think," says Honus in a quiet voice, "that our best

option, our *only* option, is to take Malora back to Mount Kheiron, where we are in control of circumstances."

"For once, I'm with the Learned Master," Dock says.

"Dear Honus, that's *brilliant!*" Zephele says, throwing her arms around the faun's neck. "Isn't Honus brilliant, Malora?"

Malora says nothing at first. She remembers what Honus told her on the day they went to Cylas's shop to commission her disguise. If the hibes of Kahiro ever discovered her humanity, they would *kill her with kindness.* Is this what her own friends, however well-meaning, would do to her now? Take her back to Mount Kheiron and keep her in a satin bag, like some precious treasure? "What about Sky?" she asks.

Her friends stare at her sadly and one by one shake their heads.

"You heard what the Dromad said," Neal says. "He's a living god. Leave him to his new life, and let's get you back home. But not before I go in there and fill these two flasks, because I, for one, like the taste of gaffey and have never once in my life had a single vision from it, ill or good. And do you know why?" he asks, glaring at Orion and Zephele. "Because I'm a sensible, rational, thinking individual who doesn't subscribe to supernatural theories."

They hurry to check out of the inn and leave Kahiro in the early afternoon, stopping only after nightfall to pitch camp on the banks of the river. Leaning on her serpent stick, head blessedly free of the horns, Malora stands and stares across the Neelah. Above her, the fronds of date palm trees, laden with copper fruit, rattle in the evening breeze. Honus comes to stand beside her.

"That may very well have been the quietest meal of the entire trip," he says, puffing to get his pipe going.

"What lies on the opposite bank?" Malora asks. She is fairly sure she knows, but she needs Honus to confirm it.

"The last leg of the Dromadi caravan route," he says, gesturing with the point of his beard.

"And the Downs?" she asks.

"You can't see them now, but you will in the morning," he says.

She squeezes the Kavian snake staff in her right hand. Her Dream Wound throbs constantly now. It is like a drumbeat, inciting her to action. But she knows she must wait a little bit longer.

"Thank you," Honus says to her.

She turns to look at him. "For what?" she asks.

"For putting our concerns about you above your own about Sky," he says. "For so graciously letting us take you home with us."

She turns back to the river, her face burning with guilt. Honus has misinterpreted her guile for grace. Her real intention is to break away from her friends early tomorrow morning and swim across the river to the Downs. There she will take her chances and go alone in search of Sky. When they discover she is gone, her friends will be angry with her at first, but they will forgive her in time. She only hopes they won't follow her into the Downs. She predicts that they will not. If Zephele were not with them, they might. But Malora cannot imagine them braving the sinkholes with the Apex's daughter in tow.

After Zephele has fallen asleep, Malora writes a note by

lantern light. Everything is ready. She will sleep in her clothes. Beneath her cot she has stowed her belt—the pouch full of ripe dates and flatbread wrapped in oilcloth, two flasks full of boiled river water—and her serpent stick. When she finally drops off to sleep, her dreams thrum to the rhythm of the throbbing Dream Wound.

She opens her eyes and sits up, instantly alert. Across the aisle, Zephele sleeps in her usual state of disheveled abandonment. Malora rises, slips on her boots, and straps on her belt, slinging one flask across each shoulder in a crisscross fashion. She takes up the stick and lays the note on her cot, emerging into the tail end of the night. Up above, the stars are fading. Lightning snorts at the sight of her and nickers softly. Malora rushes over and silences her with a few whispered words, promising to return with Sky. Then she is off to the river.

On the riverbank, she stares across at the Downs, rising up like a range of small mountains made of sand. On the near bank, weaverbirds are up early, busily building nests in the papyrus.

Lifting a big rock, she heaves it into the middle of the river. The rock lands with a deep *gathunk,* making waves that lap at both banks. The weaverbirds rise up and fly away. When neither hippos nor crocodiles surface, Malora deems the river safe to swim across. For a brief moment, she considers removing her knife from her ankle-sheath and clasping it in her teeth as she swims, but she is afraid she might let water into her mouth or cut her lips. She is hampered enough by the flasks and the staff, the clothes on her back, and the boots on her feet. She wades into the shallows and walks until the water comes up to her chin, the flasks bobbing behind her, the stick held one-handed over her head. Suddenly, something wraps around her ankle and yanks her down into the water and the river grass and the mud.

In the murky water, she makes out a rope net surrounding her, its neck yanked closed by the line around her ankle. She struggles and thrashes but the harder she fights to escape, the more tightly the net binds her. Her Dream Wound bleeds through the bandage, turning the water red. Through the cloud of blood, she sees crocodiles angling toward her through the water.

It is only then, as her lungs throb with the strain, that the sickening understanding comes to her: *This is Shrouk's prophecy!* Scarcely has she set forth on her rescue mission than she is snared in some hibe hunter's hippo net. She reaches for her knife, but she is so tangled in the net that she cannot get to her own boot. If only she had held the knife in her teeth, she would already have cut herself loose. *If only* . . . Then she goes still, the blackness closing in upon her, until her body convulses as she begins to suck in the water that will flood her lungs and kill her. Her last thought is: Please let me be dead by the time the crocodiles get to me.

CHAPTER 14

Better than a Man

Someone is cradling her body as she has not been held since she was a small child. She gasps and stares up into eyes that are huge and burnished and as silver as his hair. He whispers down at her, words she has heard him say before: "Oh good. You're alive."

Lume! She tries to speak, but her throat burns. Water gurgles up and drowns her words. He pulls quickly away as she lurches, heaving up river water. Flipping her onto her belly, he holds her while she continues to convulse until her body is wrung out. Then he rights her and lowers her back onto the riverbank. He rises to his feet and looks down at her, his face flooded with relief.

As she returns his gaze, she thinks, Something is terribly wrong. But before she can put it into words, a tide of exhaustion bears her off.

* * *

The next time she opens her eyes, she is lying in a sling between the branches of two scrawny, leafless trees. The remnants of her tunic hang from her shoulders like tattered skin.

Dawn lights the sky. *Or is it dusk?* She climbs out of the sling and pads over to a stone wall. One glance down sends her reeling backward. She steals a second look, her heart thudding.

She is staring down at the tops of mountains so far below her that uncountable layers of clouds float in between. She wonders: How high up must I be? And how did I get here? The sun is setting over the faraway sea. It is dusk, she thinks. But on what day?

She backs away from the treacherous view and warily scans her surroundings. She is on a flat stone terrace—the sheared-off top of a mountain—surrounded by walls that are nowhere near high enough to make her feel secure. In the center of the terrace is something that looks like a large, overturned nest. It is woven from salvage, from sticks of silvery driftwood, scraps of fabric, and hanks of fishnet, all bound together with rope and vines and metallic wire. As she stares at the heavy, intricately carved double doors, they swing open and through them he comes, ducking under the lintel. Her heart lifts at the sight of him.

He is smaller than he was in her dreams—still half a head taller than she is but no giant. Shoulders and arms are roped with muscle, legs long and lithe, skin smooth all over, the color of wild honey. He is naked except for a faded black loincloth. Carrying a chipped blue plate and a cup, he hunches oddly like a peddler beneath a load. That is when she sees it, the *something wrong* she had detected earlier. She tries to tell herself that he is wearing a white-feathered cape, but she knows better.

Lume has a set of wings neatly folded behind him.

Lume is a hibe.

Lume is not a man.

Honus was right. It was foolish of her to entertain hopes that there could be a human mate for her. Disappointment weighs in her gut like a river rock she has swallowed whole.

"What are you?" she asks in a tight voice.

He sets the plate down on a tree stump, his mouth forming a bitter line. "I knew it," he says.

Unlike his voice in her dreams, which was soft, whispery, and melodic, his voice now is a flat drone, devoid of all emotion. "What did you know?" she asks.

"That you would be disappointed." He shoves the plate toward her. "Eat."

"I'm not hungry. Why should I be disappointed?" She bristles that he should read her mind so easily.

"I could see it in your eyes, when I held you on the riverbank. You thought I was a man, the hero who had rescued you from the crocodiles. But now you know different. I am, as you can see, a Wonder."

Her mouth gapes. Can he be that pompous?

"No," he says, with an irritated shake of his head. "That is what I am *called:* I am a Wonder. But I am the last of the Wonders. Just as you are the last of the People."

"What makes you so sure?" she asks. She hears herself ask this and marvels that she can still hold out hope that she is not the last. Better to set hope aside and be grateful for all she has: the centaurs and Honus and the boys and girls.

Lume stares off into the distance. She sees now that his silver eyes have flecks of gold in their depths. "I saw my entire colony—father, mother, sisters, brothers, cousins, neighbors— murdered by the Leatherwings, just as I saw the People of your Settlement perish. So you see, whether you like it or not, the two of us have something in common." He turns his sad-dened eyes toward her. "You and I, we are the last of our kind. And Leatherwings wiped out our kind. You really should eat. It will make you stronger. And perhaps less cross."

"I'm not cross," Malora says.

"Oh, but you are. I am, too, but that is the way I often am," he says, unperturbed. "I offer no apologies. But you . . . you have been blessed with a sunnier disposition, especially considering all that you have endured."

Malora hunkers down before the tree stump and starts to eat. She realizes that Lume is right: she *is* angry. Irrationally so. Is it Lume's fault that he is not a man?

"As it happens, I am *better* than a man," he says, crossing his arms across his chest as he watches her eat.

"Oh, really?" She crooks an eyebrow at him.

"Can a man hear from five hundred paces the crack of a lion's jaw when she yawns and stretches before setting out on her nightly prowl?"

Malora shake her head slowly, chewing.

"Can a man take wing and fly clear around the Narrow Earth, soaring over jungle and plain and ruined city, setting his feet down a mere once a day?" he asks.

Malora continues to shake her head as she washes down the salty fish without taking her eyes off of him.

"Can a man see across vast distances? My eyes are powerful."

"Really? What can you see with your eyes?" she asks.

"I have used them to watch you for years."

She nearly spits out a mouthful of fish. "You *watch* me?"

"I have watched you court death since you were a little girl," he says flatly. "I find it amusing. And sometimes alarming."

"I *don't* court death," she says.

"It seems to me that you do . . . in so many ways that I have lost count. Let me see now." He props one foot on the terrace wall and leans on his knee, counting on his fingers. "The stingrays in the sea, the scout on the pier, the lion in the camp, the elephants in the glen, the rhinos under the bluff, the asp by the fire, the army ants, the scorpions, even Sky (at least when you first rode him!), not to mention the Leatherwings. There, I have run out of fingers, but I know there's more—and so do you."

"Why?" she asks.

"Why what?"

"Why do you watch me?"

"That's a fair question," he says. He sits on the wall and stretches out his legs, staring at his toes. Like her, he has ten of them. Unlike hers, however, the bottoms of his feet are smooth and clean. There is nothing birdlike about him, she thinks. Only the wings destroy the illusion.

His eyes flick over to her, and his mouth forms that same

bitter line, as if silently recording the insult. "If you must know, I watch you because I feel a kinship with you."

"Or maybe," she says, looking around the terrace, "you're just lonely."

"Not I," he says, straightening up. He wraps his arms so tightly across his chest, he seems bound by them. "I prefer being alone. I like it up here, above the clouds. I spend days out roaming, beholden to no one, but I am never happier than when I return home. I am my own best companion."

"How sad," she says. Home for her is a house on the river-bank, surrounded by friends and horses, not an isolated mountaintop. Malora cannot imagine living in such stark solitude. Even in her loneliest days of wandering, she still had Sky to keep her company. The thought of Sky brings her back to what she had set out to do when she first waded into the river.

"Can you take me back to the Downs?" she asks.

He nods. "I have every intention of doing so, as soon as you are rested and recovered. After all, try as you sometimes might, it's not every day that you die."

"I didn't die," she scoffs. *Obviously.*"

"Oh, you died," he said. "The river claimed you before the crocodiles could. I felt your spirit leave your body as I laid you on the riverbank. I breathed the life back into you. I have powerful breath." He taps his chest. "I can dive under the sea, to the deepest depths in search of the fish that I favor. So I simply put my lips over yours and emptied the air out of me and into you . . . I actually enjoyed it." For the first time, he smiles, and it is as if the sun has broken through gray clouds.

His teeth are even and white and a dimple dents his left cheek. It is a smile as beguiling as Zephele's.

"Thank you," she says. She is also perversely grateful to know that she did die. She has satisfied Shrouk's prophecy, and now she can continue to go about her business without the shadow of death looming over her, at least any more than it ever has.

He nods, acknowledging her thanks. Malora is sorry to see his smile fade. "And now," he says, "you are in a hurry to go and free your horse from the wild centaurs."

"How did you know?" she asks, then answers her own question. "Of course: you watch." Then she remembers the white bird she kept Neal from killing on the road to Kahiro.

He holds up a hand. "The centaur's arrow would never have reached me," he says. "But thanks for your kind consideration."

"Do you know *everything* I'm thinking?" she asks.

He shakes his head quickly. "Not at all. Just the odd thought that bobs to the surface, like a fish's fins flashing on the surface of the water. Anyway, that's not important. What is important is that you save your horse. Your horse is a living miracle. He survived an attack of the Leatherwings. He continues to survive the wild centaurs. And after you have freed him—if you are so lucky as to do this, and I do believe you are one of the luckiest individuals alive, just as I am—the three of us can work together to defeat the Leatherwings, avenge our kin, and drive this scourge from the face of the Narrow Earth!"

His eyes ablaze, he stands over her. His wings have puffed out, making him seem bigger than a man—if not, as he deems, *better* than a man—and quite formidable.

"You don't understand," Malora says. "I have friends. I have people who love me in Mount Kheiron. I want to get my horse back, return to Mount Kheiron, and live a long, happy, peaceful life, free of Leatherwings."

He heaves a sigh. His wings droop. "I am disappointed but not surprised. Very well, then," he says, rallying. "It is your privilege to choose not to join me in my crusade. But know this, Malora Thora-Jayke: you may not always have the luxury of a choice in the matter. With each new massacre, the Leatherwings grow stronger. In the meantime, I caution you to beware of the centaurs of Ixion. They are not the docile, civilized centaurs of Mount Kheiron. They are a breed apart."

"So I am told," Malora says, smiling ruefully. "But at least they're not Leatherwings."

"I have watched them," he says, "and I have seen unimaginable savagery. Be on your guard."

"I will," she says. A shadow passes over and she looks up, expecting Leatherwings, but it is only a cloud.

"Don't worry," he says. "They can't fly this high. The Leatherwings are ground-huggers. Ground-huggers and blood-suckers. Now, what is it that you need for your journey?" He eyes her tattered tunic. "Besides something to wear."

"I'll need a stick."

"Yes, of course," he says. "Your friends have taken the Kavian snake staff with them back to Mount Kheiron. Who could blame them, when that is all of you that they have left?"

"What do you mean?" she asks.

"I removed the message you left for them on your cot," he says.

Her face heats up. "*What have you done?* I told them I was going into the Downs after Sky! Now they won't know *what* happened to me!"

"Stop blustering and listen to me. I hovered over their camp long enough to see them find your snake stick and your bloody clothes lying all about and conclude that the crocodiles got you."

"The crocodiles!" Malora blurts.

"Which they most certainly would have," Lume says, "if I hadn't taken your knife and sliced the net."

"You have my knife?"

"I left it on the riverbank. Your friends found that, too. And a single bloody boot. The blood from your hand was *everywhere.*"

Malora looks down at her hand. It is white around the Dream Wound, temporarily bled out. It depresses her to think that her friends are mourning her right now.

"It's better this way," he says softly. "They won't be following you into the Downs, which they certainly would have had they read your note. It is your choice to court death, but to make *them* do so . . . You wouldn't really want that, would you?"

"No," she whispers.

"Come," he says, striding toward the double doors. "Let's find you a proper stick."

Malora follows him into his home, which seems even bigger from inside. She stops on the threshold. Her first thought is that Honus would love this place. Above her, the woven roof soars, hung with baskets of herbs and berries and strips of dried fish. The stone slab floors are covered in animal skins:

zebra, giraffe, impala, lion, leopard, and many more she doesn't recognize. Objects are displayed on driftwood-plank shelves: crockery shards and old bottles and urns, tiny birds' and wasps' nests, crystals, seashells, sea stars and urchins, nubs and other coins, delicate animal skulls, teeth and horns, and ancient, rusty pieces.

"Relics of the Scienticians," Lume says.

Malora has seen similar objects for sale in the marketplace of Kahiro. Taken singly, none of the items on display are what Malora would call valuable or even beautiful. But the cumulative effect is beautiful and fascinating.

While he rummages about, she wanders over to a curtain made from braided rags and peers through to see a low, oval-shaped nest larger than a centaur's bed, feathered with down, dried grasses, and wildflowers. It looks comfortable—almost luxurious—and it smells as fresh as a meadow. She drops the curtain and turns to find him contemplating a large urn that is chock-full of sticks, hand-carved walking sticks, tree limbs worn smooth by water or wind, and a stout club with an ugly round head.

"Come choose one," he says, crooking a finger.

She joins him, quickly settling on a cane with the head of a fierce serpent and eyes of emerald.

He frowns. "That one's my favorite," he says.

"Then I'll pick another," she says quickly.

"No," he says reluctantly. "I asked you to choose one and you did. I could have left that one out of the selection, but I didn't. I dug it up from a ruined palace at the far side of the Narrow Earth. It is special. See?" He unscrews the dragon's head and unsheathes a small sword.

"Are you sure you want to part with it?" she asks. His look, as he shoves the sword back into the cane, tells her she had better accept the offer.

"Thank you," she says.

"Use it well. You'll find something that fits you in there." He sweeps a hand toward a large willow basket overflowing with salvaged articles of clothing. Setting down the sword cane, she begins to sift through the items, drawn to something that looks as if it might fit her. She lifts it out and examines it. It is a shirt made from impala skin, stitched together with sinew.

"That looks like my work," she says. There is a pouch sewn into the side of it, where she once kept seeds and berries. "It *is* my work! You *stole* this from me!"

He stares at her, expressionless.

"I thought a lion took it," she says.

"A lion *might* have taken it," he says carefully. He busies himself wrapping berries in a square of cloth. "And you with it. But I harried her off while you slept. You had just broken your arm. You were hot with sickness. Call it my reward for saving you."

She shakes her head. "How many other times have you meddled in my life?"

He wraps salted fish in another square of cloth. "Not very many. I'm sorry," he says, "the next time a lion wants to rip you apart, I promise not to meddle." He hands her the two packets of food, his expression bland.

She takes them, her anger melting. How can she remain angry with someone who has saved her life, not just once, but how many times she doesn't even want to know? Tucking the packets into the pouches of her impala shirt, she follows him back out onto the terrace. She watches as he stands at a barrel cistern and fills a goatskin bladder with water.

He fits the woven sling carefully over her head. "There. You are ready now," he says, his voice heavy with reluctance.

"How will you fly with me?" she asks nervously.

He shrugs. "I hold you in my arms. I drop down off the wall. I pick up a brisk current of air. If I'm lucky, I'll ride it clear to the mouth of the river. If not, I'll switch to another headed in the right direction."

But Malora is stuck on the *holding her in his arms* part. "Don't you need your arms to fly?" she asks.

The dimple reappears. "I find that's where the wings come in handy."

She shakes her head, feeling foolish. "Of course. Let's fly, then," she says, nearly overcome with dread as her eyes dart over the side of the wall into nothingness. "Try not to drop me," she mutters.

He gestures to the double doors behind them. "I flew across two and a half oceans carrying those. Somehow I think I'll manage with you."

With very little ceremony, he steps behind her and lifts her up, his arms encircling her just above the waist. When he hops up onto the wall, she lets out a feeble cry as she looks down.

"You will be easier to transport if you relax," Lume says, jouncing her up and down as if to shake the tension out, which only makes her more nervous. "Perhaps a blindfold?"

"Please, no. I'll just close my eyes," she says, before realizing that he has made another joke. His humor is dryer than her mouth after eating the salted fish.

She feels him bracing to leap.

"Wait!" she says.

He relaxes. "What now?"

"Where are you taking me?" she asks.

"To the banks of the River Neelah, where I found you," he says.

"If it's so easy for you to fly with me, why can't you take me directly to the wild centaurs?" she says. "It would save time."

His arms tighten around her. "Oh, I will take you directly to the wild centaurs," he says. "I will even help you rescue your stallion. But only if you promise to help me fight the Leatherwings afterward."

"No," she says.

"I thought you'd say that. Then to the shores of the River Neelah we go. I'll take you to the western bank. I wouldn't want you to get caught in any more hippo nets," he says.

"Very well," she says stiffly. "I'll fall down a sinkhole instead, thank you very much."

Ignoring this last, he says, "We go."

Before she can draw another breath, he has leapt from the wall into the air. Her stomach rises as quickly as she falls. She is just about to open her mouth and scream when she feels the tug of his wings as they unfurl and lift them upward. He catches a current of air that carries them smoothly forward like an invisible river. She can hear the rushing of the wind through his wings. It sounds like the surging of sea tides.

"You can open your eyes now," he says. She feels his voice more than hears it, rumbling in his chest behind her neck.

"I never closed them," she calls out to him.

"Brave girl," he rumbles back.

She can't be sure whether he is mocking her. She doesn't *feel* very brave. She feels helpless and in dire peril. Unable to see either above or below, she finds herself in an alien world, cold and clammy, filled with smoky clouds. She is grateful for the warmth of his body seeping into hers.

Much later, she awakes to thinning clouds and, tucked in among the valleys here and there, a smattering of settlements and ruins. It is not long before they are hurtling over the molten metal platter of the sea. On and on they race, as if they are being pulled toward the lands to the west. Then she spies the tiny city of Kahiro, huddled by the sea, the torches of the Backbone of Heaven twinkling, the soaring port arch looking so fragile, the Arms of Kahiro like twigs floating on the water. Lume follows the frothy coastline westward, over dunes and scrubland. She catches her breath as he shifts direction and starts to barrel toward the earth. It feels more like a controlled fall than flight. The river, slithering along like a silver snake, grows wider, filling her sights. With a lurch of her heart, she smells the same mud and reeds and water that nearly claimed her life.

Lume alights on the riverbank, taking a few running, skidding steps before he stops. His arms unlocking, he drops her. She lands, teetering on the balls of her feet before she finds her balance.

It is dawn, exactly one day after she "died." She is where she would have come ashore had she completed her crossing.

On the far side of the river, nothing remains of the camp. As Lume reported, her friends have pulled up stakes and left, taking her horses and her few possessions with them back to Mount Kheiron.

"I will leave you to it," Lume says.

He reaches over and fusses with her hair. "Flying has made a haystack of your hair." He stands back and gives her a mildly approving look. Then he plucks a long feather from his wing. He winces slightly and the wing twitches. Malora wonders if it hurts but isn't about to ask him.

He holds out the feather to her. She takes it, realizing with a surprising pang that she doesn't want him to leave yet. There is something sturdy and earthbound about him, in spite of the wings. He may not be her dream man, but he is beautiful in his way. And something else: he smells *wonderful.* Better than horses. Better than centaurs. Better than the sweetest flowers or essences from Orion's alchemical laboratory. She closes her eyes and holds the feather to her nose. She opens her eyes to discover that he is already running away from her, toward the river, as if he were going to dive into it. Instead, his wings extend and he floats above it. With one last unsmiling look at her, he turns to coast downriver until he seems to be nothing more than a white feather, drifting away from her.

She rakes her hair over one shoulder, plaiting the feather into the braid. Picking up the dragon cane, she walks along the dunes in a westerly direction. It is midmorning by the time she sees horse or centaur tracks forming a beaten path between two dunes. Turning into the path, she sets out to follow it.

Dunes rise up on either side of her, sparkling like gold

dust on her right, where the sun's rays catch it. She is just beginning to think that this won't be so difficult when she stumbles and sinks in sand up to her knees. More sand comes cascading down from the dune above, burying her up to the thighs. She digs the sword into the sand behind her. It takes all her strength to pull herself free of the dune. Then she inches backward on her hind end until she feels solid ground beneath her. *Now what?*

It stands to reason, she thinks, that the peaks of the dunes are safe. Otherwise the weight of the sand would form sinkholes within them. The sinkholes, like the one she just blundered into, must lie in the valleys between the dunes. If she walks on the dunes, leaping from one to the next, bypassing the valleys, she will avoid the sinkholes. *But will that be the right direction?* She could meander through the dunes indefinitely until her supply of water ran out and the sun bleached her bones. Perhaps, from the top of a dune, she might see the thread of the path she has lost or something to give her some indication of the direction she should take.

Digging the cane into the nearest dune, she starts to climb. If the cane holds her weight without sinking, it is safe for her feet to follow. She continues in this fashion, first the cane, then the foot, then the cane . . . until she reaches the summit. Sinking down onto her back, she catches her breath.

The sun beats down. Her legs ache. The sweat pours off her. At this rate, she will be a shriveled bag of skin and bones within a day. She fingers the malachite stone on the leather string around her neck. *Will I end up like my mother?* She uncorks the flask and squirts enough water into her mouth to wet her tongue and throat. Lifting her head she looks around.

All she can see are dunes, rolling away in all directions like dry waves. She knows that the sea lies directly ahead to the north and that the river is at her back to the south, but that is all she knows. Ixion could be anywhere in between.

She lifts her nose and sniffs. At first, all she picks up is her own sweat and a faint note of rainstorm coming off of Lume's feather. She concentrates on working her way past these to the very specific something beyond. The wind gusts. Sand sifts all around her. Her nostrils twitch and now she has it, a faint but complex ball of scent rolling toward her over the dunes from the northwest. It is the scent of the sea, of horses, and of woodsmoke. She climbs to her feet and angles herself toward the source of the scent, drawing a mental line across the tops of the dunes. This is her path.

She starts down the other side of the dune. She proceeds up one dune and down the next, the scent growing stronger with every dune she puts behind her. As soon as the sun sets, the air turns chilly. She stops at the top of a dune, digging herself a nest in the warm sand. After eating some of the fish and berries and drinking some of the water, she falls into a deep and surprisingly restful sleep.

She wakes up the next morning and digs herself out of the sand, her muscles sore. She freezes midstretch when she sees it to the north, glinting like a wedge of beaten silver between two dunes: the sea. From somewhere between her and the sea, woodsmoke curls into the sky. She heads toward the smoke.

By midday, the dunes have begun to harden to a combination of clay and sand, sprouting dune grass that cuts into the soles of her bare feet. Why didn't I ask Lume for some shoes? she thinks. He must have a barrel of them stashed away.

Still wary of sinkholes, she walks, cane-first, like an old woman, with her eyes on the ground. She is concentrating so hard on where she sets her feet that she fails to hear the whistling sound overhead. By the time she hears it, the noose is already over her head and down around her shoulders, tightening, pinning her arms to her sides. She pulls back with her full weight, only to be yanked off her feet, flipped onto her back, and dragged up the next bluff, stones and bushes and needle-sharp grass cutting and bruising and gouging her flesh. When she finally comes to rest on her back, covered with sand and dust, she starts to wriggle free of the rope but a hoof comes down on her chest and stops her.

She stares up into the beard-wreathed face of a wild centaur. There is not a scrap of clothing on his body, which is as sunburned as his face, scarred and painted as intricately as any temple in Mount Kheiron, his nipples pierced with small ivory bars with chains hanging down from them. Elaborate patterns are shaven into his horsehide and dyed in bright colors. His hair is gathered into a high tail the same color and texture as his horsetail and the effect of these twin tails is as dramatic and wildly beautiful as the rest of him. In spite of all these exotic trappings, Malora recognizes her captor.

"Mather Silvermane!"

CHAPTER 15

Balaal

"Mather Silvermane is no longer my name," the centaur says. "My herd name . . . is Balaal."

"Balaal," Malora says, "can you please get your hoof off my chest?"

"Sorry," he says, lifting his hoof. "I was so excited to have actually *caught* something. I never dreamed it would be you. I'm supposed to be out here roping wild horses."

"Horses? I haven't seen any horses," she says.

"That would be just my luck," he says. "To be sent out when there are no horses to be had. You can be sure the herd will find a way to blame me for that."

"It's hard to imagine you roping horses," Malora tells him.

Mather gathers up the rope into a tangled ball. "I'm not very good at it. And as you know, I don't share the Kheironite fondness for horses."

"I'd forgotten that," Malora says. Although he once confided in her his fear of horses, he had hidden it well from

192

everyone else. She sees he has made a mess of the rope, so she takes it from him and coils it properly.

"These horses are even more frightened than I am," Mather says, "which makes them quite treacherous."

"So," says Malora, handing him back the neat circle of rope. "You're a wild centaur now."

"As wild as I am able to manage," Mather says pitifully. "I tell you, there is not a single Edict we do not trample to dust on a daily basis. But if it weren't for the wild centaurs, I'd be a pile of bones in the bush. This is the home of all the centaurs who have ever been turned out from Mount Kheiron, going back generations. It is also home to centaurs for whom life in Mount Kheiron may not have been the ideal, those who were thought to have been ravaged by hippos or lions or other beasts of the bush."

Malora seizes upon these last words. "Does this include Athen Silvermane?" she asks.

Mather rolls his eyes. "Oh, Athen is not only here, he is the leader, the Alpha Stallion. He may have been a disappointment to the Apex, slow to learn, quick of temper, and fickle, but here he is loved and respected and wields immense authority."

"Herself will be so happy to learn that he is alive," Malora says. She imagines returning to Mount Kheiron with the news, banishing the look of sadness from the eyes of the Lady Hylonome.

"Oh, you mustn't tell her, Malora!" Mather pleads. "Athen would spit me over a bonfire. While I dream every night of returning to the Land of Beauty and Enlightenment, Athen quite likes his life here. As Alpha Stallion, he is as powerful as the Apex. His rule is based not on the Edicts, but on the so-called Principles of Freedom of the Natural Centaur. In Mount Kheiron, it was our human halves that we treasured, but here the horse half is held in high esteem."

"Well, there's nothing wrong with that," Malora says.

"Yes, but *your* horses are *tame*, Malora," Mather says. "One drunken feast night, Athen told me that the first time he felt truly alive was when he came to live with the herd. By the way, his herd name is Archon. And, Malora, I must tell you, Sky is in Ixion."

"I know," Malora says. "That's why I'm here."

His face falls. Then he looks suspicious. "How could you possibly know that?"

Electing not to tell Mather about Shrouk, she says, "A Dromadi hostler told me that the wild centaurs are horse rustlers and that they hold up the caravans for the best livestock."

Mather stutters. "B-b-but no one knows it is us. Athen's motto is strike hard, strike fast, and make for the Downs. *Oh, yes, and leave no witnesses to tell the tale.*"

"Apparently," Malora says, "there was a survivor of a recent raid who has told the tale."

Mather pounds his forehead with his fist. "Kheiron's hocks! That fellow *promised* me!"

"What fellow?" Malora asks.

"The Dromad whose life I spared," Mather says through his teeth. "It was my first raid. Athen ordered me to slay one of the Dromadi merchants. All the others in the caravan had already been slaughtered. I raised my sword to do the job, but I couldn't, Malora! I couldn't commit murder. It's against everything I was taught to believe. All was chaos at the scene.

So I wiped some blood from another victim on my sword and put it on the Dromad, pretending to do the deed. We made a deal, in exchange for sparing his life he was to tell no one the identity of his attackers."

Poor naive Mather, Malora thinks. "Well, the Dromad might not have held up his end of the deal, but you, Mather, were right to spare him."

Droplets of sweat have begun to run down Mather's tattooed face. He stares straight ahead of him at something terrifying. "If Archon ever finds out I was the one . . ."

Malora gently lays a hand on his shoulder, wary of startling him. "How could he possibly find out?" she asks.

He turns his eyes toward her, the tension in his features easing. "You're right, of course."

Malora takes one of the scraps of cloth Lume gave her and offers it to him. He swabs his face. When he is sufficiently calm again, Malora says, "I need you to take me to see Sky now, please."

A fresh tide of panic overtakes him. "I can't! And please don't ask me."

"Why can't you?" she asks.

"Because Sky belongs to us now. His herd name is Belerephon."

Sky, Belerephon; Mather, Balaal;. Athen, Archon. Malora says, "Does *everyone* here have two names?"

"*Most* everyone," he says. "Except the broncs, those who are born and raised here. They get to keep the names they are born with. The broncs—broncos and broncas both—can also get away with subjecting themselves to less bodily mutilation, lucky them."

This was all very interesting, but it wasn't getting her closer to Sky. "Please take me to Sky," she begs. "Now that your secret is out, it's just a matter of time before the wild centaur way of life is undone." Malora isn't at all sure that this is true, but she will say anything to get his cooperation.

Mather nods rapidly to himself. "Of course. You are Malora Ironbound, and I am no match for your iron will. But Belerephon is not easily seen. Your horse has been deemed by Archon to be a living god."

"I know that, too," she says with an impatient wave of her hand.

Mather sputters, "But that is a secret known only to the herd! How can you possibly know this? Oh, never mind, I don't want to know. At least the guilt for *that* does not weigh on my shoulders. I don't suppose there is any harm in my taking you to see Sky. But only on one condition," he says. "If you chance to fall into their hands, I will deny knowing you. And you must deny any knowledge of me. I mean it, Malora. My life will not be worth a horse's turd if you implicate me."

"Fair enough," she says. "And in exchange for your help, I promise that when I return to Mount Kheiron I will plead with the Apex to let you return."

His eyes widen. "You would do that?"

Malora shrugs. "I can try. The Apex favors me."

Mather wags his head. "But look at me!" he says. "Even if he did take me back, how can I go, looking like this? My own mother would take one look at me and renounce me."

"I'm sure she would be overjoyed to see you, no matter how you look. And, if it means anything to you, I think you look very handsome." She adds, "Zephele would declare your appearance oh so bold and daring. I can hear her now."

"Really?" he asks uncertainly. "You don't find my body glyphs off-putting?"

She wants him calm and collected when he takes her to see Sky, and so she takes a few moments, circling him slowly to admire the long, lithe body of the tigress that is tattooed down his right arm, with her head on the back of his hand and her claws embracing his forearm, and the body of a leopardess than runs down his left arm. The cats' tails intertwine in a graceful knot across his back and shoulders. "Is this decoration permanent?" she asks.

"They use the spines from a small sea creature to puncture the skin and inject the dyes. My skin will carry these markings for life. It took several sessions to complete. I must have imbibed half a cask of ferna each session."

"Ferna?" Malora asks.

"The herd's preferred festival beverage. A very strong yam brandy brewed by the Pantherians. Under the circumstances," he says, rubbing his arms, "it seemed necessary and appropriate."

"Well," she says, "your body now reminds me of the most impressive-looking edifices in Mount Kheiron . . . thoroughly decorated."

"Even though you may be saying this to make me feel better, I appreciate your kind words," he says. "If I knew that Canda Blackmane would feel the same, I'd have reason to hope that I have a future beyond this brutal place."

A brawl with a Flatlander over Canda Blackmane was the

cause of Mather's being turned out. "I think Canda Blackmane would like the new you." Malora has no idea whether this is true, but Mather looks so forlorn that she would tell him anything to cheer him up. "Can you *please* take me to see my horse now?"

He gazes up at the sky. "Soon they will retire to their stables for their afternoon rest," he says. Seeing the look of impatience on her face, he says, "Believe me, you don't want to risk running into one of them."

Malora sighs. "I believe you. So you live in *stables*?" she asks with a wry smile, thinking the wild centaurs have carried the horse culture perhaps a tad too far.

He nods. "Our domiciles are called stables. They are as crude as they sound. I sleep on a bed of straw—yes, *straw*—dreaming of the down-filled mattresses of Mount Kheiron!" He sighs wistfully. "The herd will be wondering where I am. I will say that I got my rope tangled in the horns of a wild pig, and they will believe me."

"Tell me, do you race the horses you rustle?" Malora asks.

"Not exactly," he says.

"What do you do with them?"

Mather turns away. "It is better that you not know what we do with the horses," he says sullenly.

Over the sudden roaring in her ears, Malora hears herself say "You eat them, don't you?"

"Ugh, no! What a revolting thing to say! We might be wild, but we're not *depraved*!"

The roaring in Malora's ears abruptly stops. She exhales. Well then, she thinks, what could be so bad?

Mather says, "We eat crabs, snakes, rats, rabbits, and deer.

And great quantities of fish. The fish is the worst. I prefer rat to fish. That's what I've come to. I'm a rat-eater." He shudders.

Malora tugs at his beard to make him meet her gaze. "Mather, please tell me. What happens to the horses?"

Mather sighs. "You will find out soon enough, so I might as well tell you. They are sacrificed to the Beast from Below."

Malora closes her eyes, then opens them again, not altogether certain that she heard him correctly. "The *what*?"

He nods, matter of fact. "A hideous monster lives beneath the sands of Ixion. In order to keep it at bay, the herd sacrifices a horse to it every seven days. Rumors have circulated that there is more than one beast, but one is quite sufficient for me to contemplate."

"What kind of beast is this that is so fond of horseflesh?" she asks. "A lion?"

"Oh, would that it were! We could send *you* after it, then—couldn't we?—and be done with it."

"Then what is it?"

"I personally have never laid eyes on it, thank you, Kheiron. It comes up through the sands of the Paddock, grabs its sacrifice, and disappears back the way it came. In the old days, they tell me, before I came here, it was so much worse. Every full moon, the herd would draw stones. The one who drew the white stone from among the black offered him- or herself up to the Beast from Below. Then Archon came to Ixion and had a brilliant idea that will make him a legend in time, which was to sacrifice *horses* instead of centaurs. The meat would taste more or less the same, he reasoned, the Beast would be none the wiser, and the centaurs would not only no longer be in danger of sacrifice, they had the satisfaction of outwitting the Beast. There was only one problem: horses weren't as filling as centaurs. Now the Beast comes to feed four times in every moon cycle instead of once. Every seven days a horse must be served up, so we keep a robust supply of them on hand, if you see what I mean. Or else . . ." He trails off with a shrug.

Something about this is worse than her worst imaginings. "And so Athen has turned you into a tribe of horse rustlers and horse murderers."

Mather says, "That he has. I'm glad I joined the herd after he did. With my luck, I would have drawn the white stone the first time."

"How does Sky figure in all this?" Malora asks. Her jaw aches with unexpressed rage.

"Oh, well now. Sky . . . is a legend of a different order," Mather says. "It took ten brawny centaurs to bring him in, and he killed two of them and wounded several others. But Archon figured that such a magnificent animal might keep the Beast satisfied for longer than a mere seven days. Either that or it would choke on him. So they dragged Sky to the Paddock, pegged him, and offered him up to the Beast."

Malora's fists are clenched. Only when she hears Mather say "The Beast apparently did not care for the taste of Sky" do her hands fall open.

"You've hurt yourself," Mather says, pointing to her hand. "You're bleeding. Did I do that to you?" he asks, sounding almost hopeful.

"No," she says. Her fingernails have reopened the Dream

Wound. Wiping her hand on the side of her tunic, she says, "Go on, please."

"When we went to the Paddock the next day, Sky was still there. So we simply left him there, for the next ten nights, where he remained untouched by the Beast. But on the eleventh night, the Beast came up from below and went among us. While the rest of us slept, he made off with five of the youngest centaur colts from the nursery stable."

"The Beast ate five centaur babies?" Malora asks.

Mather nods. "The mothers were out of their minds with grief. So we removed Sky from the Paddock and put in two ponies. The Beast took the ponies—and life as we know it resumed its brutal course."

"And because the Beast, for some reason, rejected Sky, you now consider him a god," Malora says. This makes a crazy sort of sense to her. Sky, having withstood the attacks of the Leatherwings, has now survived the Beast from Below. Lume was right: Sky is a miracle horse.

"That's really all I can tell you," Mather says. "And now, before I take you to Sky, do please catch me up on the news from Mount Kheiron."

Malora briefly tells Mather how the Apex made her his wrangler and how she won the Golden Horse. Even though she knows it will cause him pain, she tells Mather about the upcoming Harvest Jubilation, the first ever to which Flatlanders will be invited. It was at the most recent Midsummer Jubilation that Mather brawled with a Flatlander, leading to Gastin being expelled from Mount Kheiron.

"Is Gastin also here in Ixion?" Malora asks.

"Rorg, as he is now called, is here," Mather says, his voice heavy with resentment. "They brought him in a few days after they found me, and don't think he doesn't enjoy the fact that here we are equals."

"At home you would be equals now, too," Malora says.

"Perhaps, what with all this change in Mount Kheiron, there will be a general amnesty?" Mather says, brightening. "Perhaps those who have been turned out will be given the opportunity to return—not that many of the others will take it. They all seem very happy with what they call freedom— the life of the Natural Centaur. I myself find it rather rough going. And the Beast is more terrifying, I tell you, than a whole pride of ravening lions."

"Why doesn't the herd move away from this place and let the Beast from Below find his own food?" Malora asks.

"Ixion is the ancestral home of the centaurs," Mather says. "Much more so, the wild centaurs claim, than Mount Kheiron is to us." Mather stops and cups a hand to his ear.

All Malora hears is the sound of the wind sifting through the sand, and the waves breaking on the shore beyond the dunes.

"It's safe now," Mather says. "Stay close to me and don't wander off the path."

The ground is as hard as baked clay. They pass a pen made from upright driftwood slats. From behind the slats there arises the stench of horses crowded into close, unclean quarters. Malora hears them stir and grunt and nicker hopefully. She wants to stop and whisper words of consolation to them. But she resists. It is Sky that she has come for.

They pass three more pens, all filled with horses. "It looks

like you have a good supply of sacrifices on hand," she comments bitterly.

The narrow pathway soon lets out into a bleak valley surrounded by sandy bluffs. There is a large paddock with high rails. This is the place she dreamed about. It is the place she has struggled to find for such a long time that she can scarcely believe she is finally standing here.

"This is the Valley of the Beast," Mather says.

The words from her dream, "Feed her to the Beast!" enter her mind.

Over to one side, away from the paddock and at the foot of one of the bluffs, is a smaller round pen with high walls tightly woven from weatherworn sticks. This is Sky's prison. "You keep Sky in the Valley of the Beast?" Malora asks.

"He's almost as terrifying to us as the Beast," Mather says.

Malora walks around the pen in search of a way in. There is none. "Where is the door?" she asks.

Mather turns his palms upward. "There is none."

"You walled up *my horse?"*

He waves his hands about. "Keep your voice down!" he whispers, his eyes wide and frantic. "We blocked off the door because he got loose from the pegs and opened the latch with his teeth. By the time we caught him he had broken into two of the pens. It took us a week to round up all the horses. That stallion is very clever with his teeth. This is the only way we could contain him."

Malora simmers. So this is how they treat a god? "How do you feed him? How do you clean the pen?" she asks.

Mather has the grace to be ashamed. "We lower his water and feed down to him. We clean his pen not very successfully by standing on scaffolds with rakes with very long handles. But he bites the rakes in half. In fairness to us, your horse doesn't make it easy to care for him. One would have thought he *liked* living in his own dung."

She leans her cane against the pen and, fitting her toes into the cracks, scales the wall. She knows she is behaving precisely as she did in her dream, but she is powerless to do anything else. She peers over and sees that the top of the pen is covered with netting.

The big horse stands with his back to her, facing into the fencing in the one space that is not covered with manure. In this small clearing, there are two buckets of dirty water attached to ropes and a half-eaten pile of dried grass. Except for his tail switching at the flies, he is immobile and listless, his coat so thickly coated with manure she can barely make out the distinctive pattern of the Leatherwing scars on his back. His right rear leg is pegged to a stake.

She asks Mather, "Why the netting? These walls are high enough to hold him."

"The netting keeps him from flying away. You never told us that your horse could fly," Mather says.

Malora chuckles. Sky can jump higher than any horse she has ever ridden. But she doubts even he could clear walls this high, particularly not from a standstill.

"Oh, Sky!" she sighs. "Look at you!"

Sky swings his head around, his pale eyes seeking her out.

"Up here!" she says, making a kissing noise.

Looking up, Sky wheels around and turns to face her.

"Malora!" Mather's frantic whisper reaches her ears. "Get down! Get down *now*! They are coming! You must hide."

CHAPTER 16

Gods and Beasts

"Malora, I'm leaving you!" Mather whispers. "Forgive me!"

But she only half-hears him as she leans over the top of the pen and works a hand through the netting toward Sky's nose. She feels the warmth of his breath on her skin. Climbing up higher, she reaches down to him, bracing herself with one hand on the top of the fence. She feels a sudden sharp pain in her supporting palm where the Dream Wound has, at long last, been made real.

"I'll get you out of there," she says as she hears the shuffling of approaching hooves, a murmuring of voices. She starts to swing back down when the murmuring explodes into shouting.

Strong hands pluck her off the fence and bear her away. She stops struggling when she sees there are at least a dozen of them. They set her down on a mound of dried horse dung. A circle of curious, sunburnt faces stare down at her.

Like Mather, these centaurs are wild-haired, naked,

tattooed, and pierced, without any of the elegant draping of the Mount Kheiron centaurs. As Lume warned her, they are a breed apart.

"Oh, but she's pretty!" one of them says.

Malora finds the face belonging to the voice: a female, with a high golden ponytail and big brown eyes. Except for the delicate design of a dragonfly that adorns her shoulder, her body is without decoration. *A bronca,* Malora thinks.

"What hibe *is* she?" asks a male centaur with a sword strapped around his waist. The sword is big, made for hacking and whacking. He also holds a stout spear that is taller than she is. The Peacekeepers would not stand a chance against the wild centaurs.

"I've never seen the like, I'll tell you that!" another centaur says.

The centaurs jostle each other to get a closer look at her. Malora sees bejeweled daggers jutting from the belts of the females and enough spears to form a picket fence around her.

A new face enters the circle. Except for those who hold her, the centaurs back away to make room for him. "By my worthy horse half, it is one of the People!" he declares.

It is the Apex's resonant voice and lumbering body but with Orion's handsome face, his bright blue eyes offset by a tattooed pattern of red and orange fish scales. Just as she opted for silence in her first encounter with centaurs, so does she now.

"One of the People?" says a female with hair so fair it is nearly white. "Who knew how much like us they looked! She will fetch us a goodly sum from the scouts."

"Calm your hooves, Tam," Athen says. "We found her in

the Valley of the Beast. She is meant for the Beast. I say: *feed her to the Beast!*"

The other centaurs roar in agreement, pounding the ground with the butts of their spears. Malora hangs limp as they lift her up and carry her into the paddock. With surprising swiftness, they stake her to the ground, as once the Twani had tied her to a tree, only much more tightly. She struggles no more now than she did then. Then it was because she didn't want to hurt the Twani. Now it is because she knows she cannot hope to hold her own against so many heavily armed wild centaurs.

As quickly as they came, they go, leaving her alone with a pony tethered to a fence post across the paddock from her. The shaggy, speckled pony grazes.

Poor thing, Malora thinks.

Over the top of the bluffs from the direction of the centaurs' village, music starts up, haunting and plaintive. As if stirred up by the music, the ground begins to tremble. The pony looks up from the grass briefly and then returns to grazing with renewed intention, as if he wants to grab up all he can in the time left to him.

Suddenly the earth erupts in a giant flume of sand. The pony screams. Sand showers down, stinging the skin on Malora's arms and legs, filling her eyes and nose and mouth. When the eruption subsides, she shakes the sand from her face, blows it out of her eyes, and spits it from her mouth. She looks over and sees that the pony is gone. A torn rope hangs swinging from the fence post.

It is just a matter of time, she thinks, before the Beast returns for her. She knows that if she cries out for Sky he will do nothing. He will sense trouble and remain where he is. He has an instinct for saving himself that she does not begrudge him. But what if she were to invite Sky to come out and play? Wouldn't he do just about anything to be with her, including bash his way out of the pen with his hooves?

Putting as much welcoming warmth into her voice as her parched throat will permit, she calls out to him eagerly: "Hey, Sky! It's me again! Come on out of that pile of dung and play with me. I'm over here, boy. Just on the other side of that wall of sticks. Come on, big boy, you can do it. I know you can. They haven't built the pen yet that can hold you."

She has to raise her voice, for the music is louder now, more raucous and cheerful, as if the centaurs, sensing that the sacrifice has been taken, are celebrating the seven more days of safety it has bought them. Above the music, she hears Sky snorting and shuffling, followed by a loud, steady pounding: the sound of Sky's hooves smashing through the walls of the pen.

"That's my boy!" she urges him on.

She hears a loud splintering crack, and moments later, a dark shape looms overhead. Sky lands beside her in a cloud of dust.

"Good boy, Sky!" she says.

As the dust settles, Sky paws the ground as if to say: What are you doing lying there on the ground? I'm here, aren't I? Get up and greet me properly!

"I need some help here," Malora tells him.

Sky stomps and tosses his mane.

"You should be able to handle these knots, no?" She gestures with her chin to her wrist.

Sky paws the ground.

"What's the matter? Can't you handle it?"

He grunts and mutters, then walks over and noses her hand. His hide is lathered, and Malora is overcome by the odor of piss and dung and sweat, sweeter at this moment than all of Zephele's wild jasmine. Up close he looks smaller than she remembers, and the bones of his shoulders and his hips seem oddly angular. He doesn't look malnourished so much as *different*.

Sky clicks his teeth.

"Untie this knot, please," she says. "The Beast may come back any time."

His lips, warm and velvety, twitch against her wrist, then his teeth work at the knot until the rope falls away. Malora shakes her numb hand back into usefulness.

Untying the other three knots herself, she rises and stomps the blood back into her feet. Sky nuzzles her.

"Oh, Sky!" Tears spring to her eyes. She throws her arms around his neck and squeezes him so tightly that he lets out a snort of protest.

"I can't help it," she says, standing back and wiping the tears away. "I was afraid I'd never see you again."

He tosses his head toward the place where the pony was.

"I know," she says. "We have to get out of here."

She leads him quickly out of the paddock, stopping to dig through the splintered sticks and find the dragon cane. There is only one way out of the Valley of the Beast: the path between the bluffs that Mather showed her. Sky noses her neck and shoves her into the side of the bluff. Laughing softly, she stops and turns. "Oh, my beautiful boy. I am so happy to see you again. I have missed you so much," she whispers into his mane.

Sky blows out, licks his lips, and fits his big head into its accustomed place: chin in the crook of her arm, muzzle bent toward her heart. For a short while, they stand this way, drawing strength from each other, reacquainting themselves with each other's scents and pulses. She cannot believe she has him again, this horse who, day after day, year in and year out, wandered the plains with her. While the Silvermanes and Neal and Dock and West and Brion and Cylas and even Lume have all taken up places in her heart, this big black stallion occupies the place of honor.

Finally, Sky has had enough. He wrenches his head free and paws the ground: *let's get going.*

"Patience," she tells him.

Malora waits for the bonfire and the music and the sound of voices to die down. Sky wallows on his back in the sand, rocking from side to side. When he is finished, and coated with sand, he stands up and presents himself to her. Malora creates a scrub brush from dune grass and, rubbing his hide in a circular motion, scours away the layers of sand and dung and filth. Then she combs out his mane and tail with her fingers, picks the burs from his ears and the gunk from the corners of his eyes and nostril hairs, a grooming ritual that he never did more than tolerate. She does all this by feel, for the moon is just rising over the dunes. She glories in reacquainting herself with the swirls and eddies of his hide, with the long bands of powerful muscle that lie beneath, and with the Leatherwing-inflicted scars that stripe his back, radiating from his shoulders to his haunches, in perfect symmetry. It is not surprising that the wild centaurs have such an affinity for her horse, given how they scar their own hides. She remembers what her mother said: "Scars tell the story of how you have lived your life." Malora wonders whether the wild centaurs, scarring their bodies on purpose as they do, aren't *contriving* their stories rather than *earning* them the way Sky or Neal or she has. She is struck anew by the change in her horse since she last saw him on the Ironbound plains. He is still a huge horse, and yet he seems smaller. Or is it lighter? Even the mighty dishes of his hooves are nearly transparent at the edges.

"Just wait till you taste the grass in our paddocks," she whispers to him.

When she no longer sees the glow of the fire over the top of the bluff and silence has settled over the village, Malora walks swiftly, leading Sky. When she gets to the first pen, she stops. It had always been her intention to take Sky and leave Ixion. But that was before she had seen with her own eyes what is in store for these other horses. Now it is impossible to leave this place without taking the horses with her.

She hesitates, then looks at Sky and says, "I have to do this, don't I?"

Sky grunts, as if he has no doubt of it.

Unlatching the gate, she swings it wide. The horses inside have sensed something afoot, because they are piled up, ready and waiting to leave. They exit in a long, steady stream. She counts nineteen of them: Lapithians, Magnesians, Athabanshees, and three dusty Ironbound Furies.

Ivory! Thunder! Stormy!

These are the three that jumped the city wall and ran away from Gift, the Apex's incompetent wrangler in chief. If she had any doubt about doing this before, she has none now. These are *her* horses! She and Sky allow themselves a brief moment of reunion. The Furies seem sound, although their ribs stick out. When one of the other mares takes a jealous nip at Stormy, Stormy lets out a muffled squeal. Malora hushes Stormy while Sky, ears pinned and eyes flashing, chases the mare off.

"No *nonsense!*" Malora whispers to the lot of them. They stare at her contritely and lick their lips.

Sky snorts and stomps, confirming the directive.

Then they are all off to the next pen to free another ten horses and the nine from the pen following that one. Malora is impressed with how quietly the horses all move. The three in the last pen are nothing but hide and bones, either sick or starved or aged or all of that. Nevertheless, they bound out of the pen like spring colts and take their place at the back of the herd, except for a bay mare with a deep swayback. She trots up to Sky and rubs noses with the stallion. Sky snorts and blows but his ears poke forward in a friendly fashion.

Malora runs her fingers through the old gal's tangled mane. With her kind, limpid eyes and long bony head she is a female Max. The dowager mare takes her place beside Sky, slightly to the rear of him and just in front of the other three Furies, where no one disputes her place.

Malora leads the herd away from the village, retracing the steps she took with Mather, until she finds the spot where they met up. By moonlight, she follows the drag marks back to where Mather first roped her. She orients herself with the ocean at her back and raises both arms up, pointing west and east. Her nose points southwest, the direction they must travel over the dunes. Then she walks back among the horses and arranges them, noses to the south, tails to the north, in a single long line.

She returns to the head of the line, to where Sky, Old Gal, Thunder, Stormy, and Ivory have been waiting patiently for her. She takes her place in front of Sky and starts to move forward. The horses follow at a walk. When the clay softens to sand, she raises her hand and calls out to the herd, "Whoa!"

She pokes the ground with the cane before setting her foot down. She makes a kissing sound to signal the horses to follow her. They proceed more slowly now as she leads them up the face of the first dune. The horses struggle, their slender legs sinking down into the sand, but she keeps them moving up one side of the dune and down the other until she is a few steps shy of the valley between this and the next dune, where she calls another halt.

"All right, Sky. The others will follow you, so do what I say and you'll all be safe." Placing both hands on his nose she tells him to stay. She backs away from him—frowning and wagging a finger to reinforce her command—then as quickly as she can, turns and leaps across the valley, landing safely on the other side.

"All right, Sky," she says again, kissing and pointing up the dune with the sword cane. "Jump!"

Sky collects himself on his haunches and launches his body over the valley, landing on the other side.

"Good boy!" she says. Malora clicks her tongue and points up the dune with the cane. Sky scrambles up the face of the dune. She commands Old Gal next to jump and she flies across. Thunder, Stormy, and Ivory follow suit. The next few

horses, like liquid poured from the same bottle, flow across. The horses that follow flail but manage to make it across. The horses who have already jumped the gap wait for the others in a clump on top of the dune. When all the horses have made it across, she resumes the lead and they follow her down the other side to the next valley. This goes on all night. Every so often, she stops at the top of a dune to sniff the air and make sure the ocean is still at her back. The sun, when it rises on her left, tells her that she has been moving in the right direction.

Under normal circumstances, it would be a welcome sight, but it is as if daylight has revealed to the horses that they are in a place that is without two things they require: something to chew on and something to drink.

Rebellion breaks out. The horses, hungry and thirsty and tired of staying in an obedient line, begin to jostle each other and mill about, to nip at each other's tails and to break ranks. Malora works her way back, pushing and shoving and pounding them back into line, elbowing them hard and even punching them if they refuse to obey.

"Do you *want* to fall into a sinkhole and die?" she yells.

But they are not interested in what she has to say. They neither sense nor understand the danger. She watches as the gray mare three horses ahead of where she now stands cuts around the horse in front of her and runs down the embankment. Instead of jumping the valley, as she has all previous times, the mare staggers directly into it. Perhaps she thinks there is water there. She sinks in sand up to her shoulders until she disappears from sight, drowning in the sand. The three horses who are witnesses rear up, but this only sends them toppling and sliding down the side of the dune after the mare, their forelegs flailing, their eyes wide and unbelieving as they, too, sink beneath the sand.

Malora loses six horses before she can calm the rest of them down. This is difficult to do, since every muscle in Malora's body is screaming with tension. The thought of freeing all these horses only to lose them to the sinkholes is intolerable. But fear makes them now obedient. They do as they are told, and by midday they are once more meekly filing down the dunes, jumping over the valleys, and filing up the next.

When the River Neelah comes into view she has to shout and wave at them to keep to a walk. She herself wants to flit across the dunes toward the river, an inviting powdery blue in the near distance. But she manages to restrain herself over the last two dunes—keeping up the slow and steady pace she has set—until her feet touch the solid ground of the Dromadi caravan track. Then she breaks into a run, the horses overtaking her, Sky nipping at the ones who threaten to trample Malora.

Some of them wade into the river up to their withers. Others get down and wallow on their backs on the sandy banks. They shake out their manes and twitch their hides and bow their heads and tear up big fat mouthfuls of the plump green papyrus that grows on the bank and in the shallows. The air is alive with the sound of horses blowing. There is an air of celebration. Even the hide-and-bones horses have great mouthfuls of reeds sticking out of their snaggly teeth at all angles. Malora starts to strip off her clothes so she can join the bathers, but she remembers what happened when she took her last swim in this river and decides to stay in the shallows and keep her clothes on. Besides, she knows she needs to put more distance between herself and the wild centaurs. Now that she and the horses are out of immediate danger, her need to get home is keen.

She grabs a handful of mane and heaves herself up on Sky's back, calling out to the other horses, "Get up and get going, boys and girls! We're not home safe yet! In Mount Kheiron there'll be plenty of grass and water and oats with imported molasses!"

The horses lift their heads and stare at her, water dribbling from their lips. One by one, they crow-hop onto the bank, assembling themselves behind Sky.

When the last horses have taken their last pull of grass, they are off again at a lively trot. Sky's gait feels smoother and more buoyant than she remembers it. Every so often, he breaks into a gallop that feels so light, it is as if he were floating above the ground. Behind them the other horses try to keep up but seem by comparison clumsy and earthbound. They follow the river until the sun is nearly behind the ragged rim of the bush. Malora decides to move on through the night, she and Sky patrolling the advancing perimeter of horses to make sure no predators are about.

They rest in the shade of trees during the heat of the next day. Just like in the old days, she makes a nest of cloud grass and sleeps next to Sky, the other horses wrapping themselves around the two of them in a tight circle. Before she closes her eyes, she looks down at the palm of her hand, where she is so used to seeing the gouge.

Her palm is smooth, without blemish or scar.

Malora has the horses up and moving again in the late afternoon. A hundred times, she swivels her head and reas-

sures herself that they are not being followed. Still, she is reluctant to stop for very long. The horses, oblivious to any
danger, grab river grass on the move, but Malora isn't so lucky.
Hunger gnaws at her. The dragon cane's blade is dull. It is useless except as a shovel to dig up roots. The tartness of the bush
fruit she finds burns sores on the insides of her mouth. She
remembers the meals in Kahiro she let sit partially uneaten on
her plate and vows from now on always to clean her plate. In
some ways, it is as if she has never left the bush, except that
she is softer now. She longs for her canopied bed and her
feather mattress and her malachite tub. Even Barley Surprise
would taste good.

Fifteen days later, the golden dome shimmering at the top of
Mount Kheiron appears on the horizon. The Flatlands, as she
leads the horses across them later that same day, are curiously
deserted.

Where is everyone? she wonders. Her alarm mounts as
she passes her own paddocks and finds them empty. Could
the wild centaurs have somehow overtaken her and arrived
here already, plundering her paddocks and laying waste to the
centaurs of Mount Kheiron? She tortures herself with visions
of bloodshed and mayhem. Arriving at the gates of Kheiron,
she draws to a halt. The horses pile up behind her.

She is infinitely relieved when Margus Piedhocks stumbles out of the guardhouse. His eyes bulge. "Malora Victorious!" he sputters. "You are *alive!*"

"Of course I'm alive," she says.

"But—but—" he stammers, and points up at the
mountain.

Malora looks up and sees, rounding one of the lower ring roads, a procession winding its way down toward the gate. The sound of flute music comes to her on the breeze along with the hollow thumping of drums.

"Oh," she says.

Now she understands why the Flatlands and the paddocks are empty.

Everyone is up on the mount.

She is not sure whether to laugh or cry but doesn't have time to decide because Margus is lifting his hand to clang the bell that signals that Mount Kheiron is under attack.

"Don't do it!" she yells.

But it is too late.

CHAPTER 17

The Homecoming

The bell clangs. Moments later, a band of Peacekeepers thunders toward Malora, led by Neal Featherhoof brandishing a spear. Sky pins his ears, and the horses behind her wheel and prepare to run.

"Easy, boys and girls," she tells them. "Believe it or not, *this* centaur is friendly."

Neal stops when he sees it is Malora, raises his hand, and brings the Peacekeepers skidding to a halt behind him in a cloud of dust. "You're alive!" he says, approaching her on his own.

"I am!" she says with a wide grin.

Neal tilts his head. "I *thought* it was strange when we didn't find any bones," he says. "But they were so ready to believe that Dromadi windbag. They thought—"

"I had been devoured by crocodiles," Malora finishes for him.

Neal chuckles. "Apparently not." His jovial expression fades. "Zephele has been *inconsolable.*"

"I'm sorry," she says. In the next day, she will hear herself repeatedly apologizing for being alive.

"I see you found Sky," he says. "I can understand why you wanted him back. He's a magnificent animal."

Sky's ears flicker. Aware that he is being praised, he lowers his head, blows out, and licks his lips.

"Where did you get the rest of these horses?" Neal asks.

Malora blinks. For all the time she has had to brood upon it, she hasn't decided yet what she will tell the centaurs of Mount Kheiron. "I found them," she says with a casual lift of her shoulders.

"You *found them*?" Neal says over the steadily rising sound of drums and flute.

Malora's eyes dart to the arched entry to the city, where centaurs clutch bouquets of orange poppies. In the wake of the ringing bell, they look around in confusion, not sure whether to continue or take cover from invaders. The procession rushes around the corner in a series of orange flashes. Orange, Malora remembers, is the centaurean color of mourning. She sees the Apex and Herself at the head. Herself's head is wrapped in orange netting. The Apex wears an orange band across his gray wrap.

The Apex glares at Margus Piedhocks. He can see the horses, but he can't yet see Malora. Behind the Apex is his wagon, pulled by a Beltanian team outfitted in an orange harness. On the back of the wagon, Malora's malachite bathtub has been fitted with a malachite lid and transformed into a coffin. It would be a disturbing sight if it weren't so absurd.

The bathtub coffin is sprinkled with wildflowers. Orion, Zephele, and Theon, wrapped in orange, follow the wagon. Orion carries the Kavian serpent staff and Theon her knife. Zephele, empty-handed, sobs and stumbles, and her brothers reach for her elbows. Malora sees that Zephele's hooves are bare and that she has painted them gold in the style of the late Capricornian scout. Following them are West and all the wranglers herding the boys and girls who have orange ribbon braided through their manes.

It is Shadow who first notices her. Ignoring West's protests, she breaks away from the others and trots under the arch and right up to Sky. The two horses nuzzle.

West, in pursuit, stops in his tracks when he sees Malora. He sweeps off his orange-banded hat and draws a paw across his eyes, as if unable to believe what he sees. "Boss," he says fondly. "You're still with us. Suddenly it's the best day, rather than the worst!"

Orion and Theon and Zephele come pounding toward her through the gates. Zephele has wept all the paint off her face. Her eyes and her nose are red from weeping. "Malora Ironbound, how *dare* you show up at your own funeral!"

"I'm sorry," says Malora. She slides off Sky's back and goes to her friend with arms extended.

Zephele clenches her fists and pommels Malora lightly on the chest. The centaur maiden's mouth is pinched and white. "You have aged me twenty-five years!" she says. "And I look perfectly *hideous* in orange!"

"You do," agrees Malora, taking Zephele's hands in hers and bringing them to her lips. "But I like the gold-painted hooves."

"Do you? Oh! Let me *hug* you, my dearest darling girl!" Zephele says, throwing her arms around Malora. "You shall have to remain locked in my embrace all day long. It's the only way I can reassure myself that you're really with us again."

Orion stands nearby, shuffling his hooves. Malora catches his eye. He is smiling, his blue eyes bloodshot, with new creases at the corners. I have aged him, too, Malora thinks. She mouths the words again: *I'm sorry!*

"No. Forgive *us*," Orion says softly. "We have been through some very dark days. But it appears they are at an end now."

"I hope you can put the shroud I weaved for you to better use," Theon says with a shy smile.

"Theon!" Zephele pulls away from Malora and punches her brother's arm. "Brother, you will burn it to ashes immediately," she says. "I will not be able to *stand* the sight of it."

"Make way for the Apex!" someone shouts.

The crowd of horses and centaurs parts to admit Medon and Herself. The Apex wrenches off the orange band and flings it aside. His face is flushed with happiness. "Welcome home, Daughter!" he says, striding toward her with arms outstretched.

Herself, lifting the veil, trots over to Malora. "My dearest child," she says.

Zephele mutters in Malora's ear, "I suppose I shall have to share you now," as she steps aside for her parents.

Herself kisses Malora on the forehead and on each eyelid. "At this stage of life, one is *so* prepared for loss," she says in a thin, reedy voice. "After losing Athen, it seemed only natural I should lose you, too. . . ."

Malora has already decided not to tell Herself about Athen. Herself will never see her son again. Knowing that he is alive but in self-imposed exile would only be torture for her.

Malora stands still while the Apex's big, calloused hands rove over her head, her shoulders, her arms, her hands. "You are unharmed?" he asks, his gray eyes misty with concern.

She nods. "Just hungry," she says with a happy smile.

The Apex pulls away from her. He lets out a roar and raises the hand that holds the Eye of Kheiron. "I now declare this day of mourning to be a day of thanksgiving! Malora Ironbound has returned to us!"

The crowd erupts in cheers. Malora finds herself once again lifted up on the shoulders of the centaurs and borne along like a trophy. When her feet return to the ground, she is staring at Honus, clutching his flute.

"I am wrung out. I don't think I've ever wept as hard as I have in the last days," he tells her.

"I'm sorry," she says once again.

"There is nothing to be sorry for. So," he says, tucking his flute away and turning to take the measure of Sky. "This is the Horse. I must say, he has about him an otherworldly look."

"Ixion *is* an otherworld," Malora says.

"You will tell us how you came to win Sky back," he says. "But first, let's restore your bathtub to its rightful use."

"I have to take care of the new boys and girls first," she says, looking around for them. New horses and old are mingling. Here and there are shrill eruptions of discord. She spies Zephele feeding the wildflowers from her casket to the Old Gal and to Stormy and Thunder.

"West and the others will see to them," Honus says. "You are home now, and your friends are eager to help you."

"Home," Malora says, savoring the word.

She rides home on Sky's back, stopping to let him graze on the rich grass of the riverbank.

"Didn't I tell you it was delicious?" she says to the horse's bowed head. Then she stares up at the mount, humming with life, and sighs with contentment.

"You're going to like it here, Sky," she tells him. "It's the easy life, and Kheiron knows you've earned it."

By the time she approaches the paddocks, she has already decided not to insult the stallion by putting him in with the other horses. She leaves Sky grazing in the front yard and walks into her house. She stops on the threshold. Everything is bathed in the golden light of the setting sun. It is so beautiful! And it is hers! Across the Flatlands and up on the mount, she smells food cooking over wood fires and hears joyful music. The music sounds so strikingly similar to that of the wild centaurs that she closes her eyes. Suddenly she finds that she is overwhelmed by fear and dread.

What have I done? What will the Beast do when there are no horses to eat?

But it is too late to undo what she has done. Even if she could, she would not. The wild centaurs can defend themselves, she thinks. Horses cannot. I had to do it . . . didn't I?

She shakes the image of a vengeful Archon from her thoughts as she strides into the bedroom and shucks off the impala shirt. Slipping her robe on over her shoulders, she pats the cake of soap in each pocket, then heads out to the garden. Unbraiding her hair as she goes, she lays the white feather on her dressing table. She takes for granted that her malachite bathtub has already been reinstalled and filled with hot water . . . *strewn with rose petals, yet!* She removes the robe and lowers herself with a satisfied sigh into the hot fragrant water. When she is finished scrubbing herself clean, she immerses her entire self except for the tip of her nose. *This is me: home safe at last.*

She remains submerged, growing drowsy, when something dark looms over her. *Wild centaurs!* She heaves up out of the water with a loud gasp.

It is Sky. The stallion has found his way through the undergrowth into her garden. He dips his nose in the tub and sucks up the water.

She strokes his head, allowing her violently beating heart to return to normal. "I don't suppose a little lavender and lime will hurt you."

Leaving the water to Sky, she climbs out of the tub and slips back into her robe. As she sits at her dressing table, untangling the knots in her hair, she marvels at how quickly she went, a few moments ago, from relaxation to panic. Honus would say it is my uneasy conscience, she thinks. She picks up Lume's white feather and runs it between her fingers, then beneath her nose. She wonders whether the entire episode in Ixion was just another case of her "courting death," as Lume calls it. She doesn't think of herself as a reckless person, but perhaps she is. Still, this is the first time her reckless behavior might have consequences for others.

While Sky browses in the honeysuckle, Malora dresses slowly and afterward walks around her house, touching everything. If anything, she appreciates her new home even more now that she has been away from it. Someone has left a bowl of Barley Surprise on the table. She eats half of it, then wanders over to the shelf that holds her collection. She runs her hands over the statue of Sky and the sapphire egg Zephele purchased for her at the marketplace in Kahiro. The seashells she collected on the shore are lined up, along with crystals Honus found on the way to Kahiro. Most surprising is the leather pomegranate stuffed with ruby seeds. If they thought she was dead, why did they leave these things here? she wonders. Even during the darkest days, did they hold out hope? Or had this become a memorial?

She hears a thumping sound. Someone has come onto the porch. Malora whips around to see Sky, his head and shoulders thrust through the window, his nose in her dinner.

Relief washes over Malora. She laughs. "I'm glad you approve of Barley Surprise," she tells him, removing the spoon so he can lick the bowl clean.

She sits at the table, feeling a drowsy stillness settle over her. Sky nudges her with his nose.

She reaches up and strokes his ears. "I'm all right, boy, considering that I escaped death twice in almost as many days and arrived home in time for my own funeral."

Dusk has darkened to night and still no one comes for her. Outside, she hears West giving orders to the wranglers in a voice calculated not to disturb her. I should go out and help, she thinks. But she finds she doesn't want to get dressed again or leave her house. She goes to sprinkle Breath of the Bush on her canopy, wondering as she does so whether this is a wise idea, given what happened last time.

It's fine, she says to herself. Sky is safe with me. She hears him out in her garden, browsing in the honeysuckle.

"You'd better not leave any surprises for me out there!" she warns him as she climbs into her bed and douses the lantern. Sleep. Sleep is what she needs. Sleep will mend her frazzled nerves.

Wild centaurs move stealthily through the night, moonlight dappling their tattooed flanks and flashing on the hilts of their great swords.

This same dream wakes her over and over again in the night. She longs for the night to be over and put an end to it.

The first thing she does when she wakes up in the morning is put the flask of Breath of the Bush at the back of her wardrobe. Then she visits the horses, Sky at her heels. West has moved Max and his two mares to the much smaller paddock reserved for ailing horses. He has put the new horses, including the three Furies, in Max's old paddock. Old horses and new eye each other belligerently across the fence line.

"We're going to take them out one by one over the next few days," West tells Malora. "Give them a good going-over, deworm them, and clean them up. Meanwhile, Stormheart's crew will build us a new infirmary paddock. Hope we won't need it but can't think that we won't. Some of those horses are in a sorry state."

"Thanks, West. I know it's a lot to handle."

"They're good horses, boss," West replies. Has West ever met a horse that wasn't good?

Malora climbs the fence and takes Max's head into her

hands. "I'm sorry to put you in such tight quarters." Max sniffs at her pouch, nosing around for treats. "And I'm sorry I don't have anything for you, but I'll get some Maxes today, I promise," she tells him. "I brought Sky back. See?"

Sky remains aloof, but Malora knows what he is thinking. "These two mares are off-limits," she tells him. "They belong to the Champion. Even if he doesn't remember what to do with them."

Sky mutters as if to say, *I would know* exactly *what to do with them.*

"Yes, we all know what a big man you are," she says, stroking his neck. She says to West, "I want you to put armed guards around the paddocks, day and night."

"Yes, boss." He has not asked her where she has been or why this is necessary. Nor has he asked her how she came upon all these horses.

"The Apex wants to see me. I should be back by midday," she tells West.

As Malora rides Sky through the city gates, waving at Margus Piedhocks, it occurs to her that this is the first time she has ridden on horseback through the streets of Mount Kheiron. Sky trots blithely up the ring road, and centaurs hail them in passing, some handing her up small bouquets of flowers (blessedly not orange), which Sky promptly devours, reaching around and snatching them from her grasp. Others press Maxes upon her. Sky doesn't seem to care for the spearmints any more than he does for their namesake. It seems Malora has a new title. No longer Malora Victorious, she is now Malora Resurrected. She smiles graciously down upon the centaurs when they call her this, even though she dislikes it more than the last title. On Sky's back, she towers over the centaurs.

When she arrives at Medon's house, she dismounts. "You need to stay outside," she tells Sky with a frown, wagging a finger and backing away, then turning to leave. She is halfway down the gallery when she hears a swift *clip-clop* and turns to see Sky following her at a jaunty jog. Malora doesn't have the heart to scold him and send him back. "All right. Try not to leave any messy surprises behind you," she tells him, just as he lifts his tail and pushes out a fluffy yellow-green cascade. "Sorry," she says as a Twan rushes forward with shovel and scoop.

"Our pleasure," says the Twan, as if he were scooping up nuggets of gold.

Ash stands at the double doors. "They are waiting for you inside," he tells her, peering up at Sky through his eyeglass. "My, my, my, my, my, my, my—"

"My horse," Malora says.

"A horse and a half, I'd say," Ash declares. "The blue eyes are a bit unnerving."

Sky reaches down with his nose and flips the glass from Ash's eye. It swings on its black string.

"Oh well!" says Ash, fingers fluttering after the glass. "Better not to view you in sharp focus. Blurry is far more benign." He pushes open the doors to the Hall of Mirrors and announces, "Miss Malora and Master Sky!"

They are all here: Zephele and Orion, Honus and Neal, standing in a tight half circle before the Apex and Herself. If they are surprised to see Sky, they don't betray it. They do betray, however, with their guilty looks, that they have just been talking about her. It must be a hard habit to break, she thinks.

"Good morning!" she says brightly.

They move to make room for her and Sky.

"I trust you are settled in and rested," the Apex says. His eyes are on Sky. Beside her, Malora feels Sky basking in the Apex's admiration. Or is he, like me when I first came in here, fascinated by his own reflection?

"Yes, I am," she says. "Thank you. It's good to be home."

The Apex waits. When Malora doesn't say anything more, he adds, "Then you are sufficiently fortified to tell us your story."

Malora nods, taking a deep breath and letting it out slowly. How she wishes she had written down "the story" last night, the better to remember which bits she is going to tell and which she is withholding. She looks around at the others, dreading that something she doesn't want them to know will slip out. She has no idea what her friends have already chosen to tell the Apex. She settles for starting with a half-truth.

"I'm sure the others told you that we heard in the marketplace of Kahiro that bands of wild centaurs living in the Downs were rustling horses."

"They have," says the Apex.

"We—or at least I—assumed they had Sky."

Sky grunts.

The Apex makes a winding motion with his hand to tell Malora that he knows this already and wants to hear more.

"The Downs being riddled with deadly sinkholes, the others didn't want to go in," she says.

"I have already congratulated them on their levelheaded-ness," the Apex says with an approving scowl.

"I know I was foolish, but I couldn't come home knowing that my horse was captive to the wild centaurs. So I decided to go alone."

The Apex's brows bristle. "That was rash of you, Daughter."

"I know it was," Malora says. "But I had to get my horse back." She runs a hand down Sky's mane.

His eyes on Sky, the Apex says, "Understandably. He is a magnificent creature."

Sky bows his head modestly and licks his lips.

"To get to the Downs, I had to swim across the River Neelah. But trappers had set a snare for hippos and crocs in the river bottom. I got tangled up in it halfway across the river. It pulled me down under the water. I struggled—"

"Malora!" Orion cries out. "You could have died!"

"Actually," she says, with a wry smile, "I *did* die."

CHAPTER 18

Retaliation

They all stare at Malora in dumbfounded silence.

"Then it was all true!" Zephele bursts out. "Shrouk was right."

"Who is Shrouk?" the Apex booms.

"This old Dromad we met with," Zephele says dismissively. Then, turning an avid look on Malora, she says, "Do tell us how you died, Malora."

"And came back to life," Orion adds.

Malora continues to deliver her story in the same matter-of-fact tone. "I couldn't escape from the net, and it wasn't long before I ran out of breath. The last thing I saw was the crocodiles coming for me."

"No!" Zephele brings her fingers to her mouth.

"I was unconscious when Lume rescued me. He tells me that he harried off the crocodiles, cut me loose from the net, and brought me up on the riverbank, where he breathed life into me."

"Lume? Who is this *Lume*?" the Apex booms.

"A*ha*!" Zephele says, recognizing the name. "Lume is the man of her dreams, Father! And her dreams, it would seem, have come true, the lucky girl!"

"Actually," Malora says, "it turns out Lume is an avian hibe called a Wonder."

Zephele's enthusiasm wilts. "Oh, my poor dear!" she says. "You must have been *ravaged* by disappointment."

Malora feels a sudden irrational need to defend Lume. "I was happy to be alive. And Lume is very nice. He has very powerful eyes and ears and breath."

"Apparently," Orion says, laughing uneasily.

"But what about the blood?" Honus asks. "It was *everywhere*."

She holds up her hand. "My old wound bled when I struggled against the trap."

They all take a moment to stare at her hand, which is smooth and unscarred.

"You heal quickly," says the Apex.

Orion and Honus confer in a whisper.

Zephele, ever willing to tease out the best in every situation, says, "Even if he is a hibe, I think it's romantic that he breathed life into you."

"I'm not familiar with this particular hibe," Orion says.

"You wouldn't be," Malora says. "He is the last of his kind."

"Just like you!" Zephele beams.

"He flew me to his home, high up on a sheared-off mountaintop," Malora continues.

"Extraordinary!" Honus puts in. "Most avian hibes are earthbound. He *flew* you to his aerie, you say?"

"So I could recover," Malora says. *And fight the Leather-wings with him,* she adds silently. Neither does she make any mention of his "watching her court death."

Honus says, "Then, like your ancestors, who once rode the air currents in sleek metal contraptions, you now know what it is to fly."

"I do," Malora says, turning to Honus. "And I found it *terrifying.*"

"Terrifying or not, what I wouldn't give to experience it!" Honus says.

"Did this Wonder accompany you into Ixion?" Orion asks.

"Ah, no," Malora says. "He had something else he needed to do." She goes on to tell about her journey through the Downs, minimizing the danger of the sinkholes because she knows it will upset everyone to hear how close she came to slipping into one. But Neal won't let it go.

"You traveled into the Downs, without a guide, without a map, and without your Kavian serpent staff, and made it in and out of there alive?"

Malora nods. "With Sky and the other horses," she says.

The Apex swings his head toward her. "The horses you came home with are the property of the wild centaurs?"

Malora nods reluctantly.

Honus bursts out. "You rustled the rustlers' horses!" His face is alight with pride. "Good for you!"

The Apex's brows lower like twin thunderclouds. *"This is not good!"* he says.

And now Malora must say what she has not wanted to say: "I freed the horses because the wild centaurs were going to destroy them."

The Apex looks bewildered. "Why would they do that?"

"They sacrifice them," she says, "to their god, the Beast from Below." She doesn't add that, unlike Kheiron and the Doctors Adam and Eve, this god is *real.*

Herself shudders. "Such savagery! In that case, you did well to rescue them, Malora."

The Apex turns to his wife and snaps, "Did she now? Will you say that when those same savages come sweeping down from the north to retrieve their stolen horses?"

The Apex, having given voice to Malora's deepest fears, strikes the room silent.

Finally, Malora says, "Knowing what was in store for those horses, I had to save them." She looks around at her friends. "Don't you see?"

They stare back at her in reproachful silence. Only Honus seems to approve of her actions. He raises a finger, and says, " 'Whoever destroys a single life is as guilty as though he had destroyed the entire world; and whoever rescues a single life earns as much merit as though he had rescued the entire world.' By any standard I can think of, Malora, you are a hero . . . many times over."

"Hero or not," Medon grumbles, "if the wild centaurs show up at the gate and demand their property, I shall have to return it to them."

"Father!" Zephele cries out. "You *wouldn't!*"

"You would do this," Malora says, her anger flaring, "knowing what is in store for them?"

"Know this, all of you!" the Apex says as his eyes travel around the room and come to rest on Malora. "I will do anything, *anything* to keep the peace. I learned a lesson when I won the Hippodrome. And that is this: centaurs are more important than horses. Better sacrifice the lives of a hundred horses than lose a single centaur life."

"The Apex has spoken," Zephele says later that day, lounging on Malora's porch and sharing the wedges of an orange with her. "I remained behind, after the rest of you left, and had a perfectly hideous row with him. I told him if ever there was a good reason to take up arms, this was it."

"And what did he say to that?" Malora asks. Sky, poking his nose between the porch rails, rejects the peel of an orange Zephele offers him with an affronted snort.

"He said that when *I* became Apex, I could wage all the war I want," Zephele says, tossing the orange peel.

"And you said . . . ?" Malora prompts.

Zephele sets her chin. "I accused him of being afraid of the wild centaurs because he feared that very same wildness in himself. Rather than owning up to it, he denied it with his usual bombast. I told him that what he thinks of as his strength has grown into weakness and that I was deeply disappointed in him, both as father and as leader." She deflates suddenly. "I suppose I will have to drag myself back in there and apologize. At least Herself and Orion tell me that I should. Neal agrees with me, by the way."

"With what?" Malora asks. She reaches for the flowers Zephele brought for her and plucks one to feed to Sky. Sky takes it in his mouth and chews. He pokes his nose back through the slats for more.

"Oh, really, Sky! You are too, too greedy. You haven't even swallowed the first one." Zephele feeds him the rest of the bouquet, one flower at a time, holding back the next flower until he has finished the last. "Has your horse *always* been this greedy?"

"A big horse has a big appetite," Malora says. "You were saying about Neal?"

"She was saying that Neal is the most ruggedly handsome centaur she knows," Neal says, ambling up onto the porch. He is off-duty, wearing his ragged impala vest. *Ruggedly handsome* is as good a description of Neal Featherhoof as any Malora can think of.

"I was saying no such thing," Zephele says, her smile warm and welcoming. Neal's eyes, when he looks at Zephele, have lost their hard glint. Things have changed between them, Malora thinks.

"Neal agrees," Neal says, popping the last wedge of the orange into his mouth and chewing it, "that to return the horses to the wild centaurs would be an admission of weakness." He spits a pit over the rail. Sky gives him an icy look.

"My brief impression of them," Malora says, "is that they wouldn't do us the courtesy of *asking*. They would be much more likely to *take*. And probably help themselves to the rest of the boys and girls while they were at it."

"Of course they would," Neal agrees, "which is why I have fortified your Twani paddock guard with a full compliment of

Peacekeepers. Not new recruits, either, but my most seasoned soldiers."

"I hope they are well armed," Malora says. "The wild centaurs carry swords that make yours look like toothpicks."

"Is that so?" Neal says with a jovial grin.

Malora describes in detail the hacking, whacking swords of the wild centaurs.

Neal's expression turns gloomy. "I'm familiar with the make. The southernmost Pantherian tribes forge them in fires fed from thousand-year-old trees. They are said to use them to slice off the horns of charging Cape buffalo."

"A shame we didn't pick up some of those buffalo-whackers while we were in the Arsenal," Zephele says.

"It's not as simple as that," Neal says. "These swords are heavy. You have to have the stamina and muscle to wield them. I'd have to retrain my entire force. Malora isn't joking when she calls them hackers and whackers. Brute force, rather than finesse, is called for."

Zephele flips a careless hand. "You strike me as quite sufficiently brutish already, Master Featherhoof."

Neal bows gallantly. "M'lady, you spoil me with compliments."

"On that note, this lady will take her leave," Zephele says, climbing gracefully to her feet. "My friends are expecting me in the stitchery. They are eager to hear all the gossip about Malora Resurrected."

"What will you tell them?" Malora asks.

Zephele's eyes widen. "Why, that you can fly through the air and walk across the Neelah without wetting your pretty little People toes."

Malora's jaw drops. "Really?" she asks.

Zephele leans over and kisses Malora. "Of course not, dearest. I never gossip about you. And besides, I wouldn't dream of stoking their already overheated imaginations. Will you be resuming your training at the forge?"

"Brion expects me tomorrow," Malora says.

"Excellent. Well then, perhaps Swiftstride will let you forge a buffalo-whacker for your next project," she says, tripping gaily down the porch steps.

Neal watches her until she rounds the side of the house, her golden hooves flashing, her braided tail swinging saucily. Neal sighs.

"You two seem *friendly*," Malora says when they are alone.

"When you left us, we thought you were gone for good," Neal says. "As it happens, I was able to comfort Zephele as few others could."

"I'm glad," Malora says.

"Grief revealed depths in her I had not known existed," Neal says.

"They were always there," Malora says.

Neal shakes his head quickly, as if clearing it. "Let's talk about the wild centaurs."

Malora eyes him closely. *Does he realize I know more than I have told?* "What do you want to know?" she asks warily.

"If the wild centaurs are as formidable as you say, perhaps you really should forge me a sword so that I, at least, stand a chance against them," he says.

She searches his face to see if he is joking. He isn't. She says, "Making a little knife was one thing. I could be turned out for making a weapon, especially now that I am on the Apex's bad side."

"You're right, of course," Neal says hastily. "Forgive me for even asking such a thing."

"Apart from the guard on the paddock," Malora says, "you might want to post a lookout—"

"Already taken care of, pet," he says. "I've gotten special dispensation from the priests of the temple to place a lookout in the dome. Kheiron's glorious golden dome will, at long last, be put to a *useful* purpose."

Malora has dragged a bale of hay in a sack up the mountain to keep Sky occupied while she works. Setting him up in the yard outside the smithy, she opens the creaking doors and enters. Sky peers into the shop and shakes his mane, as if the attraction of this foul-smelling place eluded him. The smells of smoke and metal and sweat welcome her like old friends. Groping around in the dark for her apron, she ties it on and pads across to the furnace, her boots sinking into the fine sand. She lays her palm against the stone, which still holds the heat from yesterday's fire. On the hearth lies a row of finials. She packs wood shavings into the cavity just above the firepot and uses the firebrand to kindle the shavings. Once the fire has caught, she lays some sticks of oak on top of that. When the bigger fire catches hold, she rakes the coke over the fire and works the bellows until the fire glows red-hot.

"That blue-eyed monster of yours seems to have made himself at home," Brion says. "Welcome home, Malora."

Malora turns from the forge and smiles at the blacksmith. "I'm glad to be back," she says. A clap on the shoulder from him is the extent of their physical contact. They set to work on the finials, as if she has never left the shop.

He will be hurt, she thinks as they work, if I do not tell him my story. While they weld the finials onto the fence posts, Malora tells Brion her story, concentrating on the wild centaurs and the escape with the horses.

"That was a brave deed," Brion says.

"Foolish, if it winds up bringing an army of wild centaurs down upon us," Malora says.

"Don't you worry, Daughter. Neal Featherhoof and his crew can make fast work of them," Brion says.

"Not without the right weapons, they can't," Malora mutters, more to herself than to him.

But Brion has heard her, and he turns to her slowly, one side of his face reddened by the fire. "What would be the right weapon?"

She hesitates momentarily, then describes the hacking and whacking swords of the wild centaurs.

Brion goes over to the pile of stock in the corner and picks up a big, heavy bar. "A hefty sword needs to come from a hefty bar," he says. "What do you say we start with this one?"

Malora hesitates. "The Apex would put us both out," she says.

"The Apex would hand your horses over to those idol-worshipping savages," Brion says.

"But the fence . . . ," Malora says.

"The fence can wait," Brion says. "We have more important work to do here in this forge. Build up that fire, will you, Daughter? We're going to need some big heat to make this hacker and whacker."

After Malora has built up the fire, Brion starts by thrusting the bar into the fire and heating it to red-hot, then flattening it along the blade area, drawing it out into the general shape of a sword's blade and checking with her occasionally to make sure that he is on the right track. He heats it and draws it out, folds it over, then heats it again and folds it.

"I'm going to let it cool without working it this next round to make sure that the metal stays strong," Brion says, lifting his tattered hat off his head and wiping the sweat from his brow. "We'll work on the finials while the blade cools."

They work on the sword for nearly a month. Malora finds that the very act keeps her Night Demon thoughts at bay. When the weapon is finished to Brion's satisfaction, he says, "Now what can we do for you? You can't expect to hold off the wild centaurs with that wee knife of yours."

Malora has already given this some thought. She won't feel evenly matched with a wild centaur unless she is seated on Sky. She is unschooled in wielding a sword. She is afraid she will lop Sky's head off by accident. She needs to fight from a distance so that she and Sky are kept away from the sword blades. "I could use a spear," she says. "Something I can break down and carry in two pieces in my saddlebag but put together quickly if needed."

Brion's eyes light up with the challenge. "I have seen such things in the Arsenal," he says. Over the next few days, they work on the spear. They make it with a metal shaft and barbed point with a hardwood handle, wrapped in waxed twine for easy gripping. The handle screws into the shaft, and the unit, disassembled, fits neatly into her saddlebag. If the barb sticks in her opponent's flesh, she will use the little knife to dig it out, assuming she has the time. When Malora points out that other jobs have begun to pile up, Brion dismisses them with a wave of his hand. "This comes first," he says.

She says nothing of this to her friends, who visit her at the house every night. One night, Honus comes alone for the evening meal, bringing a covered bowl of lemon pood. While she sets the table, Honus examines her collection shelf.

"I'm surprised Zephele hasn't confiscated the ruby pomegranate now that you have returned," Honus says.

"I tried several times to give it back to her, but she won't take it," Malora says.

"Lume's?" Honus asks, holding up the white feather, which she has added to her collection.

She nods.

"It is a splendid specimen," he says, running it through his fingers. "The longest feather I have ever seen, and quite the whitest."

"He has lots of them," Malora says. "I'm sure he would part with another, if you ask."

"Will you be seeing him again?" Honus asks.

Not a day passes that she does not search the sky for him. She wonders if he watches her from afar. "I hope to," she says.

Honus gives her a long, searching look, which she avoids by concentrating on her food.

After the meal, they sit out on the porch and watch the horses gambol in the paddocks.

Honus gets the fire going in his pipe and then tilts his head and settles back. Malora senses a lecture in the offing. "Once upon a time," he begins, "hibes of different types found themselves attracted to one another and indulged in certain *intimacies*. As a result of these *intimacies,* monsters were born, most not surviving their infancy. That is the reason, many say, that the Houses of Romances were started. They provided places where interhibal intimacy could be practiced," he says carefully, "without fear of the consequences."

Malora gives him a quizzical look. "Why are you telling me this now?" she asks.

Honus lifts his slender shoulders and avoids meeting her eyes. "It's part of your ongoing education." He pulls hard on the pipe.

She narrows her eyes at his profile, limned by the embers from his pipe.

He goes on, "It is natural for you to wonder what might happen should you, at some point, when the time is right, wish to practice intimacy with a mate who is a hibe . . . which he, after all, inevitably would have to be."

"Is that what you think will happen?" Malora asks. "That my children, if I have them, will be monsters? Even though I myself am not a hibe?"

"I cannot say so with certainty, but it is an educated guess," Honus says.

"Thank you for your educated guess," she says stiffly, just as Orion rounds the side of the house at a gallop, his eyes wild.

Both she and Honus leap to their feet.

"Come immediately, both of you!" he says, leaning on the porch railing to catch his breath. "The worst has happened!"

CHAPTER 19

The Worst

With one conspicuous exception, they are all back in the Hall of Mirrors, where they had stood when Malora first returned from the dead. The Apex and Herself huddle over the clutter of papers on the table, looking pale and shaken. Across from them, Neal gives his report. His buckskin vest is untied, his hair disheveled, and his eyes bloodshot.

"Sunshine sustained a fatal wound but did not live to tell what happened. Farin Whitewithers was found murdered at the gate," Neal says. "There are no other casualties . . . that we know of at this time. I don't understand," he says, raking his fingers through his curls. "I don't understand how they could have gotten past the city gates!"

"Has anyone told Lemon?" Malora asks.

"Ash has gone to sit with the poor fellow," Neal says.

Malora is awash with pity for the dour little Twan, who must have died defending her mistress. Either that or Zephele's abductors didn't want to take her with them and were eliminating a witness. She worries that Zephele saw the murder. Wherever she is now, Malora imagines her friend grieving and raging by turns.

"This is the work of wild centaurs," Malora says, reciting from memory Athen's motto, according to Mather: "Strike hard, strike fast, and make for the Downs. *Leave no witnesses to tell the tale.*"

"That much is obvious," the Apex says. "What is less obvious is *why abduct Zephele?* Why not just take what was theirs and leave? And how in Kheiron's good name did they even know where to find her?"

The Apex casts his eyes around at them one by one, settling on Malora. "Well, Daughter?" he asks, his gray eyes boring into her.

Behind her, Sky prods her forward with his nose.

Malora avoids meeting the Apex's gaze. Instead she watches as her reflection in the mirror turns a deep pink. She clears her throat. "Athen?" Her voice sounds small and defenseless.

"Athen!" Herself echoes, astonished. "What causes you to invoke my son's name?"

The Apex growls: "Explain yourself, Daughter!"

Malora braces herself. If the Apex is angry now, when she reveals the entire story he will *explode.* But she has spoken, and now there is no unsaying it. "Athen would know where to find his sister . . . wouldn't he?" She looks around. Her friends stare at her as if she were a stranger.

Orion says, "Explain to us, I beg you, Malora, what you mean."

"I was waiting for a way to tell you all this, but Athen," she says, taking a deep breath, "is with the wild centaurs."

At first, no one speaks. Finally, Herself says, "If you knew this, why did you not liberate him along with your precious horses?"

Because Herself's tone stings, Malora delivers the next information more bluntly: "Because Athen doesn't need or want liberating. He is happy where he is. Happier than he ever was here in Mount Kheiron."

"Ah!" Honus says softly, nodding, as if this makes perfect sense.

"I don't believe you!" Herself's voice breaks. "How could he be *happy* living among such savages?"

"He is the leader of those savages," Malora says. "The Alpha Stallion."

"Of course he would be!" says Honus.

"What are you saying?" the Apex whispers.

Malora goes on. "Athen is a mighty and respected ruler of the wild centaurs, from what Mather told me. He—"

"Mather?" Orion cuts in. "Mather is with the wild centaurs as well? Our cousin is alive?"

Malora nods. "If not exactly happy, at least alive." She turns to the Apex. "Almost all of the centaurs that you—or any of the Apexes before you—have ever turned out have taken refuge in the Land of Ixion."

"Why did you not tell us this when you first came home?" the Apex asks in a soft voice she finds even more threatening than his roar.

"I'm sorry I didn't tell you," Malora says. "I couldn't find a way to tell you that would not cause you pain. I wanted to spare you additional grief. Telling you that Athen, or even Mather, was still alive seemed unkind. I was afraid that for you it would be like losing them all over again." Malora bites her lip. Herself is crumpled and weeping in her husband's arms.

"But I'm even more sorry," Malora says, "that I took the horses. If I hadn't taken the horses, Zephele would still be safe in Mount Kheiron and the wild centaurs would never have come south. All of this is my fault. I hope that you will forgive me, but I do not expect you to."

The whites of Medon's eyes redden suddenly. "First my son and now my daughter! This is a *catastrophe!*"

No one disagrees.

Orion says, "I'm sure Athen won't harm our sister." He says this with so little confidence that he adds, "They took her as ransom . . . or as retaliation. Surely, she is worth more to them alive than dead."

"Orion is right," Neal says, only half convinced.

"I've gone into the Downs once," Malora says. "I can do it again. I'll go after them and get Zephele back safely. I promise."

"*I* will get her back," Neal says. "You have done quite enough damage as it is."

"I will return the horses," Malora says stubbornly. "I love Zephele, too, and I will do anything that's necessary to get her back." Except give them Sky, she adds silently. Never Sky. "I want to help. I *need* to help."

"I don't want or need your help," Neal says in clipped tones. Malora winces.

"Nonsense, Featherhoof!" the Apex thunders. "Don't be proud! You need her help. The two of you: head north immediately and bring me back my daughter."

"With all due respect, sir," Neal says, "the trail leaving Mount Kheiron does not lead north to the Downs. It seems to lead south."

"South?" everyone echoes.

"When I went upriver I found only tracks leading *to* Mount Kheiron; none *away.* I also came upon a clay pit in the riverbank, where I found evidence of a scrum."

"What is a scrum?" Orion asks.

"A mess of hoofprints in the wet clay. It looks as if the wild centaurs stopped there to use the clay," Neal says.

"To cover their tattoos! *That's* how they got into Mount Kheiron. They passed as native!" Honus says.

"But why kill Farin Whitewithers?" Neal cocks his head, then answers his own question: "Oh, yes. I see now. Whitewithers caught them leaving with Zephele and threatened to give them away."

Malora shakes her head sadly. Poor, foolish Farin Whitewithers was altogether too fond of ringing that bell. He paid dearly for that fondness.

"The clay helped them, but now it will help me," Neal says. "With clay on their hooves, they will be easier to track."

"But why would they go south?" Honus says.

"Who cares *why?*" Medon blusters. "Follow the trail wherever it leads! They have a day's lead on you. Don't waste another moment. I can and will resign myself to the idea of Athen choosing such a life. But the thought of my daughter among those heathens . . . And to think that she and I had harsh words the other day. If anything happens to her . . ."

"There there, Father," Herself says, taking Medon's big head onto her shoulder and stroking it. "We will get our girl back. Somehow or other, Neal and Malora will find her and bring her home to us, you'll see."

The others have left the Hall of Mirrors, but Malora and Sky remain.

The Apex says to Herself, "I am not surprised to learn this. From the day he was born, Athen was a wild one. Oh, he had a dark, dark soul."

"You never gave him a chance!" Herself cries out.

"We gave him a dozen chances every single day," the Apex says softly. "And he squandered them all."

Medon's eyes find Malora. "As you can see, in matters that concern Athen, my wife has a blind spot."

"He was my first child!" she wails. "My beautiful! My beloved! I adored him. I still do."

"And what of your *youngest* child!" the Apex rumbles. "Athen has a dark soul, whereas Zephele . . . radiates warmth and light!"

"I promise you I will find her and bring her back . . . ," Malora says. All she can think is that if she hadn't taken those horses, Zephele would still be safely in Mount Kheiron. Sunshine's death, Farin's death, Zephele's abduction, it is all, every bit of it, on her head.

As if she has read Malora's thoughts, Herself reaches out and rests a small, cool hand on Malora's shoulder. "Don't be too hard on yourself, Daughter," she says soothingly. "You did what you thought was best. You can't have known that your actions would have such consequences."

Malora might not have known, but she should have. She should have calculated the risk of more than just her own neck—and those of the horses. She should have come away only with Sky. Sky is hers, just as she is Sky's. But these other horses were not hers to take. She is a thief and a liar and she doesn't deserve the friendship of these kind centaurs. "I will find her and bring her back," she says in a voice that frays at the edges. "I will do that, I promise."

As she is leaving the Hall of Mirrors, Herself calls out after her, "If you see Athen, please tell him I never stopped loving him."

"I will," she says.

"Do not hurt him," Herself adds, "I beg of you."

Malora nearly laughs, the reverse being far more likely the case.

Orion is waiting for her outside the door.

"Don't!" Malora says, covering his mouth with her hand. "Don't tell me this is not my fault."

Orion smiles sadly and clasps her hand. "I wasn't going to. I was going to wish you good luck. And to tell you that Neal will forgive you, in time. He's just lashing out."

Malora says, "I don't deserve his forgiveness, but thank you for your good wishes. We will need them."

He holds her head and presses his forehead to hers.

"We will get her back," he says.

She nods.

"Do not underestimate my brother," Orion says, pulling away and walking with her down the hall.

This time Malora does laugh, bitterly. "Believe me, I don't," she says.

Neal waits for her under the portico, scuffing one hoof against the marble floor.

"We need to stop at Brion's shop," Malora says.

"There's no time," he says.

"There's time for this," she says.

Reluctantly, Neal follows her there. The bundle of skins lies on the hearth. Unwrapping it, she holds it out to Neal. Neal stares down at the hacking, whacking sword in its sheath. He takes it from her, unsheathes it, and holds it up to the light from the doorway. "I thank you for this," he says grudgingly.

By the time they set out on the white road winding south, there is little daylight left. They walk along the river in silence. Malora does the tracking, following the clay-rimmed hoofprints of what appear to be three adult male centaurs and a smaller set they assume belongs to Zephele. Malora wants to say to Neal that if they overtake their quarry, they will need a plan of action, but Neal's silence brooks no invasion. His way of preparing to meet the wild centaurs is to practice with the new sword. As he walks, he tests its heft, wielding it in a weaving motion with two hands, cleaving the air before him as if it were teeming with wild centaurs, their lopped heads rolling underfoot. By dusk, Sky has gotten used to the whooshing sound the blade makes and no longer twitches or balks when it whistles past his ears. Her own weapon, the spear, is in her saddlebag, but she has no need to practice. She is ready.

When Malora can no longer see the prints clearly, she raises a hand to signal a halt. They camp in a grove of orange trees. Sky wanders off to find something more appetizing to browse. Neal continues to work with the sword in darkness. Malora eats by herself as she watches him in the dying light, slicing through the bright orange blossoms without mercy. Later, he comes to lie down with his head on the other side of Sky's saddle. The crowns of their heads are almost touching, and yet they seem a great distance apart tonight.

As she breathes in the tangy fragrance of the grove, Malora remembers when she rode through here with Orion and the Silvermane cousins as she approached Mount Kheiron for the first time. She can tell that Neal is still awake. "How long?" she asks.

"How long?" he repeats. She notices that his voice has lost its hard edge. He sounds unutterably weary.

"How long are you going to stay angry with me?" she asks.

Neal sighs. "Zephele thought you'd done the right thing, taking those horses."

She knows this, but she waits to find out where Neal is going with this.

"She wouldn't want me to be angry with you," he says. "In fact, she would disapprove heartily."

"But you're angry with me anyway," Malora says.

"Oh, the truth is that I'm angry with *myself*," he says. "You just happened to get in the way. She also would not want us to give the horses back, so put that out of your mind. We will get her back, but we won't horse-trade for her."

Silence falls again, but it is less awkward now.

After a while, he says, "Shrouk had a prophecy for me, too, you know."

"Oh?" Malora says, smiling up at the sky. "And you actually believe whatever steaming pile of elephant dung she had to offer?"

"After you had your session with her, I went in to fill my flasks. I thought she was asleep, but she was wide awake and waiting for me. She asked me if I wanted a reading. I told her exactly what I thought of her readings, but she said I'd want to hear *this* one. It was a prophecy of love, not death. She told me—are you ready to hear this?—that I would fall in love with and wed the daughter of the Apex."

Malora smiles. "That's nice."

"That's all you have to say?" Neal asks. "Aren't you shocked?"

"Not at all. You have no idea how overjoyed Zephele would be to hear that prophecy," Malora says.

"You're lying! She'd be *outraged*! A Highborn lady marrying a Flatlander!"

"You're wrong, Neal," Malora says. "She is in love with you, too. As far as I can tell."

Neal rolls to a sit-up. "Really?"

"Really," Malora says.

He lets this sink in. A smile spreads slowly across his face. "Well then, in that case," he says, "here's to the windbag's prophecy, and to rescuing the bride." She hears the hiss of the brown liquid shooting into his open mouth, then sees the zebra-skin flask swing toward her. It is a gesture of fellowship she hates to resist, but resist it she will.

"No thanks," she says. "I have sworn off gaffey."

In the morning, they move through the olive groves, then on through rolling fields of flax. By midday, they have passed out of Mount Kheiron and into the bush. The day turns overcast and humid. The smell of rotten meat hangs in the air. She looks over at Neal. Neal nods warily. He smells it, too. They are so busy scanning the bushes for predators that they almost miss the spot where the tracks veer away from the river and head in a westerly direction.

"I wonder what drew them away from the river?" Neal asks as they leave the river behind and the air grows thicker and more noxious.

"They may be circling back and heading to Ixion on a path to the west of Mount Kheiron. Or else . . ." Malora squints into the distance.

"What?" Neal asks.

"There are ruins in the foothills about a day's ride from here. Perhaps they have holed up there and will send someone out with a demand to exchange Zephele for the horses," Malora says. "If that is their purpose."

"Let's hope that it is," Neal says. "They must know we'd empty every stable in Mount Kheiron to get her back. Even if we won't," he adds hastily.

It seems that the tracks do lead to the ruins. Nearly halfway there, Malora feels Sky's back muscles go rigid. He starts to shimmy and balk. She bangs her heels into his ribs to keep him moving forward apace with Neal.

"What's the matter with him?" Neal asks.

"I don't know," Malora says. Then to Sky, "What's wrong, boy? It's too early to stop. We've got to keep going. We've got to find Zephele."

Her legs tire of kicking him and she saws at the bit instead. Sky's mouth foams, and he backs up six paces for every two going forward. Malora wonders whether he has eaten a plant that might have sickened him, but Sky knows better.

They come to a large, round concavity in the earth. It looks like a vast abandoned elephant wallow from which the water has evaporated. But these are not elephant tracks that she sees printed in the hardened cake of mud. They are the same centaur tracks they have been following. Hooves have churned up the earth, which is dark red in places. This, Malora concludes with a sickening thudding of her heart, is what they have both been smelling: blood turning rancid in the sun's heat. Sky starts to trot around the bowl, as if trapped by an invisible fence. He pauses now and then to give off a foal-like whinny.

Neal stands in the middle of the bowl and scans the ground, then looks up and warily follows Sky with his eyes.

Sky rears, his hooves churning the air. Malora hangs on, waiting until all four hooves are back on the ground. Then she slips off his back before she is dumped off.

"Calm down, big boy. It's all right," she says. But it is far from all right, she thinks. She continues to speak to him in a low, soothing voice.

Muttering, Sky gradually settles down, his ears flicking forward as he listens to her instead of his fears.

"Good boy," Malora says softly. Then to Neal, "They were here."

"I know," Neal says. "But what happened here?"

Malora hands Neal Sky's reins. "Hold on tight. He may spook and bolt."

Neal nods and takes the reins, making calming sounds to Sky.

"*He* knows what happened here," Malora says. She walks in slow circles examining the churned-up ground.

Finally, she returns to Neal and Sky. "It's the Leatherwings," she says. "Leatherwings attacked the centaurs here."

"You're absolutely sure?" he asks.

Malora nods slowly, not wanting it to be true.

Neal looks around, his mouth a grim line. "But wouldn't the Leatherwings leave tracks?" he asks.

"They don't touch down," Malora says. "They swoop and pluck up their prey." And in her head, Lume's words echo: "They are ground-huggers and blood-suckers."

In stunned silence, they stare up at the sky, hoping something will appear that will contradict this heart-shattering conclusion. Gradually, they both become aware of the sound of pounding hoofbeats drawing closer. They look toward the river and see Orion galloping toward them, flanked by two of the Peacekeepers. Orion's white wrap is mired with dust, and his black curls are plastered to his forehead with sweat. Has he run all the way from Mount Kheiron? Malora wonders.

"Finally!" Orion gasps, skidding to a halt and clutching his chest with both hands. "You had a day's lead on us. I thought we'd never catch up to you! We have news!" He stops to lean an arm on one of the Peacekeeper's shoulders as he fights to catch his breath. "We were wrong!" he says, panting.

"About what?" Malora asks.

"About the wild centaurs," Orion says. "All this was just to throw us off. While they made their getaway north with Zeph."

Malora and Neal exchange a look, mouths agape. Then they collapse into each other's arms, limp with relief. Neal growls at Orion over Malora's shoulder, "You had better be right about this, Silvermane."

Orion says, "Believe me, I am. The port captain brought in one of his workers. The hauler had been lying unconscious behind some bales of flax. He'd been clobbered over the head—by two male centaurs dragging a female along the docks. The female had *gold-painted hooves* and a burlap sack over her head."

Neal claps Orion on the back. "Did you hear that, Malora?" Neal says to her. "The Leatherwings didn't eat our girl, after all!"

"I heard!" Malora says happily.

Orion narrows his eyes at them. "What in the world are you two going on about?"

"Nothing!" Malora says.

"Never mind," Neal says, grinning.

Giving them both a wary look, Orion goes on, "They stole a pack boat and are probably halfway to the Downs by now."

"Then what are we standing around here for?" Neal says with a lusty clap of hands. "After them! Onward to Ixion!"

That the Leatherwings have begun to range far north of the Ironbounds and have made an attack within a day's ride of Mount Kheiron is something Malora can give no further thought to right now. Finding Zephele comes first.

"To Ixion!" Malora cries.

CHAPTER 20

Knobkerrie

Malora leads Sky along the docks toward the Apex's blue-and-white-painted barge, bobbing on the river's current. When her traveling companions—Neal, Honus, and Orion—see her coming, they shake their heads in unison. The message from them is clear: *Sky stays.*

"Not this time, pet," Neal says. "It's bad enough that the Learned Master is coming along."

"I heard that," Honus says, looking up from a crate of food he is tying down with a rope. "You never know when having someone *learned* along will come in handy."

Malora says, "Even if I wanted to leave him behind—which I don't—he wouldn't stay."

"But a stallion on a barge . . . ," Neal says helplessly.

"Is it really so different from a *centaur* on a barge?" Malora asks.

"It is not. But two clumsy quads aboard are more than enough, thank you," Neal says. "Turn around and take him back to the paddock. West will figure out what to do with him."

"Sky doesn't listen to West. He only listens to me," Malora says. "Believe me, you want him along. The wild centaurs are afraid of him. Do I have to remind you that they think he's a god?"

Neal gives Sky a pointed look. "Will *you* listen to reason, even if *she* won't? You'll hate being on the water. I know I do, but I have no choice. It's the fastest way to the Downs."

Sky stretches out his hind legs, lifts his tail, and sends a stream of urine splashing down onto the dock.

"*Another* excellent reason for banning horses on board this vessel," Neal says. "At least the rest of us know to aim our streams overboard."

Malora makes one last attempt. "He'll remember the safe route through the Downs better than I will."

Neal tosses up his arms in surrender. "Keep him directly amidships and *make sure he stays there!*"

"Thank you, Captain," Malora says, leading Sky on board.

After she has parked Sky's saddlebag and her Kavian snake stick, she and Sky pick their way around the deck. She lets him sniff and poke his nose into everything, discovering in the process that there are four crossbows, two spears, Neal's buffalo-whacker, a Bushman's Friend—the long dagger with a snakeskin hilt that is poking out of the top of Honus's trousers—and that Orion carries what she thinks is a Pantherian blowgun.

She asks Orion, "Do you know how to use that thing?"

Orion smiles ruefully. "A little."

"He's too modest," Neal says. "Silvermane's a sharp-shooter. We used to play at being river pirates. We both had blowguns. Orrie here could hit a frog between the eyes from fifty paces. Pushing off now. Brace yourselves, everyone."

Malora stands next to Sky as Orion casts off. She feels Sky plant all four hooves as the deck beneath them starts moving and rocking. Never having been on a boat herself, Malora feels almost as leery as Sky. She has thrown Jayke's rope around Sky's neck, just to be safe.

"With any luck," says Honus, "we will collide with Zeph-ele's abductors before they even arrive at Ixion."

"I doubt that," Neal says grimly. "But we will make the best possible time."

As they are floating upriver past the paddocks, Malora waves to West and the other wranglers, who raise paws in salutation. The horses gallop back and forth along the fence line. Shadow calls out to Sky as if to say, *Where are you going? You just got here!* The horses from Ixion say, *Take us with you! We don't care how dangerous it is!* Thunder merely tosses his mane and says, *Don't tell me you're going back there! You must be crazy!* Sky, ever his own horse, doesn't answer any of them, but Malora can feel the tension in his body as he braces his legs and growls low in his chest.

It isn't long before waves of nausea overtake Malora. She wonders if the dates she ate for breakfast were bad. She leans into Sky and closes her eyes, hoping it will pass. She dozes woozily on her feet. Suddenly, she staggers as Sky erupts from under her. She hears Orion and Neal call out just as Sky leaps over the barge's rail into the river. Malora is left holding Jayke's rope in her hand.

"Sky!" Malora runs over to the rail. "Come back here!" But Sky is swimming steadily toward the bank.

"Well, *that's* a relief," says Neal.

"Will he return to the paddocks?" Honus asks.

Sky wades up onto the bank and shakes himself from mane to tail. "I hope so," Malora says. But Sky faces north and begins to amble along the riverbank, keeping pace with the barge.

"He seems to be following us," Orion says.

"Oh, Sky! No!" Malora says. "He'll never be able to keep up with us. Maybe I should get out and go with him."

"Not a good idea, pet," Neal says.

Neal is right. As badly as Malora wants to dive off the barge and join Sky, she knows it's important to stay with the others. The quickest and surest way to Zephele is by water. A barge doesn't have to stop to graze and sleep.

"Take care, Sky," she calls out as the barge overtakes him.

Malora spends a good portion of the rest of the day with her head hanging over the side, emptying the dregs of her stomach into the river. "You had the right idea, Sky," she says bitterly as she stares down into the murky waters of the Neelah.

Orion offers her a scent from his traveling case. "It's largely ginger," he says. "It will calm your stomach."

But her nausea is stronger than Orion's scent, which only makes her gag.

There is a brazier in the cabin where Honus cooks their meals. The aroma of this, too, makes Malora retch. But Honus brews her cups of chamomile tea, and eventually she is able to keep them down along with a few crusts of bread. She finds that if she fixes her eyes on objects along the shore, her gorge rises. But if she allows her eyes to relax and skim the landscape at the same rate the boat is moving, her stomach settles.

The others stay busy. There is always one of them in the prow to keep watch and one of them in the stern manning the rudder, which is also an oar. It is nighttime when Malora is able to move around without feeling sick. She joins Honus in the prow, where he sweeps a lantern back and forth over the river before them. The smells—weeds and mud and fish—nearly set her off again. They remind her of her death or, as she prefers to think of it, *near death*. The familiar smoky tang of bush sage and river lilies calms her. And if she looks directly overhead, she is actually soothed. It is like gliding down a river made of stars. She wonders where Lume is right now. She wonders where her horse is. She asks Honus, "Have you seen Sky?"

"Oh, he's out there. Every so often, the lantern catches the flash of a blue eye," Honus says.

"Oh good," Malora says, squaring her shoulders. "Well. I think I'm ready to be useful now."

"Excellent," Honus replies. "I was just about to go river-blind." He hands her a whistle and the lantern. "Keep a look-out for menaces to navigation—branches, sandbars, rocks, elephants, crocodiles, hippos, what have you. If you see something, blow the whistle and guide the helmsman around the obstacle. We're moving quickly, so reacting quickly and signaling clearly are essential. I will go below and brew you up a stimulating tea."

After Honus delivers her tea, he stays to enjoy a pipe. Malora swings the lantern toward the dark bank. "What was Athen like when you knew him?" she asks.

Honus says, without taking his eyes from the river, "He was my first pupil, my greatest challenge and my greatest failure. He was, in some fundamental way that I will never understand, *untutorable*. Once, he was so frustrated that he picked me up bodily and threw *me* across the room. He was always apologetic afterward. But even when he was happy, there was always the threat that it would not last."

"He was difficult to live with," Malora says.

"I'm not sure the Silvermanes will ever admit this—even to themselves—but it was a relief when Athen 'died.' It was as if a great, dark cloud had blown away, letting in the sunshine." After a moment, Honus says, "My guess is that Athen came to believe the Apex was behind the theft of his horses."

Malora nods, not needing Honus to be any more explicit than this. She flies the Apex's colors over her paddocks. Athen came to claim his horses and saw the flag. Athen concluded that the Apex had sent Malora to Ixion to liberate the horses. Rather than simply taking the horses back, Athen sought revenge on his father by taking Zephele hostage. She asks Honus, "Do you think he will harm Zephele?" It is hard for Malora to imagine anyone being angry with Zephele.

"Athen is a good deal like the Apex in many respects. Zephele knows how to humor the Apex. She should be able to handle Athen."

"I hope you're right," Malora says.

She remains on watch for the rest of the night and sleeps

much of the next day. While she sleeps, she senses Sky following along the bank, wading in the river, grazing on the grass, rolling in the dust. She wakes up to the sight of the Hills of Melea sliding past, purple against the pale blue sky.

That night, Orion takes the first watch while Neal works the rudder. Malora joins Orion.

"You should get some rest before your watch," he tells her.

"I slept all day," she says. The river sweeps past, black and cloaked in a smoky mist that reminds Malora of her flight with Lume. After a while, she says, "I'm sorry I didn't tell you about Athen."

"You did what you thought was best," Orion says, his pale eyes unreadable in the darkness.

"I shouldn't have kept secrets from you," Malora says. "You're my friend."

"We all keep secrets," Orion says. "Even from friends."

They both fall silent, lulled by the river and the lantern light rocking back and forth. At some point, Orion says, "I was dazzled by Athen, even though I was half his age and outshone him in the classroom. He was very strong and sure of himself—and he had a wicked sense of humor. He had Zephele's gift of being able to light up any room he walked into, but he had to be in the right mood. If he wasn't, he cast the most terrible pall. He had a band of friends, mostly from the Flatlands. I always thought he was born to be a Flatlander, but now I see that he was born to lead his own 'herd.'"

"Mather says he has never been happier," Malora says. "Life for the wild centaurs has improved under his rule, even if it is at the expense of horses' lives."

They settle into another silence. A baboon heckles. Wild dogs howl. Orion says, "I've never told this to anyone before."

Malora waits. Finally, he begins: "This was years ago, a year or so before we lost Athen. I was on my way back from the Flats one evening, where I had been playing with Neal. I saw a centaur moving along the riverbank. At first, I thought it was a Flatlander gathering herbs or cress, but then I saw it was Athen. And it wasn't herbs or cress he was gathering. It was rocks."

"Why rocks?"

"He told me he was going to fill his wrap so that when he walked into the river they would weigh him down and he would drown." Orion digs thumb and finger into his eyes and holds them there briefly before removing his hand and continuing. "He told me that life was agony for him, that he brought only misery to those he loved, and that he had decided to end it."

He laughs bitterly.

"He even asked me to help choose the heaviest rocks. Not only did I refuse to help him, but I begged and pleaded with him not to harm himself. I told him that if he destroyed himself our mother was as good as dead. I told him we all loved him." He stopped, as if struck by his own words. "I meant it, too, when I said it, in spite of all the pain and grief he had visited upon us. Finally, he put down the rocks and came home with me, almost docile. Later on, when he disappeared and everyone said the hippos had gotten him, I simply assumed he had finally succeeded in finding enough heavy rocks to do the job."

Malora sees tears standing in Orion's eyes. She takes his

free hand and squeezes it gently. "I'm glad he didn't kill himself," she says.

"Yes," Orion says. "No matter what happens, I am, too."

Early in the morning, eight days later, the mist is thinning so that Malora, from the bow where she is on watch, can finally see Honus at the stern. She hears a loud whinny and spots Sky on the eastern bank.

"Shhh!" she calls out to him, because the two centaurs are still asleep.

But it quickly becomes clear that this is not a social call. Sky is agitated, pacing, rearing higher at each turn. She tests the air with her nose. It isn't lions. It is something else. It is the musty scent of mice trapped in walls. Then she hears it, a drone like a giant swarm of angry bees headed their way. She fumbles for the whistle, but no sound comes. She spits out the whistle and shouts, "Take cover! Leatherwings!"

The centaurs heave up from their bedrolls, wide-eyed and yelling. Malora abandons her post to fetch her spear, colliding with Orion in search of his own weapon. Neal stands on the deck, hooves planted, sword gripped in both hands, facing skyward. As she is screwing the spear together, she glances back to see that Honus is no longer at the stern. Where is he? The next moment, there is the sound of splintering wood. The barge has collided with something. Malora is slammed to the deck, her left elbow catching the impact. Waves of pain run up her arm. She gasps, shakes out the arm, and hoists the spear just in time. All at once the world seems to darken, the sky lowering. The air is alive with beating wings.

One of them swoops down upon her. As a girl, she had

never dared look up for fear of drawing Sky's eye to them, but now she stares directly into the crafty black eyes of her foe. His small round head, eerily mannish, is topped with tufts of dusty brown fur. Fangs pinch withered black lips. His outstretched arms, encased in the leathery wings, dip down to envelop her. His hind legs cycle fiercely as the talons protract and prepare to seize her. She jabs the spear at his protuberant underbelly, what her mother had once counseled her was the weak spot. But he shrinks away from her spear point, sneering and hissing. A moment later, he rears up with a shriek, his head exploding in a bloody cloud. She staggers backward as the Leatherwing settles onto the deck before her with a sigh, as if he were just resting, but she knows he is dead.

The noxious odor of the Leatherwings is temporarily washed away by the familiar, ever-so-much more wholesome storm-scent. Lume lands on the deck next to the body. He wedges a foot beneath it and casually kicks the corpse overboard. Then he rinses the blood off the rounded knob of a wooden club in river water that now swamps the deck.

"Thank you, knobkerrie," he says, bowing to the club's knob.

Taking Malora's arm, he says grimly, "You. You're coming with me."

CHAPTER 21

Wings

Malora casts about frantically. Five more Leatherwings have swooped down upon them. Neal has sliced off the end of one wing, and Orion is holed up in the amidships cabin, the barrel of his blowgun poking out, aimed upward. She cannot see Honus and fears he may already have been seized. It is happening all over again. Leatherwings will destroy everyone she loves.

"No!" she tells Lume, shaking her arm free of his grip.

Lume moves behind her, elbow hooked around her shoulders and neck. She feels his lips at her ear. "Look there, Malora Thora-Jayke. See?" he rasps. "This is what happens when you try to live your long happy life in Mount Kheiron with your friends. You're coming with me."

She struggles against him, but she is no match for him. Gathering her up, spear and all, he lifts her from the deck of the sinking barge, weaving his way through the Leatherwings. Almost instantly, he sets her down on the riverbank.

Sky has whipped himself into a frenzy. He runs toward them and begins to circle, mane and tail whipping. Turning, she watches him helplessly. How can she calm him when he is right to be mad with terror? She sees his blue eyes flash with fear and something else. Outrage. She hears the creak of his leg joints, the air whistling in and out of his mouth and nose. She can smell the ripeness of his sweat. The lope escalates into a gallop.

"There. See?" Lume raises one arm and points at Sky, and that is when she sees it. It is as if the scars from the Leather-wings have come alive, dancing and whipping above Sky's back like black lightning.

"Kheiron's *hocks!*" Malora shouts.

Sky gallops on as the black lightning extrudes further and forms itself into a set of great black wings.

"My horse!" she cries, and looks to Lume for an explanation.

"I first saw this happen when I was flying over Ixion," he says. "The wild centaurs were so terrified, I thought they'd turn tail and run into the sea. But Archon ordered them to catch him in a fishing net. I don't think your horse quite knew what to make of the wings at first, but I think he does now, don't you, Horse?"

Sky grinds to a standstill before them, the great black wings half-furled behind him. They are not beautiful, white-feathered wings like Lume's. They are tough and leathery and black like those of their enemy. Sky snorts and tosses his mane.

"What are you waiting for?" Lume says to Malora. "Mount your horse and follow me into battle."

Malora isn't sure she wants to get on Sky's back. What if he begins to show other traits of the Leatherwings, like fangs or talons? Can this really be her horse?

"While you stand here dithering," Lume says, "your friends are losing ground to the Leatherwings. They've already got the faun."

Sky noses his way into her armpit and blows out, as if to reassure her that he is still himself—and hers.

"Okay," she whispers to him, stroking his neck. "Okay. Honus will have an explanation for this later, but right now he needs saving." She backs away from him slowly. As if he knows what she wants, he folds one wing out of her way. With the spear, she vaults onto his back, grabbing his mane with her free hand. He spreads his wings as Lume takes flight back toward the melee on the river. Sky follows Lume in a soaring arc. Malora's body braces to absorb the shock, as it would if the horse were still earthbound. But there is none. She might be riding the horse, but the horse is riding the air, and the sensation is strangely weightless. Her feet, resting on the roots of his wings, ground her better than any stirrup ever has. She lifts the spear and cocks it over her shoulder as they follow Lume flying well above the Leatherwings. She cannot see through the chaos to the centaurs below. Are her friends holding their own?

"Up here!" a strangled voice cries out. Malora looks up and sees Honus's hooves dangling high in the air above her, kicking feebly. Then she sees his terrified face staring down at her, pale and slack with shock. A Leatherwing's talons grasp him by the back of his coat, lifting him ever higher. The fabric saws at his neck as he struggles.

Lume shouts back to Malora, "I'll harry him toward you! Maim him however you can, and I will catch the faun!"

He had better catch the faun, Malora thinks, or the fall will kill him as surely as the Leatherwing. And how is she to maim him when Honus's body protects the creature's underbelly? Lume circles around and flies above the Leatherwing. He blocks its ascent with the force of his beating wings, which are wider and overpower those of his opponent. Then he darts behind him and thrashes the creature's barbed tail with his club, chasing him toward Malora. Honus has covered his head with his arms. She waits until she can feel the carnivorous heat of the Leatherwing's breath and looks for a spot to pierce. His head is too small, and he flicks it constantly back and forth. The tendons in his neck are thick and radiate down from his head like the spokes of wheel. She looks below the neck and thinks she can see where his heart beats a hand's breadth above Honus's cowering head.

"Don't move, Honus!" she calls out as she aims the spear and, heeling Sky, drives it forward and upward to meet the Leatherwing. The spear finds its mark.

Her foe lets out a strangled cry. Blood rains down upon her. Before she can pull back and free the point of her spear, he has a death grip on it. Even if she were willing to relinquish her weapon, his dead weight has settled on Sky's neck, dragging all three of them earthward. I have the wrong weapon, she thinks too late. She only hopes Lume made good on his plan to catch Honus, for they are all falling together. At the last moment, Sky gives his head and shoulders a mighty rattle, breaking the Leatherwing's lock. The spear cracks in half. Lume swoops down and plucks Honus from the limp talons. The Leatherwing spirals headfirst, splashing into the Neelah. Sky, wings pumping, climbs upward.

Afterward, they sprawl on the western bank. The barge has sunk. The crocodiles have arrived, having passed up the temptation of eating the six Leatherwings, whose corpses the current had carried downriver. But the crocodiles have made it impossible to salvage any of the cargo. Malora and company have managed to escape with their lives, most of their weapons, Jayke's rope, an oilcloth bag of salt, two flasks, and the leather satchel containing Honus's journal, writing implements, and toilet kit.

Sky grazes calmly nearby, tail switching, as if none of this ever happened. No one has made any mention of his wings, which seem to have vanished into the scar tissue on his back.

Orion and Neal lie on their sides bickering listlessly over which of them killed more Leatherwings, Orion with the darts from his blowgun or Neal with his sword.

Lume, who has flown off to make sure there are no more Leatherwings, returns just in time to settle the dispute. "You each got one and a half. I finished them off with my knobkerrie."

"Is that what you call it?" Neal says.

"It's an executioner's club, from the far southern reaches," Lume says. "I find it serves me well."

"Crude but effective," Neal says, giving the club a grudging nod of approval. He heaves himself up to a sitting position and raises his left hand palm out, placing the other over his heart. "Neal Featherhoof. I am pleased to meet you. You must be Lume, the Wonder Boy."

"Lume will do, soldier," Lume says coldly.

Orion, groaning, sits up, too, and manages to salute. "Orion Silvermane," he croaks.

"Son of the Apex of Kheiron," Lume says. "And alchemist."

Orion shrugs, as if neither of these were of much consequence. He waves in the general direction of Honus. "That's Honus. Polymath."

"The polymath and I have met," Lume says. He sinks to the ground, his wings folding neatly behind him like a pair of crossed quivers.

"Gallant Rescuer," Honus says with an airy salute. He rubs the ugly red mark around his neck but is otherwise unharmed. Twirling a blue flower in his fingers, he contemplates the *Triteleia grandiflora* with a nearly blissful expression.

Malora knows how he feels. The pleasure of being alive pulses through her limbs. But it isn't just that. After a lifetime of fearing the Leatherwings, of watching them destroy everyone she loved, she has finally gotten some of their own back— even if it was, as Lume points out, just a small hunting party. It doesn't get her mother and father and Aron and the people of the Settlement back. But it is *something*. She wants to tell Lume how thankful she is to him for helping her achieve this sweet victory, but she doesn't want to do it in front of the others. Instead she settles for saying "I, for one, am happy to be alive."

"Hear hear," Honus concurs.

"And," Neal adds, "we even wound up on the right side of the river."

"How far away are we from the Downs, do you reckon?" Orion asks.

"At least six days on foot," Neal replies, "maybe seven, *and* we have no supplies. I hate to say this, but we should consider returning to Mount Kheiron to reoutfit ourselves."

"No," Malora says firmly. "We've come this far. I can get us the rest of the way. This doesn't have to change anything."

"Oh, excellent," Orion says, lying back down.

"What are you talking about?" Lume bursts out. "This changes *everything*!"

They stare at him in surprise.

"What's wrong with you all!" He is on his feet again, staring down at them as if they have lost their minds. "You must return to Mount Kheiron without delay and warn them of the danger."

Malora remembers the evidence they saw of a Leatherwing attack even closer to Mount Kheiron than this one. But neither she nor Neal breathed a word of it to Medon. Rescuing Zephele has always been their only thought. It still is. Lume doesn't understand.

Neal says, "We will warn them. *After* we find Zephele and bring her home. I think the Apex himself would condone our making this a priority."

"She *is* his favorite," Orion adds.

Lume looks to Malora to make sense of this for him. "Zephele is but one, and the Kheironites are many."

Malora climbs to her feet and goes to him. "We have to do this, Lume. We can't let the wild centaurs have Zephele. You said yourself they're capable of unspeakable savagery."

Lume's head droops in defeat.

As gently as she can, Malora adds, "You don't know what it's like, to love someone so much you can't bear the thought of losing her."

He gives her a long and deeply resentful look.

"I'm sorry," Malora says, flustered. "Maybe you do know, in which case you should be able to understand why we're doing this."

He sets his jaw and shakes his head quickly. "Very well. I will fly to Mount Kheiron and warn them myself."

"Well done, Wonder!" Honus crows.

"But will they believe you?" Orion asks.

"They'll disbelieve him at their own peril," Neal says. "Demand an audience with the Apex. Tell him exactly what happened. Spare no detail. Tell him to station the Peacekeepers along the wall and four more in the dome facing in each direction. Tell him to enlist every blacksmith in the city to start forging weapons. Brion knows what we need. Everyone must be—"

Lume interrupts. "Soldier, I can only give him the warning," he says. "I cannot tell the Apex of Kheiron what to do."

"You're right," Neal says ruefully.

"But a little friendly advice won't hurt," adds Orion.

"I'll do what I can," Lume says. He turns toward the river. In another moment he will be gone.

"Wait!" Malora says. She takes his hand and draws him farther away from the others.

"What now?" he says, frowning. "I'm in a hurry, as you can see."

Why does being near Lume make her feel thrummingly alive and yet like a large clumsy child with a tongue full of knots?

Seemingly unaware of her difficulty, he looks beyond her to the others. "So these are the friends that had you scurrying home to Mount Kheiron."

She nods. "Along with Zephele, yes."

"I like them," he says. "I had fun with them."

"I thought you said you didn't need company, that you were your own best companion," Malora says boldly.

His eyes sweep briefly over her. "So I did. I must be changing. Look, I really have to go now. There is no time to lose."

She blurts, "We wouldn't have made it out alive without you!"

"That's true," he replies evenly. "See that you take care, since you will be without me for the foreseeable future."

"After this, I think we could survive anything," she says.

His frown deepens. "It's dangerous even to *think* that. Returning to the wild centaurs is folly. Your friends are as stubborn and foolish as you are. You have no idea—"

She cuts in with force: *"I'm trying to tell you how thankful I am to you for helping us!"*

A smile breaks through the frown. The dimple in his left cheek appears. She wants to move closer and run her lips over that dimple.

There is a glint in his eye, as if he were daring her to act on the impulse. Taking a step closer to her, he says in a very soft voice, "If you want to thank me, Malora, just say the words."

"Thank you!" she says, feeling more foolish than ever.

"There. That wasn't so hard, was it?" He lifts his hand and works his thumb along her jawline. "You are very welcome, Malora Thora-Jayke. And if you were not covered in Leatherwing gore," he says, "I might even be tempted to kiss you."

He turns away from her, and with a powerful stroke of his wings he is up and soaring away without so much as a backward glance.

Each time he leaves, she thinks, she misses him a little more. Sky goes dashing off after him, whinnying up at Lume, as if to call him back.

Malora trudges back to her friends.

"So that's Lume," Orion says musingly.

"That's Lume," Malora says, turning to watch his dwindling form.

"Do you think Sky will follow him all the way back to Mount Kheiron?" Neal wonders.

"Birds of a feather," Honus says breezily.

Kneeling by the river, Malora washes the blood off her face. "I doubt it," she says, rising and wiping her chin on the hem of her tunic. "I think Sky's just seeing him off. I think he likes the Wonder."

"Sky isn't the only one," Orion says, gently teasing.

Malora blushes and loops Jayke's rope over one shoulder. She looks around at them. "Well!" she says, just to be filling the silence.

Honus says, "I know *I'm* in love." He is only half-joking.

"You just say that because he saved your life," Neal says.

"That might have something to do with it," Honus muses. "But he's an engaging fellow. And those dazzling white feathers . . . I wonder if he'll take me up with him again sometime. Under less stressful conditions . . ."

Neal, narrowing his eyes in thought, turns slowly to Malora. "Is he the one I nearly shot with my bow and arrow?"

Malora blushes. "Turns out, it was."

A slow smile spreads across Neal's lips. "Good thing you stopped me."

She shrugs. "He claims you would have missed," she says.

"Hmmm . . ." Neal strokes his beard thoughtfully.

"Wonder all you like about the Wonder," Orion says, getting to his feet. "This isn't getting Zeph back."

Honus rises with a groan. They gather up their meager supplies and, as quickly as that, are on their way again on foot.

In the aftermath of the attack, they are all hungry. Neal's sword is useless for hunting, and they agree not to risk losing any of Orion's remaining darts on game. There are no ostriches here, so there will be no lassoing them with Jayke's rope.

"I'm a hunter, not a gatherer," Neal says, deferring to Malora.

Now that they are back on land, she is comfortable leading and sets to gathering what's edible as they go—wild berries and hard, tart-tasting fruits and plants whose gritty roots she digs up with her bare hands. That night, their stomachs are hollow and growling. As if that weren't bad enough, it rains, and they sleep huddled miserably together beneath a tree. Malora has the first watch, followed by Neal. At sunrise, she is the last to wake up to the sight of everyone staggering toward the river to drink. She stops them with a shout.

"Give the silt time to settle to the bottom!" she says.

Neal spits out a mouthful and nods. "Of course. I knew that."

She is pleased to share what she knows with her friends. While they walk along and wait to slake their thirst, she teaches them how to fold a leaf and make a cup to scoop up the drinking water. When she finally gives them permission, they fall to their knees and scoop up cup after cup. Malora fills the flasks.

By the end of the second day, their mouths have broken out in sores from the tartness of the fruit.

"Is there anything else on the menu?" Neal says plaintively. "I'd settle for bugs at this point."

"I will see what I can do," Malora says.

They watch as Malora hunts around the weedlike shrubs that grow along the riverbank. "Flannel bush," she explains as she cuts several stems and begins twisting them up. She looks up from her work and says, "Can someone catch me some grasshoppers?"

Orion makes a face. "We're not going to eat them, are we? Neal was just joking."

"Grasshoppers happen to be very tasty, roasted over a fire," Malora says. "But no, they're just bait."

Orion and Neal stumble all over each other chasing a single grasshopper along the riverbank, but it is Honus, the collector, who manages to catch several in his cupped hands and deliver them to Malora.

"Orion, can you please fetch me a big thorn from that acacia over there? Watch you don't hurt yourself, they're sharp."

Orion brings back the thorn, and they watch as she ties it to one end of what is now a long string fashioned from the twisted stems of the flannel bush.

"You *are* good," Neal says in grudging admiration. "I am officially in awe. Without you, I'd have been guzzling mud and chewing clods of dirt by now."

"An entire fishing apparatus, improvised from nature. What a remarkable feat!" Orion says.

Malora grins crookedly. "Only if the fish actually bite."

Honus says, "Are you ready for your grasshopper, Malora?"

She nods. Honus opens his hands long enough for her to pinch one of the grasshoppers between two fingers.

Impaling it on the thorn, she tosses the end of the line, twitching grasshopper and all, into the middle of the river, then settles back on the riverbank to wait. "This may take some time. Honus, do you know a puzzle bush and a silver bush when you see them?"

"I most assuredly do," Honus says.

"Go and find them. With your Bushman's Friend, cut me a straight branch from each. Your puzzle bush is the twirling stick, and your silver bush is the rubbing stick."

"We're going to make *fire*!" Honus says with zeal.

"*You're* going to make fire. I'm going to hold this line and wait for a fish to get interested. Neal, see if you can find us some dry tinder beneath the bigger trees. And some stones for a fire circle. And, Honus, after you've found me the fire sticks, see if you can't track down a velvet raisin bush. Orion, go with him and collect everything from it: leaves, branches, roots, stems, seeds, fruit."

"Whatever for?" Orion asks.

"Everything!" Malora says cheerfully.

Orion smiles at her. "Thora's daughter watches over us!"

Over time, with the help of another six of Honus's

grasshoppers, Malora manages to pull three big bass from the river. They flop and leap about on the bank like living silver. One by one, she whacks them against the rocks and guts them and scales them with her knife. When the fire is ready, she coats them with salt, wraps them in damp leaves, and sets them in the coals to steam. When the fish is cooked, they sit around the fire eating it, all except for Orion, who looks on with a squeamish expression.

Malora says to him, "I know you have never eaten the flesh of a living thing, Orrie, but you won't be much good to Zephele if you can't keep up your strength."

She arranges some of the flaky white meat on a fresh green leaf and places it in his hands. "Try it. For Zephie."

"For Zephie," he agrees. He tastes it tentatively, then with more enthusiasm. "A little muddy-tasting, but not bad at all!"

Afterward, they sit around and pick their teeth with twigs from the velvet raisin bush, propped around the fire shoulder to shoulder.

Having real food in their stomachs makes them more talkative than they have been since they set out on foot. Neal leads the way: "Tell us, pet, did you know all along that your horse was a hibe and just neglected to mention that niggling detail to us?"

Malora says, "When I got him back from Ixion, I noticed a change in him. It was as if his bones had been altered. But I thought it was malnutrition, or something the wild centaurs had done to him."

"Then he was some sort of latent hibe?" Orion asks.

"He's not a hibe," Honus says.

They all turn to look at him. He holds a stick in his mouth, favoring it as if it were his pipe.

"Then what is he?" Neal asks.

"My guess is that when the Leatherwings attacked him years ago, the wounds they inflicted festered and introduced some sort of toxin into his system. A lesser creature might have died, but Sky's body fought the invasion by gradually taking on some of the physical properties of his attackers. It is a kind of defensive mutation."

Malora recalls aloud Lume's words: "He's a miracle horse."

"Do you mean," says Neal, "that if the Leatherwings scratched me, I'd grow wings, too?" His face is suddenly alight with the possibilities.

Honus says, "It is not beyond the realm of possibility."

"In that case," Neal says, leaning back with his arms crossed, "I regret defending myself so successfully. Next time, I'll let the Leatherwings have at me."

"Then again," Honus adds blithely, "you might just die instead."

"True," Neal says wistfully. "Still, it would be worth the risk to have wings."

"I think Zephele might think otherwise," Malora says.

Neal heaves a wistful sigh, whether over Zephele or wings it is hard to tell.

The next morning, they are awakened by the sound of approaching hoofbeats. Sky trots into their camp, covered in dust, trailing a baby zebra in his wake.

"You've found a new friend!" Malora says to the horse.

"Well, look at that!" says Neal. "A mount for Honus."

Malora grins. "Honus can ride with me on Sky."

Honus looks intrigued. "Do you think Sky would let me fly on his back sometime soon?"

"Maybe. But something tells me it takes a crisis to bring out the wings," Malora says.

Honus holds up a hand. "In that case, I'll settle for riding on the ground for now."

CHAPTER 22

The Gallery of Masterpieces

"Step only where Sky steps," Malora cautions Neal and Orion endlessly.

Since dawn, they have been working their way through the Downs, Malora leading the way on Sky's back with Honus clinging to her like a burr. In keeping with her theory of sinkholes, they leap from dune to dune, bypassing the sinkholes that might lie in the valleys. The zebra, whom they have taken to calling Baby, wallows in their wake, in spite of Malora's attempts to chase her off. *Poor thing doesn't know what she's gotten herself into.*

Malora has just caught the first whiff of the sea, when Baby clamors ahead of them, up to the top of the next dune, and turns to wait for them. Sky is just reassuring her with a low nicker that he is coming when the baby zebra begins to sink into the top of the dune. Sky leaps forward.

"No, Sky!" Malora screams.

But there is no controlling her horse as he lunges to the

aid of the zebra. The zebra is sinking fast. Only her black-and-white head shows, mouth agape, as she bleats in terror. And then it is as if the entire dune were collapsing in on itself, bringing down Sky with Malora and Honus on his back. Orion and Neal struggle to free themselves, but they go down, too. Malora grabs hold of Sky's mane and feels him falling down, down into the darkness, with Honus nearly strangling her in his own fear and desperation. Sky falling faster than she does, she quickly loses her seat. They continue to fall, and Malora is thinking, the farther we fall, the harder we will hit, when she lands on her side with a jarring thud that knocks the wind out of her and Honus's grip loose from her neck.

Darkness, stillness, silence follow. Malora catches her breath, surprised to be breathing air rather than sand. She moves her joints and tests her bones. Nothing seems to be broken. Beneath her is sand. It is the sand that cushioned her fall and saved her from fracturing every bone in her body. She hopes the others are as lucky. She is just about to call out to them when, from somewhere in the darkness, Neal says in a calm and conversational tone of voice, "So much for Malora's Theory of Sinkholes!"

She sits up, gropes around, and bumps into something hard.

"I beg your pardon?" Honus says.

It is his horn. She finds his face and pats it. "Are you all right?" she asks him.

"I'm not yet sure. I seem to have someone's hoof in my armpit."

The next moment, Malora hears a sharp little bleat.

"Baby!" she says. "The others?"

"The others," Orion calls out, "appear to be intact."

"Speak for yourself, Silvermane," says Neal. "And do you mind removing the tip of your blowgun from my ear?"

"Sorry!" Orion says.

"We're alive!" says Malora.

"Apparently," Neal says.

"The sinkholes aren't deadly, after all," Malora says.

"I'll believe that when we're back in the sunlight again," Neal says.

"There *is* sunlight," Malora says, squinting upward and pointing. "Look."

A thin shaft of sunlight beams down on them from above. As her eyes adjust, she can make out her friends in a grayish light, lying in a tangle in a pile of fine white sand.

But there is no Sky! Cupping her hands to her mouth, Malora calls him, her voice echoing strangely.

Relieved, she hears a dull *clip-clop* as Sky trots into view and shakes the sand out of his mane. He's been exploring. Malora says with a smile, "Show us the way out of here, big fellow."

The zebra bleats, heaves herself up out of the sand, and goes to Sky. Sky noses the zebra, making sure she is not hurt.

Sky turns tail and starts walking away from them, Baby tripping at his heels. Malora gets up to follow them and nearly slips and falls on her face. Sky turns around, concern in his eyes.

"I'm all right," she says. "Watch the footing," she warns the others. She reaches down and touches the floor. Through the thin film of grit, it feels slick and slippery. "It's like glass," she says.

The others get up slowly and dust the sand off, one by one easing themselves off the sand pile. Honus kneels and examines the floor. "It *is* glass." He looks around. "This entire place seems to be made of glass. And look there! Signs of habitation."

Honus points to the torches burning brightly in iron brackets, their orange-blue flames reflecting off the glass walls of what appears to be a vast underground cavern. He turns in a slow circle. "My guess is that all of this was once sand. When the meteor crashed, the heat from the impact was so intense that it turned everything that was sand into glass. Minerals in the sand cause the colorful streaking,"

"It's beautiful!" Orion says. "Like frozen fire!" He reaches out and runs his hand along the glass wall. "Ouch," he says. Pulling back, he holds up a finger, wet with blood.

"Let me see to that," Honus says, reaching for his kit in the pouch around his waist.

"It's just a small cut," Orion says.

"Nevertheless," Honus says, taking charge of the wound, "it wouldn't do to have a cut fester down here. The rest of you, don't touch the walls. The surface is irregular and has edges that can cut."

They wait in wary silence while Honus applies salve and a bandage to Orion's finger.

"I wonder," Neal says, "who put the torches down here."

"And who keeps them burning," Orion adds.

"Who else?" Malora says. "The wild centaurs. Ixion is up there somewhere."

"Either that," Honus says, "or the Beast from Below lights his own lair."

The thought makes them move closer together. Only Sky and Baby seem impatient to move off. They have both begun to paw at the gritty floor.

Malora says, "We need to find a way out of here before . . ." She stops short of finishing her thought: . . . *before the Beast finds us.*

As if Neal were thinking the same thing, he says, "Let's take stock of our weapons."

Neal still has the sword. Orion has the blowgun and four darts. Honus has his Bushman's Friend. Malora has Jayke's rope and the knife in her boot.

"And let's not forget," Orion says, "that we have a winged stallion that is held by the wild centaurs to be a god."

Malora, who has just stepped in a trail of the god's turds, mutters, "Wings won't do us much good under the ground. I'm thinking that Ixion should be somewhere northeast of here."

"But where is *here*? What's more, where is *north*?" Orion says.

"And east?" Neal adds.

"I have no idea, but let's just get moving," she says.

"The Ironbound Resolution: keep moving no matter what!" Neal says.

The fact is, she feels trapped and just this side of panicking. But the others expect her to continue to lead the trek, so lead she does. They move through a torchlit corridor as wide as the River Neelah. At times, the corridor widens so that the torches on either side wink in the distance. Now and then, they come upon a pile of bones, sometimes horse, sometimes centaur, along with other animals, large and small, all more or less intact skeletons.

"This is what would have happened to us if we hadn't landed in such a deep pile of sand," Malora says.

"Yes, but what ate the flesh off the bones?" Honus asks.

"Maybe there are rats down here," Malora says, peering into the shadows.

"Maybe it's the Beast," Orion says.

"It could be," Neal says. "But it seems to me that the Beast would have dragged the bones off to his lair."

"What if this entire place is his lair?" Orion asks.

Refusing to be spooked, Malora says, "I'm still thinking that scavengers had at these bones. Something small."

Malora strikes out again, picking up the pace. The air is stale and makes her feel light-headed. What if they wander down here until they starve? Time, when there is no real light to measure, stretches interminably. When the footing isn't sandy, her impala-skin boots get reasonably good purchase on the glass floors. Every so often, someone tells her to slow down.

"If one of us slips' and breaks something, it will bad," Neal says.

Malora slows down, but eventually she always speeds up again. She wants to see the sun or, if it's night now, the stars and the moon. She wants to feel the fresh sea air on her face. Behind her, the hooves of her companions move as soundlessly as her own feet, except for when they hit a patch of sand, and then they make a gritty, grating sound that plays on her nerves. Everyone wants to save the water in the two flasks.

Who knows how long they will be trapped? The cavern widens and brightens.

"Interesting!" Honus says.

They have come to a place where torches burn atop tall pillars set in a wide circle. In the center of the circle is a marble plinth with a large statue resting on top of it. The statue is of a giant lion sitting on its haunches. The lion has wings and the head of a woman, painted gold. The eyes are widely spaced and tightly shut, boldly lined with kohl, with the eyelids painted the bright blue of lapis lazuli. She wears a golden headdress studded with gems. Strewn at the foot of the boulder are all manner of bones and skulls.

Malora wants nothing to do with it, but Honus leads them closer. "It appears to be some sort of a sacrificial altar."

"Whoever made it, it's exquisitely wrought!" Orion exclaims, staring up at the statue.

"Eerily lifelike," Neal says without enthusiasm. "Let's move on."

"I'm with Neal," Malora says.

Lingering, Orion says, "Body of a lion, wings of an eagle, face of a human woman," he goes on thoughtfully, coming around to the front of the statue. He laughs uneasily. "Now *that's* a hibe you'll never see wandering the streets of Kahiro."

"No, you won't," says Honus. "But you'll hear tell of it. I believe this is the Sphinx. The legendary ancient Sphinx of Kahiro. If it is, it is certainly well preserved. And I had thought it was much larger than this, but legends tend to exaggerate."

Sky snorts in distaste and paws the floor. Malora is just about to reassure Sky that they are as good as gone from this scene, when she sees the statue's right eye twitch. "It just moved!" she whispers, her heart slamming against her ribs.

They all pull closer to Sky, who has pinned his ears and flared his nostrils. Baby scrambles to huddle beneath Sky's belly. They watch the creature on the pedestal shake itself from head to tail, as if casting off raindrops. The voluptuous lips, painted a deep crimson, part, revealing teeth sharpened to fine points. The painted eyes blink slowly and then open wide, swiveling in their sockets until they fix themselves on the visitors.

"You! Travelers!" the creature calls down to them in a hissing growl of a voice. "Remain where you stand!"

Malora reaches a hand into Sky's mane and takes a firm hold. If he runs, he is taking her with him. Honus's arm latches onto Malora. Orion and Neal edge closer to Honus. They stand in a small transfixed cluster before the creature hunkered down on the stone slab. She rises up on all fours, her long, tufted lion's tail switching, her body more than twice as large as any lion Malora has ever encountered in the bush, her wings as vast as Lume's and pale blue. A single sweep of her paw could easily separate Malora's head from her shoulders. Our weapons are useless, she thinks.

Malora hears herself speaking in a bold voice that betrays none of her terror: "You're the Beast from Below, aren't you?"

"You will call me Abu al Hul, the Terrifying One! And all who pass this way must answer any question I ask," she bellows.

"Is this a joke?" Neal mutters.

"If it is, it is of cosmic proportions," Honus mutters back.

"Honus, isn't she one of them?" Malora whispers. "You

know, one of the monsters you spoke about that results from the hibes inbreeding. Maybe this one survived infancy."

"An interesting theory, my dear," Honus says softly. "But I doubt it. The scale is too large. Besides, too much art and imagination went into the making of this creature. Far from being an accident, this creature here is what you might call a masterpiece."

"A masterpiece of *what*?" Neal asks, skepticism and disgust mingling in his voice.

"Of myth. Of imagination. Of whimsy. Of science. She is a masterpiece of the Scienticians. That would be my best guess," Honus says.

"I am waiting," the creature calls out, "for someone to volunteer to answer my question!"

"I'll try," Orion says, his hand shooting up.

"Shut up, Silvermane!" Neal snaps, slapping his hand down. "Can't you tell it's a trick? We're not answering any of your questions!" Neal calls up to the creature.

"Oh, you will!" the monster says silkily. "Or at least you will attempt to. The pretty little centaur stallion has volunteered to answer, so let us begin."

"No!" Honus speaks up. "Let *me* answer the question instead."

"Too late, goat-boy!" says the Sphinx. Turning to Orion, the creature says, "These are the rules, my delectable centaurean morsel: if you answer my question correctly, you may pass and continue on your journey. But if you answer it incorrectly, and you will, I get to eat you—one by one. I will start with the horse and work my way down, in order of descending size, picking my teeth with the bones of the little striped one. But first I will play with you. I do love to play with my food. I get so very bored down here, and food must serve as both entertainment and sustenance," she says, her mouth opening in a wide yawn, then closing with a snap.

Sky spooks and slews to the side, pulling the rest of them along with him.

"Judging from that pile of bones," Neal whispers to the rest of them, "it looks as if she's been very sufficiently entertained."

"Think very carefully before you open your mouth to answer the question," Honus cautions Orion.

"There may not be much meat on his bones but the little goat-man has a good head on his shoulders," says Abu al Hul.

"Thank you," Honus says.

"I shall look forward to picking your brain from the pan of your skull."

Honus pales as the creature sinks back onto her haunches. Then she folds her tail, crosses her paws, settles her shoulders, and stretches her neck. She clears her throat and stares at Orion: "Ready?"

Orion nods gravely. His eyes are wide. There are beads of sweat on his forehead and the dark stubble of his upper lip.

"Here is your question, then: what creature has the legs of a horse and the wings of a bird?"

Orion shakes his head, his face flooded with relief as he looks around at the others. "But this is too easy. The answer is simple: the horse standing here with us."

"That is *not* the correct answer!" the Sphinx says, her face flooding with greedy delight.

"Oh, but it is," Neal says. "Show the Sphinx your wings, Sky."

Sky dips his head mulishly.

"This horse has no wings," the Sphinx says with contempt.

Malora stares at Sky in dismay. Never has her horse looked more earthbound. "Please, Sky. Please show the nice lady your wings."

They all watch Sky, who stretches his hind legs and sends a small waterfall of urine splashing to the floor.

Malora shakes her head. "It's not a trick he can perform on command."

"No worries," Honus says. "I suspect the Sphinx has another, more classical, answer in mind. And it's an answer that you can supply, Orion."

"I can?" he asks, wide-eyed.

"Think," says Honus.

Orion turns away, covering his face with his hands.

"Don't worry, Silvermane," Neal tells him. "Do the best you can. If you get it wrong, I'll just go up there and lop off her head."

"I'll help," Malora says. She doesn't know about Neal, but for her it is all bravado. It is all she has.

The creature, overhearing Malora, laughs. "I look forward to seeing you try."

"And she looks forward to it as much as I do," Neal says.

"BE QUIET!" Honus says, in a much louder and more nettled tone than Malora has ever heard him use. "Let the lad *think*. Our lives depend upon this. You know this, Orrie."

Almost comically, considering the circumstances, Orion peers out at Honus from between his fingers. "I do?"

"Yes," says Honus. To the Sphinx, he says, "Am I permitted to offer him a small hint? The first letter, perhaps?"

"Do and I'll rip your head off and bowl the others over with it like pins," the Sphinx says with a lick of her crimson lips.

Honus flinches. "I am very sorry to say for all our sakes that you're on your own, my boy," he says miserably.

Orion has squeezed his eyes shut now in concentration. The sweat dribbles down the sides of his face and his flanks. "I know this!" he says. "I know this!"

"Of course you do. Remember? You read it in a book," Honus says to Orion. Then, quickly to the Sphinx: "That was not a hint. That is a fact."

The creature's long red forked tongue darts out and she spits. "Oh, a book! What is a book?" she says with a sneer. "Can you eat a book? Can you crush its bones beneath your teeth and grind it to powder? Can you lick its juices from your lips after you have finished devouring it? Your time is nearly up, little centaur. I can practically taste the fresh red horse meat now. I will start with the tenderloin, tearing it away from his spine while his heart is still beating."

Sky's head jerks up and he growls. He pulls violently away from Malora, leaving wisps of mane hairs trailing between her fingers, and launches into a brisk jog, circling the torches.

"Calm your horse!" the Sphinx screams. "Agitation will taint the meat!"

Sky lets out a shrill whinny as he picks up a lope.

"He's going to do it," Malora whispers, eyes on her horse.

"He'd better do it soon," Neal says, his own eyes on the Sphinx, who has begun to rise from her crouch.

"If ever there was a crisis," Honus says, "this would be it."

The flames of the torches bend and sputter as Sky sweeps past them, mane and tail whipping.

"Hold still, I tell you!" the Sphinx cries.

As she has once before, Malora can hear the steady creak of Sky's leg joints, the air whistling in and out of his mouth and nose.

"Look!" says Honus, his finger following Sky. "He's doing it! He's *doing* it!"

And now Malora sees it, too. The scars from the Leatherwings have come alive, dancing and flying above Sky's back like black snakes.

"That's my boy!" says Neal.

The Sphinx screams as, with a crackling sound, two huge sleek black wings emerge from the bed of the Leatherwings' scars and unfurl above the stallion's shoulders.

Meanwhile, oblivious to all this, Orion opens his eyes and raises a finger. "I have the answer. It is the winged horse, Pegasus!" he shouts. He looks around for his congratulations but instead sees that Sky has, in his way, beaten Orion to it.

"It's a trick!" the Sphinx growls.

"No, it's not," says Malora, bathed in relief. "And now you don't get to eat us."

Honus turns to the Sphinx. "Madam, you see with your own eyes the irrefutably correct answer to your question: the creature with the legs of a horse and the wings of a bird is standing before you as big as life. He is Malora's stalwart stallion, Sky! And, completely unnecessary, but correct nevertheless, the centaur lad has given you the answer you sought in the first place. It is Pegasus. We are right on two counts, and your banquet is hereby canceled."

"All of you! Get out of my sight!" the Sphinx hisses.

"Gladly," says Orion.

"Happy to oblige," says Neal with a mocking bow.

"Wait," says Malora, holding up a hand to the others. "Before we leave, I have a few questions for the Sphinx. Information."

"Oh, ask and be gone!" the Sphinx snarls.

"Tell me how you came to be in this place?" Malora says.

"That's an easy question. This place is my realm. The gods made me and set me down here for all eternity," says the Sphinx. "We are one of a kind. We were so perfect, the gods needed to make only one copy of each of us."

Honus nudges Malora and nods as if to say, *I was right, wasn't I?*

"The Scienticians, you mean," Malora says to the Sphinx.

She nods. "They are father and mother to me, god and goddess." A tear rolls out of the corner of one painted eye. "Alas, we are all that is left of them."

"And the centaurs of Ixion worship you," Malora says. "And keep your larder stocked."

The Sphinx shrugs. "By an ages-old compact, they see to our needs. They feed my brother, and he feeds us. Our brother doesn't mind going up. We do. We hate it up there in the Narrow World."

"We?" Orion says.

"Me and my sister," she says.

"So there are *three* Beasts from Below," Neal says grimly.

"Why can't you hunt your own food?" Malora asks. "You seem fierce enough."

The Sphinx's head swivels left and right. "Do you see any herds of impala running through here? The sinkholes deliver us up only the occasional prey but not enough to sustain us. Even children of the gods must eat. And if horse meat is the order of the day, horse meat is what we will eat."

The Sphinx licks her puffy lips and points to the bones lying all about. "My brother prefers centaurs, but I myself don't care to eat anything with a human face," she says.

"That's comforting to know," Neal mutters.

"As a rule, I toss the human half aside and leave it for the rats to gnaw at," she says.

"Not so comforting," Neal mutters.

"Do the wild centaurs come down here often?" Malora asks.

"To refuel the torches. Now and then one of them tries to get at the treasure," she says.

"What treasure?" Honus and Orion chime in.

Malora asks, "Where is this treasure?"

"We're not here for treasure, pet," Neal warns.

"We might need it to bargain for Zephele's life. *In place of horses,*" Malora adds.

Neal nods, then speaks up: "You heard her. Where is this treasure, Hul?"

"*Abu al* Hul—and wouldn't you like to know, my handsome little lion-stalker!" she says, her heavy-lidded eyes flirtatious.

"Actually, we all would," Malora says. "And if you tell us, I promise to go away and bring you back a delectable horse to lick. The most wonderful horse you have ever tasted."

The Sphinx's face lights up. She smacks her lips. "Do tell!"

The others stare at Malora as if she has taken leave of her senses, but she continues. "This horse is really something special. It is the prized possession of the Apex of Kheiron. Everyone who sees it covets it. It's a stunning golden steed with rippling muscles and a fiery spirit."

The Sphinx salivates.

Malora says, "Tell us where the treasure is and the horse will be yours. I will personally return and present it to you."

"My brother, the Minotaur, guards the treasure at the heart of his labyrinth," says the Sphinx. "Keep following the torches and eventually you will find him! If he doesn't find you first." She chuckles nastily.

"Thank you! We'll be going now," Malora says as she backs away from the circle of torches. She finds that she is soaked in sweat. She will not turn her back until the Sphinx is no longer in her sights.

"Have you completely lost your mind?" Orion whispers. "Promising to bring her a horse of all things!"

"I never said I would bring her a *real* horse," Malora says. "I was talking about the Golden Horse of Kheiron. The Apex will be more than happy to make a gift of his trophy to her, especially if her information leads us to the rescue of his daughter."

CHAPTER 23

More Masterpieces

The torches are spaced farther apart now, and the travelers find themselves groping along in the near darkness that stretches out between. The floor begins to tilt downward, so gradually that no one notices it at first. Then Honus slips and falls backward, his head hitting the glass with a thud.

Malora and Orion kneel beside him. Orion gathers him up in his arms. Honus groans. Malora gently probes the back of his head. "There's a lump rising, but there's no blood."

Honus revives himself and sits up. "Onward to Ixion!" he says gamely. And on they go.

Ahead of them, Sky, his wings retracted once again, continues to advance in small, shuffling steps. Baby slips and slides behind him. Malora gets down and inches along on her bottom, as does Honus. Orion and Neal creep forward on their haunches. The incline steepens and Sky falls onto one hip, continuing to slide as the heavier centaurs move out in front of Malora and Honus. Soon they are all careening down the steep glassy chute. Malora has the sensation of falling through space as the slide grows ever steeper. Faster and faster she flies until she crashes once again into a big powdery pile of sand, her face planted in Sky's neck.

Sky rolls one blue eye toward her as if to say, *What have you gotten us into now?*

"I'm sorry," she whispers to him.

Baby clamors to her feet and trots ahead. Sky heaves himself up and follows.

"However deep beneath the earth we were before," Honus says grimly, "we are deeper still now."

They get up slowly, dusting the sand off, and forge onward. The ground is level again, and they no longer have to crawl. They stop now and then to wet their tongues from the flasks. The fish they packed in leaves is so full of sand they leave it behind for the rats.

After another eternity, up ahead in the tunnel they see flashes of lightning, followed by a thunderous roar that sounds like the ocean crashing against the shore. Malora is wondering whether the cavern might be leading them to the sea, when Sky and Baby come racing back, nearly bowling her over. Sky's sides heave. His hide is lathered, his eyes rolling up to the whites.

"Easy, big boy," Malora says, making calming motions with hands that feel anything but calm.

Sky snorts and pulls back, refusing false comfort.

"He saw something that scared him," Orion says.

"Any other glaringly obvious observations you'd care to make, Silvermane?" Neal says.

"I'll go and see," Malora says. "Sometimes the things that

spook horses are really nothing." While she doesn't believe this for a moment, she says it anyway.

Malora makes her way slowly forward. As she rounds a bend in the corridor, a wall of intense heat rolls toward her, followed by a deafening roar that knocks her onto her hind end and sends her scrambling backward. Through a smoky haze that smells of her own singed hair, Malora peers up at the monster.

There is no germ of human being here. She has the head and body of a lion, with a goat's head sticking out of its back and a long, thick serpent's tail. Smoke trails from her mouth as she draws herself up and glares down at Malora.

"We mean you no harm," Malora calls out in a trembling voice.

The monster gives no sign of having understood. Malora has never seen a lion with such a malignant look. Her eyes are huge and white and spindled with black. Her shaggy head is twenty times bigger than that of a normal lion.

All the breath goes out of Malora as she watches the monster puff up her chest. She opens her mouth and emits a loud bawling noise, equal parts roar, howl, and hiss. A long forked serpent's tongue pokes out and a column of fire shoots from the back of her throat. Malora dodges the flame and rolls over. She has just enough time to sit up before the monster howls again. Moments later, another gout of flame comes rolling toward her. She scuttles backward as the creature howls, and this time she feels the bottoms of her boots half-melt away. The smell of singed impala skin, and her own flesh burning, fills her nostrils. Choking, she staggers to her feet and hobbles back around the bend.

"I gather it's not nothing," Neal says, sizing up her appearance.

"It's huge!" Malora says, panting. "Vicious. Our weapons will be useless against it. And there's no way through this tunnel but past it."

"We'll never make it back up the chute we slid down," Honus says.

"We're as good as stuck here," Orion says bleakly.

Neal draws his sword. "We'll see about that."

"No, Neal," Malora says, her hand shooting out to stop him. "You'll never get close enough to use your sword. You'll be roasted alive."

"Roasted?" Orion echoes, his pale eyes huge.

"She spits flames," Malora says.

Honus is the only one who doesn't look stunned and terrified. Instead, he is deeply thoughtful. "Exactly what does this monster look like?"

They listen as Malora describes the creature that blocks their passage.

"What an indescribably fifthly mess of a hibe," Orion says.

Neal turns away and spits, as if ridding his mouth of a foul taste.

"Ah, and yet it is a masterpiece," Honus says.

They stare at Honus in bafflement as the faun begins to pace. "I begin to see what the Scienticians were up to," he says, his eyes shining. "They must have amused themselves at first with the likes of us, the simple splicing of horse and human, goat and human, amphibian and human, and so on and so forth. But after a while these primitive forms must have bored them. They wanted to create something mythic. Like us, but more powerful, more frightening, and more monstrous. So they created the Sphinx. They created the Minotaur, whom we have yet to meet. And they created the fire-breathing monster we now face: the Chimera. I know it seems hopeless, but I have good tidings for one and all."

"Then stop lecturing and tell us," Neal says, throwing up his hands in exasperation.

Honus stops pacing. "I know how we can slay it."

"How?" Malora asks.

"Orion, can I trouble you to give me one of your darts?" Honus asks.

Orion digs a dart from his belt and hands it to Honus, a doubtful expression on his face.

"What are you up to, Polymath?" Neal asks.

Honus has untied the pouch at his waist. He rummages around in it one-handed as he mutters to himself. "I know I have it, I placed it in here after Malora salvaged it from the barge, along with my quills and my flask of ink. Ah! Here it is! And to think I almost jettisoned it as useless." He pulls out a small red plug of sealing wax. He takes the dart and trots over to the nearest torch, but it is too high on the glass wall for him to reach it. "Neal, come here, please. I'm going to need to stand on that sturdy young back of yours, if you would be so kind."

Neal obliges, and Malora boosts Honus up onto his back. Honus teeters.

"Ouch," Neal says. "Easy with those sharp little trotters."

Malora braces Honus with one hand as the faun reaches up and holds the plug of red wax to the torch's flame until it softens and begins to drip. With the other hand, he turns the dart slowly, letting the wax drip down onto the tip. When it is completely covered with red wax, Honus hands it to Malora and asks for the remaining darts so he can do the same with them. When he is finished, he says, "Very good. You can help me down now, if you would, Malora. Thank you for the use of your back, Neal. I trust it will be worth the temporary discomfort of being trod upon."

Honus turns to Orion. "All right. You, young sir, are the master of the blowgun, are you not?"

"So Neal has always told me," Orion says glumly.

Malora steps forward. "I'll do it," she says. "Orrie, teach me how to use the blowgun."

Neal says, "Don't be ridiculous."

Orion says, "It would take more time to teach you than we have. Didn't I wing at least one Leatherwing with my sharpshooting?"

Orion bangs the shaft against the glass floor, knocking the sand out. He peers with one eye down the barrel. Then he inserts three darts into his belt. He kisses the fourth before he loads it into the blowgun.

"Aim for the heart," Neal says.

"If only I knew where that was," Orion says ruefully.

"On its goat side," Honus says, frowning. "Or is it its lion side?"

"I shall aim for any part that looks tender," Orion says.

"We're counting on you," Neal says.

"Worse luck for all of you," Orion says with a sad smile. "Nevertheless, I shall endeavor not to disappoint. On the whole, I think I preferred answering the Sphinx," he adds.

Neal says, "Give me hand-to-hand combat any day."

"Hand to *paw*," Orion says.

"Or is it *claw*?" Honus ponders.

Malora finds their banter oddly comforting, and is glad that Orion seems to as well. There is a kind of foolish bravado in it, and she thinks that she has never loved them all more than she does at this moment.

"She howls first, then almost right away shoots the flame," Malora says. "Try to get your shot in *after* the howl but *before* the flame."

"Sound advice." Orion hands the blowgun to Honus and walks a few paces. He shakes out his arms from shoulders to hands, and then shakes out his hands. "They've got the right idea," he says, indicating Sky and Baby, who have discovered a few hardy blades of dune grass poking up through a crack in the glass beneath a shaft of sunlight. "Would that I could be as easily calmed."

Malora notices that his hands seem steady enough. If someone had told her when she first met him that this gentle centaur would one day be fending off Leatherwings and Beasts from Below, she would have told them they were crazy. But Orion appears ready and willing to defend them all.

Orion holds out his hands. Honus lays the blowgun across them. Now it is Orion who is ready to court death, she thinks while she watches, much as Lume watched her all those times.

Blowgun in hand, Orion ventures slowly around the corner. The others move along behind him. Orion steps out into the open. Rounding the corner, Malora's heart begins to race at the renewed sight of the monster. She can only imagine how Orion feels.

Orion creeps forward, one careful step at a time, the blowgun at his side. The Chimera cranes her head, slowly capturing Orion in the scope of her eerie spoked eyes. Malora can see Orion working to make his breath steady and even. It is much harder, she reflects, thinking of Lume, to watch someone do something dangerous than to do it yourself. The tawny chest puffs up with air and the monster opens her mouth wide. *First the howl, then the flame.* She sees a row of short, sharp teeth with two long fangs in front, like a viper. Her forked tongue snakes out between the fangs. If it were Malora's shot to make, that's where she would aim.

"Do it *now*, Orion," she whispers. She realizes that she is holding Honus's hand so tightly that it must hurt. She eases up but almost immediately renews the pressure.

Orion raises the blowgun to his lips and sights down the long red tunnel of the creature's throat, right between the two fangs. The monster lets loose with the howl. The fire, Malora knows, will soon follow. Orion inhales deeply and empties his lungs in one powerful burst as the dart shoots out of the end of the barrel and flies directly into the creature's open maw.

The howl is cut short as the monster gags on the dart. She rises up on her tail, reeling in agony. Malora's heart twists with pity. Then pity vanishes as the monster seems to recover herself. She puffs up her chest and opens her mouth, revealing blood-stained fangs. This time, the howl is tinged with pain and outrage. Malora watches Orion wait in helpless dread for the monster to let loose the deadly gout of flame. The next moment, the creature's head bursts into flames. Orion staggers backward, away from the heat.

Malora, Neal, and Honus leap up and down, pounding

each other's backs and shoulders and cheering hoarsely. Orion looks back at them with a shy smile before taking one last, thoroughly impressed look at the damage he has done with one little dart.

The creature has collapsed. The air stinks of singed fur. A broadening puddle of gore seeps from her mouth, burning like oil.

They surround Orion. Even Sky and Baby abandon the grass to see what the fuss is all about.

"Sharp shot, Orrie!" says Neal.

"Got it the first time!" Honus adds.

"Orion Victorious!" Malora says proudly, removing the blowgun from his trembling hand. "The title is now yours."

Orion is drenched with sweat. He exhales, then turns to Honus. "All right. Now I'd like to know why you were so sure the wax-tipped dart would do the trick. That was a very small dart and a very big beast."

Honus smiles. "I think you all know the answer to that question."

"I know!" says Malora.

Then all three of them say it in unison: "You read it in a book!"

They laugh. It is as much a release of tension as it is a response to the joke.

"Guilty as charged," Honus says. "Didn't I tell you that having a book-learner along for this expedition would come in handy?"

"I don't know about the rest of you," Neal says, "but if we get out of here alive, I intend to make an effort to read more books."

CHAPTER 24

The Sweet Beast

The glass walls gradually run to dull rock, ramping steadily upward as the footing softens to sand. Malora takes this for a sign that they are nearing Ixion. Up ahead two torches burn. The torches' handles are gold, inlaid with gems, and they are set on either side of an arched doorway framed in elaborately carved wood.

She peers down a stone-lined passageway lit by more torches. Honus peers around her. "This must be it," he says. "The entrance to the labyrinth."

She removes one of the torches from the wall and shines it on the floor. "The Beast's droppings," she says.

"His footprints, too," Neal says. "He's a monster." He bends over and holds a hand over the droppings. "They're still warm. These tracks are fresh."

"Maybe they'll lead us to the treasure," Malora says.

"And to the Beast as well," Honus says.

Malora remembers lying bound in the paddock and the

explosion of sand when the Beast came up to claim the sacrifice. She reaches down into her boot and removes her knife. The Sphinx was terrifying, the Chimera even more so, but it is the Minotaur who comes to claim the sacrifices. Terrified as she is, she has a personal grudge against this monster.

Neal draws his sword. The corridor is narrow and they proceed along it single file, Malora leading the way with Honus, Orion, and Neal following, Sky and Baby bringing up the rear.

The corridor has been bored through solid rock. Each turn in the maze branches out, offering the travelers another choice and often three. But Malora trusts that the Beast whose tracks they follow knows the way. She can smell him now: a dark, rank odor.

"The passage is getting narrower," Orion says uneasily. "I don't like it."

"Shhh!" Honus says.

Above the rankness, Malora smells something sweet and spicy and familiar. Could it be wild jasmine? Then Malora hears a new sound. She stops and turns around. "Which one of you is making that noise?"

"What noise?" Orion says.

"I'm not making any noise," Neal says.

Malora puts her finger to her lips and points to the corridor behind them. Sky and Baby squeeze past the two centaurs and Honus and go to stand behind Malora. When the shuffling of their hooves settles, they all listen, their eyes bright in the torchlight. It is a rustling, snorting sound, and it is coming from somewhere behind them in the labyrinth.

"We're being followed," Malora whispers.

She eases past Sky and Baby and continues to lead the way, moving more quickly now, burrowing deeper into the labyrinth.

After countless twists and turns, first Malora, then Sky and Baby, come tumbling out of the corridor into a space that feels so wide open that for a brief instant Malora thinks they have arrived aboveground. Then she cranes her neck and sees that there is still a ceiling of rock above them. In the center of the space, a heap of debris rises up at least four times higher than their heads. It seems to be glowing from within. As she approaches it, she sees that it is a mountain made entirely out of treasure: a gaudy tangle of jewelry and coins and crowns and breastplates and mirrors, and more precious gems than in all the marketplace stalls of Kahiro.

The others pile out of the tunnel and, one by one, gasp in amazement. Sky and the zebra bend their heads to nose around in it, looking for something edible.

The rest of them walk around it in speechless wonder. Malora is so dazzled that it takes a moment for her to register the voice calling out to her. "Yoo-hoo! Malora, dear! It's me! Up here!"

They all look up. She is waving to them from atop the mountain of treasure. Wearing a golden crown, she is bedecked with necklaces, bracelets, bangles, and rings.

"Zephele!" they cry out.

"I'll be right down," she says breathlessly as she comes scrambling down off the mountaintop, setting off a small, tinkling avalanche of treasures. Arms outstretched to them, jingling and sparkling, she says, "You came! You came to rescue me. I told my host you'd come—and here you are, big as life."

Tucking away their weapons, the travelers crowd around her, taking turns hugging her, except for Neal, who holds himself back.

"Little Sister, thank *Kheiron* you're all right!" says Orion.

"Did they sacrifice you to the Beast from Below?" Malora asks. "Is that how you got down here?"

"Oh, goodness me, no," Zephele says, clapping a hand over her heart. "I got up in the middle of the night to use the convenience. Duna told me I was to wake her up if ever I needed to go in the night."

"Duna?" Malora says.

"My bronca host. She's lovely, but I fear she had far too much ferna at the bonfire feast. The wild centaurs *love* their feasts. I doubt I could have roused her even had I rung a gong over her head. So I went by myself, and that's when the Sweet Beast waylaid me on the path."

"Sweet Beast?" Orion asks.

"That's what I call him. The wild centaurs call him the Beast from Below, but what sort of name is that? Call someone a low-down Beast and without a doubt he will behave like one. So far, my Sweet Beast is behaving like quite the gentleman. I told him you'd eventually come for me. How clever of you to have tracked me down. Tell me how you did it!"

"It's a long story," Orion says.

Zephele looks tantalized by the prospect of hearing every word of it. She tugs fastidiously at her white wrap, which is soiled, and snugs a white kid shawl around her shoulders.

Leave it to Zephele, Malora thinks, to appear radiant and fashionable even as a prisoner.

"I see you admiring my dragonfly," she says, pointing to the embroidery work on the shawl. "Aren't the thread dyes gorgeous? Wild centaur work. I did the needlework myself while I was with the herd."

"With the herd?" Orion asks.

"The wild centaurs think of themselves as a herd. Isn't that cunning? And—prepare yourself, Orrie—their leader is none other than our apparently not-at-all-dead brother, Athen. But call him Athen at your own peril. His name is Archon now, thank you very much. He's a bit of a grumble-guts, like our father, but he has his softer-hearted moments. The wild centaurs are quite frolicsome in their way. They have races and bonfires by the sea, and they even ride the waves. I have tried it myself! Imagine, Malora, me, swimming in the sea! I think my brother quite expected me to remain with the wild centaurs for the rest of my life. . . ." She stops and nods at something that just occurred to her. "Not that I would ever dream of doing so, but there is a quality of freedom they enjoy here that we in Mount Kheiron would find difficult to grasp."

"Freedom?" Neal speaks up in a surly tone of voice. "Free to plunder and murder."

Zephele sighs. "Ah, that is altogether too true. Still, it's all rather *complicated.*"

"But you yourself are unharmed," Neal says.

Zephele cocks a hand on her hip. Her eyes flash. "Why don't you come a little closer and see for yourself, Flatlander."

The others fall away as Neal approaches her, examining

her with hungry eyes. "I see a few scratches, but you seem perfectly fit, I am very glad to see."

"Just how glad are you, Master Featherhoof?" Zephele asks, raising an eyebrow.

Neal breaks down and sweeps her up in his arms. "Oh, my dear girl," he says into her hair. "I have never been so glad of anything in my life than I am to see you."

Malora and the others turn discreetly away as the two embrace and whisper back and forth. Sky, feeling no such constraint, trots up and nuzzles Zephele's neck.

"Sky!" she cries, pulling away from Neal, blotting away the tears with the edge of her kid shawl. "You came back for me, too! What a brave horse you are! And who is your little friend?"

"That's Baby," Neal says.

"Come here and let me hug you, too, you adorable little striped darling!" Zephele says.

Baby cowers behind Sky's front leg.

"Baby's shy," Orion explains. "She wandered away from her herd, and Sky adopted her."

"Oh, Sky!" Zephele says, stroking the stallion's nose. "Your heart is as soft as your nose."

"Sky does have a big heart," Neal says. "But he also has a rather substantial set of wings, we've recently discovered."

"Is that a fact?" She laughs shortly. "Mather told me he did, but I thought he was just being silly and superstitious. You were holding out on us, Sky. And speaking of holding out, Malora Thora-Jayke, why didn't you tell me we had so many kith and kin amongst the wild centaurs?"

"I thought it would be too painful for you to know," Malora says.

Zephele frowns. "What am I? A delicate rose? This rose has thorns, I'll have you know." Zephele throws up her arms, her jewels rattling as she bursts into a wide smile. "But all's forgiven now that I'm rescued!"

"The Beast's treasure becomes you," Neal says.

Zephele's smile dims as she lowers her arms. "Yes, well. He likes to see me wearing his ill-gotten gains." She pauses and holds up a finger. A snorting sound echoes in the passageway. She whispers, "That's him now. It's too late for you to hide. Oh dear. I fear he will be jealous."

They all turn to the labyrinth exit, just as the Beast strides through it.

"There you are, my dear Sweet Beast!" Zephele calls out in a gentle voice. "I thought I heard your footfall. We have visitors, as you see. I would like you to meet my friends from Mount Kheiron. This is Honus, my teacher, and Orion, my other brother, and Malora, my best friend, and Neal . . ." She trails off. "You've heard me speak of all of them. He's not much of a conversationalist," Zephele says in an aside. "He's more of a listener . . . and a snorter and a pawer. But, all in all, he hasn't been bad company."

Malora's mouth goes dry at the sight of the Minotaur. He stands twice as tall as she does, on stout human legs that end in black cloven hooves five times the size of Honus's. His bull's head, springing from human shoulders that look too narrow to support its weight, is large and black and blockish. He has wide, round nostrils linked by a large golden ring, sickle-shaped horns that look lethally sharp, and big, dark eyes that combine animal ferocity with human cunning. His body is muscular but tapered, and he has about him an air of fierce dignity, in spite of the fact that he is laden with a rush broom, a rake, and a dustpan full of his own droppings. The Beast is very neat, Malora thinks. Then, with a sinking heart, she realizes that the sound she heard behind them in the labyrinth was the Minotaur sweeping up his droppings and erasing their way out of the maze. The Minotaur flings aside his cleaning tools, snorts, and paws at the earth.

"Now what did I tell you about the snorting and pawing business?" Zephele says to him sternly. "Settle down, Sweetness. Haven't you been listening to me? These are *friends*."

"Somehow, I don't think he cares," says Orion.

"Orion's right. He wants you all to himself . . . and he's getting ready to fight for you," Malora says, reaching down to her ankle for her knife.

But Neal stays her hand. "This one is mine, pet!" he says, pulling his sword from its scabbard.

The Minotaur snorts and rounds on Neal. Zephele holds up her hand. "Please don't!" To the others, she adds, "I don't think I've ever seen him this upset."

"Of course he's upset," says Neal, never taking his eyes off the Minotaur. "He knows we are here to take you away from him. He's like everyone else you have ever met, dear girl. He is in love with you. He is also smart enough to see that I love you, too. Tell me you love me, Zephele Silvermane, so Sweetness here knows exactly where you stand."

"Somehow I don't think that's a good idea," Malora says, seeing the reddening eyes and flaring nostrils of the Minotaur.

"It's a fine idea," Neal says. "What do you say, Zephie? Of course, if you don't love me, I'll still fight for you. . . ."

"I *do* love you, Neal!" Zephele bursts out. "You know I do. I love you deeply with all my heart. I've always loved you. But right now, my darling, I fear for you!"

Neal smiles happily. "Did you hear that, Orrie? She called me *darling*. Your highborn sister has fallen for a Flatlander."

"I'm pleased to hear it," Orion says warily, "but I'd prefer that the Flatlander left here in one piece."

"Oh, I fully intend to!" Neal says with a broad grin. "Now that I know that I am loved by Zephele Silvermane, I will risk all."

"I wish it didn't have to come to this," Zephele says, clutching at Malora's hand.

Neal says, "Oh, but it must, my love. It was always going to come to this. It's the only way any of us will get out of here alive."

Keeping an eye on the Minotaur, Neal backs away toward the other side of the treasure heap. "Follow me, my fine friend," he says to the Beast, beckoning with one hand. "We wouldn't want any innocent bystanders to be harmed in the scuffle."

Zephele, Malora, Honus, and Orion edge away but not so far that they can't see the combatants. Sky and Baby huddle in the doorway, peering anxiously out of the shadows.

"Oh, do be careful, my darling!" Zephele whispers. And once again, Malora finds herself in the position of watching rather than doing.

The Minotaur paws the earth, lowers his head, and charges at Neal, the points of his horns aimed at the centaur's chest. Neal springs forward to meet the Minotaur, blocking him with the length of his sword. The Minotaur skids to a halt and backs up, bellowing in frustration. He wheels around and jogs several paces away from Neal, coming around to face him once again.

"Do you see, Zeph?" Malora points out. "He can't back up and he can't make sharp turns. Neal is more nimble."

With Neal back in his sights, the Minotaur paws the earth, lowers his horns, and charges again. Wielding the sword in both hands, Neal swings the blade sideways, striking sparks on the horns but failing to block the charge. Neal lifts a leg and kicks the Minotaur roundly in the head, sending him reeling backward.

"Nice work," Orion says.

Shaking his shaggy head, the Minotaur snorts, then launches a fresh attack. Once again Neal holds the Minotaur off with the long edge of his sword and this time backs him into the wall. The Minotaur lifts his head at the last moment and with a toss of his horns flips Neal's sword into the air.

The sword wheels off and lands in the sand. While the Minotaur's eyes are on the sword, Neal feints to the right and begins to circle the Minotaur. The Minotaur turns to keep Neal in his sights, but Neal breaks clear and lunges for the sword, sweeping it up in his hands at a swift trot.

The Minotaur charges again. This time, Neal pivots on his hind legs, removing himself from the path of the charging horns. The Beast runs past Neal and slams into the wall. One horn sticks in the door frame. He digs into the dirt with his hooves and, grunting and heaving, struggles to pull himself loose.

"Finish him off *now,* Featherhoof!" Orion shouts.

Had Malora been in Neal's place, she would have come up from behind and sunk the point of the sword between the Minotaur's shoulder blades. But Neal has other ideas. Maddeningly, he stands and waits for his opponent to free his horn. Once freed, the Beast shakes his head and turns to face Neal. The Minotaur paws the earth, snorts steam, and glares at Neal through bloodshot eyes. Lowering his horns, he comes at Neal with the speed of a charging rhino. Neal rears up and, with a downward slash of his sword, tears open a long red slit on the side of the Minotaur's neck.

Zephele gasps, burying her face in Malora's shoulder. The Minotaur howls in outrage, turns around, and takes a reckless run at Neal, broadside. Neal pivots on his forehand, haunches slewing to one side as the Minotaur's left horn grazes Neal's flank.

"It's not fair," Zephele whimpers. "He's got two weapons to Neal's one."

Malora gets an idea. Kneeling, she removes her knife from her boot.

"What are you going to do?" Zephele asks. "You're not ganging up on him, are you?"

Malora shakes her head and moves closer to the fray. Opening her mouth, she shouts, "Hey, *you!* Beast!"

Startled, both Minotaur and centaur turn to look her way. Malora hauls back and throws the knife, sinking the blade into the door frame just over Neal's head.

Neal grins. "Good arm, pet!" he says, and reaches up to pull the knife out of the wood. Sword in one hand, knife in the other, he circles the Minotaur. Neal is pale and dripping with sweat, while the Minotaur, apart from the wound on his neck, looks as powerful as ever.

Honus murmurs to Malora, "Is there any way you or Orion could get in there and spell Neal for a bit?"

"Neal would never stand for it," Orion says grimly. "He wants to do this himself or die trying."

"Oh, Orrie, please don't say that!" Zephele says.

The Minotaur charges at Neal. Neal sidesteps, his foreleg buckling as he collapses to his knees. Sword and knife fly from his hands. He lunges forward and wallows in the sand to reach his weapons. The Minotaur lowers his head and charges at Neal from the side.

The others shout out a warning. Just as Neal is about to grasp his sword, the Beast gores him beneath the arm. Neal cries out.

"Oh, dear Hands, no!" Zephele whispers.

Horn snagged in Neal's armpit, the Minotaur lifts him up over his head and spins around twice, pinning Neal against the wall. Neal, standing on his hind legs, gnashes his teeth. The Minotaur wags his head and digs the horn deeper into Neal's flesh.

Malora can't bear to watch.

"Sky!" Malora calls out. "Here!"

Sky stirs and trots over to her. "Give me a leg up, Orrie."

She needs the help because she doesn't trust her trembling legs. "Honus, fetch me Orion's sword!"

Orion, eying the Minotaur fearfully, makes a stirrup of his hands and swings Malora up onto Sky's back. Now that she feels Sky beneath her, the tremors in her legs lessen. Honus scampers over to retrieve Neal's sword and hands it up to

Malora. The sword is so heavy she is afraid it will drag her off Sky. She needs both hands to hold it.

The Minotaur flings Neal aside and turns to face Malora.

"I must go to him!" Zephele cries.

"No!" Malora shouts. "Stay clear!"

Obediently, they all edge toward the doorway.

Squeezing Sky with her knees, Malora directs him to move away from where Neal lies sagging against the wall. If Neal is still alive, she doesn't want to trample him to death. On Sky's back, she now has the advantage of height. But she has more than that. She can see it in the Minotaur's eyes as he regards Sky with bloodshot eyes.

"Do you see that, boy?" she whispers to Sky. "The Beast is afraid of you."

She leans back and cues Sky with a series of little kicks to back up to the wall, as far away from the Minotaur as they can get and still keep him in view. "Just think," she leans forward and whispers into his ear, "of all the poor innocent horses this monster has eaten."

Malora straightens, feeling Sky brace himself beneath her. She holds the sword in both hands, cocked over one shoulder. *Like the blacksmith's hammer.* The weight on her wrists and biceps is almost unbearable. She digs her heels into Sky's belly, urging him forward, hanging on with the muscles of her thighs as he lunges forward. She sights just over the Beast's left shoulder. The Beast lowers his head to charge. But then he simply stands and stares at Sky, dumbstruck. Malora pulls up short before the Beast. Sky stretches his neck clear of the sword's path. Malora swings the blade down and slices into the top of the Minotaur's skull, between the horns.

The Beast opens his mouth and lets out a dull roar. Shuddering, he sags to his seat, legs splayed out before him. The sword is stuck fast. Malora leaves it there and slides off Sky's back. Sky trots away, head high. Planting a foot to either side of the sword, Malora pulls back and yanks the blade free of the monster's head. Blood blooms from his skull. Then she summons her remaining strength, swings the blade sideways, and hacks off the Minotaur's head in one stroke. The head rolls onto the sand, splattering blood. Malora bends over and wretches up a long string of bile.

"He was already dead. Why ever did you cut off his head?" Orion says.

Malora raises her head and wipes her mouth on the sleeve of her tunic. "Insurance," she says, leaning on the sword as if it were a crutch.

Zephele runs to Neal, flinging off her jewels as she comes. Kneeling next to him she takes him gently in her arms. In no time, her white kid shawl is stained with Neal's blood.

"He's alive! My darling is alive!" Zephele announces. "Honus! Orion! Help me stanch the bleeding."

"The Minotaur has been slain in his labyrinth," Honus says quietly, bending over Neal's body. "Behold, our modern-day Theseus."

Malora stares down at the Beast's head. His eyes are open, still transfixed by Sky.

"That was *fine* work, Malora," Orion says as he hurriedly tears up his wrap to make a bandage for Neal.

"He didn't even put up a fight," Malora says in a daze. "He was afraid of Sky." Suddenly, she feels light-headed and weak. She doesn't think she could lift the sword again if her life depended on it.

Neal says, lifting his head from Zephele's arms, "You should have seen the look in Sky's eyes when he charged. It was *murderous*."

"Darling! How lovely to hear your voice again!" Zephele coos, kissing the top of his head.

Neal winces as Honus cleans his wound. Then Honus wraps the bandage around Neal's shoulder and under his armpit. Afterward, Neal lies on his good side, looking pale and pinched.

"Open your mouth and stick out your tongue," Honus says.

Neal obeys and Honus places a small tar-colored pellet on his tongue. "Chew this to dull the edge of your pain," he says.

Slack-jawed, Neal does his best to chew, his eyes riveted to Zephele's face.

Zephele smooths his golden curls and covers his face with gentle kisses. "Are you all right, my darling?"

"I'll be fine," Neal says, and adds, "It's nothing. Only a scratch." Then he blacks out.

Zephele raises her eyes to Honus.

"The wound is deep," Honus says, "but not fatal."

Zephele nods quickly, as if she already knew this but needed it confirmed. She looks over at what is left of the Beast. "He tried so hard to be the perfect host. In his way, he was just like my brother. He hoped that I would remain here as his guest forever. But it never would have worked out." She sighs and turns away.

CHAPTER 25

Onward, to Ixion

Orion says, "I don't think I can carry him very far without wrenching something."

"I won't be much help," Malora says. It has taken her last burst of strength to lop off the Beast's head. She suspects the half-dead weight of a full-grown centaur is a little more than she can handle, even with help from Orion.

"I have an idea," Orion says, holding up a finger. "We'll rig a sling."

"Good idea." Malora sighs, sinking onto folded legs, her head dropping down over her lap as she holes up in a tent of her hair. She doesn't want to say this aloud, but she screams it in her mind: *If Sky had not scared the Beast stiff, I would have lost that fight!* The fact was, the Chimera, too, was beyond her ability to even imagine defeating. Only the Sphinx failed to frighten her to her core. Just very nearly to it. And the Leatherwings . . .

And yet she peers out through a gap in the tent of her hair

and sees Orion, calmly rummaging through the pile of treasure. Zephele and Honus hover over Neal, whispering comfort and encouragement and even making little jokes. And didn't Lume say that fighting Leatherwings alongside them had been *fun*? The hibes, all of them, seem to be taking this monster-ridden adventure in stride. Why? Is it because both hibes and monsters are the children of the Scienticians? Would it be like feuding with a brother or a sister or a cousin? Having had no brothers or sisters or cousins, she cannot say. All she knows is that her hands still tremble.

"This will do nicely," Orion says as he reaches for a bronze staff that is sticking out of the treasure heap. Moments later, fishing around with both hands, he cries out in triumph as he begins to pull an enormous robe made of ermine from the pile. Then he takes staff and robe and blowgun and, settling onto his haunches, sets to work.

Malora bursts out of her tent. "You're using the blowgun to make the sling?" The same blowgun that slew the mighty Chimera, the scariest, most hideous animal Malora has ever seen or imagined. It is enough to make her weep.

Orion looks up at her with a look of mock severity. "Now, Malora. You know that this is a much better use for it."

Malora makes no comment. The last time she saw the wild centaurs, they were preparing her to be the Beast's next meal. There is probably no way out of this underworld without passing directly through Ixion. Malora will have to make do with her knife and Neal's sword—not that she has any confidence in her ability to wield that sword against the wild centaurs, most of whom have probably *teethed* on such swords. She is sitting up now, taking an interest in Orion's project. He has lashed blowgun and staff into a V and is now arranging the cape to stretch across the V.

"Can I borrow your knife?" he asks.

Malora reaches into her boot for it and passes it to him, handle-first. Orion gives her a look of sympathy when he sees how her hand shakes. She watches as he uses it to punch a neat line of holes in the cape. He hands the knife back to her, then threads the silver wire through the holes, wrapping the wire around the poles and making a secure sling with just enough give in it to absorb the shock to Neal's body when they move him. It is as good a job as she would do. Better, in fact. She compliments him.

He looks up from his work with a crooked smile. "You seem surprised."

"Well, it's just that . . ." She isn't sure how to say it.

"How could I possibly be so adept with my hands when I spend so much of my time dreaming and listening to the notes of scent in my head?"

Malora shrugs, embarrassed, but that is it exactly.

"Ah, but you see, I grew up with Neal Featherhoof." Then he adds, "I'll expect you to help me with the harness for Sky. I wouldn't want to design anything that might bind. Jayke's rope will suffice?"

Malora nods.

"We can pad it where you see the greatest danger of chafing."

She is touched by his consideration. "Thank you," she says. "I'm sure Sky will appreciate that."

Malora arranges the rope around Sky's neck and chest and pads it here and there. Orion attaches the ends of the harness to the sling. When Malora has moved Sky around so that the sling is as close to Neal as they can get it, they hoist Neal into it. It takes all of them working together to do this, including Neal, who sucks air through his teeth with every move. Moments after they have settled him into the sling, he passes out once again, whether from the pain or the painkiller, no one is sure.

As they work their way out of the labyrinth, Malora walks next to Sky to regulate the pace, not to lead him. Sky is the only one who knows the way out. The stallion moves steadily, pulling the sling with care around each corner without jostling his passenger. The sling supports Neal's upper body, while his hooves drag along behind, the tip of the blowgun bumping and grinding along with them.

The path runs uphill now. Sky slows down and scrambles as the footing softens. His hide foams with the sweat of his exertion. When Malora catches her first glimpse of blue sky, she bends over and removes her knife from her boot. Then just as quickly, she returns it to her boot. She imagines the wild centaurs snickering at her little knife.

"We're almost there," she says to the others. Orion and Zephele are following close to the sling in case Neal starts sliding off. Sky's feet churn as he hauls his burden up the steepest stretch of footing they have yet encountered. Mercifully, Malora can see the end of the path, in a cave that looks out on the paddock in the Valley of the Beast.

What will they call it now? she wonders.

As she guides Sky past sharp rocks toward the cave's mouth, a lone sentry leaning against a dune wall springs to attention, his eyes widening with shock. He runs off and returns with four more centaurs. Soon, a mob of wild centaurs fills the valley, crowding in around the paddock. There are males and females, children and old ones. Except for the latter two, they are all heavily armed. Malora hopes that the presence of children and ancients will dispose the wild centaurs toward civilized behavior. Then again, they might just want to set a good example for the young ones by showing how to punish interlopers and horse thieves. Weapons notwithstanding, they don't look as if they are contemplating slaughter. They are talking in low, animated voices amongst themselves. No one makes a move to speak to any of them. The travelers remain isolated in the paddock, more like prisoners than visitors.

Malora stands in the safest place she can think of, next to Sky. Orion stands next to her, and Honus joins Orion. Zephele tends to Neal. When a sandy-haired centaur with a big blue fish tattooed on his upper torso ambles into view, Zephele raises a hand and wiggles her fingers at him. "Hello, Drift darling!" Then she says to the semiconscious Neal, "That's the wild centaur who reminded me so of you. His name is Drift. He taught me how to wave-ride. Hello, Drifty dearest, were you all ever so worried about me?"

"Duna took it hard. But we thought Archon would bellow down the heavens, he was so angry with the Beast for taking you. We had given you up for dead. We were going to seal up the cave first thing in the morning, treasure and all. It's good you got out when you did."

Malora realizes that he is younger than Neal, not much more than a boy. Still, the resemblance is remarkable.

"Could Neal have had a child?" Malora muses aloud.

"Cauterize your tongue, girl," Zephele says, her eyes flashing.

Honus laughs softly. "I wager Drift is the offspring of Neal's uncle Markon, who was turned out for wife-stealing when Neal was just a tyke. I believe his lover went with him voluntarily. And is that Mather I see with the extraordinary body art across his shoulders and arms?"

Mather raises a limp hand in greeting but makes no move to join them.

"They call them body glyphs," Zephele says. "If I hadn't been taken by the Beast, I would have my first glyph by now. Athen thought it would help me get in the wild centaur spirit. Ah, there's my dear brother now!"

Archon is shouldering his way through the centaurs. Like the Apex, he is a head taller than the tallest centaur there. When he arrives at the front of the crowd, he stops and stares at Zephele.

"So it's true. You're alive!"

"I am," she says.

His eyes sweep coldly over the rest of the group and come to rest on Malora.

"You again," he grunts.

Sky mutters.

Athen's eyes flick to Sky.

"And you, too, Belerephon? I thought I'd seen the last of you."

Sky snorts as if to say that he is not particularly happy to be seen.

"His name is Sky," Malora says.

But Athen's attention has shifted. "Honus," he says, with a dip of his bearded chin.

"Athen," Honus says.

"Archon," Athen amends.

"Of course," Honus says, inclining his head. "Archon."

He returns his attention to Zephele. "Had I known that you would go wandering off in the night, I would have tied you into your stall."

"This was the part of wild centaur life I didn't particularly favor," she says to her companions. "Very uncomfortable living quarters. One might even say squalid."

"You made your opinion known from the start," Athen says curtly. "As I made mine: those of us who truly live in our bodies have no need for creature comforts. I assume, Orion, that you are responsible for rescuing our sister? Always the savior. I trust you didn't aggravate the Beast while you were at it."

Orion, who has charge of the blue velvet pillowcase, consults Malora with a look.

Malora nods.

Orion upends the bag and out rolls the head of the Beast.

The wild centaurs move closer to peer at it. When they see what it is, they gasp and pull back. The level of chatter rises, then subsides quickly as the bloody head comes to rest at Athen's feet.

Neal lifts his head from the sling. "I'd say that's *very* aggravated," he says, then flops back.

Zephele and Malora exchange relieved grins, glad that he is feeling well enough to make a joke.

Orion says, "It was Neal Featherhoof and Malora who did the deed. Neal is in need of a healer's ministrations, as you can see."

Athen ignores the plea and looks down at the head. "His sisters will starve now," he says.

There is such a note of tenderness in his voice, Malora almost hates to tell him, but she does. "There's only one sister now."

Athen looks up quickly. "You slew the Sphinx, too?"

"No," Malora says. "We spared her. She seemed harmless enough," she lies.

Athen's eyes bore into Malora, his eyebrows furrowed. As bushy as his father's, they are pierced all along with tiny golden rings that glint in the sunlight. "You have slain the Chimera?" he asks, his voice faint and tinged with respect.

Orion clears his throat.

Malora says, "I'd love to take credit for it, but Orion slew the Chimera."

Athen squints at his brother, as if trying to imagine it. He gives up, shaking his head in mystification.

"Najeeb!" he roars. Herd and visitors alike jump. He sounds so like the Apex that Malora expects Ash to come scurrying forward instead of this ancient centaur, older than Cylas Longshanks, who comes hobbling forth from the back of the crowd.

"Follow me, my dear," he tells Zephele in a parched voice.

"Drift!" Athen now bellows. "Sound the conch!"

Drift lifts a large pink seashell to his lips and, throwing back his curly head, blows into it until his face turns bright red. The sound, loud and deeper than the cry of bull elephant mourning, fills the air.

When the noise dies away, Athen says, "Our guests have given us a reason to celebrate!"

Maybe it is just the fearsome glyphs, but he looks as if he would rather throttle them than invite them to a celebration. But the wild centaurs seem happy and enthusiastic. They rear up in unison, then settle back on their hooves, drumming them rhythmically on the ground. "Bon. Fire. Bon. Fire. Bon. Fire!" they chant. Those whose faces are tattooed look as if they were wearing jubilation masks.

"Go now," Athen says, indulgently, shooing them off. "Prepare a great roaring fire, and show our guests," he says, flashing a resentful look at them, "that we wild centaurs know how to enjoy life."

Malora pulls Orion to the side and crooks an eyebrow.

"This may be as friendly as it gets," he whispers to her.

"But they are thieves and murderers," Malora says.

Orion looks around. "I see many familiar faces here, distant relatives, friends of friends, descendants of those long turned out. It is disturbingly like being back home. A home I could never have dreamed of in my wildest imagination . . ."

"Exactly," she says. "They are savages."

"Whatever they may have done," he says, turning to her and meeting her look, "they did it because they were being held hostage by the Beasts. Now that the Beasts are all but gone . . ."

Malora turns away. Where is Zephele? Zephele cannot possibly feel this charitably toward her abductors. But Zephele is leaving the valley, leading Sky and Neal's sling in Najeeb's wake.

"Where are they going?" she asks.

Honus says, "Calm yourself, child. They are seeing to Neal's wound."

Reluctant to let Sky out of her sight in this place where he was trapped by fishing nets and held prisoner, she hurries to catch up. The centaurs she passes smell like horses and salty seawater. She feels their eyes on her, fascinated and a little frightened. Do they know she stole their horses or has Athen kept that from them? She follows Zephele down the same sandy corridor through which she and Sky once escaped. They pass the horse pens, which stand empty now. Have the wild centaurs failed to replenish the supply, or did Athen let them loose when he decided to bury the monsters alive? She catches up with Zephele just as they are passing beneath a high white arch lined with jagged teeth.

"That is the jawbone of a sperm whale," Zephele says, her eyes flashing with amusement.

"Where are you going?" Malora says, in a tense whisper. Two young male centaurs are serving as escort and Malora doesn't want them to overhear.

"To Najeeb's stall. To see to Neal. You may come along, if you wish. But please don't glower so. You have slain monsters. You and Neil and Orrie have freed the wild centaurs from their terrible yoke. You should be pleased and proud."

"You would trust Neal's life to these thieves and murderers?" Malora says.

Zephele laughs. "Najeeb is neither thief nor murderer," she says. "He was put out of Mount Kheiron for blasphemy that gave rise to public brawling when he stood up one day in the temple—he was a priest, you know, and a noble-blooded Goldmane by birth—and announced that the Scienticians were the only gods we hibes could ever legitimately lay claim to. Isn't that so, Najeeb?"

Najeeb shrugs. "I was a bit of an upstart. This way, please."

They are in a field of sand and dune grass, densely packed with rectangular huts made from sticks of driftwood lashed together with sinew. The skins stretched across the frames are decorated with colorful designs: flowers and shells and birds and insects. Crushed seashells forming more decorative patterns pave the paths between the stalls. It flashes through Malora's thoughts that this is a primitive version of Mount Kheiron.

"What about Sunshine?" Malora says.

Zephele freezes. She turns slowly, her eyes filling. "My poor, foolish Twan, in an attempt to save me, charged my abductors. She impaled herself on one of their spears before he could stop her. I saw it with my own eyes. The wild centaur was very sorry."

"Did Farin Whitewithers also run into a spear?" Malora presses.

Zephele turns away. "I wouldn't know. I had the sack over my head. They insisted upon it even though I put up no struggle. Archon considered what you did to be an act of war, and I was a prisoner of war. But as soon as we got here, all he wanted to do was show off Ixion to me so that I would appreciate how superior life here was to that in Mount Kheiron."

"And do you find it superior?" Malora asks.

"Of course not," she says with a laugh. "Not for me, at least. But there are very many for whom it is."

They pass a hut that looks no less humble than its neighbors. "Archon lives here with his wife, Tam. Their children stay in the nursery stable, along with all the other young ones. The children here are very happy. Happier than the children of Mount Kheiron, I dare say. Better fed than the Flatlanders and freer than the Highlanders."

"Your brother has *children*?" Malora asks.

Zephele's face softens. "I am an aunt five times over." She claps a hand over her mouth. "I have forgotten to tell Orrie that he is an uncle. Oh well, he will find out soon enough."

They come to a stall that looks nearly twice as large as the others. "Najeeb does a brisk business there."

"Business?" Malora asks.

"He is a needler as well as a healer," she says.

"What is a needler?"

"He makes the body glyphs," she says. "He is an artist. Aren't you, Najeeb?"

"I am a *pain* artist," he says with a wicked cackle. A single tooth overlaps his upper lip like a snake's fang. His face and head are as rough and sparsely hairy as a coconut, but his eyes are beady and intelligent.

Every inch of the stretched parchment is crowded with pictures set at odd angles, squeezed in without regard for composition.

"These are some of the designs one can choose from," Zephele says.

While Malora removes the makeshift harness from Sky, she scans the pictures and recognizes snakes and rabbits from the bodies of centaurs she has seen in the crowd. She sees the leopard and tiger that decorate Mather's arms as well as the delicate dragonfly that Zephele has embroidered on her shawl.

Najeeb holds aside the skin door as the two centaur escorts, careful not to touch the wounded arm, help Neal out of the sling and into the stall. Neal sags against them. Zephele and Malora follow them into the dim interior. They pass a worn wooden table at the center of which embers glow in a brazier. A pot of water boils, tended by a female centaur very nearly as old as Najeeb. Around the brazier is a rush mat spattered with colored ink. Seashells in a neat half-circle hold the inks next to a tray displaying a lethal array of needles. Gingerly, Malora picks one up.

"The spines of sea urchins," Najeeb explains.

"The wild centaurs embroider their flesh," Malora says, setting the needle down with distaste.

"You might say that," Najeeb says, grinning. "They glory in their bodies."

"You say 'they,'" Malora says. "Aren't you one of them?"

"Yes, but I am old," he says. "I was old when I came here and I am older still now." He gestures to his thin arms and legs. "There is very little left to glory in. I can at least help others glory in theirs."

The centaurs have taken Neal to the back of the stall, where a bed of straw is covered with a clean blanket. They lower him down onto the side that is not wounded.

"Thank you," Najeeb says, dismissing the young centaurs.

The old female centaur wordlessly brings forth the pot of steaming water. Najeeb lifts Neal's arm. He groans as the healer unwraps the wound. He dips a sponge in the water and swabs the wound. Zephele, averting her eyes, holds Neal's hand. She has turned very nearly as pale as Neal.

"The horn of the Beast makes a very clean cut!" Najeeb declares with relish.

When he is finished, he wraps the wound in a fresh, clean cloth. The old female, who has been brewing something rank-smelling over the brazier, hands Najeeb a cup. Najeeb lifts Neal's head. Neal slurps up what is in the cup. Although he makes a terrible face, the lines of pain etched around his mouth and eyes begin to ease.

"He will sleep, and while he sleeps he will sweat out the toxins. Nakira will stay with him and ply him with water."

"Can I stay with him, too?" Zephele asks.

"You should rest, my child. You have been through a terrible ordeal. But I am glad to see that the Beast has left you unharmed."

He looks down at Neal and smooths the damp hair off his forehead. "As for this young brave, he is to be congratulated. He has liberated us from the monstrous masters from below. And now, what will we do with ourselves?" He chuckles softly to himself.

"Stop killing horses?" Neal murmurs without opening his eyes.

"Thank you!" Malora says, for she could not have said it better herself.

"Ah yes," Najeeb says, his bright eyes finding Malora. "You are the miscreant who stole all of our horses, leaving us defenseless."

"I *saved* those horses," Malora says.

"After we discovered the horses were all gone, we sent out

a raiding party. But as luck would have it, there were no caravans passing through and no horses to be found within ten
days' ride. Archon refused to hold a lottery. That would be
marching backward into barbarism, he claimed. Instead, he
posted a guard of twenty on the empty paddock, including
himself, and when the Beast came up for his horse, they went
at him with everything they had. When the dust settled, three
of the centaurs lay gored and dying. Another was dragged
down below to the Beast's lair, screaming." As he speaks, Najeeb smiles at Malora in a strangely gentle fashion.

Malora stares back at him, numb with shock. She hadn't
given much thought to what would happen to the wild centaurs without the horses. She assumed they would simply
round up more in time for the next sacrifice.

"Come outside in the sunlight, dearest," Zephele says.
She rubs Malora's arms as if she were cold rather than guilt-
stricken.

The sun in Malora's eyes nearly blinds her. Sky and Baby
are waiting. Sky nuzzles her, and Baby butts her knee. She
strokes them both absently, in a daze.

"Please don't fret," Zephele says. "I still think what you
did was right. And everything turned out perfectly in the end,
didn't it? The monsters are dead, at least the two most fearsome ones, and the world is now a safer place for centaurs,
horses, and caravans. I wonder what will happen to the third
beast? They will mostly likely bury her alive in the morning.
Imagine how flattered I was to learn that my brother was so
angry to have lost me, he was willing to give up the treasure.
The treasure was just legend, of course. None of them had
ever seen it with their own eyes, although many have died

trying. I think the wild centaurs thought of it as being theirs. And I suppose it is, now."

"*Four* centaurs . . ." is all Malora can say.

Zephele bows her head. "Archon took pains to introduce me to their widows and mothers when I first came."

Malora rouses herself enough to remark in a dull voice, "You call him Archon."

"I do, don't I?" Zephele seems surprised. "I suppose that's how I think of him now. Malora, I know it's terrible that the wild centaurs sacrificed horses and, worse, killed witnesses at the scene of their crimes, but this is my brother and my cousin and my uncle's brother and my mother's friend's daughter, and my best friend's older sister. . . . They are a bit rough around the edges—some of them even savage, yes—but they are also my kin and my countrymen, and I have tried very hard to understand the forces that caused them to behave in such a reprehensible fashion."

Malora stares at Zephele so intently that Zephele, catching her lower lip in her teeth, adds, her voice laced with doubt, "Isn't that the right thing to do, rather than be angry and vengeful? Isn't that what Kheiron would want me to do?"

Malora smiles. "I don't know about Kheiron, but I am very proud of you."

CHAPTER 26

Wave Riding

"Will Belerephon bite?" A pretty little centaur hovers outside Najeeb's stall. She has a fountain of rippling golden hair and big brown eyes. A firefly glyph adorns her shoulder. Malora recognizes her from the circle of centaurs that bore down upon her in the paddock.

"His name is Sky, Duna, not Belerephon, and he won't bite," Zephele says. "He is a very good horse."

"Archon told me I would find you here. I am so happy that you are alive, Moonbeam!"

"Moonbeam?" Malora says, darting Zephele a look.

Zephele shrugs. "That was my tribal name. This is my hostess and stall mate, Duna. Isn't she the most impossibly pretty thing?" Zephele fusses with Duna's hair, tucking errant strands back into the ponytail. "Duna and I did nothing but talk, talk, talk, didn't we, dear? She is quite curious about the world outside of Ixion. And I was curious about Ixion, so it suited. Duna dear, this is the extraordinary friend I told you about. This is Malora."

Duna steeples her fingers beneath her chin. She clears her throat expectantly. At a suggestive nod from Zephele, Malora steeples her own fingers.

"I, Duna, am at your service," she says, bowing over her steepled hands, her golden ponytail flopping over her face.

"I, Malora, am happy that you are," Malora says, for want of something better to say.

"Archon wants me to show you to the seaside, where we are preparing for the feast," Duna says.

"Didn't I tell you the wild centaurs loved their feasts?" Zephele says. "I never saw such a group for celebrating. We Kheironites are staid and restrained by comparison."

"Shouldn't you rest?" Malora asks.

Zephele makes a face. "Why? Neal and I are alive and in love. I have my own cause for celebration."

Duna leans in close and whispers behind her hand, "I would very much like to meet your brother. You told me he was handsome, but I never imagined he was *this* handsome! I saw him being led down the seaside path. We can catch him if we hurry."

"Oh, my brother is quite the catch, all right," Zephele says, her smile impish. Zephele is in her matchmaker mode and, thinks Malora, wanting nothing more than to dash the hopes of so many eligible females back home.

"We mustn't waste any more time," Duna says. "Come!"

They follow her away from the field of stalls along a winding path through the dunes. The sun is hot as it beats down on the top of Malora's head, but the breeze blowing in from the sea cools it. She finds the combination almost unbearably sensual. How long had they been underground? A day? Two days? She has no idea. She wants to soak up the sun like a sea sponge.

They emerge from the dunes and there it is, shining like a million diamonds on a vast tray: the sea. Sky and Baby wander off in search of edible plants. Malora follows Zephele and Duna in a state of bedazzlement. The sun on the sand sparkles. The shore is swarming with life. Seagulls dip and squawk and skim the surface of the ruffled sea. Smaller birds scamper along the wet sand, chasing the waves on twiglike legs. A group of young centaur stallions near the shoreline is playing a game with some sort of a gourd wrapped in a net. They are galloping back and forth, shouting and kicking up a great deal of sand.

"Sand rally," Duna says. "The object is to touch the ball with only your head and hooves."

Malora sees centaur children making sand sculptures and older ones digging a pit in the sand. Others stand beneath a canopy sorting catch on long driftwood planks: tiny silver fish and shells and crabs. Further down the shore, Malora sees Athen, along with others, wading into the surf and hauling a huge dripping net loaded with fish.

"Look there," says Zephele, pointing at the waves closer at hand.

A group of young male centaurs is submerged in the water just beyond the line of the breaking surf. Their ponytailed heads rise and fall with the churning sea. One of them— Malora thinks it is Drift—shouts and waves at Zephele and Duna. Then, seemingly as one, the young centaurs rise up on a swell and ride the curl of a large wave as it rolls toward the land and breaks on the shore. They stagger up onto the shingle, pausing just long enough to hoot and shake the water from their hides and ponytails. Then they dash back into the surf with fearless abandon.

"That, my dear, is wave riding," Zephele says.

"I want to try it," Malora says.

"Oh, you will, I'm sure," Zephele says.

"There he is!" Duna says, pointing inland.

Orion and Honus are farther up the shore where the dunes start, helping wild centaurs to stack driftwood. Orion waves them over.

"How is Neal?" he asks Zephele as they approach. His eyes take in Duna in a way Malora has never seen him look at the females back home. There is, she thinks, a suggestion of heat in those cool blue eyes.

"Sleeping," Zephele says. "Najeeb says it is a clean wound."

"That's good." He turns to Duna, steeples his hands, and bows to her. "I, Orion Silvermane, am at your service."

The way he says it, it seems to mean rather more than wild centaur custom would dictate. Duna blushes to the roots of her hair and returns the greeting. Malora catches Honus's eye. He winks.

"Our hosts have favored us with a little refreshment to tide us over until the feast," the faun says, bringing forth a wooden plank tray on which there are juicy sections of cut fruit and flakes of dried fish along with something dark green Malora doesn't recognize.

"Dried seaweed," Honus says. "It's nutty and quite good."

Orion asks Duna polite questions about her hobbies (embroidery, sand rally, stringing shells) and interests (the sea, the stars, the clouds), while Zephele and Malora help themselves to what is on the plank tray.

"I've quite gotten used to the taste of dried fish," Zephele says, chewing a piece. "Do try it."

Malora shakes her head. Dried fish reminds her of Lume. She wonders how Lume's audience with the Apex went, if he has even had it yet, or whether more Leatherwings waylaid him. She wonders why Lume isn't here. Lume should be here with me, she thinks.

After they have eaten, they walk up and down the shore collecting more wood for the bonfire. Orion and Duna wander off together so far down the shoreline that Malora can no longer see them. They reappear some time later with the lowering sun at their backs, without so much as a stick of wood. They are holding hands.

"I can see you didn't need our help," Orion says, gesturing to the pile of driftwood towering high above the dunes.

"We managed somehow without you two," Zephele says with that same wicked smile.

Just then, five little centaurs tumble before Zephele in a giggling pile.

"Hooray! It's Aunt Moonbeam!" they cry. They push at each other and roll and wrestle in the struggle to be the first in line to greet her.

"The Beast didn't eat you all up!" says the first in line.

"No, he didn't, Fin," Zephele says. "I am quite alive and happy to be so."

Fin is shampooing sand into the hair of the little female he has clasped tight between his legs.

"Let your sister be. Pay attention. I want to introduce you all to Archon's little brother."

They giggle and punch each other as they stare up at Orion.

"What's so funny?" Zephele asks.

The little girl who has gotten up to shake the sand from her hair says, "Because he's not little. *We're* little."

"But not for long!" one of the boys boasts.

"What is your name?" Orion asks the little girl with the sandy head.

"I am Sandy," the little girl says.

"How very fitting," Orion says, helping her brush out the sand. "Are you the eldest, Sandy? You seem very grown-up to me."

"I *am* grown-up," Sandy says. She has fair skin and hair so pale it is almost white, to match her creamy white flanks. "And this is my little sister, Plum. But we call her Plumkin."

Plum has sea-green eyes and a wild thatch of black hair and black flanks speckled with gold. "I am the smartest," she says gravely.

The others shove her hard into the sand.

"Are not!" Fin says.

"Am too," Plum says, scrambling to her feet with dignity. "I can read."

"You can?" says Orion.

"Like Duna, I can read the *stars*!"

"Oh!" says Orion, nodding solemnly. "And who are you?" he says, turning to the next little centaur.

"I'm Bark, and I can run the fastest." He is small and wiry

with light brown hair and flanks and fierce gray eyes like the Apex. "Want to race?"

"In a bit, perhaps," Orion says. "But I want to meet your little sister first."

The others push the little one forward as if she were a special offering.

"This is Rose," Sandy says. "She's shy."

Orion kneels in the sand so that his face is level with the little centaur's. Rose has a wild thicket of black curls that escape from her ponytail, and rosy cheeks. She sucks her fist and stares at Orion out of big, startling blue eyes that are a match for her uncle's. "Is it true?" he whispers. "That you're very shy?"

She nods, drool dripping down her wrist from her chubby fist.

"Well, Sandy, Fin, Plum, Bark, and Rose, how would you like to come with me and Duna and look for seashells?"

Rose holds out the slimy fingers she has just been sucking. Orion accepts them as the gift that they are. Duna claims his other hand. The others trip along behind.

Zephele says, "I thought *I* was smitten. And wait until Herself gets her hands on them. She will spoil them rotten."

By the time the sun has set and the moon has risen, the fire is blazing, giving off sparks of bright blue and green and pink that break loose and rise up to mingle with the stars. The centaurs have given their guests the place of honor. They sit with their backs settled comfortably against the dunes directly in front of the fire. Archon sits next to them, along with his children and their mother, Tam. Malora recognizes, with a mild jolt, that Tam is the same fair-haired centaur who suggested selling her to the scouts. When Malora reaches down to draw up her outrage, she no longer finds it in her.

While the food is cooking in fire pits nearby, they sit and watch two male centaurs, their muscular bodies oiled, moving gracefully in the firelight, to the accompaniment of musicians on drums and pipes and stringed instruments. They are like mirror images of one another. They lock arms and appear to be struggling. Then they break their hold on each other and circle, first one way, then the other. Malora is hard-pressed to understand whether they are fighting or jubilating.

Archon leans over and explains. "They are dueling for the hand of their ladylove across the way." He indicates a red-haired female centaur standing on the other side of the fire. "The winner will walk off with her tonight."

"And the loser?" Malora cannot help but ask.

"Will live to duel another day," Archon says. "I know what you were thinking, that they were going to fight each other to the death. No, it is a civilized competition. Each is simply showing himself off to his best advantage. At the end of their exhibition, the lady will choose."

"I see," Malora says.

After the blissful couple has wandered off into the moonlight, three centaurs on one side of the fire and three on the other tug at a rope in an attempt to pull the opposite team into the fire. But the fire burns through the rope, and in the end all of them fall backward into the sand, laughing and kicking their hooves. A female centaur runs forward with a skin flask and squirts ferna into each centaur's open mouth.

"Is anyone ever burned playing this game?" Malora asks.

Athen says, "Rarely. As you can see, it is all in good fun. There was so much darkness in our lives, I felt it necessary to legislate good times whenever I could."

"Very sensible," says Honus.

Malora wonders whether, with the darkness now gone, the good times will be as much fun.

Later, everyone lines up beneath the canopy. Malora doesn't realize how hungry she is until she discovers all there is to eat. There is sea chicken and boar sausage baked in seaweed. There are crabs and clams and mussels and at least fifteen varieties of fish, which Honus is at pains to name. Malora fills her seashell plate three times over. Neal, awake from his rest and freshly bandaged, nestles in the sand next to Zephele. The color has returned to his face. Zephele feeds him with her fingers. Tam is with Archon, Duna is with Orion, Zephele is with Neal, Najeeb is with Nakira. Honus is conducting a spirited conversation about religion with Mather. Even Sky and Baby have wandered off together. Everyone seems to have paired off with someone, except for her. She lies alone in the fire-toasted lee of the dunes and stares up at the sky, wishing Lume would come. Is this the way it is going to be from now on? Will she spend the rest of her life staring up at the sky and pining away for him? If this is the case, then she would just as soon not care for him quite so much. She was better as she was before: single and happy to be that way. Someone handles her a skin of ferna and she squirts some into the back of her mouth. She chokes a little. It burns like fire.

"I'd watch that stuff if I were you, pet," Neal says from the cozy circle of Zephele's arms.

Awash in self-pity, she allows herself another squirt, and another. When the flask is empty, she finds another.

She awakes at dawn. Above her, seagulls wheel and dive, picking at the remains of last night's feast. The fire has burned down to embers. Her head half-buried in the sand, she has a vague recollection of dancing with Honus around the fire, along with a bunch of stomping, singing wild centaurs, some of whom were laughing when Malora kept falling down. The affront to her dignity is nothing compared to the pain in her head, which feels as if it were writhing with poisonous snakes. Around her, centaurs sleep, including her friends from Mount Kheiron. Honus has a smile on his face.

She wants to shake him awake and say, "What are you smiling about?"

Instead, she staggers away from the fire and finds the water bucket she filled for Sky and Baby sometime last night. She remembers Duna leading her to a well and giggling as Malora leaned over it and called out, "Lume! Are you down there?" This morning, the bucket is half full. She lifts it and tips it into her mouth, swirling the water around and spitting it out. Then she pours the rest of it over her head.

Tossing the empty bucket aside, she heads for the ocean, her body knowing what it needs before her mind knows what she is doing. As she walks, she strips off her clothes and drops them behind her. The water surging around her bare legs is so cold, she stops and for a moment thinks better of this idea. Then she recalls how the wild centaurs charged straight into the waves. With a quick shake of her head, she faces the sea and runs in. The sea here is colder than it was in Kahiro. It boils all around her, so freezing cold that it feels hot. The waves are bigger, too. The farther out she goes, the more monstrous they seem, bellowing like something alive as they plow their way shoreward. A particularly monstrous wave rises up and charges toward her. She looks to the shore. Everyone is still asleep. No one will see her if the wave knocks her over and dashes her to a pulp. Her heart races. Then she remembers what the wild centaurs did. She pinches her nose and down she goes, beneath the crashing wave. The underwater world is eerily peaceful: pale green and as sudsy as soap foaming beneath the roaring tap of her tub. She hears the wave that she has just evaded crashing like a thunderclap on the shore behind her. The wave sloshes back out toward her, its power spent.

Malora bounces back to the surface. Grasping for breath, she finds that she is grinning. What is more, her headache is gone! She swims out behind the line of crashing waves, paddling with arms and legs. Then she lets the rolling waves carry her back in, nearer to where the waves are breaking. Just when the waves seem to be collapsing over her head, she begins to swim with all her might, racing to stay ahead of the cresting wave. She feels the wave scoop her up and nearly swallow her, bearing her high above the land and then speeding her toward it. She is as weightless as a bird in flight. Then, just as she is about to tumble face-forward into the rattling pebbles, the wave spits her out and sends her stumbling and splashing and laughing up onto the shingle.

No sooner is she up on the shore than she is running back into the surf. This is far too much fun to do only once. She wants to do it a hundred times more.

She swims out in search of the next wave to ride. She has just spotted a nice plump one rolling her way when there is a tremendous splash in the water nearby. She lets out a startled shriek and looks around. The water seethes with froth.

"Sharks!" she gasps.

Suddenly, something big breaks the surface.

It is Lume, his silver hair spangled with droplets.

She smacks the water near his head with the edge of her hand. "You frightened me half to death."

He shakes the water from his hair. "Not half as frightened as I was when I saw you courting death *again*. There happen to be at least a dozen sharks circling, just over there." He points out to sea.

She yelps and leaps into his arms, wrapping her legs around his waist and her arms around his neck. "Where?" she says, head swiveling, searching for the deadly fins.

He smiles lazily. The dimple pops out.

And that's when she knows. She narrows her eyes at him. Her hands curl into fists. "There aren't *really* any sharks in this water, are there?" she says.

"Well, I wouldn't go so far as to say *none*. It's a fairly large body of water and I'm sure there are quite a few . . . for instance, down the shore a ways, where the nets are."

"But none here," she says.

He frowns and nods. "None whatsoever. I checked very carefully. *Someone's* got to look out for you. You certainly don't do a very good job of it. Swimming alone by yourself *again*."

When she tries to pull away from him, he holds her even closer. His storm-washed aroma mingles with the scent of the sea and makes her want to lap the seawater from his skin. And yet she braces her hands against his chest. "You tricked me," she says.

"You have to admit . . . ," he says, his voice trailing off as he bends his head and begins to plant small kisses down her neck.

"What?" she says with a small shiver as her neck arches and her wrists collapse against him. "What do I have to admit?" she says faintly.

"That my trick worked awfully well." He kisses her along her jawline, where he nearly kissed her once before, where ever since she has imagined him kissing her. "Now that you're here, where both of us want you to be, I hope you'll stay."

"I just might do that." She settles into his embrace with a happy sigh as they drift off together into the undulating swells of the wine-dark sea.

Cast of Characters

Akbar: Kavian proprietor of the Backbone of Heaven, the inn in Kahiro where Malora and her companions stay

Aron: half-wit stable boy and Malora's childhood friend in the Settlement; deceased

Ash: Apex's servant

Neal Featherhoof: captain of the Peacekeepers

Dugal Highdock: also known as Dock; former head of the Peacekeepers and bodyguard on the trek to Kahiro

Honus: biped hybrid of goat and human; Medon's pet and tutor of the Silvermane children and Malora

Jayke: Malora's father; deceased

Kheiron the Wise: patron and founder of Mount Kheiron

Lemon: Sunshine's mate; Orion's servant

Cylas Longshanks: master cobbler

Lume: one of the Wonders, the last of his kind

Malora: one of the People, the last of her kind

Margus Piedhocks: Flatlander who replaces Whitewithers as night-duty guard of the gates of Mount Kheiron

Shrouk: Dromadi seer

Lady Hylonome Silvermane: wife of Medon

Medon Silvermane: Apex of Mount Kheiron

Orion Silvermane: son of the Apex and Hylonome

Theon Silvermane: son of the Apex and Hylonome

Zephele Silvermane: only daughter of the Apex and Hylonome
Sunshine: Lemon's mate; Zephele's servant
Brion Swiftstride: blacksmith
Thora: Malora's mother; deceased
Anders Thunderheart: owner of the Thunderheart Stable
West: once Orion's servant, now Malora's wrangler-in-chief
Farin Whitewithers: Highlander and former night-duty guard
 of the gates of Mount Kheiron

Ironbound Furies
Sky
Shadow
Coal
Lightning
Silky
Raven
Blacky
Posy
Charcoal
Ember
Smoke
Fancy
Streak
Stormy

Rescued Horses
Oil
Flame
Ivory
Star
Butte
Sassy
Thunder
Cloud

Light Rain
Beast
Mist
Max

Athabanshee
Bolt

Rescued Zebra
Baby

Wild Centaurs
Archon: formerly Athen Silvermane, now leader of the centaurs of Ixion
Balaal: formerly Mather Silvermane
Children of Athen and Tam: Sandy, Fin, Plum, Bark, and Rose
Drift: bronco who teaches Zephele to wave-ride
Duna: bronca host of the captive Zephele
Najeeb: body glyph artist and healer
Nakira: Najeeb's mate
Rorg: formerly Gastin
Tam: Archon's mate and mother of five

Masterpieces of the Scienticians
Abu al Hul: also known as the Sphinx and the Terrifying One; has the body of a lion, the head of a human, and the wings of an eagle
Chimera: fire-breathing hybrid of lion, serpent, and goat
Minotaur: also known as the Beast from Below; a biped hybrid of human and bull

Glossary of Terms and Places

Aleur: quadruped hybrid of human and big cat

Apex: chosen leader of the centaurs, first among equals

Arsenal: aisle in the marketplace of Kahiro where weapons are sold

Athabanshee: small, delicate breed of horse known for its speed, originating in the deserts of the Sha Haro

Backbone of Heaven: enormous rock in the harbor of Kahiro, the vestige of a meteorite collision; also the name of an inn

Beehive: notorious House of Romance located on an island in the harbor of Kahiro

Belerephon: name given to Sky after the wild centaurs captured him

body glyph: wild centaurean tattoo

Bovian: biped hybrid of human and cow

bronc: wild centaur born in Ixion

Bushman's Friend: hunting knife crafted by Pantherian weapon smiths

Caldera of Neelah: tidal lake outside of Kahiro

Capricornia: biped hybrid of human and sheep

centaur: quadruped hybrid of human and horse

Church of the Latter Day Scienticians: religion observed by the majority of hibes outside of Mount Kheiron

Doctors Adam and Eve: patron saints of the Church of the Latter Day Scienticians

Downs: vast area of sand dunes and sinkholes west of Kahiro, where the wild centaurs live

Dromad: quadruped hybrid of human and camel

Edicts: founding laws of Mount Kheiron

ferna: fermented beverage favored by wild centaurs

Flatlanders: less-privileged centaurs born on the flatlands surrounding Mount Kheiron

gaffey: beverage brewed by the Dromad Shrouk, said to bring on visions

Grandparents: ancestors of the People

Great Ice: ice age brought about by the collision of a large meteorite

Hand: centaurean trade; entails making things that can be seen, such as alchemical potions, paintings, tapestries, sculptures; or studying things that can't be seen, such as law, religion, philosophy

hibe: hybrid of two species, usually human combined with animal

Highlanders: more-privileged centaurs, born on Mount Kheiron

Hills of Melea: mountain range to the northwest of Mount Kheiron, where Kheiron the Wise was once said to have lived as a hermit

Houses of Romance: brothels where hibes may intermingle without fear of creating monstrous mutations

Ironbound Furies: name given by the centaurs to the breed of large black horses that run wild at the foot of the Ironbound Mountains

Ironbound Mountains: mountains to the south of Mount Kheiron

Ixion: ancestral home of the wild centaurs, hidden in the dunes along the coast to the west of Kahiro

jubilation: centaurean celebration, usually involving a ritual dance wherein the males wield a staff

Ka: biped hybrid of amphibian and human, native to Kahiro

Kahiro: port city and capitol of the Kingdom of the Ka, north of Mount Kheiron

Kamaria: name of the People's city on the site that is now Mount Kheiron

Leatherwing: predatory hybrid of bat and human

Loxidant: biped hybrid of elephant and human

merfolk: aquatic hybrid of fish and human

Narrow Earth: habitable remains of the earth to the north and south of the equator

nubs: currency of Mount Kheiron

Otherian: centaurean term for any race that is neither centaur nor Twani

Pantherian: biped hybrid of lion and human

People: last pure-bred human beings on earth

recognition: ceremony officially conferring upon a centaur his or her Hand

River Neelah: consists of the upper and lower segments; runs from the Ironbound Mountains in the south to Kahiro in the north

saruchi: long skirt favored by the fashionable sheKa

Scienticians: group of People, half mage and half scientist, who created the first hibes

Sealie: aquatic hybrid of seal and human

sheKa: female Ka

Suidean: biped hybrid of boar and human

talent scout: individual charged with recruiting or kidnapping workers for the Houses of Romance

Twani: hybrid of cat and human that serves the centaurs

wave riding: body surfing, as practiced by the wild centaurs

Wonder: winged hybrid of human and raptor

About the Author

Kate Klimo is making the transition from corporate career woman to barn wench. In her barn in New Paltz, New York, she is host to a paint gelding named Harry and a quarter horse named Fancy. When she isn't mucking or writing or riding, she likes to travel with her husband (also named Harry) and see the world from the back of a horse. She hopes that one day she and her horses will be so attuned to one another that they will, together, achieve a unity of movement that is nigh onto centaurean. Kate is also the author of the Dragon Keepers series for middle-grade readers. You can visit her at KateKlimo.com.